WEAVER

TIME'S TAPESTRY: 4

WEAVER

TIME'S TAPESTRY: 4

Stephen Baxter

GOLLANCZ
LONDON

Weaver © Stephen Baxter 2008
All rights reserved

The right of Stephen Baxter to be identfied as the author of this
work has been asserted by him in accordance with the
Copyright, Designs and Patents Act 1988.

First published in Great Britain in 2008 by Gollancz
An imprint of the Orion Publishing Group
Orion House, 5 Upper St Martin's Lane, London WC2H 9EA
An Hachette Livre UK Company

ISBN 978 0 57507 8 642 (Cased)
ISBN 978 0 57508 2 045 (Trade Paperback)

1 3 5 7 9 10 8 6 4 2

Typeset by Input Data Services Ltd, Frome

Printed in Great Britain by Mackays of Chatham plc, Chatham, Kent

The Orion Publishing Group's policy is to use papers that
are natural, renewable and recyclable products and made
from wood grown in sustainable forests. The logging and
manufacturing processes are expected to conform to the
environmental regulations of the country of origin.

www.orionbooks.co.uk

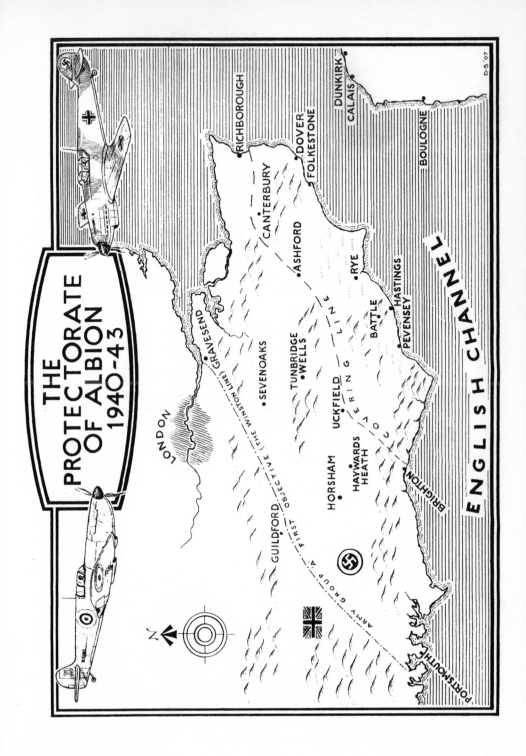

THE PROTECTORATE OF ALBION 1940-43

ENGLISH CHANNEL

LONDON
GUILDFORD
GRAVESEND
SEVENOAKS
HORSHAM
HAYWARDS HEATH
TUNBRIDGE WELLS
UCKFIELD
CANTERBURY
ASHFORD
RICHBOROUGH
DOVER
FOLKESTONE
RYE
BATTLE
HASTINGS
PEVENSEY
BRIGHTON
PORTSMOUTH
DUNKIRK
CALAIS
BOULOGNE

FIRST OBJECTIVE (THE WINSTON LINE)
HERING LINE
A ARMY GROUP

D·S ·07

Time's Tapestry
AD 1492

'As mapped by myself; in which the long warp threads are the history of the whole world; and the wefts which run from selvedge to selvedge are distortions of that history, deflected by a Weaver unknown; be he human, divine or satanic ...'

FRIAR GEOFFREY COTESFORD OF YORK

	War	Deflection	Weft
AD 1492	The Destiny of Cristobal Colon	*The Codex of Aethelmaer (AD 1042); the Testament of Eadgyth (AD 1070)*	A War of the Religions
AD 1242	The Mongols at Vienna	*The Amulet of Bohemond (AD 1242)*	A Mongol Empire
AD 1066	The Battle of Hastings	*The Menologium of Isolde (AD 418)*	A Northern Empire
AD 732	The Battle of Poitiers	*The Testament of al-Hafredi (AD 732)*	A Moorish Europe
AD 314	The Survival of Constantine	*The Prophecy of Nectovelin (4 BC)*	The Church Disestablished

The Prophecy of Nectovelin

4BC

(Free translation from Latin, with acrostic preserved.)

Ah child! Bound in time's tapestry, and yet you are born free
Come, let me sing to you of what there is and what will be,
Of all men and all gods, and of the mighty emperors three.
Named with a German name, a man will come with eyes of glass
Straddling horses large as houses bearing teeth like scimitars.
The trembling skies declare that Rome's great son has come to earth
A little Greek his name will be. Whilst God-as-babe has birth
Roman force will ram the island's neck into a noose of stone.
Emerging first in Brigantia, exalted later then in Rome!
Prostrate before a slavish god, at last he is revealed divine,
Embrace imperial will make dead marble of the Church's shrine.
Remember this: We hold these truths self-evident to be –
I say to you that all men are created equal, free
Rights inalienable assuréd by the Maker's attribute
Endowed with Life and Liberty and Happiness' pursuit.
O child! thou tapestried in time, strike home! Strike at the root!

The Menologium of the Blessed Isolde

AD 418

(Free translation from Old English, with acrostic preserved.)

Prologue

These the Great Years	of the Comet of God
Whose awe and beauty	in the roof of the world
Light step by step	the road to empire
An Aryan realm	THE GLORY OF CHRIST.

I

The Comet comes	in the month of June.
Each man of gold	spurns loyalty of silver.
In life a great king	in death a small man.
Nine-hundred and fifty-one	the months of the first Year.

II

The Comet comes	in the month of September.
Number months thirty-five	of this Year of war.
See the Bear laid low	by the Wolf of the north.
Nine-hundred and eighteen	the months of the second Year.

III

The Comet comes	in the month of March.
The blood of the holy one	thins and dries.
Empire dreams pour	into golden heads.
Nine-hundred and thirty-one	the months of the third Year.

IV

The Comet comes	In the month of October.
In homage a king bows	at hermit's feet.
Not an island, an island	not a shield but a shield.
Nine-hundred and seven	the months of the fourth Year.

V

The Comet comes in the month of May.
Great Year's midsummer less nine of seven.
Old claw of dragon pierces silence, steals words.
Nine-hundred and twenty-one the months of the fifth Year.

VI

The Comet comes in the month of February.
Deny five hundred months five Blood spilled, blood mixed.
Even the dragon must lie at the foot of the Cross.
Nine-hundred and five the months of the sixth Year.

VII

The Comet comes in the month of July.
Less thirty-six months the dragon flies west.
Know a Great Year dies Know a new world born.
Nine-hundred and twenty-six the months of the seventh Year.

VIII

The Comet comes in the month of September.
A half-hundred months more. At the hub of the world
Match fastness of rock against tides of fire.
Nine-hundred and eighteen the months of the eighth Year.

IX

The Comet comes in the month of March.
End brother's life at brother's hand. A fighting man takes
Noble elf-wise crown. Brother embraces brother.
The north comes from south to spill blood on the wall.

Epilogue

Across ocean to east and ocean to west
Men of new Rome sail from the womb of the boar.
Empire of Aryans blood pure from the north.
New world of the strong a ten-thousand year rule.

The Testament of Eadgyth of York

(Free translation from Old English.)

(Lines revealed in AD 1070)

In the last days
To the tail of the peacock
He will come:
The spider's spawn, the Christ-bearer
The Dove.
And the Dove will fly east,
Wings strong, heart stout, mind clear.
God's Engines will burn our ocean
And flame across the lands of spices.
All this I have witnessed
I and my mothers.
Send the Dove west! O, send him west!

(Lines revealed in AD 1481)

The Dragon stirs from his eastern throne,
Walks west.
The Feathered Serpent, plague-hardened,
Flies over ocean sea,
Flies east.
Serpent and Dragon, the mortal duel
And Serpent feasts on holy flesh.
All this I have witnessed
I and my mothers.
Send the Dove west! 0, send him west!

PROLOGUE
APRIL 1940

I

The boy slept beside the calculating engine.

Rory walked into the room. The sleeper, Ben Kamen, lay slumped over his desk, bulky volumes of physics journals opened around him, pages of foolscap covered with his spidery Germanic handwriting.

Crammed full of the components of the Analyser, the room smelled sharply of electricity, an ozone tang that reminded Rory of the wind off the Irish Sea. But this was Cambridge, Massachusetts, and he was in MIT, an oasis of immense concrete buildings. He was a long way indeed from Ireland. Nobody knew he was here, what he was doing. His heart hammered, but his senses were clear, and he seemed to see every detail of the cluttered, brightly lit room.

He turned away from Ben to the bank of electromechanical equipment that dominated the room. The Differential Analyser was an engine for thinking. There were tables like draughtsmen's workbenches, and banks of gears and wheels, rods and levers. This clattering machine modelled the world in the spinning of these wheels, the engaging of those gears. Earlier in the day Rory had fed it the data it needed, carefully tracing curves on the input tables, and manually calculating and calibrating the gear ratios. He ripped off a print of its results. The Gödel solutions were ready.

And Ben Kamen was ready too. Sleeping, Ben looked very young, younger than his twenty-five years. There was nothing about him to suggest his origin, as an Austrian Jew. One hand still held his fountain pen; the other was folded under his left cheek. His features were small, his skin pale.

Rory looked over what was assembled here: the brooding machine, the boy. This was the Loom, as he and Ben had come to call it, a machine of electromechanics and human flesh which – so they believed, so their theories indicated – could be used to change the warp and weft of the tapestry of time itself. And yet none of it was *his*, Rory's. Not the

Vannevar Bush Analyser which was being loaned to the two of them by MIT; they were students of the Institute of Advanced Studies at Princeton, and they had come here to Cambridge ostensibly to run complex relativistic models with the Analyser. Not the dreaming boy himself – and still less the contents of his head. All that Rory O'Malley owned was the *will*, to bring these components together, to make it so.

Rory pulled a lock of black hair back from Ben's brow. He wore it too long, Rory thought. Ben didn't stir, and Rory wasn't surprised. The sleeping draught he had poured into Ben's midnight coffee was strong enough to ensure that. Ever since their time together serving in the International Brigade in Spain Rory had always been fond of Ben, poor, deep, intense Ben. But he needed him too, or at least the peculiar abilities locked up in that head of his. Rory saw no great contradiction in this mixture of manipulation and affection. He was intent after all on nothing less than a cleansing of history, a reversal of the greatest crime ever committed. What was a little subterfuge compared to that?

He pulled a scrap of paper from his jacket pocket. It bore a poem of sixteen lines in English, translated roughly into Latin. He scanned it one last time. This was the core of his project, a mandate to history laden with all the meaning and purpose he could cram into it. Now these words would be sent out into the cosmos, crackling along Gödel's closed timelike curves like Morse dots and dashes on a telegraph wire – all the way from the future to the past, where some other dreaming head would receive it. All he had to do was to read to Rory, read out the Gödel trajectories computed by the Analyser, read the bit of doggerel. That was all, like reading to a child. And everything would change.

Ben stirred, murmuring. Rory wondered where in the many dimensions of space and time his animus wandered now.

Rory began to read. '"Ah child! Bound in time's tapestry, and yet you are born free/Come, let me sing to you of what there is and what will be . . ."'

The boy slept beside the calculating engine.

And then—

II

Julia Fiveash seduced Ben Kamen. No, she consumed him.

She took him inside three days of her arrival in Princeton from England. He couldn't have stopped her if he'd tried. He wasn't a virgin, with men or women, but after she pushed him to the carpet of his room and wrapped him in her long English limbs he felt as if he had been, before.

The second time they made love it was actually in the study of his mentor, Kurt Gödel. And Ben started to fret about her motives.

He lay on Gödel's sofa, his jacket pulled over his crotch for modesty. Julia, boldly unclothed, stalked around Gödel's room, flicking through the papers on his desk, running her delicate fingertip over the books on the shelves. Many of the books were still in their boxes, for Gödel had not been here long; reluctant to leave his beloved Vienna, he had hesitated until the last possible minute, when the Nazis had already started to roll up Europe like a giant carpet.

Julia's golden hair shone in a shaft of dusty sunlight. She was tall, her limbs long and muscular, her belly flat, her breasts small; she walked like an animal, balanced, confident. Her body was the product of a lifetime of English privilege, Ben thought, a life of horse-riding and tennis, her sexuality mapped by one healthy Englishman after another. She had conquered Ben as easily as the English had conquered much of the planet.

He longed for a cigarette, but he knew he dare not light up in Gödel's own room.

He plucked up his courage to challenge her. 'What are we doing here, Julia? What do you *want?*'

She laughed, a throaty sound. She was twenty-eight, three years older than he was; her age showed in her voice. 'That's not a very nice question. What do you think I want?'

'I don't know yet. Something to do with Gödel. You used me to get you in here, didn't you? Into this study.'

'Can you blame me for that? Kurt Gödel is the world's greatest logician. He's building a new mathematics, so they say. Or dismantling the old. Something like that, isn't it true?'

'You're a historian. You're attached to Princeton University, not this institute of math and physics. Why would *you* care about Gödel?'

'You're ever so suspicious, aren't you? But those suspicions didn't make you fight me off. He's such a funny little man, isn't he? Short and shabby with that high brow and his thick glasses, scuttling like a rabbit in his winter coat.'

'He's been known to take lovers among his students. Despite his unprepossessing looks. I mean, he's still only in his thirties. Back in Vienna—'

'The first time I spotted Gödel he was walking with Einstein. Now you can't miss Einstein, can you? Do you know, he was walking in carpet slippers, out in the middle of the street! Is he friendly with Gödel, do you know?'

'They met in 1933, I believe. Friends – I don't know. Einstein is the most exotic of the European beasts here in this American zoo, I suppose. But even Einstein had to flee Hitler.'

'Ah, Hitler! I've been in his presence, you know.'

'Whose?'

'Hitler's. I shook his hand. I wouldn't claim to have *met* him, exactly; I doubt he remembers me at all. I was an exchange student. I wanted to see for myself what the Germans were up to, rather than swallow the usual horrid propaganda. The transformation of that country from economic ruin in just a few years is remarkable. They made us very welcome. Hitler has a very striking presence; he has a way of looking *through* you. Goebbels, on the other hand, pinched my bum.'

He laughed.

'And now you've all come scuttling here, haven't you? Running from the monster, all the way to America.' She wrinkled her nose. 'Such a poky, dusty room, to be lodging a world-class mind. Gödel should have come to Oxford. Einstein too. Better than *this*. I mean, they have cloisters built of brick! Bertrand Russell says that Princeton is as like Oxford as monkeys could make it.' She laughed prettily.

'Perhaps Einstein and Gödel feel safer here than in an England which contains such people as you.'

'You're not very nice to me, are you, all things considered? Anyway Gödel would be under no threat in the Reich. He's not even a Jew.' She began plucking books from the shelf, and flicked through their worn pages.

Ben gathered his clothes from where they had been scattered on the floor, and began to pull them on. 'You've had your fun. Maybe it's time you told me what you want from me.'

'Well, there are rumours about you,' she said smoothly. 'You and your professor. Look at these titles. *Being And Time* by Martin Heidegger. *An Experiment With Time* by John William Dunne. *On the Phenomenology of the Consciousness of Internal Time*, Edmund Husserl. You worked with Gödel in Vienna, and now that he is here at the IAS you're starting to work with him again, aren't you? But not on the outer reaches of mathematical logic.' She glanced at a pencil note on the flyleaf of the Husserl, scrawled by Gödel himself. 'My German is still poor ... "The distinction between physical time and internal time-consciousness." Is that right?' As she leafed through the books there was a scent of dust, and stale tobacco – of Vienna. 'Ah. *The Time Machine* by H.G. Wells. Thought I'd find *that* here!'

He began to feel defensive, shut in, a feeling he remembered from Vienna, when he had been the target of the 'anti-relativity clubs' and other anti-Semitic groups. 'How did you find all this out? Slept with half the faculty, did you?'

She smiled at him, naked, entirely composed. 'And I know what else you've been working on. Something even Gödel doesn't know about. Something to do with relativity, and all this mushy stuff about internal time and the mind ... Something that goes beyond mere theory. And I know you haven't been working alone. I'm talking about Rory O'Malley.'

'What do you know about Rory?'

'I have a feeling I know more about your Irish friend than you do.' She ran a languid finger up the length of his bare arm; he shivered, despite himself, and buttoned his shirt. 'Come on, Ben. Spill the beans. The rumour is—'

'Yes?'

'That you and your Irish boyfriend have built a time machine.'

He hesitated. 'It's not like Wells's fantasy, not at all. And we played with ideas – concepts – that's all. We went through some of the calculations—'

'Are you sure that's all?'

'Or course I'm sure! We haven't *done* anything. We decided we mustn't, in fact, because—'

'Rory O'Malley isn't terribly discreet. Surely you know that much about him. *That's not what he's been saying.*'

As the import of her words sank home, Ben's stomach clenched. Was it possible? But how, without his knowledge? Oh Rory, what have you done?

Julia saw his fear, and laughed at him. 'I think you'd better give Rory a call. We've a lot to talk about.'

III

'I studied physics,' Rory said slowly. 'I was a bright kid. I was fascinated by relativity. I bet there weren't so many other fifteen-year-old students in Dublin in the 1920s who owned a copy of Einstein's 1905 papers – still less who could read them in their original German.

'But I was drawn to history as well. Why was a man like Einstein singled out for his Jewishness? Why, come to that, had the Christian church – I was an Irish Catholic – always been in such dreadful conflict with the Jews? So I began to study history. Religion. Philosophy . . .' He spoke uncertainly, plucking at his fingers.

Rory was dark, darker even than Ben. He joked that the Irish strain had been polluted by swarthy Spaniards washed ashore from the wreckage of the Armada. There was a trace of scar tissue at Rory's neck, the relic of the Nationalist bullet that had nearly killed him in Spain. Rory was a stocky, bullish man, an Irishman who had made himself a place in America, and had embraced mortal danger in Spain. Yet he seemed intimidated sitting before Julia, who was dressed in her customary style, an almost mannish suit of jacket and trousers, with a shirt-like blouse and a loosely knotted neck-tie, her perfect face framed by cigarette smoke.

The three of them sat in Rory's apartment, here at the leafy heart of Princeton. The living room was small but bright, with long sash windows pulled open to admit the green air of an American spring day. They sat on battered, grimy furniture amid loose piles of books, volumes on physics and history, on the roots of Christianity and the philosophical implications of Einstein's relativity. It was a jumbled, disorganised, dusty room, but it reflected Rory O'Malley, Ben thought, as if it were a projection of his own mind.

It had taken a couple of weeks for Julia to set up this meeting. She hinted darkly that she had wanted some time to verify some aspects of Rory's 'account' for herself, and she had arrived today with a slim briefcase, presumably containing the fruits of that research. Ben found himself gazing at the briefcase with dread.

And he felt uncomfortable at how Rory was opening up his soul, and Ben's, to Julia's interrogation.

He said sharply, 'You don't have to talk to her if you don't want to, Rory. I mean, who is she?'

Rory looked at him bleakly. 'Don't you *know?*'

Julia just smiled.

'I'll tell you who she is,' Rory said. 'She's an officer in the fucking SS. That's who she is. She's done more than shake Hitler's hand.'

Ben stared at her, appalled.

Julia extracted a fresh cigarette from the silver box she carried. 'Oh, don't look so shocked, Benjamin. I apologise for keeping it from you. But you'd hardly have slept with me if you'd known, would you? Let's get on with it. You met in Spain, during the Civil War.'

Hesitantly, uncomfortable, Rory spoke.

When only twenty-two, Rory had moved to New York from his native Dublin, ostensibly to study. But, a strong-minded idealist, he had quickly made a name for himself as an outspoken columnist. Then he had gone to Spain to work on a book on the seven-centuries-long history of coexistence and conflict between Christianity and Islam in the peninsula.

'I was in Seville when it all kicked off. The Civil War. The city fell to Franco's Nationalists within days. The bloodshed was worse *after* the cities fell, as the Nationalists took reprisals. So I fled north, to the Republican areas.'

'And there he met you?' Julia asked Ben.

Ben said reluctantly, 'I had already seen enough of the fascists in Germany. I went out to fight in the International Brigades. I never went back to Austria after that. I got some help from the Americans in my brigade, and they eventually got me into the country, and a place here at Princeton to continue my studies.'

Julia said briskly, 'I've never been terribly impressed by the Spaniards. They had all that wealth, a global empire, gold from the Incas and the Aztecs. And they blew the lot on dynastic wars within a century of Columbus. As for their Civil War, what a pointless conflict that was!'

'Three hundred and fifty thousand died,' Rory said angrily. 'Many of them to German and Italian bombs and bullets.'

'New ways of fighting wars were rehearsed. An imperial nation was reduced to a testing ground for the weapons of superior powers. So much for Spain!'

Ben snapped, 'You're damn cold, Julia.'

Julia laughed. 'No. Just realistic. Were you lovers?'

They spoke at the same time. 'No,' said Rory, and, 'Only once,' said Ben, more wistfully.

'And it was in pillow talk in Spain, I suppose, that you began to dream of time machines.'

'It was a pooling of interests,' Ben said.

Rory said, 'Studying history, I had come to feel a vast dissatisfaction. It need not have been this way! All the suffering, all the blood spilled – especially that provoked by religions, by prophets of peace. I wondered if it need be so – I longed for it not to be so.' He glanced at Ben. 'Then there was Ben's idle talk of Gödel, this eccentric mathematical genius who twisted Einstein's equations and imagined it might be possible to reach out, around what he called "closed timelike curves", to *touch the past . . .*'

'That and my dreams,' Ben said.

Julia eyed him. 'What dreams?'

'I have always had intense dreams. Often they are like memories of visits to scenes in the past – and the future. Once or twice—'

'Go on.'

Rory said, 'There was one dream, of the bullet which nearly killed me.' He touched his neck.

'You are precognitive,' Julia said to Ben.

'So John William Dunne might say. He might speak of my animus floating free in a multidimensional spacetime.'

'Is that what you believe?'

'No.' He sighed. 'I'm one of the most rational people you're likely to meet, Julia. I don't even believe in God. And yet others believe such powers of me. Isn't that an irony?'

'And so from all this,' Julia said, 'from hints of precognition, from Gödel's speculation about travel into the past, you began to design a time machine.'

'Not a machine,' Rory said. 'Though we gave it a machine-like name.'

'The Loom.'

'Yes. But it's a method, really.'

'A method for touching the past. For changing it. Is that right? And after Spain you came to this institute, where you worked together on realising your "method". You went so far as to wangle time on a calculating engine in Massachusetts. And you, Rory, began to work out, *if you* could make a change to the history that you found so unsatisfactory, exactly *what* change should be made.'

Rory fell silent. Ben stared at him.

'Oh, come now. If you don't tell him, I can – and will.' She patted her briefcase.

'Very well,' Rory blurted. 'It was Nicea.'

Ben was bewildered. 'Nicea?'

Julia smiled. 'You're clearly not as intimately acquainted with Christian history as your little friend here, Ben. Nicea, 325 AD. Where the Emperor Constantine convened his great Church council.'

'Constantine!' Rory spat. 'It was all his fault!'

IV

'Ah, the Romans,' Julia said. 'They were Aryans, you know, without a doubt. Hitler has the scholarship to prove it . . . Before Constantine,' she sneered, 'Jesus was a god of the slaves. By establishing the Church as the state religion of Rome, Constantine saved Christianity for the future.'

'Only by making it into a reflection of Rome itself! And it is that Roman autocracy and intolerance that has been at the root of the evil done in Christ's name ever since.'

'And so you had the temerity to cook up a plan. Didn't you? A scheme to use your Loom of time to unpick a few threads of history.'

'You told me none of this,' Ben accused Rory.

'Of course not,' he said miserably, still avoiding his eyes. 'Because you would have stopped me.'

'He worked out a message to send to the past,' Julia said brightly. 'A sort of retrospective prophecy, yes? You meant to send it to the age of Emperor Claudius, I gather, and his invasion of Britain. It was going to contain news about the future – and a little comical nonsense about democracy—'

'The republican age was the best of Rome,' Rory said defiantly. 'It inspired America centuries later. I wanted to give them hope.'

'Who?' Ben demanded.

'You know how it works, Ben. We can't target an individual in the past. We can only broadcast. And hope there are minds as receptive as yours – natural radio receivers, waiting to pick up news from the future.'

Julia said, 'You put in the prophetic stuff as a sort of lure, didn't you, Rory? You sent it back beyond Claudius to the year of Christ's birth, to catch the attention of the early Christians. You hoped to snag your dupe in the past by giving him a bit of foreknowledge that could make him powerful or rich, for instance about the building of Hadrian's wall. And you hoped that that power would be used as you intended: to fulfil your ultimate command.'

'To do what?' Ben asked.

Julia grinned. 'Why, to *kill* the Emperor Constantine!'

Ben found himself on the edge of panic. 'Rory – we discussed the dangers – what gives you the right to make such choices?'

'What gives us the right *not* to use such a gift?'

Ben thought fast. 'But this is just fantasy. Just talk. For Constantine was *not* cut down before Nicea, was he? And the Church was *not* restored to some state of innocence. The Pope still sits in Rome.'

'Rory failed,' Julia said.

'Well, I can't deny that,' Rory said.

'But *he made the attempt*, Ben.'

'That's impossible.'

'No.' She smiled. 'I have proof.'

Rory's eyes narrowed. 'What do you mean by that?'

'The Party has a rather good research institution. It's called the Ahnenerbe – it reports to Himmler, you know. Some quite innovative research into racial origins. I wrote to them . . .' She opened her briefcase and extracted a battered volume. It was a history of Rome.

Her Nazi scholars had not been able to retrieve Rory's testament in full. But elements of it had been recorded in an autobiographical work by the Emperor Claudius. That work too was lost, but there were references to it in other histories, from which, with a little care and some guesswork, some of Rory's lines had been reconstructed. She passed her book to Ben, opening it at a marked page. He read in disbelief, the text pale on old, yellowed paper:

Remember this: We hold these truths self-evident to be —
I say to you that all men are created equal, free
Rights inalienable assuréd by the Maker's attribute
Endowed with Life and Liberty and Happiness' pursuit.
O child! thou tapestried in time, strike home! Strike at the root! . . .

'By all that's holy,' Ben said, his heart hammering.

Julia smiled. 'Life, liberty and the pursuit of happiness. How delightfully gauche!'

'It seems I did it,' Rory said, his own eyes wide. 'These are my own words, cooked up in 1940, transmitted through the centuries, and now written down in this battered old history book. I never saw the proof before. I failed in my plan – Constantine survived – *but the Loom works*.' He laughed, but it was a brittle sound.

'You could not have done this,' Ben said weakly. 'I am an integral part of the Loom - my supposed precognition—'

'He drugged you,' Julia said simply. 'Drugged you, and used you in your sleep. Would you have stopped him?'

'Of course I would.'

'Why? Because you're a fan of Constantine?'

'No.' He looked at Rory with gathering horror. 'Because I have come to believe that the Loom, if ever operated, is a monstrous danger. The Loom is a weapon that destroys history, not creates it!'

'Yet it works,' Rory said flatly.

'Yes,' Julia said. 'Hitler despises Christianity, you know. He says it amounts to the systematic cultivation of failure. I think he'll rather approve of your attempts to destabilise the faith, Rory.'

'What do you mean by that?' Rory snapped.

'I really believe the Ahnenerbe is the place to carry forward this project of yours, don't you think? With proper funding and some decent researchers – not some half-trained Irish monkey and a mixed-up Jewish dreamer – with a better calculating machine than the antiquated gadget at MIT—'

'You want to give a time machine to the Nazis?' Ben felt weak. 'Oh, that's a good plan.'

Rory asked, 'So you're planning to support Hitler?'

Julia shrugged. 'What do you care? Ireland is neutral in the war.'

'But your own country isn't.' Rory stood up. 'You English aristocrats are all the same. You and your bloody empire. Now it's better Hitler than a Labour government, eh? Well, you're not going to give my work to that gang of thugs.' He raised a fist and closed on her.

It happened in an instant. From somewhere Julia produced a gun. Ben had time to notice how small it was, how exquisitely made, how expensive it looked. She raised the pretty, silver-plated pistol. She shot Rory in the heart. Rory looked surprised, and he stared down at the bloody mess of his chest. He shuddered; he crumpled and fell.

'Well, that's a bit unfortunate,' Julia said. 'We have made rather a mess of the apartment, haven't we? I don't need him. No doubt every-thing's here among these books and papers. But, of course, I need you. She turned to Ben and smiled. 'You and your dreams.'

'You want to hand me over to your Ahnenerbe. To the Germans.'

'They're here already. All around the building.'

'They'll love you in Nazi Germany,' he said.

'Oh, they will. They do! Now, will you come with me quietly or—'

He was still holding the heavy history book. He slammed it as hard as he could against her temple. He moved suddenly, giving her no notice at all. She fell, even more quickly than Rory, her gun spilling from her hand.

Ben looked at the mess, Julia sprawled across Rory's legs, the silver gun on the floor. He ought to destroy any evidence of their work. Take the gun. Kill Julia.

He knew he could not. His head was filled with flight, nothing more. All he wanted was to run until he could run no further, out of Princeton, out of America – all the way to England, perhaps, where at least he could be sure there were no Nazis.

But first he had to survive this day, uncaptured. He headed for the door, watching for Julia's German supporters.

I

INVADER
MAY–SEPTEMBER 1940

I

31 May – 1 June 1940

Mary Wooler heard about the desperate evacuation from France on the evening of the Friday, 31 May, on the BBC news. It was the first time the public had been told about it. The operation had already been underway for five days.

She spent a sleepless night, mostly on the phone to the War Office, trying to find out what had become of her son. It sounded as if the struggle to evacuate the British Expeditionary Force from Dunkirk was failing. It was chaotic, an unfolding disaster. Nevertheless she was told that elements of Gary's division were scheduled to be brought back to Hastings, on the south coast, if they made it back at all. So that was where she had to be.

On the Saturday morning she set off from her rented apartment in London in her hired Austin Seven, with its white-painted bumpers and plastic visors on the headlamps, to drive down to the coast.

The drive ought to have been simple enough. Her plan was to head roughly south-south-east, passing through Croydon, Sevenoaks and Tunbridge Wells, before cutting through the Sussex countryside until she came to Hastings via a little place called Battle, where the English had once faced the Normans. That was the theory.

But she never knew where the hell she was. Even as she drove she saw gangs of workmen cutting down direction markers, and unscrewing metal plates with village names. No names! She was a journalist and historian who had always made her living from words, and she thought how odd it was that to protect their country the English were stripping it of its words, of the layer of meaning that gave the landscape its human context: words that were a mish-mash of Norman French and Norse and Old English and even a bit of Latin, relics of other tumultuous days, words like bullet holes. Well, it might or might not confuse General Guderian and his Panzers, but it sure as hell confused Mary.

Still, the sun was a beacon in the clear sky. She took her bearings from that and just kept on running south. It wasn't that big a country, and she had to hit the coast in the end.

And meanwhile this first day of June was exquisitely lovely, one of those early summer days that England served up so effortlessly. Over a crumpled green carpet of fields and hedgerows, the birds soared like Spitfires. It didn't make sense, Mary thought. How could all this coexist with the horrors of the European war, unfolding just a few tens of miles away? Either the war wasn't real, or the summer's day wasn't; they didn't fit in the same universe.

Once she was through the last of the inland towns and neared the coast, the signs of war became more evident. There were pillboxes at the road junctions, some of them so new you could see the concrete glisten, still wet. She was nervous every time she crossed a bridge, for the Home Guard were mining the bridges, Great War veterans and kids too young to be conscripted who might or might not know what they were doing with high explosives.

And then, when she got close enough to glimpse the sea from the higher ground, she came upon more traffic. Most of it was heading the other way, inland, a steady stream of private cars, families, mum, dad, the kids, the dog and the budgie in its cage, with roof racks piled high with suitcases and even bits of furniture. Despite the official orders to 'stay put', as Mary had heard the new Prime Minister Churchill saying on the BBC, whole towns were draining northward, looking for safety. And in among the fleeing English were refugees who must come from much further away, buses and lorries full of civilians, women and children and old folk, and a sprinkling of men of military age. Jammed in, grimy, exhausted, they stared out at the glistening English landscape as they passed.

At one crossroads there was a hold-up. An Army truck had thrown a tyre, and a couple of soldiers were labouring to replace it. The soldiers had stripped to their khaki shirts in the heat of the summer sun, and as they struggled with the heavy wheels they bantered and laughed, cigarettes dangling from their lips. The traffic had to inch past, the laden buses and trucks bumping up on the verge to get by.

Mary found herself stuck opposite a bus that was marked for Bexhill and Boreham Street. She looked into the eyes of one little boy, who sat on the lap of a woman, presumably his mother. He was maybe eight or nine. His hair was mussed, and the dirt on his face was streaked by dried tears. He wore what looked like a school blazer, but the colour was odd – bright orange, not the English fashion. He said something, but she couldn't make out his lip pattern. But then he could be speaking French, or Dutch, or Walloon – maybe even German. She mouthed back, 'Welcome to England.'

II

At last she came to a coastal town. But which one?

She tracked a rail line until she reached a small station. No name signs. A train stood here, evidently kept back for troops; somebody had chalked 'WELCOME HOME BEF' on the side of a wagon. It made sense that once you had the troops back you would rush them inland, away from the dangers of the coast. But there were no troops to be transported; the train stood idle.

She got to a sea road and turned left, following the line of the coast. To her right the sea lay steel grey and calm, glimmering with highlights, studded with boats. The tide was low, and there was a beach of shingle and rocks, covered by tangles of wire and big concrete cubes. These coastal works were just the outer crust of an entire country turning into a fortress, with hundreds of miles of coastline reinforced, and elaborate systems of defences reaching far inland. The beach just ran on as far as she could see, curving gently into a bay ahead of her, to the east. Hastings had a harbour, but there was no harbour here; she wasn't in Hastings.

She wasn't sure what to do. She'd driven non-stop from London. She was stiff and thirsty and, having had little sleep, was conking out.

She parked the car roughly at the beach side of the road and clambered out. It was about noon now. The light of the sun, the salty sea air hit her like a strong gin. The coast road was busy with vehicles, and there were plenty of the uniforms she had got used to in London – Army khaki, the Navy's deep blue, the lighter slate blue of the RAF, and women in the uniforms of the ATS, the Auxiliary Territorial Service, or the Navy Wrens.

She walked a little way along the beach. Signs ordered civilians to keep off, and warned that the shingle was mined. And if she looked out to sea, this brilliant summer day, she could actually see the war in Europe, the glint of aircraft swooping low, and she heard the distant crump of guns. A pall of smoke rose up, towering, remote. She found herself noting her impressions for when she next filed some copy. She had barely ventured out of London since the day war had been declared back in September. She tried to imagine this scene being played out in her own homeland, the Atlantic coast fortified in this way.

But the evacuation was in progress too. In the deeper water Navy ships glided, blue-grey silhouettes, while smaller ships filed steadily towards France and back again, trawlers, drifters, crabbers, shrimpers, fishing smacks, a few lifeboats, and many yachts and small motorboats. Big barges lumbered, emblazoned with the name 'Pickfords', intended to haul cargo around the coast. Some of the beach line had been cleared so the boats could ground, the barbed wire cut and pulled back, the tank traps shoved aside. Waiting on the shingle there were stretcher parties, she saw, and the WVS, the Women's Voluntary Service, had set out tables done out with little Union flags and signs saying 'WELCOME HOME OUR BOYS'. Tea boiled in huge urns, and sandwiches piled up on plates. But the tea went undrunk, the sandwiches uneaten.

This was Operation Dynamo, the evacuation from France. The BBC had been playing this up all night, the little ships of England sailing to France to help the Navy bring home a defeated army. But the little ships were, shockingly, coming back empty.

'You can't park here, madam.' She turned to face a man, quite young, in a heavy black jacket and a tin hat that looked like a relic of the Great War. He had a rifle, a canvas gas-mask pouch slung over his shoulder, and an armband with 'ARP' stitched into it. Air Raid Precautions, another of Britain's new volunteer armies. 'We're trying to keep the beaches clear, and the run into town.'

'Yes, I can see that. I'm sorry. Look—'

'And you ought to have your gas-mask with you.'

'Well, it's in the car.'

'The rule is, carry it at all times.' His accent was what she thought of as neutral English; he sounded quite well educated. He was looking at her more closely now, suspiciously. 'May I ask what you're doing here? You seem lost.'

'I'm trying to get to Hastings. My son is coming home with the BEF, or I hope he is.'

'And you don't know where Hastings is?'

She tried to keep a lid on her temper. 'I don't even know where I am. Look, if you could just point me at Hastings—'

'Where are you from? Canada? I know there are Canadian units in the BEF.'

'No, I'm American. Easy mistake to make.'

His eyes narrowed and he stepped towards her. He limped slightly; maybe that was what had kept him from the call-up. 'No need for that tone, madam. You're in Bexhill.' He pointed east, along the coast road. 'Hastings is a few miles thataway. Just keep on through Saint Leonard's and you can't miss it.'

'Thanks.' She hurried back to her car.

In her rear-view mirror she could see him stand there and watch her pull out. She reminded herself that she was at the besieged coast of a country where there was a strong suspicion that the enemy wasn't just coming but might already be here, in one disguise or another. He fixed his helmet and continued his patrol along the sea front.

It was a straightforward drive east, though the coast road was crowded with trucks and buses and other transports, and, ominously, ambulances.

She came into another town. She saw a pier, with boats clustered around its great feet. The pier had been severed so it couldn't be used by invading Germans. She kept pushing forward until the road passed the base of a hill, a stratified cliff on which sprawled the ruins of a castle. This was a seaside town, with hotels and a bandstand. She saw no children around on this summer Saturday. All evacuated inland, no doubt, because of the invasion scare. Still, it was eerie. And ahead of her an unlikely sight loomed, a school of tremendous silvery fish straining on tense cables into the air. They were barrage balloons; evidently air attacks were expected.

Soon she saw a harbour wall jutting out to sea. But she wasn't able to reach the harbour itself, for the coast road was blocked. Uniforms swarmed everywhere. Once more at a loss she turned inland, scanning for information points and police officers.

She passed an open space that seemed to have been set up as a medical triage centre for refugees, where bewildered-looking civilians were tended to by kindly nurses and other volunteers. A white-coated doctor sat with one woman, gently trying to prise something from her. As she drove past, Mary saw that *it was an arm*, the severed arm of a child, blackened and burned. The sight bewildered Mary. She was supposed to be a journalist, at least pro tem. How could she write about this?

She came to yet another hold-up, ahead of a piece of wasteland. This was the anchor point for one of the barrage balloons. The steel-grey monster, an envelope of hydrogen sixty feet long, loomed quite low over the rooftops, in the middle of being deployed. It was tethered to the ground by thick steel cables, and its crew was struggling to control the cables' release from massive winches. Most of them were women, straining and sweating, in the colours of the ATS, the Wrens, and a few

WAAFs, the Women's Auxiliary Air Force. An officer, male, stood by, steadily counting to give the crew rhythm as they heaved. Mary stared, amazed at the sight of this miniature zeppelin rising up from the streets of this seaside town.

One of the WAAFs lost her hat as Mary watched, and bright red hair tumbled loose. Mary thought she knew who she was. She parked hastily, ignoring the shouts of yet another ARP warden, and she got out of the car and ran forward. 'Hilda! Hilda Tanner!'

The young WAAF turned. Mary waved, still pushing forward. The WAAF had a word with the officer, and he released her from the crew with a brisk nod. Hilda picked up her cap, crammed her red hair beneath it, and hurried towards Mary.

Mary felt relief gush. It wasn't Gary, but it was one step closer. 'Hilda? Look, you don't know me. We haven't met. I only knew you from the photographs—'

Hearing her accent, Hilda evidently guessed who Mary was. 'You're Gary's mother.'

'He did speak of you, and how he'd met you here – I was stuck in London, you see – and then the embarkation came—' Unaccountably her vision blurred.

The girl took her arms. 'Here, don't take on so. Come with me. Here, sit down.' She led Mary to a bench; some of its slats had been removed, maybe for firewood, but it was possible to perch on it. Sitting there, in the sharp sunlight, Mary felt the last of her energy drain out of her.

Hilda was as pretty as her photographs had suggested, but with a long, rather serious face, a strong nose, and a determined set to her chin. She didn't seem to be wearing any make-up; that bright red hair, struggling to escape from her cap, was the most colourful thing about her. 'What are you doing here, Mrs Wooler?'

'Mary. Call me Mary, for God's sake.'

'It's Gary, isn't it?' Her voice rose. 'Has something happened to him? I've had no news since—'

'There's nothing bad, that I know of.' She told her what she had learned from the War Office.

'And so you came.'

'Yeah. The trouble is I don't know what to do now I'm here.'

'Then it's lucky you found me,' Hilda said firmly. 'We'll ask my dad.'

'Your dad?'

'You'll see.' Hilda took Mary's hand, stood, and led Mary away from the sea front and into the town. But as they walked she glanced across at the work unit still labouring at the balloon.

Mary asked, 'Are you sure you can get away?'

'Oh, they can manage without me. Tricky job, mind. If the wind changes you get a bag of hydrogen coming down in the middle of town, and one fag-end and it's blammo. Of course we WAAFs could manage it alone, but the men would never admit to that.' She turned her palm to show what looked like rope bums. 'They call us "amazons", you know. In the papers.' She laughed, quite gaily.

'I'm partly responsible for that, I suppose. I'm a journalist of sorts, a stringer for the *Boston Traveller.*'

Her eyes widened. 'You are? Gary says you're a historian.'

'A historian by profession. I, we, happened to be here when the war broke out. I looked for something more useful to do.'

'Just as Gary did.'

'To tell you the truth, I tried to stop him joining up. I mean, America isn't in this war.'

'Do you wish you'd tried harder now?'

'No,' Mary said, thinking that over. 'No, I'm proud of him. He did what he thought was right.'

Hilda nodded. 'Look, here's my dad.'

Her father turned out to be a policeman, a constable in uniform. Today, complete with his gas-mask slung over his shoulder, he was on duty outside the town hall. With various uniforms hurrying to and fro, the building was evidently serving as some kind of information station for the evacuation operation.

'Dad!' Hilda broke into a run for the last couple of steps, and, suddenly girlish, let him give her a quick uniformed hug.

'Hello, love.' The father took off his heavy bobby's helmet, to reveal a square, deeply lined face, greying hair cut short and smoothed flat with pomade. He must have been in his late forties. Mary thought she could see something of his daughter in him; he must have been a looker once. 'What's up? Lost your toy balloon?'

'It's Gary. Dad, he's back—'

'He might be,' Mary put in.

The father eyed her, surprised by her accent. 'And you are?'

Hilda introduced her quickly.

The father shook her hand; his grip was warm, firm and sure. 'Call me George.'

'Mary.'

'I saw little enough of your son before he was shipped away. But he went off to fight for a good cause. And now you say he's back?'

'It's possible. All I really know is that elements of his division should have been brought back here. What I don't know is where I might find him.'

George Tanner rubbed his chin. 'The evacuation's being going on for about six days already. There are shot-up soldiers all over town – I don't mean to alarm you, Mary – not enough of them by half, things have gone badly over there. Look, I have contacts of my own. Wait while I nip inside.' He tucked his helmet under his arm and went into the town hall.

With her father gone Hilda asked solicitously, 'How are you bearing up? Would you like a cup of tea?'

'Maybe later,' Mary said. 'I'm glad I found you, Hilda. Without you I don't know what I would have done.'

'Somebody would have helped you. People are like that. Besides, we haven't done anything yet.' She was staring at the town hall door. 'Come *on*, Dad.'

George came hurrying out of the hall, fixing his helmet hastily on his head. He carried a slip of paper in his hand. 'Look, we need to go to the hospital. It's that way.' He pointed. 'It's only half a mile. I could get a car but it's going to be quicker to walk it.' He eyed Mary, uncertain. 'Are you up to that?'

'I'm tougher than I look.'

Hilda led the way, hurrying.

Mary said carefully, 'So you found him.'

'There's a record in the log, yes,' George said, with what sounded like a policeman's caution. 'They've got everything buttoned down in there, those ATS ladies, it's quite remarkable. Every last soldier logged in, cross-checked, filed and indexed. If only the generals had done as well in France.'

Her relief that Gary was here, that he had come through the funnel of the evacuation, was tinged with fear. 'But he's in the hospital, you say.'

'When the evacuation started, they cleared out all the hospitals ready to receive the wounded. They set up a few field stations in the schools too. As it turned out there were far fewer coming back than had been planned for.' He said carefully, 'You mustn't read anything into the fact that he's in hospital. It's a case of first come first served, not medical need.'

'We'll know soon enough,' Hilda said, hurrying forward.

'Afterwards we'll sort you out,' George said. 'Find you somewhere to stay. You can be with us if you like. There's just the two of us, Hilda and me. My wife passed away a dozen years ago.'

'I'm sorry.'

'Long time ago. Look, is there anybody you'll need to call? We don't have a private phone, and the public lines are blocked – well, you know that – but if you want to make a call I'll take you to the police station. You have a husband – Gary's father?'

'I'm afraid we're divorced, George. But, yes, I'll need to speak to him at some point. Depending on – you know.'

'We'll sort you out, don't you worry.'

'You're being very kind.'

III

At the hospital entrance ambulances pulled up and drove off, and there was a steady stream of stretcher parties. Nurses fussed around, and a doctor seemed to be on hand to greet every arrival. Green Army blankets were spread over the stretchers. The staff looked strained, the doctors' white coats ominously stained with old blood.

At a desk inside the entrance an ATS volunteer, a woman of about sixty with a helmet of steel-grey hair, was doing her best to block the way to all non-essential visitors. But George the copper, big and bluff and authoritative, easily talked his way past her. Further in they found an information desk manned by a Wren, who was able to give them the number of the ward they needed. The hospital was busy, and there were soldiers everywhere, in grimy uniforms and bandages. But even so there were a lot of staff and arm-banded volunteers standing around, looking fretful, with nothing to do.

There was a dreadful smell, a heavy iron stink. George saw Mary react, and he touched her arm, and Hilda's. 'That's dried blood. I remember it from the last lot, the first war. The men are turning up here with old wounds, days old some of them. You never forget the smell. But you just have to put it aside and get on with things. All right?'

They both nodded, and went on. To Mary, knowing that Gary was close, somewhere in this crowded, busy building, these last moments, this walk down the corridors with their shining floors, seemed endless, as if time was stretching.

At last they came to Ward Twenty-Three. There were two rows of beds before a big sash window that had been flung open to allow in the light and air of a garden. The beds were all full of broken-looking bodies, lying still. Mary couldn't bear to look at their faces. She marched forward, looking at the names on the medical notes fixed to the iron bed frames.

And here was his name, WOOLER, GARY P., with his British army serial number. He lay on his back covered by a thick white blanket, his eyes closed. A skinny young man with thick black hair and wearing a white coat sat on a hard upright chair beside the bed, eyeing them.

Gary looked asleep. His face was clean, though Mary could see some bruising, but his blond hair, scattered over the pillow, was matted and filthy. A drip stand stood beside him; a clear tube snaked into a vein in his arm, the needle covered by a bit of bandage. Mary was hugely relieved that at first glance he looked *whole*: two arms, two legs, no hideous medical apparatus strapped to his body.

But Hilda was crying, with great silent heaving sobs. Mary felt her own tears come, and she buried her face in the girl's neck, smelling the starch of her uniform.

When they broke, Mary turned to the young man on the chair. She whispered, 'Nurse? When will he wake up? Can we speak to him?'

He stood. 'Well, I'm not a nurse. Just a volunteer.' He grinned, and showed her an armband with a red cross. 'My name's Benjamin Kamen.'

Both Hilda and George stiffened at hearing his accent. 'You sound German,' Hilda said, wondering.

'I'm Austrian,' said Kamen. 'An Austrian Jew, in fact. I came to Britain to fight. They wouldn't let me join up. Flat feet! So I'm doing this instead.'

'And why are you here?' George asked, still sounding suspicious.

'Because I've got this accent,' Kamen said simply. 'Makes the English uncomfortable. So I try to help out with the international brigades. Half of them don't recognise my accent, or if they do they feel like outsiders anyhow. And when I got to know Gary, when he was brought in – he spoke about you, Mrs Wooler.' He faced Mary. 'I recognised your name. I used to read your pieces in the *Traveller*, and I know about your work before the war. I've been waiting here to meet you.'

Mary was bewildered. 'Thank you—'

'Mrs Wooler, there's something I need to talk to you about. You might be able to help me. It could be urgent.'

George snorted. 'More urgent than this? For God's sake, man.'

'I'm sorry.' Kamen backed off, hands raised.

'But is he all right?' Hilda asked.

Gary stirred. 'You could try asking him yourself.' His head turned, and his eyes flickered open.

Mary grabbed her son's hand and squeezed it, pressing it to her face. 'Oh, Gary, my God. What a day you've given me!'

'I'm sorry.' His voice was very dry, cracking. 'Mind you, I've not been at a picnic myself, I can tell you that.' He turned his head to Hilda, who was suffering that odd silent sobbing again, and he stroked her face. George, standing massively, rested a hand on his daughter's shoulder.

'He got off lightly,' Ben Kamen murmured. 'Believe it or not. The troops are turning up raw off the beaches of France. When they come in it's more like a battlefield dressing station here than a hospital.'

'And you,' Hilda said, stroking Gary's brow, 'look as if you need more sleep.'

'Yeah.' But he faced his mother, wanting to tell her. 'Listen, Mom. They tore across the country in those tanks of theirs. There was nothing to stop them. We did nothing but retreat – a fighting retreat, but a retreat. The Brits just weren't prepared for what hit them. I heard some of them bitching that it wasn't like this in India. And, Christ, the things we saw. Women and kids mown down from the air—'

'It's all right,' Mary said.

'Well, we got to the coast. The Germans had us pinned. And then we heard that Guderian was coming, with his First Panzers. We all knew what that bastard had done in Poland. They say he reached Gravelines, and secured bridgeheads over the river there. He waited one day. This was last Friday. I don't know why he paused. It let us start the evacuation. But then, on the Saturday, he came for us.

'Mom, we set up a perimeter. *We fought back*. But it was a slaughter. You had the Panzers ripping into our flanks, and the damn Luftwaffe coming at us from overhead, and we just couldn't get on those ships fast enough. I was in a line for three days, a typical goddamn English queue, waiting for a place on a destroyer. No food, no water, nothing.

'I got away. I was lucky. The scuttlebutt here is that ten per cent might make it home, out of four *hundred* thousand on those beaches. That's half the damn English army, Mom. I can't see how much of a fight they can put up after that.'

'Hush,' Mary said, for he was becoming agitated; she tried to calm him, smoothing his brow.

'He didn't sleep for five nights, I think,' Kamen murmured. 'He has a lot of healing to do.'

But Gary was still distressed. 'I think maybe the English have lost their war already, Mom. Lost it, on the beaches of France. Next thing you know they will be here. The Nazis.'

George shook his head. 'They won't come. Hitler wants an armistice. That's what they say.'

Gary actually laughed, though it hurt him. 'An armistice? After all this?'

A nurse came then, and a doctor; they administered a sedative. Mary sat with her son until he slept.

The strange medical volunteer, Ben Kamen, waited for his chance to speak to her.

IV

It was another glorious day in this long, glorious summer. And in occupied France there was nothing more glorious than to be a soldier of the Reich.

Ernst Trojan was on a rest day, and he wanted to use it well. He would have come here to Claudine's little apartment even if not for the sex; sooner the sweet breath of Claudine than the gusty farts of some fat Bavarian pig of an obergefreiter in the Wehrmacht's tent city – or, worse, a few more hours of drunken mockery by his elder brother and his drinking partners in the SS. And yet, as the heat climbed in the middle of the day, as he lay naked with Claudine on her bed and the light slanted through the shutter slats into the dusty, scented room, he longed to be out in the world.

'Get dressed,' he told Claudine with a grin. He threw a bundle of clothes at her, and hunted for his pants.

She lay there watching him. Claudine Rimmer was tall, taller than he was in fact, her limbs long and her torso slim; she lay naked on her bed, her legs parted slightly in unconscious, unafraid invitation. Her dusky complexion and rich black hair would have made him think more of a girl of the Mediterranean than of Boulogne, of the northern coast. That was how he would have thought two or three months ago anyhow, but he had never even left Germany back then, and now he was learning fast. And when they made love, he had learned that she was not as delicate as she looked.

When she saw he was serious she sat up with a sigh, hunted through her clothes, and found a bra of impossible delicacy. 'Getting bored with me, are you, Gefreiter Trojan? We're not running out of sheaths, not yet.' She brushed her hand over a pile of the things on her bedside table. They were actually English army issue, the spoils of war, far better quality than the standard Wehrmacht supply.

'Of course not. It's just that it's such a beautiful day – here we are in the middle of history – even love can wait!'

She pulled her blouse over her head, but she kept arguing. 'Are the hours unsuitable for you? I can be flexible.' Her German was good, though her accent sometimes made him pause. 'I am a teacher, but quite junior, Ernst. I can find cover. It's not as if there is any great enthusiasm for education just now, and soon the summer vacation will come. My timetable is subordinate to yours.'

She always spoke to him briskly, challengingly, with no hint of weakness or dependency in her voice. He told himself that he would not have chosen any girl if he could not have had that. But was this some subtle rejection? His old inadequacies bubbled up inside him. Suddenly he was no longer a soldier of the all-conquering German army, but just poor foolish Ernst Trojan from Munich, he of the spiky hair and sticking-out ears. 'You seem troubled,' he said. 'Do you think I would be ashamed to be seen out with you?'

'Not that. It's just that what we have – whatever *that* is – others might not see it the same way, Ernst.'

'If others judge us, into the sea with them! All that matters is us, and what we have together. And *we* know what that is, do we not, Claudine?'

'If you say so,' she said evenly. She pulled on the stockings he had given her, and rummaged for the cosmetics he had bought her, and tucked the pile of marks he had given her into her purse.

They walked through the old town, heading towards the sea. The district was surrounded by walls left by the Romans. Ernst had grown up in a place the empire had never reached; his imagination was caught by such antiquity. And today there were Party flags everywhere, red with a bold black swastika on a circle of white. He commented on the splashes of colour they lent to the buildings from which they were draped, the Hotel de Ville, the wall gates. Claudine said nothing. Ernst held Claudine's hand, and as they walked her body swayed against his, brushing easily. She was so beautiful, he thought, suffused with the summer light that shone through the fabric of her blouse. He felt proud to be walking with her, he in his Wehrmacht uniform, his cap on his head. Yet he could never forget, even on this beautiful morning, that she was taller than he was, taller and older.

They walked down to the coast road, the Quai Gambetta, and set off north, heading towards the harbour and ultimately the road to Calais. And here they saw the most remarkable sight in town: the invasion fleet.

The harbour was full of river and canal barges, drafted for the purpose and floated down the Seine and the Rhine. They were lined up like logs on a river, jammed so close that you could have walked across the harbour from one sea wall to the other without getting your feet wet. These clumsy vessels would not provide a comfortable ride across the Channel; they would have to be towed, and looked horribly vulnerable to attack. But the crossing would be short, he had been assured by his superiors, over in less than half a day. Out at sea heavier craft, motor transports and others, stood at anchor, grey shadows on the bright water.

They walked further, reaching the beaches north of the town, where the men were going through landing exercises. The landing boats ran onto the beach, one after another, and the infantrymen jumped out into the shallow water and waded to the shore, laden with packs and weapons. One squad of men was struggling to haul a field gun up the beach. Elsewhere unhappy horses were being led through the shallow water. Despite the sudden fame of the Panzers, the German Army was basically horse-drawn; there would be one horse for every four men, so that twenty-four thousand of the animals would be shipped across the Channel in the first three days alone.

A boat-load of soldiers tipped over, leaving the men splashing in the surf, laughing like children.

Claudine laughed too. 'I'll tell you something. You Germans are hopeless on the ocean! All summer I've seen you flounder around like this. Your commanders even seem to be baffled by the tides!'

He shrugged. 'We're not a nation of sea dogs, not like the British. But we have mounted one successful seaborne invasion before, when we took Norway. Why can't we do it again?' He gestured at the Channel. 'It will be an unlucky man who loses his life to that miserable ditch.'

She pulled a face, and he saw age lines around her eyes and mouth, caught by the sun. At twenty-eight, she was five years older than him. 'But that "miserable ditch" held back Napoleon. Well, good luck. And if you Germans know so little of the sea, what on earth will you make of England when you get there?'

He snorted. 'We know all we need to know of England. It is a land of plutocrats in fine houses, who leave the defence of the nation to the shambolic old men of the Home Guard, while the working people cower in fear of our parachutists.' He rummaged in his jacket and produced a picture book. 'This *bildheft* has been given to every man.'

She flicked through the book. It showed pretty little harbours, country houses, romantic ruins. 'How attractive,' she said drily. 'Does England have no factories, then? No major roadways, no big cities? Well, I suppose you're going to find out.' She looked at him. 'But why do you do this, Ernst? Not Germany – *you*. You are a clever man, I know that much.'

He shrugged. 'I hoped to be a teacher, like you, or a scholar. I studied mathematics, though when I was drafted I was not advanced enough for my skills to be useful to the war effort.'

'But why do you fight?'

'For my father,' Ernst said simply. 'My brother might tell you differently, but *he* joined the SS. My father fought in the first war. He saw the ruin of the country after the unjust Versailles settlement. And he nursed an old wound that made it impossible for him to work. We were impoverished. He was a proud man, my father. He died bitter. I was pleased when the war came. I fight for my country, for my father.'

'But the soldiers in England have fathers too.' Claudine found one image in the book, of a place called Hastings. It was evidently taken from a postcard; it showed a shingle beach crowded with families. 'I wonder if children will ever play on these beaches again.'

'There is no reason why not,' Ernst said primly. 'Provided that such play does not conflict with the goals of the occupation.'

She laughed again. 'Ah, Ernst. Perhaps it will be mockery that defeats you Germans in the end, not guns.'

They were distracted by a new noise from the sea, a throaty roar. A different sort of boat ripped across the water, running parallel to the shore; jet black and sleek, it created a wake that sent lesser craft bobbing. The men on the beaches whooped and applauded.

Claudine swore softly. 'And what is *that*?'

Ernst's heart sank. 'It is a *schnelleboote*. Powered by an aircraft engine. Designed to roar across the Channel and dance up the beaches of England. More noise than performance . . .'

'It's stopping,' Claudine said. 'Look. Somebody's waving at us!' She waved back.

'And that,' said Ernst, his gloom deepening, 'is my older brother. Who can't leave me alone for one day.'

'Oh, don't be so grumpy. How exciting, a brother in the SS!'

The *schnelleboote* turned and made for the shore.

And a flight of planes, the bombers and fighters of the Luftwaffe, poured suddenly over their heads, making them duck. It had been going on since the beginning of the month, assaults on English ports and railways and aerodromes and factories, all part of the great softening-up. The planes roared on, wave after wave, a three-dimensional armada that towered thrillingly into the sky.

V

Josef, in the crisp black uniform of the Waffen SS, was nothing but good manners. 'Mademoiselle,' he said correctly, in German. 'How you must illuminate the shadowy life of my stunted brother!' He bowed and kissed Claudine's hand, holding it just a little too long, Ernst thought.

Claudine laughed in her pretty way, laughed with Josef. Of course Ernst knew they were laughing at him. His brother was ten years older than Ernst, that bit taller, that bit better looking; he and Claudine, side by side, looked as if they belonged together much more than Ernst and Claudine ever did.

It made it worse that Josef had turned up with a girl still more stunning than Claudine. Tall, blonde, she too was in uniform, that of an SS-unterscharfuhrer; she carried a small canvas bag. Her name was Julia Fiveash, and she was, surprisingly, English. She was in an SS unit called the Legion of St George, made up of British subjects. She barely seemed to notice Claudine, and she looked at Ernst haughtily. But she made the black SS uniform she wore almost unbearably glamorous.

Josef brought them to a bar near the harbour. They sat in the open air, at a polished table with a pretty lace covering, and Josef ordered coffee and cognac for them all. The servile barkeeper insisted he would take no payment from an officer of the SS; Josef, just as politely, insisted that he would, and handed over crisp mark notes.

When Julia spoke to Ernst her German was crisp and precise, with barely a trace of an English accent. 'Josef is an SS-standartenfuhrer, which I believe corresponds roughly to colonel in the English army,' she said. 'Whereas you, Ernst?'

'I am a gefreiter,' he said uncomfortably. 'A Wehrmacht rank—'

'Different from the SS. Lower than a corporal? But then you are so much younger than Josef, aren't you? One must make allowances, I suppose.'

Josef laughed. 'Even Julia outranks you. She has already risen to unterscharfuhrer.'

Julia said, 'Or as we would say, sergeant. In fact we generally speak English in the Legion ...'

The barkeeper brought their drinks; he laid them out as quickly as he could and scuttled away, head averted.

'Of course,' Josef said to Claudine silkily, 'you don't have ranks in your profession, as such, do you?'

That confused Ernst. 'She is a teacher.'

'Ah, but I meant your new profession, my dear.' He reached down and casually lifted up Claudine's skirt.

Claudine did not flinch, or show any fear.

Ernst slapped his brother's hand away. 'Leave her alone. It's not like that.'

'Oh, come, Ernst, don't be naïve. All collaborators are whores; it's just a question of the price. I mean, do you really imagine a girl like this would be seen with a man like you if not for the war?' He winked. 'It's not as if you need to spend your money, you know. The SS will soon have their brothels set up. I could get you a pass. Come to that, as we are of good Aryan stock, it would be doing your country a service to spend your seed between the thighs of some busty blonde maiden.'

Julia laughed, blowing out smoke. 'It will be an Aryan paradise when the SS gets things sorted out, will it, Josef?'

'For us it will be, yes, my dear.' He peered at Claudine's complexion disapprovingly, and plucked at a lock of her hair. 'I suppose this one will do for now. I doubt if she will meet the racial criteria. Pity. I wouldn't mind riding her myself.' Ernst grew angry, but before he could speak Josef sipped his coffee, then spat it out on the ground. 'Ach, what is this muck? Made from acorns, is it?' He called more loudly, 'Are you trying to poison us, barkeeper?'

The barkeeper hurried to pour out replacements.

Julia poked Josef's elbow. 'Don't be so cruel to the poor old man.'

'Well, he deserves it. I mean, look around you. I could have been posted to Paris. Boulogne! This must be the arsehole of all France.'

Claudine said evenly, 'And you are the turd that is passing through it, I suppose?'

Ernst gasped. Even Julia looked shocked.

Josef stared at her, then laughed out loud. 'My word, Ernst, this half-breed of yours has a bit of spirit!'

'Yes, she does,' Ernst said testily.

'So, Ernst, your training is going well? All that seasickness and lumping it up the beaches?'

'The preparations are proceeding,' Ernst said neutrally.

'Yes, they are, in fact, at levels more elevated from *you* than the eagle flies,' Josef said. 'The Fuhrer has issued a final directive, I am told. The invasion of England even has a name now. Operation Sea Lion! But the details are still being argued over among the military command. I need something to draw on.' He patted his pockets. 'Damn.' He lifted the cups and glasses from the table, and pulled away the lace tablecloth to expose a surface of old wood, dark and so polished it had the look of satin. He took out a pocket knife and with brisk strokes scraped a map into the table's surface. 'This will have to do.

'Look here. *This* bit of coastline is the most suitable to mount an invasion, for it is here that Europe comes closest to England. One can simply hop across the Channel and assail the coasts of Sussex and Kent, and be only a few hours' drive from London. The Navy want to plan on the basis of a narrow front, for that is more defensible from the sea than a long stretch of the Channel; the Army, though, don't want to be bottled up on land, and argue for a wider front ...'

He continued to sketch with his knife, drawing attack lines and defensive perimeters, cutting and splintering the tabletop. Ernst watched the faces of the women; neither of them reacted to this bit of petty vandalism.

Claudine asked, 'You are a mere standartenfuhrer. Why would you know all this? Perhaps you are simply trying to impress a woman you have called a whore.'

'You do have spirit, don't you? I am here advising the Waffen SS. The military arm of the SS, which strictly speaking is a Party organisation. But I work with the Ahnenerbe.'

'Which,' said Julia, 'is Himmler's research and cultural institute.'

'I have worked with Himmler himself. So you see, my dear, your lover's brother has contacts in high places. Aren't you impressed?'

Claudine said, 'It is already a month since the surrender of France. By waiting so long you have given the English time to prepare.'

Josef nodded, impressed again. 'Actually some have said exactly that. General Milch, Goering's second-in-command, for example. It is a basic principle that one should pursue a defeated enemy. Milch argued we should have mounted an airborne invasion as soon as we reached the ocean, in June.'

Julia said, 'I think the Fuhrer continues to hope that my countrymen will come to their senses. After all England's land army is severely depleted after the bulk of it was lost at Dunkirk.'

'It's true Hitler has made peace offerings,' Josef said. 'With sensible terms: a free hand in Europe in return for the security of the British

Empire. All ignored or rebuffed. How unreasonable! Especially when you see how well we treat the conquered French.' He grabbed the top of Claudine's thigh and squeezed it.

'You're a pig, Josef,' Ernst murmured. The talk of war seemed unrealistic, a fantasy in the bright summer sunlight, amid the gentle sound of voices, the clink of cutlery and glasses. 'Do you think we *will* invade, Josef, when it comes to it?'

'Well, what do you think? The invasion fleet is in the harbour just over there. That doesn't come cheap, you know; every barge that's brought here can't be lugging machine parts or coal up and down the Rhine.'

'True. But we need a show of strength to keep the British on the ropes, don't we? If the barges ever sailed, the Royal Navy would overwhelm the Kriegsmarine – it has a ten-to-one advantage. We would be chopped to matchsticks.'

'But it could be even worse,' Julia said. 'After France fell Churchill ordered the Royal Navy to sink the French fleet in its Algerian ports. But his cabinet overruled him; the Navy was ordered back. And so Germany took the French Navy, one of the most powerful and most modern in the world. What a mistake for the British!'

'Yes,' Josef said. 'They lacked the confidence to strike – or the foolhardiness.'

'The English are all cowards,' Julia said lightly.

That stung Ernst, who had fought the English in the Low Countries. 'And what is it you want, madam, save for the prostration of your own people?'

She was unperturbed. 'On the contrary, it is what I offer him that interests Josef in me, I think.'

Josef grinned. 'Don't think she wants me for my body. I hope that we will soon be engaged in a great enterprise together.'

'What madness are you cooking up now, Josef?'

Julia dug into her canvas bag and brought out a couple of books. 'Do you read English, Ernst? I'm afraid I have no German translations, not yet.'

He fingered the books. One was a battered volume titled *If It Had Happened Otherwise*, published in 1931, edited by somebody called J.C. Squire. The other was actually a magazine, he saw, with a garish cover; it was called *Unknown*. It was a year old.

Julia said, 'The Squire book is a collection of essays, speculations on how history might have developed differently if certain key events had taken another course. What if Napoleon had won at Waterloo, for instance?'

Claudine glanced at the book. 'There is an essay here by Churchill!'

'As for the magazine—' Julia tapped the contents page with a manicured finger. 'This is the item of interest.' It was a contribution from an author called L. Sprague de Camp, and it was called 'Lest Darkness Fall'. 'De Camp's serial imagines a man gone back in time to a Rome on the point of falling to the barbarians. What if that collapse could have been averted?'

Ernst clumsily translated the title into German. 'What is all this, Josef?'

His brother clasped his hands behind his head. 'Do you ever have the feeling that history went wrong, Ernst? I mean, everything we do is entirely shaped by the past. If not for our ignominious defeat in the west in the first war, if not for the spiteful settlement of Versailles, *we* would not be sitting here now – yes? And take that further. What if you could *change* history so that, for example, Germany did not lose the first war?'

'History developed as it did through necessity.'

Julia sighed. 'Your brother really is rather unimaginative, Josef.'

'Well, I warned you about that.'

Julia said, 'There are plenty of ways things could have gone differently. If the British had been persuaded to stay out of what was essentially a continental war, for instance. If that had been so, the Kaiser could have won, in the sense of achieving his central goal of an economic union of the European peoples centred on Germany. Wouldn't that be a better history than the one we endured? I mean, all those lives lost on the killing fields of France – your own father's invaliding—'

'Be careful what you wish for,' said Claudine. 'If not for the turmoil that followed Germany's defeat, surely you Nazis couldn't have risen to power.'

Josef applauded ironically. 'Well, I don't necessarily agree with your conclusion, but you have the right idea, unlike my brother.'

Ernst shook his head. 'What is the point of this conversation? Even if you wished to change history, you could not.'

'Ah.' Josef glanced at Julia. 'You might think so, mightn't you? But Julia assures me that it is not so. There is a peculiar technology, developed in America—'

'America! I might have known. You have proof of this, I suppose,' Ernst snapped at Julia.

'In fact I do,' Julia said. 'Proof intelligible to a historian anyhow. But I don't yet have the means to deliver an operational technology. There is a component I lack . . . a human component.'

'Strictly speaking, subhuman,' Josef said.

She smiled at him fondly. 'I am confident that when England is in German hands, that component will shortly be found and brought to me.'

'And then,' Josef said, 'the possibilities are unlimited.'

Ernst said, 'You always were an ambitious bastard, Josef. You plan to sell this fantasy of a time manipulator to Himmler, do you?'

'Well, you know he would be receptive. The Reichsfuhrer dreams of super-weapons. A plane that could strike at America. The Hammer of Thor! What would he make of the greatest weapon of all? For what enemy could stand before us, if his very past could be cut away?'

Ernst shook his head. 'You're mad. It's as simple as that.'

Josef sighed. 'How disappointing you are, brother, as you have always been. And yet I love you even so. And that is why I want you to share my great adventure, even if you are incapable of understanding it—'

A siren wailed mournfully.

'Ah,' Josef said. 'It sounds as if the RAF is coming to join the party. What a pity.' He drained his cognac, stood, and bowed to Claudine. 'Mademoiselle. Don't be too rough with my little brother; he does break easily, you know.' He glanced down at the ruined tabletop, brushed some splinters from it, and, with Julia, walked away.

Claudine touched Ernst's hand. 'You shouldn't let him upset you. It's what he wants.'

'He's had a lifetime's practice at it.'

She shrugged, and lit another cigarette. 'But while he pursues these absurd fantasies of his, you are the one who will earn an Iron Cross in England. It is you who would make your father proud.'

Perhaps, Ernst thought. If he ever got there.

A band of soldiers came into the bar. There was a good deal of laughter and banter, despite the sirens. Their uniforms were soaked to the knee by sea water, as if they had been paddling.

It was as if everybody was playing, Ernst thought, all along the Channel coast. You had to keep up a front that this was a serious operation; he'd never say anything else even to Claudine. But Ernst suspected that nobody really believed the invasion would happen, despite all this build-up. There were other ways to bring down the British, such as bombing them flat, or sinking their supply convoys and starving them out. No, the vast, unlikely barge armada would never be launched. Ernst would never see England, and he would have to earn his Iron Cross some other way.

He finished his cognac. And when they left, he gave the barman money to cover the damage to the table.

VI

The siren's wail woke Mary with a start. For a moment she had no idea where she was. The night was hot, her neck was slick with sweat, and the room was pitch dark.

She rolled over, and her questing hand knocked painfully into a bit of furniture. But she found the small electric lamp, and fumbled for the cord. The lamp came on, shedding a dim low-voltage glow. This was her hotel room. She was in Colchester, her first night here. The windows had been blacked out by being pasted over with wallpaper – cheaper than blackout curtains. No wonder she was lost. And no wonder the room was so damn hot, with the windows stopped up like that.

She lay back for a moment, reluctant to wake fully. The siren continued to howl, and now it was answered by others, more remote. They sounded like prehistoric beasts, long-necked and lonely, calling to each other across some dismal swamp.

A fist battered the door, making her jump. 'Everybody out and to the shelter!' She heard running footsteps receding down the corridor. Doors slammed, voices murmured.

So she got out of bed. She took slacks from her suitcase, which she hadn't yet unpacked, and pulled them on over her nightdress, and took a jacket down from where it hung on the back of the door. She forced her bare feet into her flat sensible shoes.

She crammed her research papers inside her briefcase and slammed it closed. Her gas-mask in its canvas bag hung on the back of the small chair before the desk. She looked around for her handbag, lost in the dim lighting of this awful power-starved English summer. She found it under the bed, next to a chamber pot. It held her identity card, ration books and US passport, all her essential papers. Her only valuable was her wedding ring, which she was wearing. What else, what else? It wasn't her first air raid, the big attacks had been going on across southern

England for a week or more, but the others had caught her in Hastings where she had been staying with George Tanner and Hilda during Gary's convalescence. Now here she was alone in a strange town, and she hadn't figured out her routine. She didn't even know where the nearest shelter was.

At the last minute she reached back to the sink, grabbed her toothbrush and stuck it in her pocket.

She opened the door. The corridor was even more dimly lit than her room, with light bulbs only sparsely placed amid gaping empty sockets. There was nobody about. She hesitated for a second, trying to remember the way to the stairs. Left, she thought. She hurried that way.

Still the sirens wailed. She wondered what her friends at home would think if they could see her now, fleeing for her very life down this shadowy corridor, her nightdress sticking out of her slacks. She dragged her fingers through her hair, trying to comb it roughly.

She came to the stairs, a shadowy well. Holding onto the banister she hurried down to the ground floor, decanting into a tiny, deserted reception area. She ran straight through and out onto the street.

The night was cloudy, the sky dark. She was in utter darkness; she felt very uncertain. The streetlights were all out, of course. The only scraps of illumination came from the odd open door or imperfectly blacked-out window. She could smell dust and ash in the air. She was only a block or so from the big old Norman castle, but she couldn't even see that.

A big ack-ack gun opened up somewhere nearby, making her flinch, and the ground shook, the noise a battering roar. And somewhere to the north a searchlight splashed a circle of light on a lid of low cloud. More gunfire barked, and a stream of sparks rose along neat parabolic arcs. By the searchlight's glow she saw a family running in the dark, hunched over, parents hanging on to the hands of their children. Scuttling in the shadows they looked like rats.

Mary set off the way she thought led to the castle, her bag and gas-mask pouch over her shoulder, her briefcase in her hand. She could see practically nothing, and she groped her way along a wall. It was a nightmarish feeling, hurrying into the dark.

She collided with somebody. There was a stink of tobacco and stale beer. 'Hello, love. Lost your way?' A hand fumbled at her waist.

She slapped the hand away, hard. 'Fuck you.' She stepped out into the street.

'Well, I wish you would.' Clearly drunk, the man laughed, but didn't try to grab her again.

When she was well past him, she made her way back to the sidewalk and the wall. She tried to hurry; she sensed she was in more danger from the horny drunk than from the might of the Luftwaffe. Then she tumbled into a doorway, and fell. Her right hand scraped down the wall and her knee slammed into the paving stone. 'Shit, shit.'

A dim light floated before her, a masked torch. 'Are you all right?'

Mary looked up. She made out a woman's face. She wore a tin helmet and a dark overcoat with an ARP armband. 'I'm OK. I just tripped.' She tried to stand, but the knee was painful, and she winced.

'Let me help you.' The girl got hold of her under her armpit and hauled her to her feet.

'Thank you. I was just trying to get away from an asshole back that way.'

'There are plenty of those about. Hey, you have blood on your hand. That's a bit of a scrape. Well, you need to get to the shelter. Do you know the way?'

'No.' Mary looked around, and realised she had got turned about. 'I'm not sure which way is which, to tell you the truth.'

'That's common enough. The nearest shelter is under the castle. Come on, I'll take you.' She held Mary's arm and led her quite confidently through the dark. But the girl limped as she walked.

Mary said, 'You're hurt yourself.'

'Kicked out an incendiary. Got a bit burned. Feel foolish, actually. I'll live.'

Mary was an independent sort, but she was happy to let the girl take charge. 'Thank you, um—'

'Doris Keeler. Just call me Doris. Are you American?'

'Yeah. Mary Wooler. Good to meet you, Doris.'

'I've got an aunt in America. Just visiting, are you?'

'Sort of.'

'Well, you picked the right summer to visit England. Here we are.' The castle wall loomed before them, and they hurried through an arched doorway. Doris shone her torch on a sign, white on black, with a large 'S', an arrow, and the word 'SHELTER'. They hurried down a narrow staircase.

VII

Mary found herself in a tunnel-like vault, with walls of brickwork. The light was dim, coming from electric lamps hung roughly on the walls, but there was a stack of candles and what looked like old-fashioned oil lamps standing by. Doris snapped off her torch and took off her helmet, revealing brown hair tied back into a tight bun. Her features were regular, strong rather than pretty; she looked competent.

The vault was already crowded, the people packed in rows on the floor like sardines in a tin, mostly women, children and older folk, and a few men of service age. They were settling in for the night, Mary saw. There were beds that looked like official provision, but they had already been occupied. Otherwise people had brought down heaps of blankets and deckchairs and bits of carpet, and were making up nests under the vault's curving walls.

The place was quite organised, with trestle tables bearing tea urns manned by WVS volunteers. An oil stove was burning, and a cooking smell filled the muggy air. One section of the vault had been fenced off by a couple of blankets; from the smell Mary guessed that the privy was back there.

Doris led Mary to a first-aid table, where mothers sat with sick children in their arms. Mary protested, but a volunteer here, a stern middle-aged woman, took a brisk look at her knee, fingering the joint – 'a bit of bruising, that's all there is to that' – and washed her scraped hand, dabbed it with antiseptic and gave her a bit of bandage. Doris said nothing about the injury to her own foot, and Mary didn't prompt her.

Doris found a bit of wall where they were able to sit, their backs to the brickwork. She fetched Mary a cup of tea, and set her helmet down on the floor between her crossed legs. They were surrounded by people, a warm fug of wriggling bodies, a stale smell of woollen clothing, a murmur of conversation. Mothers tucked in their children, three or four to a bed. A lot of people were reading, papers and Penguin paperbacks.

One old man who looked like a rabbi was reading a leather-backed holy book. It was all quite cosy, and few people seemed afraid; it had all become a routine, Mary supposed. But she could hear the deep rumble of aircraft engines, the distant slam of bombs, and the hammering shudder of the ack-ack fire. There was nothing gentle about the night.

'I needed a break,' Doris said, sipping her own tea. 'It's been a long night already.'

'It's all very organised,' Mary observed.

'Wasn't like this in the beginning. My word, after a night down here you could have sliced the air up and carried it out.'

'But, you know, speaking as an outsider I'm impressed by the way the Brits have adapted. Coping the way you do.' All this achieved by a nation, repelled by the industrialised slaughter of the Great War, that had never wanted this conflict.

Doris sniffed. 'Well, a bit of common sense and an ounce of courage get you a long way in my experience. Actually we haven't been hit so hard, not yet.'

'No. Not like the coastal towns. I've been staying in Hastings. The people there shelter in caves.'

'Really? Well, the coast's been getting it, they say, and the airfields and the like. Softening us up before old Hitler invades. So they say.'

'I don't think they'll invade.'

'No. They don't need to – that's what's said. They can just starve us out, can't they, with their U-boats in the Atlantic?'

'Do you have family? A husband?'

Doris eyed her; she'd evidently asked an awkward question. 'Well, my husband was with the BEF. He didn't come back from France.'

'I'm sorry.'

'I got a Red Cross postcard. He was in a POW camp outside Paris. They say they're now being shipped further east, off into Germany, to be used for labour.' She laughed. 'I suppose it takes even the Germans a bit of time to move a whole captive army, four hundred thousand men.'

Mary told her about her son. 'I suppose I was lucky. Gary came back in one piece, more or less. He'll recover soon.'

'And he wants to fight again?'

'Oh, yes.'

'It's all a frightful mess, isn't it? I miss my Bob, of course, and so does Jennifer. I don't suppose we'll see him before this beastly war is done.'

'Jennifer?'

'My little girl.' She opened her coat and dug out a photo, of a sunny pre-war day, showing Doris herself, a smiling, prematurely bald young man, and a little girl of five or six.

'She's pretty. Where is she now?'

'Well, I have that aunt in America. Somewhere called Kentucky, she lives. We had a bit of money saved up before the war, and we decided we didn't want Jenny off in the country somewhere, but with family. So we bought her passage. She's up in Liverpool at the moment, but she's supposed to sail next month on the *City of Benares*. She'll be safe in America, won't she? I'm afraid I don't know anything about your country, nothing but what's in the movies.'

'People are kind. Just like here. I'm sure she'll be fine.'

'Well, after she went off I thought I may as well do something useful, and I joined the ARP. But I miss her ever so much.' She was absent for a moment, and then she deliberately brightened, as if remembering to do her job. 'So what are you doing here in England?'

'Actually I was here before the war. I'm a historian; I was researching aspects of the late medieval. When the war came I stayed on, but I'm working as a stringer for a paper in Boston.'

'A what?'

'A correspondent. But actually I'm here in Colchester to do a bit of historical research. I'm following up a document somebody gave me.' It had been Ben Kamen, the young Austrian Jew who had befriended Gary. 'It concerns the Emperor Claudius. Colchester was a great Roman centre – a military garrison, just like it is now. But I've found my way to the archive of a monastery outside the town, where a medieval monk called Geoffrey Cotesford lived towards the end of his life. Funnily enough Cotesford knew a Wooler, who was maybe one of my husband's ancestors ... Oh. I'm sorry.'

Doris smiled. 'Do I look a bit lost? That's rude of me. I don't know much history. Who's this Claude?'

'Claudius. The Roman emperor who conquered Britain.'

'Wasn't that Julius Caesar?'

'No. Long story.'

'I don't even know anything about this blooming great castle we're sitting under. The Normans built this, didn't they? William the Conqueror and his lot.'

'Well, yes. But that's a long story too. This vault was built by the Romans, but it's not really a vault. Colchester used to be the capital of the ancient Britons. After the Romans conquered it they built a huge temple to Claudius, right on this spot. This vault is actually the foundation of the temple, like a big concrete raft.'

'So the Romans came, then the Normans, and now here we are hiding under it all from the Germans.'

'Well, that's history for you.'

The folk in the shelter were growing quiet now, the children shedding their excitement and settling down to sleep, some of the adults talking in soft murmurs. In the shadows of one corner near the WVS table, Mary saw one couple with their mouths locked together in passion.

Doris said softly, 'I can't hear much engine noise, can you? Maybe we'll get away with it tonight. I'll need to go back out in a minute, check that everybody is where they should be. We've got lists we have to tick off, or we get stick from the officers. But maybe tonight—'

There was a wallop, like a great fist slamming down. The ancient vault shuddered, and bits of dust and brickwork hailed from the roof. Suddenly the place was alive with noise, kids screaming, somebody with a splash of blood-red on his forehead calling for help. Doris clung to Mary's hand, suddenly scared; Mary put her arm around her.

There was another wallop, even more violent, and the lights flickered and died.

VIII

14 September

Hilda Tanner found Ben Kamen just where his Home Guard commander said he would be, out in the country a couple of miles or so north of Hastings, digging holes in the ground with a gang of other men.

She parked her car and walked through a field of corn stubble. It was a fine, bright Saturday afternoon, with just a hint of autumn coolness in the air. The field was cluttered with broken-down tractors and other vehicles, and loops of wire big enough for Hilda to have stepped through.

In the distance to the south above Hastings, an aerial battle was in progress. Hilda felt like a veteran of the air war, for the radar stations, including her own, had been getting a pasting. She recognised the way the Messerschmitt 109s were flying, in their 'schwarms' of four aircraft, and the Stuka bombers diving down onto their targets like predatory birds. The guns on the ground were firing back, releasing balls of fire that lanced up towards the planes. A big pall of smoke rose up from the ground, beyond her horizon. Perhaps one of the planes had gone down. The sky was full of smoke and colour; the Messerschmitts' tracer bullets were bright yellow and green.

It was an astounding sight when you stopped to think about it. But the workers in the field didn't even look up. Such spectacles had filled the sky around the towns and ports and airfields of southern England for a month now. There had been one day of relief, when the Luftwaffe had launched a massive raid on London: the Saturday Blitz, the papers had called it, Saturday 7 September. Everybody had hoped, shamefully unless you were in London itself, that the Germans were changing tactics, that they had abandoned the idea of winning the aerial war and were resorting to terror against civilians. But then the usual pattern had resumed, as the Luftwaffe had pursued its objective of knocking the RAF out of the war through sheer attrition.

Hilda approached the work party. Ben was working alongside an older man of maybe fifty. The other Home Guard men leaned on their shovels and wolf-whistled and larked about, showing off their puny muscles, calling in their ripe Sussex accents, 'Oi, WAAF! That uniform fits you pretty nice.' 'Hey, WAAF, what's he got that I haven't got?' 'Tell you what *he* hasn't got. A bit of skin on the end of his knob . . .'

She acknowledged it all with a tight grin and kept walking. The older man waved them silent. 'Stop drooling, you lot.' He had a faint Irish burr, and big hands, a farmer's hands, the biggest hands Hilda had ever seen.

Ben stuck his spade in the ground, wiped his hands on his trousers, and faced Hilda. 'It's lovely to see you. You came all the way out here for me?'

'Well, I've got a couple of messages for you.'

He asked intently, 'From Mary Wooler?'

'Yes, and from Gary too. Me and Gary actually.' She held herself straight, and hoped she wasn't blushing.

'Well, well. Look, I'd give you a hug if I wasn't sweating like a good'un. Tom, do you mind?'

'You take a break, don't mind me.' Tom continued to scrape at the ground.

Ben took his jacket from a heap of stakes, spread it on the ground and gestured for Hilda to sit. He squatted easily on the ground himself. He took a swig from a milk bottle full of water, and offered it to Hilda; she refused.

'Fun, is it, digging holes in the ground?'

'Oh, the glamour,' Ben said. 'But you know the theory. We're just trying to muck up every field and open space to stop planes and gliders landing.'

'It's no ruddy fun,' Tom growled. 'The ground's baked hard as concrete. You can see what we're up to, though.' He pointed to a row of completed installations; they were simple tripods of scaffolding, like the frames of teepees. 'I grow my peas and beans up poles set like that.'

Hilda called, 'Wouldn't you rather be digging your garden – um, Tom?'

'Given half a chance,' he said with a grin. 'But I'll tell you what, sooner this than route marching. First time we went marching, our Home Guard platoon, a quarter of a century just fell away in a flash. I'll swear I could smell the cordite and the mud. I was in Flanders, see. Never thought I'd be back marching again, not in my lifetime. Well, well.' He sighed, and continued to ram his spade into the reluctant ground.

'Tom's been a good mate,' Ben said. 'Keeps the other lads off a bit.'

'Give you a hard time, do they?'

'Nothing I can't handle. Funny, though, they bait me for being a German *and* a Jew.'

'But sooner here than that internment camp, from what Gary told me from your letters.'

'Oh, yes.' In late June Ben Kamen's name had come up on a list of potentially enemy aliens. While waiting for his tribunal, he had been taken off to an internment camp in Liverpool. 'It was a half-finished council estate in a place called Huyton. What a hole. But the tribunal eventually classed me as a C.' Category A were considered hostile to the war effort; B were for some reason doubtful; C were friendly and no threat. 'But even then, when I joined the Home Guard, they kept me away from the guns and handed me a shovel instead. Funny, that.'

'Well, it's behind you now.'

'I hope so,' he said fervently. 'How's your war? I think I expected to see you up there by now.' He glanced at the sky. 'In a Spit or a Hurricane. I hear they are planning to send women to the front line.'

'So they are, but I've no training. I'm working at an observation station on the coast.' She had picked up the habit of not using the word 'radar' unless it was necessary.

He looked at her. 'It's coming, isn't it?'

'What?'

'The invasion.'

'Why do you say that?'

'Just looking around. Piecing bits together. I mean, the work we've been doing, you can see the logic.' He mimed an enclosure with his hands. 'You have this crust around the coast – tank blocks, barbed wire, ditches, mines. Then further back we've been building what they call the stop lines. Natural barriers like rivers and canals and forests, but reinforced with tank traps and pillboxes. Defence in depth. You can see it taking shape.'

'I don't think they'll come,' Hilda said. 'For one thing they haven't been able to knock out the RAF. Those Me109s of theirs are too short-range. The Hurricanes and Spits can always retreat to fields in the north of England. The Luftwaffe can't win.' That was the official line. But, Hilda had heard it said at work, all the Germans actually needed to do was to beat the RAF back from the skies of southern England, and achieve 'local air superiority'. And Hilda knew from her own experience that if they kept battering at the airfields and radar stations and sector stations of the south-east, the delicate system of command and control behind the RAF's operations could soon crumble. It would actually be better for Britain's prospects in the war if the Luftwaffe turned on

London again. But she said firmly: 'No, they won't come. And all your digging will be for nothing!'

'So where's Gary now?'

'Well, he's recovered. He's been reposted, a lot of the BEF veterans have. Now he's to be with an international unit in the Twenty-ninth Brigade. He's due to join it on Friday.' She hesitated. 'They're stationed north of Eastbourne. I was hoping he'd be sent to the Twenty-first. A lot of the veterans are with them, north of London.'

'They're reserves up there, the Twenty-first?'

'Yes. But they're short of front-line troops.' Hilda had heard rumours about the troops in the field – eight divisions, something like a hundred and fifty thousand men, with another forty thousand north of the Thames. It might have been twice that if not for the loss of the BEF. It was thought the Germans could muster a force outnumbering the British by at least two to one. 'We shouldn't talk like this,' Hilda said. 'Spreading rumours.'

'But don't you feel the need to talk?' Ben said, and he laughed nervously. 'I'm cursed with an active brain, Hilda. I'm an academic, for pity's sake, I worked with Gödel himself. Now they've got me digging a hole in the ground.' He made a spinning motion by his temple. 'I can't help thinking, thinking, working it all out.'

'Yes, and you yak and yak about it,' Tom said sensibly. 'My advice to you is to enjoy the sunshine while it lasts.' He stuck his spade into the earth again.

Ben said, 'I think that was a hint. You said you had messages for me?'

'Can you come into town on Friday, in the morning? Meet us at the house. Gary's got something to say to you before he gets posted – we both have.'

Ben nodded. After the way he had helped Gary after the return from Dunkirk, the two of them had stayed close.

Hilda went on, 'And I know Mary Wooler has some material for you. History stuff.'

Ben's eyes gleamed. 'I expect the war effort can spare me for a couple of hours. I'll see you then, Hilda.'

'Good. All right—'

'Holy Mother of God.' Tom had stopped digging, and was staring south.

Over Hastings, one of the barrage balloons had been set alight. Subsiding gently, deforming, it was drifting down the sky, a brilliant teardrop.

IX

20 September

So they gathered, on a dull Friday morning, in the stuffy parlour of George Tanner's little terraced house in the Old Town of Hastings.

When Mary came downstairs, a sheaf of her research papers under her arm, she found George, Ben Kamen, Gary and Hilda standing side by side. They all held cups of tea in saucers, rather stiffly. The windows were taped, and buckets of sand stood in the corners. Everybody was in uniform save Mary, George in his copper's jacket, Gary and Hilda in the colours of the British Army and Air Force respectively, and even Ben Kamen, a bit crumpled, in the Army-like khaki of the Home Guard. It would have made a good group portrait, Mary reflected, thinking like a journalist.

Gary and Hilda hung back, shyly. 'Oh, a card came for you today, Mary.' George picked it off the mantelpiece and handed it to her. She glanced at it; it was a postcard, addressed to her in a round, unfamiliar handwriting.

Ben was eager to speak to Mary, and he stepped forward. 'Mary, Hilda said you found out something?'

Mary glanced at Gary and Hilda. 'We can talk about it later. But, briefly, I dug up a lot of stuff in Colchester, following the lead you gave me about Geoffrey Cotesford. Take a look at this.' She handed him her sheaf of documents, some copied from the archive she'd visited at Colchester, some her own notes.

Ben read hastily: '"Time's Tapestry: As mapped by myself; in which the long warp threads are the history of the whole world; and the wefts which run from selvedge to selvedge are distortions of that history, deflected by a Weaver unknown; be he human, divine or satanic ... " Oh, my.'

'This is getting *very* strange,' Mary said. 'We need to talk.'

'Yeah, but not right now, Mom, Jeez,' Gary said, breaking his silence at last. 'Look – we don't have much time. You know I'm being mobilised today. We want to give you time to get used to the idea before, well, before we all go off to our separate duties.'

George looked baffled. 'What idea?'

Gary hesitated, the silence stretching. Mary's heart pulsed with pride to see him standing there in his crisp uniform with his crimson-haired girl at his side, even if she ached to think of the damage this war had already done to him.

And Mary suddenly knew why she had been brought here. 'You've gone and done it, haven't you?'

Ben was grinning. 'Gary, you dog.'

George snapped, 'Done *what*? Will somebody tell me—'

Hilda lifted her left hand. The ring on her finger was a simple gold band. 'It was my mother's,' she said. She faced her father defiantly. 'Look, Dad, it was all a rush. We didn't even decide to do it until last Friday, when Gary's orders came through, and we knew we were running out of time. And then we went to the town hall, and found a registrar who was prepared to see to us on the spot—'

'See to you,' Ben said mockingly.

'Shut up, Ben,' Gary said mildly.

Hilda said, 'Dad, we wanted you there, of course we did. And you, Mary. But we didn't want to lose this chance before – you know. In case we didn't get another go. And besides—'

'And besides,' Mary said drily, 'you thought if you told us in advance we might have said no. Well, you're not the only wartime bride, are you?'

Gary looked at her uncertainly. 'Are you happy for us?'

'Oh, love, of course I am.' She crossed to him and hugged him, smelling the pungent scent of his new khaki uniform. 'It's a shock. But we live in a world of shocks, don't we?'

Hilda turned to her father. 'Dad? What about you?'

George's face was hard. 'Well, you haven't given me much choice in the matter, have you? Gary, you're a good boy, anybody can see that. But, Hilda – your mother's ring – and you didn't even tell me!'

Hilda's face was set. 'Yes, well, this is why, I knew how you'd be.'

As tempers soured, Ben shrank back, dismayed.

The telephone rang in the hall. It made George jump. It had only been installed a few weeks earlier, for his job; he hadn't owned a phone before. 'Excuse me.' He walked out stiffly, retreating into his role, more uniform than man.

'He'll come around,' Mary said.'

'Yes,' Ben said. 'It's just a shock, that's all. *I'm* shocked.'

Gary grinned. 'We'll do something about it when we get the time – after the war, if we have to wait that long. We'll have a reception – maybe we'll try to have a church ceremony, if we can find a tame padre to do it.'

'You'll be a war hero by then,' Ben said. 'Um, do you think you could stand a Jewish best man? ...' He had a complicated look on his face, Mary thought, as if he was trying too hard to be pleased. She knew he was close to Gary; she wondered if he was somehow jealous.

George came back into the room. His face was grey; he looked old. 'Cromwell,' he said simply.

Ben flinched. Hilda grabbed Gary's hand.

Mary asked, 'What does that mean?'

Ben said to her, 'It's a code word. The invasion.'

Mary took a moment to absorb this. In these last minutes, somehow she had forgotten the war, and now here it was intruding. 'I thought it wasn't going to happen,' she found herself saying. 'It's too late in the season for the weather. The RAF and the Navy are too strong. That's what they've been saying on the BBC. Could it be a mistake?'

Gary said, 'We have to get out of here.'

George faced his daughter. 'Hilda—'

'Later, Dad,' she snapped, still angry. 'I think you've said all there is to say for now.' And she stalked out of the room. Gary hugged his mother quickly, then he hurried out after Hilda. George and Ben followed.

Only Mary had no post to man, no obvious duty to fulfil, nowhere to go. She stood in the empty room, marvelling at how her whole world could be turned upside down by a single word.

She was still holding the postcard. It had got crumpled when she had hugged Gary. She turned it over dully. It was from Doris Keeler, the young ARP warden who had been so kind to her during the air raid back in August. They had stayed in touch since, with cards and a couple of letters, sharing their experiences. Now, Mary read, Doris had had a letter from the headquarters of the Children's Overseas Reception Bureau. On Tuesday evening the SS *City of Benares*, carrying refugee children bound for North America, had been torpedoed. 'Forgive me for writing like this out of the blue as they say with such an awful shock and I know you never knew Jenny but I'm writing to tell everybody I can think of ...' Mary imagined her, alone in her home without her POW husband and lost child, scribbling card after card, obsessively.

Somewhere a church bell started to chime, the first church bell Mary had heard in England for months. And then an air raid siren coughed and wailed.

X

Ernst sat in a crowd, all of them men of the Twenty-sixth Division of the Ninth Army, on the road above Boulogne's harbour wall. His pack was heavy on his back, and his rifle gleamed in his hands, polished until it shone. The men sat about, smoking gloomily, complaining about their officers, swapping stories about French women and wine, and tending to their feet – doing what soldiers always did. Ernst's Wehrmacht uniform was stiffly laundered, made smart for England. The men had dreaded these hours of waiting at their embarkation points, for they, and indeed the waiting fleet, were so obviously vulnerable to air attack. But there had been no sign of the RAF. Perhaps Goering had at last done what he promised, and beaten back Britain's planes for the day.

It was misty and cold. This was S-Day Minus One, the eve of Sea Lion Day itself. Ernst was looking out to sea. And before him an astounding spectacle unfolded.

Beyond the harbour the sea was crowded with ships. Heavy steamships glided in the deeper water, shadows on the sea, laden with stores and the vehicles of the motorised units. Smaller vessels plied the nearer waters, motor-boats and fishing smacks and even a few rowing boats. There were some exotic craft, such as the new varieties of assault boats like the one Josef had played with, and 'Herbert ferries', actually sections of pontoon bridges fitted with motors, stable and massive enough to carry over a complete anti-aircraft unit. All these specialised craft had been designed and built in the fever-pitch hurry of this invasion summer.

But it was the barges themselves that were the most remarkable sight. Many of them had already been towed out of the harbour, and they were forming up in great columns, convoys miles long. Black smoke rose in threads from the steamers that dragged them. There had been no rehearsal for this immense choreography of wood and iron and military force, for none had been possible.

And then yet another wave of planes went roaring overhead, sweeping out to sea: Messerschmitts and Junkers and Stuka bombers, ploughing determinedly towards England, to beat off the RAF and the Royal Navy, and to soften up the landing sites. A wave of Ju-52 transports followed, bearing paratroopers to begin the invasion from the air.

It was a magnificent spectacle, he told himself: a conjunction of forces, on land, at sea and in the air, the largest invasion across this ocean since the Romans. He would write a book about it one day. But for now Ernst felt very small, very vulnerable, a tiny disregarded piece of a vast machinery.

And somehow none of it seemed real. After the months of playful training, all the saloon-bar arguments about the relative strengths of navies and air forces and the sea-going capabilities of river barges, suddenly the order had come. It was strange to sit here and share a cigarette with a man, trying to believe that by this time tomorrow you might be in England, and there was a good chance that either he would be dead, or you would, or both, trying to believe this was serious, not just another exercise.

And here, out of nowhere, came Josef. He strode along the harbour wall, his black SS uniform standing out against the camouflage green battle dress. The men glared at him, or deliberately ignored him. Traditionalists in the Army had never accepted the SS. But Josef rose above it all. When he spotted his brother he beckoned.

Ernst glanced at his obergefreiter, who shrugged, his head wreathed in cigarette smoke. Ernst slipped his arms out of his pack, leaving it on the ground, and stood and crossed to Josef.

'Brother.' Josef shook his hand warmly. Then he studied Ernst's face. 'You don't seem very pleased to see me.'

'I'm pleased enough.' He glanced back at his unit. 'It's just, I don't know, I feel like a junior worker in a factory favoured by the manager.' In fact, that was the aura Josef gave off, with his strutting about in his glamorous uniform. But then, Ernst thought, 1940 was a good year to be a Nazi with ambition.

'Never mind these jealous dolts.' Josef said this loudly so the others could hear. 'Look, you should appreciate me being here. I've been pretty busy these last hours.'

'Doing what? Shagging that English girl?'

He laughed. 'No. Planning. Preparing. You must be aware of the detail involved in an operation like this. The Fuhrer's final commit order has been broken down in the planning until we are visualising every footfall of every soldier on every beach. As for Julia, don't mock her. She, and the rest of her Legion of St George, will be crossing in the second wave with me. I have a feeling Julia Fiveash is going to be very useful to us in the days of the occupation to come.'

'She's as mad as a rabid stoat.'

'You're much too cynical, Ernst. Look, I found you because Mother would want to know that we shook hands at least before we parted for England.'

Ernst was touched. 'Well, that's true. Thank you for finding me.'

'Not that that was easy, in a mob like this. Now listen to me, Gefreiter Ernst. You are caught up in the detail, you will be a mere pebble on those shingle beaches. But you must see the bigger picture. The Fuhrer has determined that Churchill will never be reasonable, that England must be eliminated from the war – and that we have just enough to make Sea Lion work. And so by the force of his personality he has brought his great generals together for the project. Even Goering!' He waved a hand. 'And now we are ready; you can see it. Goering has beaten back the RAF, *just enough*. The Kriegsmarine with its barriers of mines and purloined French ships can keep the Channel clear for the crossing, *just enough*. Even the weather is behaving itself – just! And so the Fuhrer has ordered that we go. Within six weeks we will have half a million men in England, the British army, weakened by Dunkirk, will be scattered, and Churchill will be suing for peace, if he has not been deposed or shot.'

Ernst said, 'Six weeks? In the ranks it is said that the Panzers will run out of petrol in three days.'

Josef snorted. 'I believe there is petrol in England.' He gripped his brother's shoulder. 'Listen to me. We will find each other tomorrow or the next day, the two of us, brothers on English soil. Yes?'

The obergefreiter nudged Ernst. 'Hey, Trojan. Smile for the camera.'

A truck was driving along the length of the sea wall, with a camera crew set up in the back, and a woman shouting directions. It was Leni Riefenstahl, who had followed the Nazis from Nuremberg to Poland, and now to the edge of the sea. The men waved and shouted cheerful obscenities.

More planes thundered overhead, in layers stacked up tall in the air, so many of them that they turned the grey afternoon sky black.

XI

Once the raid started it went on and on, the planes rumbling across the sky, and the little shelter shuddered and rattled as the bombs slammed into the carcass of the town. Mary supposed the whole south coast was getting it, a final softening-up before the invasion forces landed.

Oddly she wasn't afraid. She had lived through too many raids.

When the others had gone running off to their posts, Mary had pulled on an overcoat, collected her bag and gas-mask, and went down to George Tanner's Anderson shelter. She got there just before the first planes came over. George had made the shelter a bright little place, like a den. He had painted the interior white, lined it with canvas to keep out the damp, and brought in blankets and deck chairs and a wireless set. There was even a camping stove to make a cup of tea. But the wireless delivered only static. Maybe the raids had knocked out the transmitting towers, silencing the BBC.

She had been back to the house a couple of times, trying to remember what needed to be done. She'd turned off the lights, switched off the gas, and filled sinks and the bathtub with water in case the mains got cut off. She had her briefcase with her research materials, and she packed a small rucksack with clothes and bathroom stuff. But then it was back to the shelter. She felt useless stuck down here, contributing nothing.

There were safer places to be than this. The best shelter in Hastings was a system of caves called St Clement's, which had been fixed up to hold a few hundred. And it would be safer yet to get out of town altogether and head off inland, where she could evade both the bombs today and, presumably, the stormtroopers that were likely to land here tomorrow.

But she didn't want to leave the house. This was the last point where they had all been together, she and her son, his new wife and her father, and even poor sweet Ben. She wished she had thought to arrange a way they could contact each other.

It occurred to her that even if the house was bombed flat, as seemed highly likely right this minute, the Anderson shelter might survive. Here, then. She scrabbled in her bag for her lipstick. It was an American brand, and she used it sparingly; cosmetics were just one item in desperately short supply over here. She made an experimental mark on the white-painted wall. The lipstick was bright red; you couldn't miss it, and, in the interior of the shelter, it wasn't likely to get washed off or rubbed away.

But where should she tell them to meet? Nowhere in Hastings itself; the place would be crawling with Germans if they landed. Somewhere nearby, somewhere memorable. She held up her lipstick, and wrote clearly:

MEET AT BATTLE. MW 20/9/40.

It was just as she dropped the lipstick back in her bag that the big bomb fell.

XII

Ben and Hilda had driven off in Mary's car, her rented Austin Seven. Hilda had to get to her radar station, and Ben to his Home Guard assignment at Pevensey.

With Hilda at the wheel they barrelled along the coast road, heading west through Bexhill and onwards. They drove past the long fortified beaches with their huge coils of barbed wire and emplacements of superannuated Navy guns. The traffic was heavy, as the men of the Home Guard and the army detachments struggled to get to their pillboxes and machine-gun nests, and WAAFs and Wrens hurried to their naval gun emplacements. But the road was clogged with civilians, fleeing from the towns. There were a few cars, and carts drawn by horses and donkeys, amid files of pedestrians pushing prams and wheelbarrows heaped up with luggage and furniture. All of this got in the way of the military vehicles, and of the ambulances straining to get through.

Overhead, a war was being fought out in the air, Messerschmitts and Spitfires and Hurricanes tearing into each other over fleets of German bombers. Nobody looked up to watch.

Hilda grunted and swore as she rammed the car through the clogged traffic. Ben could see the ring on her finger, her mother's ring, just a little too big for her; Hilda, focused, seemed to have forgotten it was there.

'So, Pevensey,' she said. 'We'll reach my radar station first.'

'I can drive on from there. I'm a lousy driver, but I know the way.'

'It's an observation post, yes?'

'And a defensive point, and a headquarters ... There are a bunch of Canadians there. They fortified the old castle. I'm surprised your radar station is still operational.'

She glanced at him. 'I suppose it doesn't matter if I tell you now. The RAF is withdrawing, moving the fighters back from the forward bases. They'll operate from deeper inland now. Before sunset we'll have to decommission my station. Scrap the gear if we can't bring it back out of the threatened zone. Well, here we are.'

She lurched off the road, throwing Ben sideways.

An unprepossessing station lay ahead, locked behind a fence of barbed wire. Ben glimpsed masts, seven or eight of them, hundreds of feet high, and blocky buildings. The station had already taken damage, Ben saw; part of the fence had blown down.

'This is it. Good luck.' Leaving the engine running, Hilda leaned over, kissed him on the cheek, and hurried out of the car. Then she was gone, off at a run to her station.

'You too,' Ben murmured. He slid across to the driver's seat. He gave himself thirty seconds to familiarise himself with the strange controls of this English car. Then he turned the car around with a squeal of tyres and rejoined the traffic stream, heading west towards Pevensey.

XIII

Hot air pulsed over Mary, a compression that squeezed her chest. The whole shelter lifted and shuddered, and bits of stuff, the wireless and the tin cups, rattled and fell off their shelves. The shelter's roof clattered, as if handfuls of gravel were being dropped on it.

But the noise was muffled. She touched her ears to see if they had been stopped up by dirt or dust. They were clear. She could hear little but a ringing noise.

It made her mind up. Whatever came next, she couldn't just sit in here, waiting to be bombed out. She had her handbag with her papers, and all her cash, her gas-mask, her rucksack, her briefcase. She glanced around the shelter. She picked up the camping stove and set it carefully on the floor.

Then she clambered up the little ladder and emerged into George's garden. The soil, and George's potatoes and carrots, were covered in debris, bits of brick, wood slats, slates, and a layer of dust. There was heat in the air, and a smell of dust and sewage. Yet she could still hear little. The planes washing overhead sounded dull and distant.

She made her way through the house and out to the street. She locked George's front door carefully behind her.

She walked down the street, heading for the sea front. This was Hastings' Old Town, a tangle of streets crammed into a valley between two sandstone hills, steep and crowded, long terraces of houses assembled over centuries. Today there was chaos, brick and broken glass spilled all over the road, people running, distant screaming.

She found that the big bomb had fallen slap bang on top of a large corner house on the High Street. Mary just stood and stared. A crater had been dug deep into the ground, and broken pipes and cables jutted out like snapped bones. The house itself had been sliced open, exposing the interiors of rooms, so it looked like an immense doll's house. In one upper storey room a big iron bed dangled perilously over the drop.

There was an extraordinary, repellent stink, of dust, ash, burned meat, sewage.

People swarmed all over the smashed house. A fire tender was pulled up outside, and firemen grappled with a hose, spraying the lower floors with water. Men of a Heavy Rescue Squad were hauling their way through heaps of brick, trying to get through to rooms at the back of the house. Some worked with bare hands, and others laboured to get joists and blocks and tackles in place, to lift heavier beams and slabs of wall. They were already streaked with dirt and sweat.

And people were being brought out of the building, some walking, some not. Stretcher parties bore their inert loads, sometimes just on bits of planking. At hastily assembled first aid stations the victims were treated and marked with labels, a code Mary had come to know through her experience of such raids: X for internal injury, T where a tourniquet had been applied. Two kindly ladies from the WVS, in their bottle-green uniforms and felt hats, handed out the inevitable cups of tea, the reward for every 'bombee'. But others had been less fortunate. Mary saw a row of bodies lined up on the ground like fish on a slab. An ARP warden, a woman, was checking names off a list, and studying the bodies for identity cards and rings and other means of identification.

Somebody touched her shoulder.

It was George. His face was caked with sweat and dust and dirt, and blood was smeared over his dark uniform. He was speaking to her.

She shook her head. 'I can't hear you.' She tapped her ears.

He leaned closer and shouted, 'I said, what are you doing here? I thought you were in the shelter.'

'I couldn't stay.'

'If you're not going to a shelter, get out of town.'

'George, I can't go. Not while this is going on.'

'It's not your fight.'

She shook her head. 'But it's Gary's. Look, I'll go help those WVS women. I can pour a cup of tea.'

He eyed her, then stood back. 'All right. Your funeral.' He glanced at the sky. 'What time is it? The light's going. I don't think this is going to let up all night—'

There was another shuddering crash. They both staggered, and a bit more of the ruined property collapsed.

George ran off towards the latest catastrophe, blowing a whistle. It occurred to her that she should have taken the opportunity to tell him about Battle. But it was already too late.

She walked determinedly towards the WVS team.

XIV

20-21 September

Transport Fleet D sailed from Boulogne at 1800 hours on 20 September, S-Day Minus One. It was one of four fleets setting off that day, carrying Army Group A, the Ninth and Sixteenth Armies. From west to east, Fleet E was to sail from Le Havre, D from Boulogne, C from Calais, and B from Dunkirk, Ostend and Rotterdam. Fleet A, a figment of Wehrmacht planning, had only ever existed on paper. It was the beginning of an elaborate marine choreography, designed to land nine divisions, two hundred thousand men, on the beaches of southern England in three days.

Ernst's barge, one of a group of four, was towed by a tug out of the harbour. The men gripped the barge's reinforced sides, nervous even before they passed through the harbour mouth.

The noise was tremendous. The great guns at Boulogne had been shouting for hours, mighty twelve-inchers firing across the Channel to bombard the English defensive positions even before a single German landed, and when Ernst looked up he saw a curtain of shells flying across the sky above him.

The barge itself had been heavily modified, with concrete poured over the floor, the hull strengthened with steel plate, and the sharp prow replaced by bat-wing doors and a ramp at the front that would drop down to allow them to land. The wheelhouse was cut down and surrounded by sandbags. This barge was meant to carry grain down a river. Now it would carry seventy men and four trucks across an ocean. The barge lay low, and with every wave salt water splashed over the gunwales, soaking the men huddled inside it. The doomsayers said gloomily that the Channel surges could be twenty feet high. Every day of his training Ernst had been struck by the contrast between the sleek perfection of his Army equipment and the ramshackle nature of the transports that would take him and his gear across the Channel. The boatman, the binnenschiffer, laughed at the men's discomfort.

At last the barge joined its column. Ernst clung to the side and stared out. It was a remarkable sight in the fading light of the September day to be riding across a sea carpeted by barges and men, as far as the eye could see. Ernst's barge was one of two hundred in this column alone, towed by tugs and steamers, with an escort of heavier ships bearing supplies. While the barges carried the assault troops, the spearhead troopers, the Advanced Detachments who would be the first to land – the Heaven-Sent Command, the men called them – crossed in mine-sweepers. They would land in speedboats and sturmboats, fast, small, unarmoured boats made for river crossings. For them it would be a dawn landing, amphibious, two thousand men for each beach.

Fleet D as a whole would form a column more than a mile wide and twelve miles long – so long that the lead barges would be halfway across the Channel before the last boats left harbour. But the barges could travel at no more than three or four knots, and all the columns had to follow crooked courses, to avoid sandbanks and mines. The crossing would take long hours.

And even as the column pulled away from the harbour, the attacks began. Over Ernst's head Messerschmitt 109s were taking on Hurricanes, Spitfires and light bombers. Josef had said Goering had been trying to disrupt the RAF's command systems as much as ruin its planes and airfields; perhaps a weakened RAF was focusing its efforts where it thought it could do the most harm. For Ernst that wasn't a comforting thought.

They were not long out of the harbour when a Spitfire got through and flew low over Ernst's column, machine guns blazing. Ernst and the others cowered low in the barge, and the bullets clanged harmlessly from the hull's steel plates. The plane swept over, and when it pulled up Ernst saw how the metal skin over its wings wrinkled with the stress.

But it wasn't the RAF that Ernst feared most, as the evening darkened into night, but the Royal Navy.

For days before the barges sailed, the minelayers, protected by destroyers and E-boats, had been setting up a fortified corridor across the Channel, walled by minefields each a half-mile wide, and even now the U-boats, destroyers and torpedo boats, reinforced by ships taken from the French in Algeria, must be fighting desperately to repel the overwhelming might of the British ships. Sometimes Ernst thought he heard the booming voices of that other battle, far away, a battle on the sea just as one raged in the air. But Ernst's barge sailed on undisturbed.

The night folded over them, imperceptibly slowly, until it became starless and moonless under a lid of cloud. Some of the men were ill, though the sea was mild. They got absolutely no sympathy from the binnenschiffer, the only true sailor on the boat, a leather-faced forty-year-old river worker from Cologne. Occasionally you would hear bits of banter drifting across the ocean between the barges of the tow group, and ripples of laughter coming out of the dark. Some men huddled down and tried to sleep. Coming from one boat Ernst heard murmured prayers. The Nazis looked down on religion, but he doubted anybody was going to put a stop to that tonight. So you crossed the ocean in the dark, in bubbles of companionship, nothing but you and your buddies out on the sea. Ernst wondered if it had been this way for William's Normans, and Claudius's superstitious Romans a thousand years earlier still. But those ancient warriors had not had to endure this passage through a corridor of warfare, in the air and at sea.

Later in the night units of Fleet E, the westernmost, linked up with D as had been planned. And rumours began to spread among the men on the barges about what was really going on.

At the fringes of the invasion, the Royal Navy was getting through the flimsy defences of the Kriegsmarine. Though for fear of aerial attack the English had committed no capital ships, no cruisers or battleships, their light fighting ships had sailed from Harwich, Dover, Portsmouth and Portland. Their small motor torpedo boats, like the Germans' E-boats, had been the first to fall on Fleet E, and later the English destroyers had got among them. The German escort ships, mostly civilian ships with machine guns and a few pieces of light artillery, could do little about it. The destroyers' guns, four- or six-inchers, made short work of the steamers, and the men in the barges had to listen to boom and crash, boom and crash, as the big guns were fired, and the shells found their targets. Within minutes many of the steamers were holed, sinking, burning.

And then these wolves of the sea, travelling at thirty or forty knots, tore through the columns of wallowing river barges, crushing them, drowning them in their wash, or simply dragging them by their towing cables until they were capsized. Any surviving barges were raked with gunfire, shells and flame throwers until the sea was littered with burning wreckage. Men in the water were being wiped out systematically. The destroyers even sent up flares to light up the night, the better to prosecute their slaughter. There was no rescue tonight, no honour of the sea, no pity.

But while Fleet E died, D was spared. Perhaps it was true in the east too, the men muttered, Fleet B soaking it up to spare Fleet C. Perhaps, the men whispered, Fleets D and C would make it to their landing sites, around Eastbourne and Rye. At Brighton and Dover, the destinations for E and B, there would only be wreckage and bodies washed ashore on a tide frothing with blood.

In that case, Ernst thought, listening, appalled, those who landed alive must make these huge sacrifices count.

In the dark, with the water lapping and the tug engines labouring, surrounded by the boom and crash of the fighting planes and ships, Ernst lost his sense of time. He was startled to realise that dawn light was seeping into the sky.

And there ahead of him, a grey line sandwiched between a steel sky and an iron sea, was land. He saw prickles of light. It was 0615, already half an hour after dawn, and, after a softening-up bombardment, the lead echelons must already have landed, were already fighting and dying.

A drizzle started. The sky was murky, charcoal grey. It was 21 September, S-Day. This was England. He thought he could hear church bells ringing distantly, a beautiful nostalgic noise. Hitler had had all the bells in Germany melted down for munitions.

XV

The sound of the tug engines died, and the barge drifted. At last, thought Ernst. It was two hours since his first glimpse of land. Since then they had run parallel to the shore, before finally turning and driving in.

The sound of the long battle raging along the coast was already huge. The men lay as low as they could, sheltered by the barge's reinforced walls. But Ernst risked raising his head and looked out over the barge's fortified flank, hoping for his first glimpse of Pevensey, his landing site.

There was a murky light now, and the coast was obscured by haze and drifting smoke. But it was chaos on land and on sea. Assault-troop barges like his own were sliding in towards the shore, jostling for a place to land. On the beach more craft were stranded by a tide that was already receding, the rubber boats and speedboats of the advanced detachments. The beach itself looked littered, as if by bits of seaweed, and it was striped by peculiar black bands that ran parallel to the shore. The invaders were under fire. Ernst saw a tower to his right, and the larger guns of a coastal battery were coughing somewhere to his left; shells hissed as they flew, and landed with crashing explosions, or threw water spouts spectacularly into the air. From the area directly ahead Ernst heard the bark of automatic arms fire, and he saw the bulky silhouettes of pillboxes, fire sparking from the slits drawn in their forbidding faces.

All this was screened by smoke and a spray of water thrown up by the shells. But it was clear that the coastal defences were not subdued by the advance troops, as they had been promised. The very pile-up of boats struggling to find a place to land proved that something had gone wrong, that the beach wasn't clearing as fast as it should.

The barge's unteroffizier turned in the grey light. He was younger than Ernst, but his left cheek was darkened by a huge livid scar, picked up somewhere during the Nazis' dash across Europe. 'All right, lads. Now, we've been over the drill often enough. The first echelon are clearing the beach. They'll cover us when we land, and in turn we'll need to cover the command companies. Then we'll organise into our assault companies, get off the damn beach and through the marshy rubbish further up, and then we'll be off into the hills before breakfast.' Even as he said this, everybody could see the plan made no sense. The unteroffizier was faced by rows of wide-eyed faces, many of them pale under their blacking. 'Right, check your lifebelt,' he said. This was a bulky item like a motor tyre you wore under your gear. Ernst had his tucked up under his armpits. 'Remember what the officers said. Don't stop for wounded. Somebody else will follow up for them. Your job is to advance. Don't forget that . . .'

A motor roared, and their barge, one of a group of four, ploughed forward once more. The tug that had brought them across the Channel had to stand out to sea; a smaller motor-boat was dragging them to land. Whether the plan was defunct or not made no difference. They were going in.

As they neared the beach the barge jostled with those around it, gathering in a throng as tight as in Boulogne harbour. But now they were coming into the range of the shell fire, and Ernst ducked down, into the cover of the barge's hull. The men were splashed with water thrown up by the detonations, and once by a hail of splinters from some smashed boat.

There were screams nearby, and a rip of metal. Ernst risked another glance. One of the barges in his group was ripped open and was tipping, spilling out its men. Its flank had snagged on a tangle of scaffolding jutting out of the water, revealed by the receding tide.

Shingle scraped, and Ernst's barge rocked. It was grounded. The bat-wing doors opened, and the ramp at the front of the boat was let down. The unteroffizier jumped up. 'Off! Off!—' The shot hit him in the mouth. The back of his head detonated, and his jaw hung down, flapping, as he tipped into the water.

The men ducked down again. But now some English machine-gunner got his range. The bullets stitched the length of the barge and through the bodies of men who cried out, one after another.

'Get out!' Ernst screamed. 'We're sitting ducks here.' He stood again, and men pressed behind him, trying to get off the barge. Ernst realised he would never get to the ramp. Without letting himself think about it, he rolled his body over the side of the barge and dropped into the water.

He was submerged in water a few feet deep. The water's own bubbling filled his ears. The sea was murky and cold, and the pack on his back, his boots, felt inordinately heavy. He could see others falling into the water around him, and one burly trooper almost landed on top of him.

71

And he could *see* the bullets lancing into the water, creating trails like tiny diving birds. He thrashed, trying to find his footing. The pull of his lifebelt under his armpits helped him.

His head came up above the water, into air that was filled with shouting and the singing of bullets and the whistle of heavier shells. He thrust his hands beneath him, scraping them on the shingle, and at last got his feet under him and dragged himself up. Head down, hefting his rifle, he just ran forward. The going was hard, the stones slippery, the water dragging at every movement. There were bodies floating around him, some riddled by bullets, but some unmarked – men must be drowning as they tried to get off the boats. And he was *cold*, by God; that was something he hadn't anticipated.

At last the water shallowed, and he found himself crunching over slippery shingle. The beach was long and sloping. It looked an awfully long way to the pillboxes beyond the sea wall which still spat their spiteful fire. And the beach was already littered with men lying still where they had fallen, and by the wreckage of boats and barges.

Automatic fire hissed through the air. He threw himself flat. He landed heavily, his pack slamming between his shoulder blades like a punch.

He saw there was a low wooden wall only a few feet to his right, like a groyne. Men huddled behind it. He might get a bit of cover there, if he could reach it. He rolled towards the groyne, over and over, his pack bumping under his back. A stray bullet smacked into the shingle, only inches from his right eye, and a pebble splintered and peppered his face with a kind of shrapnel. He cried out, feeling the sting of blood.

But he got to the groyne. He pressed himself against the thick wood, which was dark and slippery with seaweed. It wasn't much protection, but it was better than nothing, better than being out there exposed on the shingle like a beached porpoise. The men already here were soaked, wild-eyed, some of them wounded. None of them was from his company.

He risked a look over the groyne. There was a pillbox directly ahead of him. He was right in its line of fire. He could not imagine the men inside it, fighting for their lives; it seemed like something superhuman, brooding, a slit-eyed monster spitting lead at him. Before it the beach was chaotic, cratered, men crawling or lying still, looking for cover in shell-holes or behind the wreckage of boats. He saw the black plumes of mortar fire, the crack of bullets, and toxic fumes and sprays of red-hot shrapnel rose up from shell falls. Overhead the aerial battle continued, much of it hidden by the murky low cloud. The RAF fighters dipped low enough to scour the men on the beach with their guns. And there were Luftwaffe planes in there too; he saw a Stuka dive bomber coming down to take on some English gun nest. There was a smell of cordite and salty sea spray and the rich, sickening tang of blood.

And there was a wall further up where more men crowded, seeking shelter, their soaked battledress dark. Ernst realised that he had joined one of the black lines he had seen from the sea: bands of black that were mortal men huddling behind whatever cover they could find, trying to stay alive.

It wasn't supposed to be like this, he reminded himself. Evidently the English resistance had been underestimated. A shot slapped the wood close to his face, and he ducked back down.

Well, he couldn't stay here. Looking around, he saw that others drawn up against the groyne had the same idea. One man, an unterfeldwebel, raised his arm.

Ernst moved with the rest. And for the first time since landing in England he raised his weapon and fired.

The troops advanced up the beach in turn. It was a long slog. It was a question of lift your head, take a shot to cover the rest, and then when they were firing take your chance to crawl a bit further forward, before ducking down again. Still the pillboxes fired. There were hazards on the beach too; Ernst nearly fell into a dugout improvised from a bit of drainpipe buried in the shingle, but the Englishman inside was already dead.

And then a mortar emplacement got its range, and the shells rained down on the beach all around Ernst. Men and bits of kit were thrown high in the air, men torn to pieces in an instant, their limbs scattered. Ernst found himself crawling desperately *over* the bodies of the fallen. You could even get a bit of cover, if you ducked down behind a corpse.

But gradually, he saw, inch by inch – life by life – the tide of the German offensive was rising up towards the defenders, and one after another their emplacements fell silent, put out of action by a rattle of gunfire or the pop of an explosion.

And as he climbed the beach, and the daylight gathered, he began to see the scale of the operation unfolding around him. To right and left, all along the four miles of this shallow beach as far as he could see, men were making their advance, fighting and dying, Twenty-sixth Division slowly achieving its objective. Back at the edge of the sea, beyond the litter of assault boats and splintered barges, more troop carriers were pressing to land, a great crowd of them still stuck off shore. But already the sapper companies were landing their heavier equipment. He saw mortars and machine guns being assembled, and a big PAK anti-tank gun, and even an anti-aircraft weapon. The first horses were landing, bucking nervously as they were led through the spray. There were even men struggling to drag the barges out to sea, so they could be towed back across the Channel to be loaded with the second wave.

When he reached the head of the beach, he had to crawl around anti-tank obstacles, big concrete cubes. And then he came to the barbed wire, already snipped and pulled back by the first wave of engineers.

At last he was almost under the face of that damn pillbox itself. It was sheer concrete that glistened as if still moist. A man rushed it, lobbed a grenade through that slit, and ducked down. The grenade detonated with a dull thud, smoke and fire billowed briefly from the slit, and the pillbox was silenced. Ernst cheered with the others, wishing he could have thrown the grenade himself.

And then one more push and he was on grass, the beach at last behind him.

He heard a throaty roar. He turned, lying on his back, breathing hard.

An amphibious tank was coming out of the water, its snorkel raised like an elephant's trunk, a monster rising from the deep. On a day of extraordinary sights, this schwimmpanzer was the most remarkable. But a wounded man, lying behind a heap of corpses for cover, was right in its tracks. He screamed and tried to crawl out of the way, wriggling. But the tank driver could not see him and he was crushed into the shingle. His guts were forced out of his mouth and his arse, like toothpaste from a tube.

XVI

Ben Kamen watched the landings from the look-out post, high on the walls at Pevensey Castle.

From horizon to horizon, as the sun rose, the beach was alight with the spark of firing. Shells came in from the sea too, where the German ships were firing on the coastal defences. There was even fire coming from big guns on the continent, massive rail-mounted Bruno-class, perhaps. And one by one the gun emplacements and Martello towers and anti-tank ditches and pillboxes that had been so hastily manned during the summer were silenced.

Ben glanced around the interior of the fort. He was at the west gate, a relic of the Roman fort. The Roman curtain wall surrounded a cluster of medieval buildings, a lesser fort within the mightier ruin. It was this vast expanse of enclosed space that had inspired William of Normandy to make his landing here, when he had made his own invasion; it had been a defensible place to land his troops that first crucial night nine hundred years back.

Well, the sea had receded since then. And now, after all this time, the fort had been adapted for another invasion, another war. The castle was host to a garrison that included Home Guard like Ben, and British and Canadian regular units. Pillboxes had been built into the ruins of the keep, and the towers of the inner bailey had been fitted out as a garrison. It was very odd for Ben to see the characteristic slit gun port of a modern pillbox cut into what was obviously medieval stonework, itself built of reused Roman masonry.

But it was the same all the way along the English coast. Martello towers had been pressed into service, more than seventy of them, hefty structures thrown up before the time of Napoleon when the British feared invasion by the French. Now, after a hundred and fifty years of patient watchfulness, many were falling silent after only hours of use.

'We're not going to stop this lot today, mate,' said Johnnie Cox. 'Not this way anyhow.' Johnnie was a Canadian.

Ben shrugged. 'Yeah, but that wasn't the point, was it?' He was aware of a faint Canadian inflection in his own voice; he had a habit of taking on the accents of others, in an unconscious strategy to fit in. 'This is the coastal crust; it's just supposed to slow them down. But when the counterattack comes—'

'What counterattack? General Brooke doesn't have the men, I'll tell you that. If the BEF wasn't locked up in jail on the continent—'

Ben shook his head. 'You know, Johnnie, I've got to know a few soldiers in my time in England, and they're all miserable bastards. But you take the biscuit. Don't the Brits have any chance?'

'Well, maybe one. It all depends on how tough they are.'

'Tough? What do you mean?'

'You got your gas-mask with you?'

XVII

It took until noon before Pevensey Bay was secured, with the railway line crossed at the halt, and the road to Bexhill taken, and the assault groups were at last able to form up, ready to move out. The tide had long since turned, and the barges and motor boats were desperately trying to reach the sea, for they were needed to bring across the second echelon, but they were having trouble finding clear water through the wreckage of boats and the tangles of corpses. The casualty rate must be high, Ernst thought, a quarter, a third of this first wave lost; he was lucky to be alive. But he had been forced to watch many comrades die.

And then, after all that, four hours after Ernst landed, the gas came.

Just one shell was dropped by a Blenheim bomber, onto the beach where Ernst himself had landed. It seemed to detonate harmlessly, causing few casualties. But then the gas spread, and men fell, crying out, clawing at their eyes and their blistering skin. Those officers with experience of the first war knew what this was: mustard gas. Fear spread through the ranks of the men, still massed tight on the beaches. They scrambled for gas-masks, fearing they might have been ruined by immersion in the sea.

But there was only that one plane, that one shell. Perhaps this attack was carried out by a rogue unit, disaffected officers of the RAF. The British did not quite have the inhumanity to use this last resort – or, some said, the courage.

Whatever, the incident served only to enrage the men. Ernst felt it himself.

He was in the group that took Pevensey Castle. The defences here were feeble, and surrendered quickly when a flame tank, a flammenpanzer, forced its way through the west gate. Ernst was one of the first into a garrison that had been built into the ruins of the inner bailey, and he himself took several prisoners.

One small man, dark, in the uniform of the Home Guard, dared to speak to them in German: 'Welcome to England.' Ernst used his rifle-butt to club him to silence.

XVIII

22 September

Around seven a.m. on the Sunday morning, the day after the invasion started, the raids let up for a bit.

The WVS coordinator was a plump, brisk woman of around fifty called Mollie. She practically shoved Mary away. 'Get some rest. You're no use to anybody dead on your feet. I dare say the Jerries will be at it again when you come back.'

So Mary complied. After all, she hadn't slept at all on the Friday night, had worked all Saturday, and had stayed awake that night too.

She picked up her stuff, her rucksack and handbag, the briefcase that she'd taken to slinging around her neck on a bit of string, and she stumbled home, to George's little terraced house in the Old Town. It took her only minutes to get there. It shocked her, actually, how close to home all this destruction and injury and death was. It was as if the whole of the war had focused down on this little bit of England, into her life.

The house itself looked intact. But the front door stuck when she tried to open it, and she had to barge it with her shoulder. She felt the frame splinter as the door gave way. The corridor was dark, and the light didn't turn on when she snapped the switch. Everything was quiet, eerily so after all the commotion outside. The carpets were covered with a patina of plaster dust. For Mary, lacking sleep, it was very odd to be here again. When she'd left on Friday night she hadn't really expected to come back, not for a long while.

She pulled off her gas-mask and rucksack, and dumped the felt hat and green WVS jacket she had been loaned. She made straight for the bathroom. Like the other WVS ladies, with embarrassed averted gazes or sometimes a giggle, she had been relieving herself behind heaps of rubble, in the smashed-up ruins of what had so recently been homes. The toilet flushed, but she could hear the cistern wasn't refilling. She wasn't surprised. Even as the raids continued she had seen teams of workers trying to patch up water mains, gas pipes, electric cables.

She looked at herself in the mirror. Her face was a mask of greasy sweat and soot, her cheeks and forehead smeared where she had rubbed them with the backs of her hands.

Nothing came out of the taps, but the water she had poured out on Friday stood in the sink, covered by a skim of plaster dust. She scraped the dust off with her palm and bent to soak her face. The water stung her hands. She saw that under the dirt she had blisters, burned patches. But the dirt floated off easily, and the cold of the water revived her a bit. She longed for a bath, and to wash her hair properly.

She made her way to the kitchen. More in hope than in expectation she tried the gas ring on the cooker, but that didn't work either. A cup of tea was off the menu, then, unless she built a fire in the living room and used the iron stand. It seemed a lengthy project, getting the coal, finding matches and a bit of paper and kindling, building the fire – she decided she couldn't face it. Anyhow there was some milk, and more scummy water, and she knew there was a bit of bread; she could make a sandwich.

She heard a clatter from the front door, a muffled curse. It was George. She walked back to the hall.

He was experimenting with the door, which wouldn't fit back in its frame. His uniform was dust-smeared and the left knee was torn badly. His face was black with dust and dirt and soot, as hers had been. He glanced at her. 'Thought you'd still be around. The door – can you see, the whole frame is distorted? It'll be a nightmare to get hold of a builder. Bloody Goering. Are you all right? You look done in.'

'No worse than you,' she said defiantly.

'What happened to your hands?' He took her hands and turned them over; his own hands were caked in dirt. 'You need to do something about these blisters. We've got a bit of ointment somewhere.'

'Do you want a cup of tea?'

He followed her back towards the kitchen. 'Is the gas on, then?'

'No. But I was thinking of building a fire.'

He shook his head. 'No time for that. Look, let's just have something quick. I need to get back to work. And *you* need to get out of here. Out of town, I mean.' In the kitchen he put his helmet and gas-mask on the wooden table, opened a few buttons of his uniform jacket, and washed his hands in the sink.

They began to make a rough breakfast together, glasses of milk, slices of bread with a pale scrape of margarine and elderly cheese.

She said, 'The Germans, I suppose.'

'Well, they've landed at Pevensey and near Bexhill, and to the east between Hastings and Rye. Actually they're all along the south coast. Today they'll be trying to get more troops across, I should think, and supplies, although the bulk of the second echelon will come over tonight. And those already landed will be consolidating.'

'And coming here.'

'That's the best guess. We're supposed to evacuate what's left of the civilian population. Let's see if we can get a bit of news.'

He went off to the parlour, and came back with his home-made wireless in its shoe box. He set it on the table, held up an earpiece scavenged from an old telephone, and began to fiddle with the settings. This home-made crystal set, by some process which non-scientific Mary regarded as a miracle, didn't need any power.

'Ah,' he said. 'There's Alvar Lidell. I wonder where *he* is now. They were talking about moving the BBC out from London to Bristol ...' His voice trailed off as he listened. He sat at the table, chewing his bit of bread, his face emptying, the old phone earpiece clamped to his head. Mary sat with him and waited.

'Well, there we are,' he said. '"The Germans have invaded Great Britain. In due course they will be driven out by our Navy, our Army and our Air Force. The Prime Minister, Mr Churchill, has emphasised that the ordinary men and women of the civilian population will have their part to play" ...' He listened further. 'Sounds like they're panicking a bit in London. They're moving the civil servants out to Lancashire and Wales. The government is talking to the Americans about "increased cooperation", whatever that means. We could do with a few tanks and guns, never mind cooperation.'

'Maybe they're doing deals,' Mary said.

'Your ambassador Kennedy thinks we should surrender.'

'Yeah, but we don't all agree with *him*. The US has no interest in seeing Britain fall to the Nazis. I know Churchill exchanged military bases in Newfoundland and the West Indies for a pack of old destroyers. Maybe they're working on something like that.'

George grunted. 'Nothing comes free with you lot, does it? Oh. The King is moving out of London, and his family. That's a bit of a blow to morale.' He put the earpiece down. 'Well, that's that. Look, Mary, just clear off. The trains are out. If you can, head out of town along the A-road towards Battle. The police are organising convoys there, to be driven up towards London and the north.'

'I was thinking of sleeping a bit.'

'Sleep. God, I could do with a bit of that. Not just now. The next hours are critical.'

81

She nodded reluctantly. 'All right, George. Look – the others, Hilda and Gary—'

'I haven't heard from them since Friday. Seems like years ago.'

'I left a note in the Anderson shelter. Said we should meet at Battle, if the opportunity arises.'

He nodded. 'Not a bad idea.'

'What about you?'

'It's my job to stay here, Mary. I'm a copper.'

'Your German is lousy.'

'I'll be fine. And so will you.' He took her hand, carefully avoiding her burns. 'You're brave. If you're an example of what Americans can do, the sooner you're in this war the better.'

'Brave? I think I'm just numb. I'll pay for all this one day.'

'Well, so will Hitler.' He'd finished his bread and cheese. He glanced down at his crystal set. 'Of course I can't take this.' He slipped off his boot, and without hesitation brought it crashing down like a hammer on the components of the set. 'Right, that's done. Come on, Mary, let's find you that ointment.'

XIX

Leutnant Strohmeyer had a map. He spread it out on Pevensey's dewy ground. Strohmeyer was a tough, humourless soldier who had served the Reich's armies across Europe, from Poland to France. And now here he was sitting before a camp fire in the ruins of this ancient fort in England itself. When one of the lads dared to make a comment on this, Strohmeyer said only, 'Funny old world, isn't it? Now shut up and listen.' He began to outline the day's objectives, Day S Plus One, for these elements of the Twenty-sixth Division.

It was another filthy, drizzling morning. Ernst, wrapped in his blanket, cradling the rifle he had been cleaning since dawn, tried to focus on what Strohmeyer was saying.

He never would have believed he would sleep so well, tucked up in a corner of this dismal old fort under no more cover than a tarpaulin. Yesterday, the day of the crossing, had been a vivid, unreal day, a day of a kind he imagined he would never experience again, no matter how long his war lasted. He supposed the raw tension of it had carried him through. But he had woken this morning to find that he was *still here*, he really was in England, and now he had to get through the first of what might be many days of combat. He felt drained, exhausted, even shivery; he woke with no energy. Even the men with him were strangers; in the turmoil of the landing he had become separated from the men he had trained with in France, and he knew nobody here.

He kept thinking of Claudine. He longed to be lying with her in her apartment in Boulogne, her long limbs beside him in the bed, so that she could soothe away the aches of his body and the trauma of his bruised mind.

The man next to him whispered, 'What's he saying? I can't see the wretched map.'

Another replied softly, 'Marching. That's all you need to know, lads. When the Panzers come over in a day or two they'll rip about the place.

But until then it's just us, and it's foot-slogging. Best not to know how far.'

So they stood, and began to form up.

Elsewhere in the fort, Ben Kamen and a couple of other prisoners from the observation post at Pevensey were roughly woken by coarse German shouts.

They rose stiffly. They were given cups of water to drink, and told in German to make their toilet in the corner of the room, if they needed it. Ben, not wanting to stand out, affected not to know any German – his bit of cheek yesterday had earned him a clubbing – and he acted dull, slow and baffled like the rest. In fact it wasn't hard, as his head was still throbbing from the blow he had taken yesterday.

They had been given nothing last night. No food or water, no blankets. Ben had slept in his clothes, huddled on the cold stone floor of one of the converted rooms. All night he had had broken dreams, glimpses of past and future, of the type that had so intrigued Rory and Julia back in Princeton. But none of them made any sense, and none was any comfort.

One prisoner, a burly Canadian, drank a bit of the water and spat it out. 'Horse's piss,' he yelled at the German corporal who had brought it. The corporal actually replied quite politely, in calm German, saying that the man's rights would be protected when the German army had the resources to grant them, and that in the meantime his best course was to behave with self-respect.

As far as Ben could see these elite-type combat troops had been reasonably civilised with their prisoners. Maybe it was true that the Germans, still intent on an eventual armistice with England, were under instructions to be restrained. But then, he reminded himself, the best of the Wehrmacht were not representative of the culture of modern Germany.

The prisoners were shortly brought out, at gun point. There were other prisoners, brought here from emplacements along the invasion shore, regular soldiers and Home Guard and a few flyers in RAF blue and leather jackets. The fort was full of activity, as vehicles were serviced, horses fed, even bicycle wheels oiled. Ben tried to listen to the snippets of German conversation around him, hoping to learn something useful, but all he heard were typical soldiers' gripes about the cold food, the lack of alcohol, and the absence of women in this soggy place.

These men were all survivors of the battles yesterday, Ben reflected; save for the odd paratrooper, not a single German could have come here any other way but across that treacherous stretch of shingle. There was a smell of war about them all, with their unshaven faces and grimy clothes, a scent of cordite and diesel and petrol and dust, of burning and of blood.

The prisoners were marched up to the Bexhill road. A column was forming up here, men, horses, vehicles, guns, even one amphibious tank. Ben guessed these units were heading towards Bexhill and perhaps Hastings. As for the prisoners, maybe they were being marched to a POW camp somewhere. Ben didn't know where he was going, and he supposed he didn't need to know; he had no choices left, nothing to do but do what he was told, and survive.

As the column set off, Ernst walked behind the single tank. It had been made waterproof for its amphibious landing, but now the protective coverings and snorkel had been cut away, and its turret turned this way and that, questing, as the crew tested out the vehicle. There were a good number of trucks, some of them with seawater stains on their canvas tops. The horses were harnessed up to carts and mobile field weapons, and the infantry marched in their files on either side of the road. Some troops rode bicycles, many of them harvested from Holland and brought over on the invasion barges. There were even a few commandos outriding on motorcycles; they were to be used as scouts, running ahead of the main column.

So they marched, north away from Pevensey. Their first objective was five miles or so inland, a place named on the leutnant's map as Windmill Hill. They soon left behind the rather dilapidated seaside villas at Pevensey. The column followed minor roads and farm tracks, but made reasonable progress over the level salt marshes beyond. The day stayed grey, even as the light gathered, and the drizzle and mist was depressing. 'If this is England, Churchill can keep it,' one man murmured.

But as Ernst walked with his comrades, swinging his arms and stepping out, he felt his blood flow, his heart pump, the clean English air filling his lungs, and he began to feel alive again. Why not? He was young, he was strong, his training was good, and he was with the best army in the world, a fact proven by accomplishment. He dared to look ahead, to the future. Perhaps he would be in London when the Fuhrer made his entrance – by barge, perhaps, along the Thames. What a grand day that would be!

The men rumbled into a marching song – 'Bomben auf Engelland', a popular favourite on the French beaches.

But this mood did not last long. Aircraft buzzed across the sky, out of sight above the lid of low cloud. Ernst winced every time one came close; he had seen troop columns strafed from the air on the continent. But no harm came from that quarter. Rumours went around the column that the RAF today was targeting the embarkation ports in France and the returning fleets of barges and tugs, trying to disrupt the invasion's second echelon.

And as the morning wore on the going became slow, disjointed. The first serious resistance they encountered was at a crossroads near a pub called the Lamb Inn, a location that commanded the levels behind them. That didn't take long to resolve, thanks to the tank. But after that the resistance became more frequent, and over and over again the column ground to a halt. Often Ernst couldn't even see what was going on up ahead. He would hear the thump of explosions, the pop of small-arms fire, occasionally a roar as the tank let loose its main gun, and see the smoke of burning petrol. Sometimes they would see one or more of their own vehicles, disabled or burned out and shoved over to the side of the road. There were a few German dead, a steady trickle; Ernst saw the bodies at the side of the road covered by tarpaulins from the disabled trucks. Medics patched up the injured.

And the troops would stare as they passed a blown-apart pillbox of piled-up sandbags, or a cleared-aside roadblock made of concrete and lengths of rail track and concrete anti-tank 'dimples', lines of little cones. The weapons in the blown-open pillboxes and bunkers, seemed crude. Ernst saw one mortar that looked as if it might have been used against Napoleon.

On they went. Every bridge was demolished, and the scouts had to find them places to ford the streams. Elsewhere there were ditches, meant to stop tanks perhaps, and the weary men scrambled down one bank and up another. These assaults were petty, but they steadily eroded the column's manpower, and took out their vehicles and horses and used up their ammunition. And, more importantly, they were slowed down.

A horse was killed by a mine in a grotesque explosion that burst the animal's carcass, showering the men with bloody fur and shredded bits of meat. The men took a break as the engineers dealt with that.

Two British troops, wounded but alive, had been taken in this place. The men sat on the ground with their hands on their heads. They wore what looked like proper army uniforms, with flat steel helmets, leather gaiters, boots, greatcoats and leather belts. One had an officer's stripes. But their arm bands read HOME GUARD. These two were *old*, Ernst saw with a shock as he passed, their hair grey, their faces deeply lined – either of them old enough to be his own father, if not his grandfather. Perhaps the rumours that had been circulating since France were true, that the British forces really were badly depleted by the catastrophe that had overtaken them at Dunkirk. Old these fellows might be, and defeated and captured, but they sat up straight like soldiers, one with

86

blood trickling into a closed eye from a head wound, and they stared every German in the eye.

'Partisans?' muttered one man.

'No,' the leutnant snapped. 'You can't be a partisan until your country has surrendered, Breitling. Until then these gentleman are to be treated as prisoners of war.'

'They should be fucking shot,' Breitling said. 'Fucking English. Why can't they just roll over like the French?'

'Don't let it get you down, lads,' said the leutnant. 'Look at what we're up against. Old men and boys, and weapons from a museum. When the Panzers get over here on Tuesday they'll roll up this countryside like a carpet.'

But later Ernst overheard the leutnant muttering with an officer about this slow progress, and how it was becoming important they found fuel before they exhausted the supply they had brought over from France.

For Ben and the other prisoners it was not an arduous walk. Stuck in the middle of the column and surrounded by guards, they plodded steadily along. They talked quietly, swapped their stories, and bummed furtive cigarettes from each other. They seemed resigned to their fate, Ben thought.

The prisoners had to shelter like the rest from the attacks by the resistance elements. This was another product of the war in Spain, Ben supposed, that great warm-up fixture where the Germans had learned how to machine-gun civilians from the air and the British had learned to make Molotov cocktails.

As the day wore on Ben's headache got worse.

One man helped him when he staggered. 'Just walk. It was like this in France, in the early days. March and march. You just have to get on with it. My advice is to think about something else.' He had a strong accent, barely comprehensible to Ben. 'You got a girl?'

'Not exactly.'

'Well, you're a bright lad. Do a crossword in your head. That's my advice.'

So Ben walked, trying to ignore the pain in his head. He tried to visualise problems in relativity, like Gödel's beautiful rotating-universe solution of Einstein's equations. But the math kept sliding away from him, the tensors with their forests of suffices blurring into invisibility.

Soon he had trouble keeping up with the pace, and drifted to the back of the little group of prisoners. The German guards thumped him with their rifle-butts, yelling at him to keep up, and even rode into the back of his legs with their bicycle wheels.

The veteran protested: 'Hey, go easy, Funf. Can't you see he's ill?' That won him shouts in German that if he didn't shut up he'd be taken out of the line and shot. The veteran understood their tone, if not their words. 'The front-line corps who captured us were gentlemen. Not like this shower. Look at them, car mechanics and horse handlers, bottle washers and sausage makers. Scum of the earth, the lot of them.'

XX

Mary prepared to leave George's house before nine o'clock, this Sunday morning.

She sorted out her belongings. She slung her handbag under her coat, so it was less likely to be grabbed off her. She hesitated a bit about taking the research papers from the briefcase. The strange allo-historical questions she had been following since meeting Ben Kamen didn't seem to matter now, didn't even seem real, compared to the vast violence all around her. And yet *not* to have taken the papers would have felt like a defeat, as if she was giving up something of herself, a bit of her identity. So she stuffed the papers into her rucksack, along with her knickers and stockings.

Then she stepped out of the house, and once more locked the door carefully. Aircraft screamed overhead, making her flinch, but at least the town wasn't coming under attack this morning. She walked out of the Old Town, down the narrow, sloping streets to the coast road, and then headed west beneath the imposing West Hill, with its Norman castle and anti-aircraft gun emplacement. She meant to cut up past the rail station and then make for Bohemia Road, which would lead to the main road out to Battle.

The heavy-lift crews had been out clearing the streets of rubble, just shoving it aside and piling it up in bomb sites and any open spaces available. But most of the shops were shut up. Some had been left with their doors open, with signs saying 'Help Yourself'. There was no food or milk, nothing she could see that would be useful now.

She heard detonations coming from the direction of the harbour. It wasn't much of a harbour, just a fishermen's port, the sea walls built by the Victorians after centuries of struggle against geography, and now mostly silted up. But George had told her of plans to defend it with guns and torpedo tubes, and in the end to wreck it. Functioning ports were key for the Germans; without harbours it was going to be hard for them to land their heavy equipment, supplies and reinforcements. Yesterday at the start of the invasion they had launched a paratroop raid on Dover, which seemed to have failed, but today there was said to be a major battle going on around Folkestone.

When she got to Bohemia Road she came upon the main flow of refugees, heading out of town, slogging it on foot with their carts and wheelbarrows and prams. They were a river of people.

There was a good bit of traffic, private cars and buses and lorries and ambulances, but at least everybody was driving the same way, to the north and out of Hastings, and there were police and ARP wardens to shepherd the pedestrians off the road to keep the traffic moving. A few bicycles threaded through the crowd; that was a sensible way to go, if you could manage it. Mary saw one lad on a bicycle hanging onto the back of a lorry, pulled along as the vehicle ploughed forward.

The police and wardens were keeping the right hand lane clear, the lane heading back to town, but there was little traffic on it. George had said that the authorities had plans to avoid what had happened on the continent, when refugee flows had snarled up attempts to move military assets into place for a counterattack, and the police had been given maps with some routes marked in yellow for the use of civilians, others red for the military. It might have worked better, George said drily, if the maps had been printed in the right coloured ink.

Mary felt reluctant to join the shuffling throng, as if it would mean sacrificing her individuality. But there was no choice. She stepped forward, and found a place behind a boy pushing a barrow, before a mother with two kids in a pram, beside an old man leaning on a sturdy woman who might have been his wife. And then she could do nothing but walk with the rest.

They passed abandoned vehicles, broken down or out of petrol, briskly shoved off the road. She didn't see many military vehicles. Mostly it was just people, walking. They trudged along with their children on their backs and their wheelbarrows and prams laden with luggage and pots and pans. They seemed stoical enough. Maybe the national myths of the bulldog breed helped them hold it together. Churchill's rhetoric, still working its magic. But there were many with drawn faces and strange absent looks – plenty of trauma, even as this dreadful day got going. How strange it was, Mary thought, that only a couple of days ago she had woken up with all these people in a town where the milk was delivered and the post and papers arrived, and you could expect the shops to be open sharp in the mornings. Now all that was stripped away, and these British subjects were refugees, as simple as that, with no dignity and precious little hope. It was a scene of a population in flight, right out of H.G. Wells.

On the outskirts of town she passed a factory. Contained within a tall wire fence, it had once manufactured components for gas cookers, but had been turned over to munitions manufacture at the outbreak of war. Now it was being systematically vandalised. A handful of women dragged equipment out of the buildings and went at it with sledge-hammers and iron bars. Every factory was supposed to have a plan to disable its equipment lest it fall into enemy hands. The women, in overalls and headscarves, drafted in to replace men lost to the forces, looked as if they were enjoying themselves. Perhaps it felt like a holiday, an end to the dull and dangerous work that had occupied them for the year of the war.

Once they got out of town towards the open country there seemed to be nobody in charge, no more police or ARP wardens, except a few who had joined the flight themselves. And still they walked, limping terribly slowly through these few miles to Battle. By now Mary was dirty, hot, thirsty, hungry, tired, and her feet ached; she felt dizzy from the lack of sleep.

A plane came looming out of the sky, following the line of the road, heading straight toward the column. The people slowed. Mary watched in disbelief.

'I think it's one of ours,' said one old man.

The plane howled as it descended.

'That's a bloody Stuka!' somebody yelled.

When the machine guns opened up people screamed and scattered. Mary threw herself off the road, into a field of stubble. Bullets sang off the road surface as the plane roared low overhead. Then a bomb fell with a devastating crash, making a kind of bloody splash in the crowd.

XXI

At noon the German column came at last into Windmill Hill. It was just a hamlet surrounded by farmland. Here Ernst heard challenges to the advance in his own language. Elements of the Thirty-fourth, who had landed at Bexhill, were already in possession.

The column broke. While sentries patrolled, the men gathered in little groups and sat around in the dirt, eating their field rations, massaging their bare feet and swapping horror stories of the landing.

A few men were detailed to break into the houses and to search the nearby farms. No food was found, no stocks of petrol in the barns, no horses, though some of the men emerged with souvenirs – a photograph of the King, English newspapers, a government leaflet offering advice about what to do 'If The Invader Comes', over which the men had a good laugh.

A motor car was found abandoned. A couple of the men spent some minutes trying to start it, but the rotor arm had been removed. Another man turned up a bicycle, so small it must have been meant for a child. But even that had been disabled, its front wheel bent out of shape and its chain snapped. Still the man tried to ride it, with his legs folded and his big knees sticking up in the air. He kept falling off, and raised a few laughs.

Ernst, wandering around, saw graffiti on one of the barns, painted in thick whitewash. There was a huge letter 'V', perhaps aping Churchill's notorious gesture. And on another, more bluntly, the words 'PISS OFF HUN'.

After an hour at Windmill Hill the column formed up, reinforced with the men of the Thirty-fourth and a few more tanks. The prisoners were sent down to Bexhill, with a detachment of guards. Ernst felt in good spirits as the column set off for several more miles' walk along the A-road towards a place called Battle – so they were assured by the spotters. All the road signs had been removed from their posts, so the ordinary troops had no real idea where they were, in green English countryside that looked much the same whichever direction you marched.

They joined a major road at Boreham Street. Again the place was deserted, but the engineers came upon a petrol station. Adorned with metal advertising signs for Shell and Mobiloil, it was abandoned, but the engineers quickly discovered that one of the big underground tanks wasn't empty. Soon they were siphoning off the fuel and filling up the trucks.

But after half an hour the first of the trucks coughed, and ground to a halt. The fuel they had taken had burned to a sticky sludge and was wrecking the engine. The fuel had been doped, with sugar maybe. Cursing, the engineers had to stop all the trucks that had been refuelled at Boreham Street, and fill them again from the column's own dwindling supply, brought from the continent. It was another delay, another hour lost, another vehicle ruined.

As the column approached Battle the country became more difficult, with narrow valleys and low hills, a carpet of fields and hedgerows and copses – ideal cover. The men proceeded cautiously, as silently as possible. Sheep grazed calmly, watching the column pass.

Suddenly they came under heavy fire; it just erupted all around them. Leutnant Strohmeyer got a bullet in the arm, and swore furiously. The vehicles pulled off the road, and the men dived into the ditches by the road. A hail of bottles came spinning out of the woods. They were Molotov cocktails; they splashed where they fell, mostly harmlessly.

'I wonder where they got the bloody petrol,' Breitling muttered.

XXII

It was late afternoon by the time Mary approached Battle itself, where the refugees had been promised a convoy of vehicles would be waiting to take them further. There were many walking wounded after the Stuka attack, people moaning as they struggled to take one step after another. Mary did her best not to think of those left behind.

But an immense plume of flame rose up above Battle, bright in the sky of this late September Sunday. Mary heard the pop of guns and the deeper booming of artillery, and planes stitched the air. The walkers stalled. Mary heard muttering. But they could not go back; they plodded forward, for there was no choice.

They approached a crossroads. The road signs had been dismantled, but Mary heard mutterings that this was the transverse road that ran just south of Battle, joining two places she'd never heard of, Catsfield to the west and Sedlescombe to the east. The refugee flow pushed on across the road junction.

But just as Mary reached the junction there was a roar of some heavy engine. People screamed and scattered back out of the way. Mary was knocked to the ground in the crowd; she landed heavily.

A tank came roaring across the junction, heading from west to east. It stopped with a grind of gears, bang in the middle of the junction. It had a square black cross on its turret. An officer, his head and shoulders protruding from the turret, stared with astonishment at the people before him.

XXIII

All that Sunday George picked up bits of news from the folk coming and going at the town hall.

There was a ferocious battle for Folkestone. The defenders were mostly a New Zealander division. Far from home, they fought well, but by two in the afternoon the Germans had taken the town. But the retreating troops blew up the harbour with its wharves and cranes.

Some German units had made it over the Channel today. But the hinge of the invasion would come overnight, when the bulk of the second echelon would try to make it across to their landing points at dawn on Monday. In advance of that a major battle was unfolding in the Channel. The RAF was strafing the flows of shipping and bombing the embarkation ports, all the while battling it out with the Luftwaffe, and trying to fend off bomber attacks on London and other inland cities. Its resources spread thin, the RAF was near collapse, so the rumours went. The Royal Navy also had split objectives, with a mandate to protect the Atlantic convoys even while the invasion was underway. But today the Home Fleet was fully deployed in the Channel. The destroyers and torpedo boats were taking on the Kriegsmarine, and were getting among the lines of barges and tugs returning from England.

And in Hastings, the Germans were here.

The first German troops arrived on bicycles at about six in the evening. They were soldiers, Wehrmacht as far as George knew, and they must have been scouts. They cycled casually, their rifles on their backs. They were unopposed. George stood at his post at the door of the town hall just off Queens Road, in his police uniform, helmet on, his canvas gas-mask bag slung over his shoulder. The scouts looked him over but otherwise ignored him.

Next came more infantry. They moved cautiously, walking so they hugged the walls to either side of the street, their rifles raised. They peered at upstairs windows, evidently fearful of snipers. But some of them kicked in the front doors of houses or smashed shop windows, and went in to emerge with clocks or bits of silver. After them came a motor-cycle detachment with route signs in German, replacements for the signs long taken down, cardboard placards which they strapped to lamp-posts and nailed to doorways.

Then followed a group of military policeman, the feldgendarmerie, with some junior Wehrmacht troopers. The MPs studied the town hall, and glared at George. Muttering in German, they picked out the building on a map. They ordered two of the soldiers to remain here, evidently on sentry duty. Then they strode on.

The men posted here looked at George, but, seeing he had no weapon and no intention of impeding them, got on with their work. They took a hammer and nails from a canvas bag, and nailed a poster to the town hall door. When they were done they took up their own position by the door, lounging, ignoring George, sharing a cigarette.

George glanced at the poster. It read,

PROCLAMATION TO THE PEOPLE OF ENGLAND:
ONE. ENGLISH TERRITORY OCCUPIED BY GERMAN TROOPS
WILL BE PLACED UNDER MILITARY GOVERNMENT.
TWO. MILITARY COMMANDERS WILL ISSUE DECREES
NECESSARY FOR THE PROTECTION OF THE TROOPS AND THE
MAINTENANCE OF GENERAL LAW AND ORDER . . .

And finally

SIX. I WARN ALL CIVILIANS THAT IF THEY UNDERTAKE ACTIVE
OPERATIONS AGAINST THE GERMAN FORCES, THEY WILL BE
CONDEMNED TO DEATH INEXORABLY.

It was signed by Field Marshal von Brauchitsch, 'Army Commander-in-Chief'. George supposed that where the Germans had up to now been a blank faceless mass, an amorphous enemy, now he would need to learn names such as this. He turned away.

Shortly after that, a more substantial column came rolling through the town: a couple of tanks, trucks, men on foot, horse-drawn carts and weapons. The troops looked weary to George; he saw salt stains on their boots.

At the head of the column was a rather fine car, a magnificent Bentley, silver grey. George wondered where they had liberated this beauty from – he could see why its owner hadn't had the heart to follow orders and disable it. A Wehrmacht soldier chauffeured it for a man in a black uniform, accompanied by a woman in a similar uniform, with bright blonde hair.

The car pulled up outside the town hall. The driver opened the car for the officer and the woman; the two sentries smartened up and saluted, military style. The man in black responded with his right arm outstretched. 'Heil Hitler.' It was the first time George had ever seen a Nazi salute, save in the newsreels.

The man and his woman companion approached George. 'Well, well,' the woman said. 'A British bobby! Years since I've seen one of these specimens. And look, Josef, he's not afraid of you.'

'Good for him,' the man said, also in English. 'Constable, is it?'

George felt confused. The man's accent was German, but the woman's was icy upper-crust English, Noel Coward stuff. And there was something very unsettling in the way she stared at him: blonde, tall, she was extremely beautiful. He said, 'I am Police Constable George Tanner, number—'

The man waved him silent. 'Yes, yes, man, I can see your wretched number on your shoulder board. I am Standartenfuhrer Trojan, and this is Unterscharfuhrer Fiveash. We are of the Schutszstaffel. That is the security service you may know as the SS. Do you understand me?'

'Yes, sir.'

'Oh, how formal,' the woman said.

George blinked. 'You're English,' he said to the woman.

'As you are,' said Trojan, 'but rather brighter, as she is fighting on the right side in this unnecessary war. So tell me, this is the centre of your town government? Your mayor is here?'

'Yes, sir.'

'I shall need to speak to him. We have much to discuss, the details of the occupation, and so forth.'

'I'll call him for you—'

'No.' Trojan held up a hand. 'Not yet. You will do for now. I think I rather like you, Constable Tanner! Now tell me – who is left in this town? It's pretty much deserted, isn't it?'

'We've tried to move out the bulk of the population, yes, sir. But there are a few who couldn't be moved – or wouldn't. The hospital is pretty full, what with the air raids and the land battles. The nurses and some of the doctors have stayed on for that. The mayor's essential staff are here, as are units of the police.'

'Very good. But why are you here, Constable Tanner? Why aren't you in the hills taking pot-shots at our tanks? Are you going to prove a useful collaborator?'

Fiveash laughed.

George stiffened. 'I have my orders. I'm here for the benefit of the remaining civilian population. Not to collaborate.'

Trojan nodded. 'No doubt that will be a fine distinction to make in the coming months.'

'I imagine it will, sir.'

'Well, we will have orders for you to implement. A census to be taken. Identity cards to be issued. Wireless sets to be collected from the population. Soon we will be arranging the delivery of food, and so forth. We will get your pretty little town functioning again, Constable!'

George said, 'What about clean-up?'

'Clean-up?'

George gestured. 'The bomb damage.' Buildings reduced to heaps of bricks and beams were visible even from here, and the air was still stained by the smoke of the fires.

'Oh, I don't think we're terribly interested in that. As long as you all have roofs over your heads – yes? Now' – he studied George – 'do you know where "Battle" is, man?'

'Of course I know. Sir.'

'I intend to drive there later this evening.' He glanced at his watch. 'Another hour or two should see the place secured. This Wehrmacht fellow of mine is rather an oaf, and a clumsy driver. We are in England; it would be appropriate for me to have an English bobby as my driver, don't you think?'

Fiveash laughed. 'Oh, what a spiffing idea! But, mind, Constable, the Germans will insist on your driving on the right, continental style.'

George kept his voice steady. 'If you order me to come with you to Battle, I'll do it, sir. But I won't drive for you.'

'Ah, that fine distinction already! Even knowing that I could have you shot in a second if you refuse my requests?'

George said nothing; he stared back at Trojan, unblinking.

Trojan turned away. 'It would be a pity to waste such a promising character so quickly. And besides, I need to give these Wehrmacht chaps something to do while the SS gets the country sorted out. Very well, then – *ride* with me, Constable. Now then, where is that mayor of yours?'

XXIV

So, at about eight p.m. that Sunday evening, George found himself gazing at the back of a Wehrmacht soldier's crisply shaven neck as he was driven in Standartenfuhrer Trojan's Bentley at speed along the road to Battle. The mayor had to content himself with a ride in a Kubelwagen following on behind. Of course this was a not very subtle slight, but Harry Burdon had shrugged. 'We'll have to put up with a lot worse before this wretched business is over, George.'

There were still refugees from the day's earlier flight limping up the road, lumps of misery and humiliation, some of them heading back to the town. Trojan insisted that the driver stick to the right, and men, women and children had to scramble out of the way; George was only glad that they got through the journey without anyone being run down.

At Battle more refugees lined up in the streets of the tiny old town, sitting on the pavements, hundreds of them controlled by a handful of strutting German soldiers. Remarkably a couple of officers were making their way through the crowd, asking questions, jotting down notes. Always methodical, the Germans, it seemed. The town itself showed signs of war damage – blown-out windows, the tarmac chewed up by tank tracks.

The car pulled up outside the Abbey gatehouse. The standartenfuhrer looked around curiously. 'So this is Battle; this is the Abbey – commissioned by William the Conqueror to commemorate his famous victory, am I correct?'

'Yes, sir,' George said uneasily. 'It's now a school ... Look, Standartenfuhrer Trojan – the refugees – there are old people. Children. The ill. Some of them are wounded from the strafing. A night without shelter will be harsh. I mean, the most fragile could be taken into the Abbey.'

'Ah, but I need the Abbey as a billet for my soldiers.'

Julia grinned. 'The Germans have a name for such people, Constable Tanner. Useless mouths!'

George flared at her. 'They are English, madam, as you are.'

Julia made to snap back, but Trojan touched her arm. 'No, my dear, let it go. And besides, we have no wish to appear callous to the British, a people with whom we have no genuine quarrel, none at all. Constable, I'll see to it that something is done for the neediest. You may advise, if you wish.'

'Thank you, sir.'

'Well, well,' came a familiar voice from the crowd. 'Just where I'd expect to find you, George – in harm's way.'

'Mary?' He turned around. She was walking towards him, limping a bit, and her hair was still grimy from the raids. But she was healthy enough. George took her hands. 'I wish I could say it's good to see you.'

'Yeah. Well, so much for fleeing; I didn't get very far.'

He forced a laugh. 'You should have stayed with me and hitched a ride in a Bentley. Listen,' he whispered, 'never mind these posturing arseholes. The invasion's not won yet . . .'

'Is that an American accent?' Trojan approached, with Fiveash at his heel.

George took a breath. 'Standartenfuhrer Trojan, this is Mrs Mary Wooler. She's a friend of mine, from Hastings. And, yes, she's an American citizen.'

'Ah. Then you have no need to hide amongst this rabble, Mrs Wooler. You are a foreign neutral, and your rights will of course be respected. Tell me, what brings you to Britain?'

'Long story. I'm a historian by profession. Since war broke out I've been working as a correspondent.'

He puzzled over the word. 'You mean a reporter? For which newspaper?'

'The *Boston Traveller.*'

'Really? Then I am very happy indeed to have met you, Mrs Wooler, at this propitious moment.'

Tired, grubby, she was wary. 'Propitious?'

'Come, please.' He offered her his arm.

Mary stared back. 'I'll come with you. But I won't take your SS-uniformed arm, Standartenfuhrer Trojan.'

'Very well. But remember, I am not your enemy. Constable, would you lead the way?'

So they walked through the gatehouse and into the grounds of the Abbey, and past the abbot's hall and the cloister. George looked out from the terrace over the shadowed hillside where once Saxons and Normans had fought over the destiny of England; now German voices echoed there. Then George led the party back through the grounds, past the ruin of the old dormitory, to the site of the Abbey's first church. It was long demolished, but there was a particular point on the ground that Trojan wanted to see.

'Mrs Wooler, you are the historian – it is here that Harold fell?'

'As best anybody knows. I mean, William wanted his church consecrated here, with the high altar right on that spot, even though it wasn't a too convenient place for an abbey. It has no water supply; it needed a hell of a lot of terracing. So here it must be that Harold fell; there's no reason to have built here otherwise.'

The SS officer walked around the unremarkable piece of ground. 'How astonishing.' He smiled, at Julia, George, Mary, the soldiers who discreetly shadowed them. 'Then on this spot I give you my pledge. I want you to write this down, Mrs Wooler, so that it may be transmitted to the world, and to posterity.'

Mary stared at him. Then she fumbled in her pockets for a pen and a bit of paper.

Trojan declaimed, 'We of the SS have come here not for conquest. We come to liberate England, a nation with proud Aryan roots, from the subjugation of the Latin conquerors. And we come to avenge the illegal murder of King Harold. I, Josef Trojan, swear by my mother's life that I will not rest until that historic catastrophe is put right, and the Aryan destiny of England restored.' He glanced at Mary. 'Did you get that? Was my English adequate?'

'You Nazis really are as crazy as they say, aren't you?'

George held his breath.

But Trojan just laughed. 'Oh, not crazy, Mrs Wooler. I mean my promise to be taken literally – and it will be fulfilled, literally. You will see.' He snapped his fingers, and to George's astonishment the Wehrmacht driver produced a bunch of flowers, late roses, purloined who knew how. Trojan scattered the flowers on the spot where the last English king had fallen. 'For Harold Godwineson!' He shouted the name, and it rang through the English dusk.

XXV

By Sunday night the POWs reached Bexhill, from where they were to be moved on by truck.

They were crammed into the trucks, some German military stock and others purloined farm wagons, maybe fifty men to a vehicle. There was no room to sit or lie down. Ben was stuck somewhere in the middle of the truck, surrounded by a forest of greatcoats that stank of cordite and mud and blood.

The truck swayed as it drove, and he was thrown against the bodies of the others, and they against him. In the night it was pitch dark. There wasn't even a glimmer of headlights to be seen; the Germans seemed to be operating under blackout rules. The prisoners had no food, no water. And of course there was no toilet. You just went where you stood, and after a while the floor of the truck swam with piss and shit and a few pools of vomit.

He thought he slept a little. It was hard to tell. The journey had the quality of a nightmare.

Once Ben slipped on a puddle of something, and would have fallen. But a beefy hand caught him under the arm, and hauled him back upright.

'There you go, mate.'

'Say, thanks, I was nearly down in the dirty stuff there.'

'You're all right. What accent's that? Canadian?'

It was the man who had tried to help him during the march. Ben could barely understand him, and couldn't see the man's face. 'Um, I spent a few years in America. But I came from Austria originally.'

To his surprise the man understood. 'You a refugee from the Nazis, then? I saw plenty of them in France.'

'You were with the BEF?'

'Yep. Barely got out of that without my arse being blown up by Stuka bombers, and after five minutes over here I've been jugged. Not having a good year, am I?'

'I guess not. I don't recognise your accent. Are you Scottish?'

'Not likely. I'm Scouse. From Liverpool. Used to be a house painter before the war.'

'So did Hitler,' someone said, and there was a rumble of weary laughter.

'Danny,' the Liverpudlian said. 'Danny Adams.'

'I'm Ben.'

'You just hold on, Ben, you'll be all right.'

'Yeah.'

When the dawn came the trucks jolted to a halt, and Ben was shaken awake. The backs of the trucks were opened up, and to German shouts the men jumped down to the ground. They were clumsy and stiff, and many fell, after a night spent standing up. But they helped each other, the fifty or so men in Ben's truck. Within a few minutes they were all standing in a rough huddle, surrounded by German troopers with rifles, and dogs, three big Alsatians, on leads.

'Bad news, lads,' someone called on seeing the dogs. 'They've shipped their girlfriends over.' That was met with a snarl in German. 'All right, Funf, keep your helmet on.'

By the dawn light Ben tried to see what kind of place he had been brought to. He was in what seemed to be an open field, coated with green grass, on a raised rectangular scrap of ground. Truck wheels had churned the turf. The earth was cut up by grassy ditches, and the whole space was enclosed by a ruined wall. At the heart of the site Ben made out a concrete platform with the remains of a kind of cross structure embedded in it. Two Germans in the black uniform of the SS were strutting about this centrepiece, pointing at it with swagger sticks and gazing around at the site.

The air was fresh; he could smell the sea. 'Where the hell are we?'

A murmur went around the men. One of them, a local, recognised the place. This was Richborough, at the very eastern extremity of Kent. Another old Roman ruin, now in the hands of the Nazis.

A party of Germans came forward, laden with shovels. One of their officers put his hands on his hips and shouted at the POWs: 'Welcome to your holiday camp, gentlemen. We must ask you to pay for your deposits by digging out your latrines.' The soldiers threw the shovels on the floor.

'Oh, good,' said Danny Adams. 'A German comedian. I feel better already.'

The men moved forward, grumbling.

XXVI

23 September

Mary was woken by a smart rap at the door, a German voice.

A crack in the blackout curtains let her see her watch; it was six a.m. Oddly she remembered what day it was, a Monday. But not for the first time recently she had trouble remembering where she was.

As an American, Standartenfuhrer Trojan had made it clear, she was an honoured guest. So on the Sunday night the Germans had given Mary this billet, a kind of store room in the school that had been built into Battle Abbey, a box with a few mops, a stink of bleach, and no furniture but a heap of English army blankets. But the power was on, and there was a bathroom nearby, with running water, thanks to the efficiency of the German engineers who had already restored the supply. Mary had been racked with guilt at the thought of the people she'd walked with, who were going to be spending the night out on the street. But there was nothing she could do for them, and, by God, she needed sleep. Now she washed quickly, used the toilet, and dressed and gathered up her shabby possessions.

No later than a quarter past six, she stepped out of the room.

The young German soldier waiting for her bowed. 'Bitte.'

She followed him out of the Abbey. It was a surreal experience, as if she were being escorted by a footman out of some old-fashioned hotel.

In the grounds, a bus was waiting. It was a mundane sight, covered with advertising panels for Typhoo Tea and Bovril. Another young German soldier sat behind the wheel. There were a few people already aboard, and the engine was running. Evidently the bus was waiting for her.

And here came Josef Trojan, brisk and smart in a fresh uniform. He bowed to her and reached out to take her hand, but she flinched back. 'Mrs Wooler. I hope you slept well.'

'I suppose I did. In the end exhaustion overwhelms everything else, doesn't it?'

'Indeed. As the armies of the English will discover in the next few days. We have provided transport for you, as you can see. Along with these others, who also have reasons to be protected.'

'Where will we be taken?'

'Only a few miles north-west of here, to a place called – ah' – he checked a schedule – 'Hurst Green. This is on the current line held by Army Group A, which we call the covering line. Do you understand?'

'You're taking me out of the occupied territory.'

'Exactly. We have been in contact with the British military authorities, over this and other matters. It is all very civilised, as you can see. At Hurst Green you will be collected by a bus to take you to, ah, Tunbridge Wells. And from then on you are free to travel on to London or wherever you wish.' He smiled at her. 'Personally I hope you will remain in Britain, and continue to report for your audience in the United States on the civilising progress we intend to make here in England, as in Europe. Now you must forgive me, Mrs Wooler, I have appointments. Please board the bus; you will be quite safe.'

What choice did she have? And, she had to admit, a large part of her longed to be out of this damn war zone.

None of the handful of people on the bus met Mary's eye. They were mostly women, some quite expensively dressed, and a couple of men, youngish, who sat near the front. What had they done to deserve this privileged treatment? Were they more foreign nationals, or collaborators of some kind?

The driver settled at his wheel. A second German soldier sat behind him with a weapon across his lap. The bus pulled out, turned, and rolled through the gatehouse.

As they passed through Battle Mary saw that the people she had walked with, after a night out in the open, were being prodded to their feet by German soldiers. She couldn't bear to look for long; she turned away in shame.

It was not yet seven a.m.

XXVII

George set off for work at the town hall. He was due at eight a.m.

It was a bright September day, a Monday morning, sunny and clear, with just a hint of chill in the air. There were no planes in the sky, and the noise of the war was distant. The only vehicles on the roads, dodging heaps of rubble, were German trucks. A bakery was, astonishingly, open, and a lengthy queue had formed, mostly old folk, all clutching their ration books. A couple of nervous-looking German soldiers watched them, rifles hanging from their shoulders. The town stank of sewage and dust, but the breeze off the sea was fresh, and he thought he could just detect the wood-smoke smell of autumn leaves.

He felt as if he was floating. He wasn't sure he'd slept a wink.

And he'd been got out of bed by a phone call from the mayor, news about the invasion. Since dawn, elements of the Germans' second echelon had been landing, all along the coast. Their losses were ferocious, the Navy and RAF pounding away, worse probably than the first wave. But nevertheless some of them were getting through. And they were managing to land their tanks and heavy equipment at ports like Folkestone, though their engineers had to clear the harbours of rubble. 'Things will get worse before they get better, George,' Harry Burdon had said gloomily.

George's head was spinning after all that had happened. The worst of it was worry for his daughter, his little girl in her WAAF uniform, caught up in the middle of a lethal conflict. He'd heard nothing of her since Friday, when they had parted in the middle of a row. But he had his duty to fulfil. He took deep breaths of the fresh air, trying to clear his thoughts.

When he got to the town hall the mayor was just arriving. He was carrying a suitcase. 'Morning, George. Sleep well?'

'As well as can be expected, I suppose, Harry. You?'

'Tossed and turned. That bonkers business at the Abbey.'

'Why the suitcase?'

'Well, I'm moving in. Orders of the SS. Me and my family. They don't use the word "hostages" but that's what it amounts to.'

'Hmm. We have to behave or you come to harm, is that the idea?'

'That's it. Of course since no bugger cared for me before the war I'm in a pickle, aren't I?' He smiled, but it was forced.

'It's bloody, Harry.'

A German truck drove up. A couple of soldiers got out, quite young, one bespectacled, talking rapidly. They hauled cardboard file boxes out of the back of the truck and walked up to the door, still talking. They entirely ignored Burdon and George, until they realised that the door was closed. Then they broke off and stared at the two of them.

George said, 'Let me—'

'No, no,' the mayor said, red-faced. He pulled the door back and held it while the two Germans passed through, without further acknowledgement.

George murmured, 'It's going to be a long day.'

Harry Burdon plucked George's sleeve. 'Listen, George,' he murmured, 'Never mind little pricks like those two. There's a bit more news.'

'Where from?'

'Never you mind. Churchill's talking to the Americans. *There may be some kind of deal.* That's what I've heard. We're not done yet, lad.'

Harry Burdon was a round, sleek sort of man, tall and a bit overweight, with a full head of greying hair and a penchant for old-fashioned waistcoats and fob watches. He looked like a munificent businessman from Victorian times: competent, solid, successful in his modest way, willing to give something back through his elected office. And yet now, behind Harry's unprepossessing figure, George glimpsed a shadow world of secret communications channels – covert phone lines, wireless sets tucked behind panelled walls. He was a man who knew who to trust. And he was a man who was preparing to accept the grim realities of his own new position, as hostage and servant of the new authority, and do what he believed was his duty.

'Thanks, Harry,' George said warmly.

'Just keep your pecker up. Now come on, let's get on with it.'

Inside the town hall the Germans were already hard at work. They were appropriating offices and setting up their own trestle tables in the hallway.

'Efficient, aren't they?' Burdon said.

'This year the Germans have had plenty of practice at the art of occupation.' It was Julia Fiveash, walking towards them. 'And they seem to have an instinct for paperwork. Of course these particular fellows know this is a cushy job compared to fighting on the front line, and they'll go at it the more enthusiastically for that ...'

She was beautiful, you could never deny that, with that shock of blonde hair swept back from a fine face, and a smile like a film star. The crisp SS uniform on an athletic body only set off that beauty. She had an unhealthy appeal, George thought, a deadly allure. But, he reminded himself, she was English, an upper-crust over-privileged Englishwoman in that black Nazi uniform, here to lord it over her own people.

George said, 'If you'll excuse me, Mayor, Unterscharfuhrer, I should report to my station—'

'Oh, I think you should stay right where you are, Constable,' Julia said evenly. 'Standartenfuhrer Trojan specifically requested your presence. He liked you, I think.'

George growled, 'Why?'

'For the way you did your job – and for that very lower-class English surliness.' She laughed at him. 'He believes you are a man with whom he can do business. Although he thinks you deserve a decent rank – sergeant, perhaps. I'm sure we can fix that for you. Marvellous, isn't it, the way war opens up opportunities? Perhaps we should talk in your office, Mayor Burdon?'

Harry Burdon led the way. Julia and George followed.

Julia said, walking, 'I need to impress on you both the importance of the work you will be doing here. The military commanders are not interested in *running* Hastings. They prefer to manage the town through you, through the appropriate local authority. Do you see? There is a great deal to be done; I'm sure you are aware of that. The first priority is to restore the harbour, such as it is. And to requisition the fishing fleet.'

'For landing supplies,' Burdon guessed.

'That's it. The estimate is that nine thousand tons a day will have to be imported from the continent in the first days of the occupation. Much of it will come through the larger ports, but Hastings will play a part too.'

They had to be desperate if they were relying on a tiny port like Hastings. And as it happened George knew the fishermen along the Stade had already sabotaged the winches that hauled their boats up the sharply sloping beach.

'After that we must consider the needs of the civilian population. The restoration of food supplies for one thing, accompanied by an appropriate system of rationing. Water, power, gas. We're aware that many citizens who fled to the countryside will surely soon return. We must prepare for them. And so on.

'The first step in all this is to gather information. That is the German way: everything orderly, everything thoroughly legal. Now. You hold census records here? And of course there is the identity card system. We will need a record of every inhabitant currently in situ in the town.'

George glared at her. 'What for? Work gangs? Looking for Jews, are you?'

Harry snapped, '*George.*'

Julia stopped and turned to George. 'Josef was right. You really are a feisty one, aren't you, Constable?'

And she stepped closer to him, breaking an intangible boundary of separation. The polished buttons on her uniform brushed his chest, and he could smell her fresh breath, a smell like apples about her hair. He was almost trembling. He was twenty years older; he could have been her father; she was everything he despised, about the English as well as the Germans. But, by Christ, she caused a heat in his loins he hadn't felt for a long time.

She knew exactly what she was doing to him. She laughed in his face. 'I think it's going to be a pleasure working with you, Constable – George, is it? – I really do.' She stepped back, mercifully. 'But for now your duty is to fetch me a coffee.'

There was a roar, and the building shook. George turned. An immense shadow passed the half-open door. Somewhere a German cheered. And then another shadow passed, another engine's roar, and another.

'It is the second wave,' Julia said. 'Landing all along the coast. Panzers, George! Panzers, on English soil. Now we will see some fun. Come, we have work to do. The first priority is to assemble work parties who will transport rubble from the town to fill craters in the airfield runways ...' She stalked away.

'Never mind,' Harry murmured. 'Remember Churchill and the blooming Yanks. Let's go and fill in her forms, eh?'

XXVIII

A few miles north of Battle the bus was pulled over. They had just passed a fork in the road; Mary had no real idea where they were.

A group of people were waiting here by the side of the road, women with kids, some men, perhaps a dozen in all. One man was in a wheelchair. Mary glimpsed a WAAF uniform among the group. More passengers, evidently. Two German troopers stood with them, just kids, very bored.

The soldier riding shotgun climbed down and spoke to his counterparts outside. They argued; Mary saw that the soldiers outside had a heavy rucksack that must have contained a field radio unit. Then the shotgun rider called up to his driver, who stood and turned to face his passengers. 'Out,' he said, his English barely comprehensible. 'Off bus. Comprenez? Um, understand?'

One of the young men at the front spoke up. 'Why the bloody hell? We're supposed to be taken out of your zone altogether. By my reckoning we've come no further than Peter's Well. What's going on?'

The soldier fingered his revolver. 'Off bus. Military. Soldiers. Understand?'

Mary sighed and stood up. 'Come on, guys,' she said. 'I don't think we have a choice.'

The passengers followed her lead, and one by one clambered down to the road. The young man who had protested moved stiffly, helped by his companion. The WAAF girl hurried forward to take his other arm. 'Let me give you a hand.'

'Thank you, miss. My bloody kidneys packing up, that's what it is, you see, and I was stuck in hospital – careful, Bill. Funnily enough I used to drive a bus like this when I was a bit younger, before following my father into his accountancy firm ...'

Mary stared at the WAAF, whose bright red hair, unruly, stuck out from under her cap. She couldn't believe her eyes. 'Hilda?'

Hilda's eyes widened. 'Mary? Oh, my word!' She rushed forward and they embraced. Hilda's hair was mussed, her eyes hollow, her uniform dusty and torn. 'We do keep running into each other, don't we?'

They stepped aside from the other passengers. 'Are you all right? I haven't seen you since—'

Hilda smiled, and lifted her left hand, waggling her ring finger. 'I know. Bit of a shock, wasn't it? Little did we know old Hitler was about to spring an even bigger surprise.'

'What happened to you? How do you come to be here?'

'Well, I made it to my station. I shared a ride with Ben Kamen—'

'I know, you were in my car.'

'Don't know what happened to him after that, poor chap. Or your car, actually, sorry about that! We were shutting the station down. Unfortunately we were a bit slow getting out of there before the Jerries arrived. Do move fast, these chaps.'

'So they captured you.'

'They copped the lot of us. We were all held at the base. We heard talk that we were to be shipped to some camp. But they processed us – interviewed us one by one – trying to find out about our radar, you see. And when they discovered I was married to an American – would you believe, I had my wedding certificate tucked into my gas-mask pouch, it had all been that quick – they said I wouldn't be held.'

'Really?'

'These big flat-footed Germans are being very careful about not offending America, Mary! *You* must have seen that. I protested, frankly. I wanted to stay with my colleagues. I'm a WAAF first, not an American's wife. But the Germans would have none of it. So here I am, on my way to Tunbridge Wells! I suppose they even arranged for you and me to be on the same transport.'

'How thoughtful,' Mary said drily.

'So what about you? How's Dad?'

Mary told her about the nights of bombing, and what had become of her following the invasion.

'Wow. King Harold! These Nazis really are crackpots, aren't they? Almost funny in a way. I bet Dad was laughing his socks off at them.'

'Maybe. But he's stuck back there now, in Hastings. He's going to have to work with them.'

'Um. Well, he's got a clear head, my dad. He always said he became a policeman so he could stop harm being done to the most vulnerable.'

'He'll have plenty of chances to do that in the coming days.'

'Yes . . .'

There was a rumble of vehicles coming from the south; they turned

111

to look that way. The bus-driver soldier approached, arms outstretched, and shepherded the passengers off the tarmac. Then an argument ensued among the Germans, evidently about whether the bus was far enough off the road.

Hilda said, 'So this is why we've been turfed off the road. Speaking of the Germans and their speedy movements—'

In moments the tanks were on them, a line of them roaring past the parked-up bus. Mary and Hilda shrank back with the others. The tanks barely slowed down, and Mary had the impression that they would just have knocked the bus aside if it had been necessary. Close to, the tanks were huge, powerful, and the roar of their engines, the dust they kicked up, their sheer rushing mass made an overwhelming physical presence. When the tanks had passed, support vehicles followed, troop carriers and mobile artillery. There were no horse, no men on foot; this was a mechanised unit of the kind that had spearheaded the blitzkrieg that had shattered whole nations in Europe.

The column took minutes to pass. Mary saw Hilda counting silently as the vehicles passed, a bit of observation. The German soldiers whooped and clapped. The other passengers just watched with hostility, resignation or fear.

As the noise died away and the dust settled, Hilda whispered to Mary, 'I think I heard the soldiers say that was a unit of the Seventh Panzers. On their way to Guildford.'

'Guildford?'

'We have an inkling of their battle plan – plenty of spies in Berlin! And we were given pretty good briefings at the station; we needed them to do our job, you see. Evidently they're now moving forward. They're planning a break-out. It might take a couple of days to get their assets in place, and then—'

'Made a right mess of the road surface, mind.' The kidney-failure man was talking to the German soldiers. He was right; the tarmac was chewed up by the tank tracks. 'The council's going to have something to say about that, I can tell you. So is that that? Can we get back on the bus now?'

The German driver blocked his way. 'Nein. No. Not yet. Look!' He pointed down the road.

Mary saw that another column was approaching, at a much slower pace.

'Oh, for heaven's sake,' said the kidney man. 'We'll be stuck here all day.'

'Now, now, Giles,' his companion, Bill, said, 'don't annoy the nice Germans. We'll get to Tunbridge Wells for tea, you mark my words.'

That won a ripple of laughter. The Germans scowled, not understanding, suspicious.

Giles, the kidney man, didn't laugh either. 'I've had enough of this lot,' he muttered.

The second column, trundling at walking pace, was led by a couple of heavy vehicles, perhaps for recovery or clearing roadblocks. Then came more vehicles, mobile guns and troop carriers, and then troops on foot walking single file, in columns alternately to either side of the road. After that came trucks and armoured vehicles, including a couple of tanks, and then a string of carts and artillery pieces drawn by horses. As the lead vehicles passed the bus, the marching troops exchanged banter with the waiting bus crew. Some of them whistled at Hilda, and she replied with sarcastic curtseys that made them laugh.

Bill, the friend of Giles, came to stand before Hilda. 'I'll tell you what *I've* had enough of. I've had enough of girls like you.' A minute ago he had been elegantly joking. Now, out of nowhere, he was shouting.

Hilda was bewildered. 'Look, what do you want?'

'I saw you smiling at those Jerries. I was in the bloody BEF. We saw girls like you in France. A Jerrybag, are you, is that the story?'

Hilda flared. 'I most certainly am not.'

The bus-crew Germans came closer, uneasy. 'What is this?'

'You are what I say you are, you little whore!'

Mary stood between the man and Hilda. 'Now, you back off, buster. I don't know what your game is, but—'

The man swung his fist. Mary ducked, but she took a blow to the temple that sent her staggering. She could barely believe it had happened.

Bill went for Hilda, reaching for her throat. He was heavier than she was, and he came at her without warning. He fell forward, knocking her to the ground, his heavy overcoat flapping.

Everybody seemed to be shouting now, Hilda and Bill, the passengers. The Germans hurried forward to grab the man, trying to haul him off Hilda.

And an engine roared. Mary looked across, startled. The bus was pulling out from where it was parked on the verge. 'He said he used to drive buses. Oh, shit.' She ran forward. 'Giles! Don't do it, you'll get yourself killed!'

The Germans had hauled Bill off Hilda, but now they realised what Giles was up to, that Bill had just been distracting them. They ran at the bus, dragging their pistols from their holsters.

Giles was turning the bus around. The German troops in the column actually continued their march, evidently unable to believe what they were seeing. But when Giles gunned the bus straight at them, the marching men scattered, yelling. The first shots were fired, by some of the troopers with the presence of mind to grab their weapons. The windows of the bus shattered, but still it came on.

Mary saw it all. The bus ploughed into the lines of men like a bowling ball into a rack of pins. Some of the troops were knocked aside, some fell under the wheels. One man, grotesquely, got pinned to the bonnet like a bit of cloth, bent over backwards. He was perhaps the first to die when the bus slammed into the tank that followed the line of infantry, or perhaps it was Giles.

The bus's petrol tank exploded, a blossoming fireball. Mary was knocked onto her back.

XXIX

Mary stood with Hilda. They were both smoking. Mary couldn't stop trembling.

The bus passengers stood in a loose group, guarded now by men from the column, who were, Hilda had overheard, elements of the Thirty-fourth Division of the German Ninth Army. Only Bill was kept apart. He was kneeling on the ground, his hands tied behind his back, his face puffy from the blows he had taken.

The Germans were working to fix the mess Giles had made. The column had moved into a defensive formation, the vehicles driven off the road, the heavy weapons deployed, the men taking loose cover in ditches by the side of the road. Engineers from the column were still labouring to bring the fire under control. The heavy vehicles stood by, waiting to shove the wrecks off the road.

The column's medics had set up a field station next to the road. There were seven dead, many more wounded, with broken bones, bashed heads, internal injuries. The dead lay in a short row, covered in blankets. Mary saw that some of the soldiers were unloading shovels from a supply truck; perhaps they meant to bury the dead. They seemed to need a lot of shovels, however.

The column commander, who Hilda thought was the SS equivalent of a colonel, a standartenfuhrer, was a big, cold man in a green Waffen-SS uniform. He was arguing with the bus crew, who were nervously going through some kind of list with him. Mary had no idea what they were talking about, and, numbed by all that had happened, found it hard to care.

Hilda said, 'The funny thing is, my dad would have loathed a man like Giles. He always said the upper-crust types would welcome the Nazis with open arms.'

'Then your dad would have got him wrong. And the Germans, and it cost them.'

'Yes. Any of us could have done what he did, I suppose. I mean it was suicidal, but he got rid of a good few of them, and he's held up this whole column for hours. Seen in that light, it's not a bad exchange for one life.'

'What an awful way to look at it.'

'"Take One With You." That's what Churchill has been saying.'

'Excuse me.' It was the SS colonel. He might have been fifty; he wore small round spectacles. He smiled at the passengers. 'If I could have your attention. I am Standartenfuhrer Thyrolf. I must ask you to step back now from the road. We will clear the bus and the tank, and there may be some risk to yourselves.' His English was crisp, heavily accented.

The passengers complied, all save Bill who remained kneeling at the feet of his guards, and they allowed the SS colonel to shepherd them into the field away from the road.

Thyrolf said now, 'Once we have the road cleared the column will move on. We will loan you one of our trucks to take you to your rendezvous with the English. So you see, you will not be too, um, inconvenient? Inconvenienced. One moment, please.' He turned to speak to the bus driver.

Mary felt exhausted, drained by it all. Something in her responded, quite illogically, to the charming manner of this SS colonel. 'He's like a hotel manager. Come to apologise because our room isn't ready.'

Hilda was frowning. 'Something's wrong. Why would he tell us his name?'

Mary took a deep breath. 'It's a relief to be away from the stink of burning fuel. Standing here in this long grass, it all seems a bit absurd, doesn't it?'

There was a discreet cough at her shoulder. It was Thyrolf with the bus driver. 'Mrs Wooler? Mrs Mary Wooler?'

'Yes.'

'And you are also a Mrs Wooler? Hilda Wooler?'

'Yes ...'

He turned to Mary. 'Mrs Wooler, may I see your passport?' She produced it from her handbag, and he inspected it as gravely as any customs official. He handed the document back. 'Now you, Mrs Hilda Wooler, are a British subject, but you recently married an American?'

'Not just any American,' Mary said. 'My son the American!'

He laughed, a charming sound. 'Congratulations. You have proof of this?'

Hilda produced her marriage certificate from her gas-mask pouch.

'Very good. If you would both come this way.' Holding Mary's arm lightly, he drew them to the road, where a staff car was waiting. Mary followed, unquestioning.

Hilda hung back. 'What are you doing?'

'The arrangements made for American citizens at Hurst Green have been adjusted. It will be more convenient for you to be carried separately. You can go on now; you do not have to wait. The others, the British, will follow soon after.'

'No.' Hilda stepped back into the crowd of passengers. 'I'll stay here. I'm British. I'm a soldier, for God's sake.'

Mary asked, 'Hilda? What's wrong?'

Thyrolf studied Hilda, his eyes soft behind his glasses. 'You are sure?'

'Yes. Mary – you go.' Hilda looked as if she longed to hug Mary, but she still hung back. 'Look, I won't be long after you. Do you know Tunbridge Wells? I'll see you there. There's a parade called the Pantiles – it has a good tea shop.' She laughed, a brittle sound. 'At least it used to be good, before the war. I'll find you there.'

'It's a date.'

Mary let the SS colonel lead her off the field, back to the road, to the staff car. Overwhelmed by his confident manner, she didn't know what else to do. She had to walk past Bill, the kneeling man. His eyes were swollen from the blows he had taken. But when she walked past, he whispered to her, 'Peter's Well.'

'What?'

'This place. It's called Peter's Well. Remember.' A rifle-butt to the back of the head shut him up.

Thyrolf actually helped her into the staff car. She sat beside the driver and settled her rucksack on her lap. Thyrolf gave her a little salute, and then waved the driver to go.

As the car pulled out, Mary looked back. Soldiers were walking from the column now, towards the passengers. She saw Hilda, her blue uniform and red hair unmistakable. She seemed to have gathered the passengers in a group. She was holding somebody's hand, an elderly man. The group was soon out of sight. Mary thought she heard singing, some mournful song, perhaps a hymn.

Mary's thinking was glacial. Only slowly was she starting to realise what was happening here.

The ripple of shots didn't even sound like gunfire. It was a distant, peaceful noise. The rooks that rose up cawing in response were more disturbing. The singing stopped, however. And then there was a series of isolated pops.

Mary turned to her driver. 'That's the clean-up. Right?'

He looked at her nervously.

'No English, huh? You didn't get your timing quite right, did you? If I'd been a bit further away, if I hadn't actually heard the gunfire, I mightn't have put it all together. I'm not as smart as poor Hilda, am I? And I'm not used to this sort of war. Well, don't worry, Fritz, I'm not going to make trouble for you. Just go ahead. I'll hold it together, you'll see.'

And she did. She held it together until they got to Hurst Green, another deserted little village, where, remarkably, a green-painted bus was waiting for her. The driver, a British soldier, actually saluted his German counterpart. The British seemed surprised to see her alone, but Mary just climbed on the bus and snapped, 'Don't talk. Just drive. And when you get me to Tunbridge Wells, find me a fucking phone.'

XXX

25 September

'Morning, ladies.' Unteroffizier Fischer came stomping through the lounge bar, his boots clattering on the pub's straw-strewn stone floor. He yanked open curtains with his gloved hands, pulling one so hard it came away from its hooks. The window was a rectangle of blue-grey. 'It's Wednesday morning, and you're still in England.'

The men under their army blankets stirred, like huge slugs. Their boots and rifles were stacked against the bar walls.

Ernst glanced at the big railway clock on the wall. Five in the morning, English time. He groaned. He heard a distant rumble, like thunder. Chances were it wasn't a storm. He sat up, rubbing his face. 'Today's the day, is it, Unteroffizier? The break-out.'

'That's the idea, Trojan. You pretty boys will have the privilege of following Seventh Panzer out of here, all the way from Uckfield to Guildford.'

'Where on God's earth is Guildford?'

'I don't even know where Uckfield is.'

'I'll tell you where Guildford is, Kieser. It's on OKH Objective One, our first operational objective. And if, when, we reach it today, we'll have achieved in five days what the Fuhrer's plan called for in ten. And then we will be out of this hedgehog country where there's a partisan in every piss-pot, and we will let the Panzers loose and it will be like France all over again.'

'We'll all get medals,' said Kieser.

'I'll pin yours on myself. Personally I would like to see Oxford. Now shift your pretty arses, we form up in half an hour.' He stomped out.

The men stirred, sitting up and pushing back their blankets. The rotting-feet stink and stale farts that had been trapped under the blankets filled the air. Kieser waved a hand. 'By Christ, lads. Fuhrer directive

119

forty-seven. Soldiers of the Twenty-sixth Division shouldn't light a fag in the mornings.'

The men moved slowly. They all knew Fischer was a bit soft, and you could grab a few more minutes' kip with impunity.

Ernst got to his feet. He was in his shorts and vest and socks, and he picked up a kit bag containing his razor and a bit of soap. He stepped over the bodies of the stirring men, making for the door. The floor was sticky with stale beer. This pub, in this place called Uckfield, had been a big disappointment to the men billeted here. Some English bastard had stolen all the spirits and taken an axe to the barrels behind the bar. 'These English partisans fight dirty,' Unteroffizier Fischer had said.

Ernst pushed out of the bar room into fresh, cold air. There was already a queue outside the lavatory, four or five men in their grubby underwear with towels around their necks, rubbing their arms to get warm. The paving stones were slick with dew, and Ernst took off his woollen socks and tucked them into the elastic waist of his pants. Better wet feet than wet socks.

He heard a distant explosion. It came from his right, the south, back towards the coast. When he looked that way there was a fading glow.

'That was a big one,' somebody grumbled. 'Must be fifteen miles away.'

Ernst heard a rumble of engines. Looking up he saw planes crossing the sky, very high, without lights, just silhouettes against the steel grey, like cardboard cut-outs, flying north to south.

'Old Goering will swat those fuckers like flies,' somebody said, yawning.

'But he was supposed to have got rid of the RAF by now.'

'Nothing to do with us, lads,' said the man at the head of the queue. He hammered on the toilet door. 'What are you doing in there, Wilhelm? We're freezing our balls off.'

More planes swept over, all of them coming from the north, wave after wave of them, without a challenge from any Luftwaffe planes, or a single anti-aircraft shot being fired.

XXXI

As Gary entered the ops room he was met by a barrage of popping flashbulbs and calls, some of them in American twangs. 'This way, Gary!' 'Over here, Corporal Wooler!' 'Gary! Smile for the folks back home, Gary!'

He stood there, uncertain, reluctant, the staff officer who'd escorted him at his side. They were behind the British lines here, in Alton, a few miles from the Petersfield to Farnborough line where Gary's own division was concentrated.

Beyond the blizzard of light the work of the ops room continued. Gary looked down on the great map table in the pit below him. The map showed southern England, a fat green peninsula pinned by the grey mass of London on the northern edge, and bounded by the pale blue of ocean to the south. This very old country was crowded with towns and villages, and by the traceries of roads that snaked around the lumpy brown of ranges of hills. But now it was disfigured by the bold red slashes of defensive lines, and harsh black scribbles that must be the perimeters of the occupied territories. Coloured blocks littered the map, representing units of men and armour, shoved across the map by Wrens with long-handled wooden shovels, like croupiers in some immense game of roulette. Along the coast from Brighton to Dover there was a cloud of toy aircraft, while little ships pushed through the Channel.

The Wrens wore headsets, and talked constantly. Telephones and radio receiving stations were set up around the walls. Officers in the uniforms of all the services watched from railed balconies, with a few civilians, ministers perhaps, puffing cigars. Still the flashbulbs popped.

None of this seemed real to Gary. The pit of light, the controlled murmur of voices, the flashing bulbs, the smell of cigar smoke, made it all dreamlike. He wasn't sure how he had kept functioning, in fact, since his mother had got through to him two days ago with the news about

Hilda. He was going through the motions of his duties. But he felt as if he were neither asleep nor awake.

An officer, Royal Navy from his uniform, marched towards Gary. Maybe forty, he looked sharp, intelligent, his face lean and ruddy, an outdoors look, and he wore a precisely clipped black moustache. 'Corporal Wooler? I'm Captain Mackie, RN - Tom Mackie, MI-14. Look, I'm sorry for this charade. I know you'd rather be with your unit.'

'Yes, sir—'

'But in this bloody war, image and news presentation are assets just as significant as boots and guns on the ground. Let's get it over with and kick this shower of hacks and bulb-wasters out of our ops room, shall we?' He grasped Gary's hand and turned to the cameras, which flashed even more furiously. Through a fixed grin, Mackie said, 'Of course we're proud you've chosen to wear the uniform of the British Army. But it's a shame you don't look a bit more American, if you know what I mean.'

'I should have worn spurs and a cowboy hat.'

'That's the spirit! Look, General Brooke hoped to be here himself to meet you.'

'General Brooke?'

'CIC Southern Command, since July. He's been shaking up our home defence and doing a bloody good job, I should say. Right, that's enough for this lot. Show these gentlemen the door, would you, Sergeant Blackwell?'

'Right you are, sir.'

Mackie touched Gary's shoulder and led him to the railing that overlooked the big ops table. 'I know you're eager to get back to your unit. But I want you to take a moment to understand the big picture, and to see why your contribution today is so important, you and your mother's. I'm with MI-14, by the way, I think I mentioned that. We're that corner of Military Intelligence dedicated to analysing the Germans' intentions. I take it you can read the map?'

'More or less, sir.'

'We know that since establishing their first beachheads the Germans have moved forward to a preliminary covering line that runs from Uckfield to Canterbury, roughly.' He pointed at the map. 'And although we've been disrupting the shipping, over the last few days they've managed to get some supplies and more men over, through the captured ports and airfields. Now we think their intention is to push forward to a deeper objective line, running from Portsmouth through Guildford and Reigate, all the way to the Thames estuary at Gravesend. Do you see? If they achieve that, they'll have sliced off the whole of south-east

England, including all the airfields. And we believe that after *that* they will make a thrust west of London, up from Guildford to Reading. London would then be pretty much at their mercy.'

'So the plan is to stop them.'

'Quite right. Now.' He pointed to the Uckfield-Canterbury line. 'We can't hold the whole of that perimeter; we can't stop them crossing the line *somewhere*. Even if we hadn't left half our bloody army on the beaches at Dunkirk, we couldn't manage that. What we're trying to do is to contain their advance. Now look, can you see our assets? What we want to do is to confine their thrust roughly to the Uckfield-Guildford corridor.'

'Why there?'

'For one thing it's at the boundary between the two armies, the Ninth and Sixteenth, that make up the Germans' Army Group A. Always a weak point, that, the hinge between two forces ...'

To achieve this containment British and allied units had been positioned to deter the Germans from advances elsewhere. The First London would block a push north of the high ground of the Weald. In the east a division of New Zealanders was trying to block an advance on Ramsgate; they were outnumbered, but had heavy guns capable of knocking out a Panzer advance. The Forty-fifth Division was positioned on the Weald itself, forcing the Germans to go west. North of the Weald were bodies of reserves, including Canadians, an armoured division and a tank brigade.

And in the west more reserves, including the Third Division under Montgomery – the division Gary had been transferred to – were ready to fall on the expected advance towards Guildford, when the opportunity rose, and carve it up.

'You see the pattern,' Mackie said. 'Now while all this is going on we've still got the RAF and Navy striking at the Germans supply lines, in their rear. They seem to have seriously miscalculated their logistics. They are still reliant on fuel and other supplies shipped over from France; the fuel especially is critical. That's the plan. It's all about logistics, essentially. We bottle them up, strike at them when they try to advance, and starve them of supplies. A kind of mobile siege.' He glanced at Gary. 'So what do you think?'

Gary considered. 'Sir, I'm just a regular corporal, and I've only been that a few days—'

'Oh, you're a bit more than that, Wooler.'

'This is above my head. It seems like it might have a fighting chance.'

'Yes, yes.' Mackie nodded. 'Well, that's how it seems to me. A fighting chance. But no more than that. You see, Wooler, the loss of the BEF was a dreadful blow, both materially and in terms of morale. We're putting up a fight. I think it's possible we can hold these bloody Germans on our soil, today and tomorrow. But it's certainly going to take more than we've got to drive them back into the sea. Which is where you come in.'

'And which is why,' Gary said coldly, 'what happened to Hilda was so *useful.*'

Mackie's face was hard. 'Yes, it was. I know how bloody this is for you, Wooler. Blame your mother, if you like. Peter's Well was sadly not the only atrocity the Nazis have committed on our soil. Himmler's einsatzgruppen, the SS killing squads, have been spilling English blood just as busily as they did on the continent. But Peter's Well was the one that was witnessed by an American. Your mother's telephone call from Tunbridge Wells was broadcast across the US by hundreds of syndicated stations. And here you are, her son and a grieving husband, an American already fighting this dreadful evil.'

'Good propaganda, right?'

'No. It's the truth, Wooler, cold and unvarnished. And it's precisely what is needed to make your countrymen realise that our fight is their fight, that the Nazis' threat to us is a threat to them. It's said that in the last twenty-four hours, despite the desperate situation, Churchill has spent more time working with the Americans than against the Germans.' He studied Gary. 'Interventionists versus isolationists – that's the language of the debates going on over there, isn't it? But didn't Jefferson himself warn that America should always fear a Europe united under a single hand? And even he didn't anticipate Hitler. Anyhow here we are. You lost Hilda, I know. But by making this contribution, you're helping to ensure there will be no more Hildas in the future.'

'I guess we all have our duty.'

'That's the spirit . . .'

There was movement at the ops table, and a stir among the listeners at the phones and wireless sets.

'They're moving,' Mackie said, his voice tight. 'They'll call this the Battle of England one day – win or lose. Watch and remember.'

XXXII

The fire roared down on the convoy from right and left, shells erupting from the fields and valleys of this folded, claustrophobic country. Once again the vehicles scattered. The Panzergrenadiers went roaring into the countryside, followed by a couple of the tanks, in search of pillboxes and other English defensive positions.

Ernst and the other men in the troop carriers leapt out to take up what positions they could find beside the road. Ernst found himself in a sort of drainage ditch, blocked by crisp autumn leaves; their smoky smell was rich.

'Where do you think we are?' Ernst shouted at Unteroffizier Fischer.

'God knows.' Fischer checked his watch. 'I know where we should be. On the other side of Haywards Heath by now.' He stumbled over the odd English name.

Ernst knew the route, roughly. From Uckfield they had headed west and north. The plan was to follow the A-class roads though Haywards Heath and Horsham and then make the long run up to Guildford. On the map it looked straightforward. But they had run into this sort of resistance as soon as they had left Uckfield.

More fire rained on the vehicles. It didn't come at random. The tank-busting shells were always targeted first at the lead vehicles in the column and the last, leaving the column trapped and ripe for further attack.

'India,' Ernst said.

The Unteroffizier snorted. 'We're going a bit slow, Gefreiter, but we're not that lost.'

'No. I mean, India is where the English learned this tactic, knocking out the lead and rear vehicles. How infantry can strike at a mechanised column. It's just what the Indians used to do to them in the Raj. I picked that up during our training in France.'

Kieser said, 'After the way they fell over at Dunkirk I never thought the English would fight this hard. Inch by bloody inch, eh, boys?'

The Unteroffizier said, 'But we're still rolling, lads, that's the thing to remember. The English are bastards, but we're worse. Right? The column's forming up again. Let's get back in the truck.'

Cautiously Ernst and the others clambered out onto the road surface. The units that had gone scouring into the hillside returned to the road, the burned-out tanks were being shoved aside by the heavy-lift vehicles, and the lorries' engines were coughing to life. A couple more vehicles lost, Ernst thought, and a bit more of their precious fuel used up.

The fuel was surely the crucial factor. The column had had no resupply since a convoy of fuel trucks had come up from the coast before it left Uckfield. There had been none of the supply dumps they had been promised, and not a single filling station had been found to contain a drop of unadulterated petrol. Already the fuel shortage was affecting the operation. Trucks had been abandoned, their tanks siphoned empty and their loads distributed among the surviving vehicles, and the flame tanks, so useful in country like this, had been neutered.

And even as he climbed back up onto the bed of his truck Ernst heard the drone of aircraft engines. The air war over the south coast had been going on all day; occasionally he glimpsed the metallic glint of a plane, or saw the bright colours of tracer fire. But this new engine noise, growing louder, was coming from behind him, from the north. He turned. A flight of Blenheims was sweeping down on the column, like predatory birds. Already the first sticks of bombs were falling from their bellies.

'Oh, shit,' said Kieser wearily.

Commands were barked out. 'Get out! Get to cover!' 'Get those anti-aircraft guns deployed!'

Once again the column had to scatter; once again Ernst found himself in a ditch. The planes were slow, but the convoy had no cover; the Luftwaffe was evidently otherwise engaged.

'Christ!' Kieser shouted. 'How do they know where we are?'

'They've got radio direction finders,' Ernst yelled back. 'That's how they know. And all these bloody partisans in the hills are reporting in every time we take a piss.'

The planes dipped lower, their machine-guns spitting fire, the bombs splashing craters into the road, and men began to scream. Ernst cowered in the dirt, burrowing into English autumn leaves, pulling his helmet low over his head.

XXXIII

The wooden blocks glided silently across the ops table, mirroring the blood and horror that must be unfolding out in the English countryside right at this moment. Gary wondered if these calm Wrens had nightmares.

He glanced at the big clock on the wall. Already it was almost two p.m.

'It's working,' Mackie said. 'It's only bloody working. Look, can you see – there's a lot of detail, but just concentrate on the Panzer divisions. You have the Tenth heading off east towards Ashford, and the Fourth pushing for Lewes. Well, they're so far from any support they might as well go back home. But the main thrust, the main line of breakout, is coming from the Seventh and Eighth, pushing up from the Sussex coast towards Guildford. Just where we want them.'

There was a fuss around the ops table, and the Wrens started sliding their blocks across the map with increasingly frantic haste.

'And it's starting,' Mackie said. 'Our counterattack. About bloody time.'

'Request leave to return to my unit, sir.'

'Of course, Corporal. I've ordered a car for you. Tell Monty to give old Hitler one from me! Sergeant Blackwell?'

'Sir. This way, Corporal . . .'

So Gary was led out of the bunker, bundled into a staff car, whisked out of the base, and rushed along roads crowded by troops and supply vehicles. There were a few civilians, fleeing north and west from the threatened towns of Sussex and Hampshire, the usual dreary parade of women and children and old folk. But such was the urgency now, and the volume of military assets on the move, that police, MPs and ARP wardens were peremptorily shoving the civilians off the road. It was all vividly real, after the monasticism of the ops room.

'Quite a show, isn't it, mate?' shouted Sergeant Blackwell, over the roar of the engines. He was a bulky man with a fat, shaven neck, and what sounded to Gary like a strong London accent. 'You pick up a lot down in that ops room. We're putting up a fight. But it's all we've got, isn't it?' Blackwell looked over his shoulder. 'What we have in the field right now. I mean, this is all there is, between the Nazis and London. Has to work, doesn't it, Corporal?'

'I guess so.'

The car rushed on, taking Gary back to his unit.

XXXIV

It was around five in the afternoon when the full-scale English assault at last fell on them. It came from the west.

The column broke again. The infantry dug in, scrambling for ditches and abandoned English foxholes. The engineers laboured to set up the field guns, and the Panzer tanks charged west, off the road, their big guns roaring.

Ernst and Heinz Kieser found themselves in an abandoned Home Guard pillbox, splashed with blood and stinking of cordite and smoke. Through a ragged slit in the scorched concrete, Ernst could see the open country the English were coming from. He saw vehicles, tanks, and scurrying troops, advancing amid the detonations of shells and the rattle of small-arms fire. This was not local defence; this was not the Home Guard. This was the English army, kept in reserve since the invasion; this was the counterattack they had been expecting all day.

And while the battle was joined on the land, over Ernst's head the aerial war was raging. It was clear that the English air force must be attacking the German advance, all along the roads back to the south, hoping to slice up the columns and then destroy the isolated elements. But now the English bombers and fighters were at last challenged by flights of Messerschmitts roaring up from the south, and Stuka dive bombers screamed down on English emplacements. The air was full of streaking planes and the howl of engines and a lacing of fire – and, from time to time, a plume of smoke, an explosion in the air, the distant drifting of parachutes. A three-dimensional war, then, in the air and on the land.

Ernst knew roughly where he was. Suffering from the attrition of the defenders' assaults, vehicles failing one by one for lack of fuel, the dwindling column had managed to push on through the towns of Haywards Heath and Horsham. The countryside was becoming progressively easier, less intensively mined, lighter and sparser defences at the crossroads and bridges and rail junctions. Now they were only a few miles south of Guildford, their target for the day, though they were far behind schedule. And if only they could go just a little further, if only they could reach the line of the Thames, the country would be open before them.

This was the crux. Ernst had the feeling that both sides were pouring all they had into this one conflict zone, that here was the spearhead, the assault that would make or break the German invasion of England.

There was a loud explosion, directly above Ernst's head. He flinched, grabbing his helmet. An English plane, a Hurricane by the look of it, had taken a strike. Its tail was gone, its right wing crushed, and it was heading straight for the ground, spinning like a corkscrew. Ernst saw the pilot struggle to get out of his cockpit, a tiny figure clambering desperately. The plane speared down, falling somewhere behind the German line, and an explosion rocked the ground.

A shadow passed over Ernst's face. He turned to look through the slit in the pillbox. Somebody was looking right back at him, not a foot away, through the thickness of the concrete. He had crept up while Ernst was distracted by the plane. The man's hand was raised. He held a grenade.

Kieser saw the same thing. 'Oh, shit!' His rifle cracked. A bullet ripped past Ernst's ear and slammed into the Englishman's hand, and one of his fingers burst in a shower of blood. He screamed.

Kieser's heavy hand slammed down on Ernst's back. 'Down, man!'

The explosion made the pillbox shudder. Leaves and bits of dirt were thrown up and then rained down.

On their bellies, they scrambled around the wall of the broken pillbox. The English soldier lay on his back, cradling a shattered hand. Kieser stuck the muzzle of his rifle in the man's face. 'Hello, goodbye,' he said in his broken English.

'Fuck you.' The English laughed, though tears rolled down his cheek with the pain of his hand. 'Fuck you for Peter's Well. And Wisborough Green. And Rotherfield. And Bethersden. And—'

Kieser's fist slammed into his jaw. 'And fuck you for Versailles.'

'Pretty boys!' They glanced over. Unteroffizier Fischer, crouching in the dirt, was waving. 'Leave him for the mop-up units. We're moving on.'

They scrambled back towards him. The three of them huddled by the side of the road, crouching, flinching from the shell fire and the bursts of automatic fire that sporadically raked the column. But the column was forming up again, the tanks and trucks lumbering back onto the road.

Kieser shouted, 'Unteroffizier? Are you serious?'

'That's the order. Listen to me. The English have fielded everything they've got, but we're still standing. And what's left of the second wave is heading our way. Always reinforce success – isn't that what the Fuhrer says? And we're the spearhead. Let the English slice away at our rear, let us lose half our bloody vehicles for lack of fuel – what of it? Mobility, that has been the key to this war – *our* mobility. If Seventh Panzer can only get into Guildford, with us following up – it's only a few more miles – if just a few of us can only get that far tonight, then we will have a chance of establishing a bridgehead. And tomorrow, when the English are exhausted, we can consolidate. Do you see?' He grinned. 'The order has come from Guderian himself, it is said. Berlin is sceptical, but Berlin is far away. What a man! Come on, get back into the truck.'

So, with the air war screaming overhead and the English assault continuing furiously from the left, the column roared on towards Guildford, led by the remnants of Seventh Panzer. The English shells hailed all around, and one by one the trucks and tanks and field guns were knocked out, and others died from lack of fuel, yet the rest simply closed up and moved on. The English desperately tried to throw up road blocks, even shoving their own vehicles across the road, but the tanks simply smashed through.

For Ernst this was a dash through hell. The men in the troop carriers could do nothing but cower, each of them waiting for the bit of shrapnel or the sniper bullet or the automatic-weapons burst from some English plane that would end his life. But they whooped and roared as the truck clattered over the pocked road, throwing them around like toys in a box, and Ernst found it impossible not to join in. This was madness. They wouldn't have the fuel even to drive back to the coast. But maybe, just maybe, this bold stroke was going to work, the English defences would be scattered and the Battle of England won.

But now they approached a crossroads. A mesh fence had been thrown across it, with barbed wire and a few tank traps. Ernst expected the Panzers simply to blast this lot out of the way and move on. He was astonished when the Panzers slowed with a grinding of their huge gears, and his own truck squealed to a stop.

Ernst exchanged a look with Heinz Kieser. Kieser just shrugged.

Unteroffizier Fischer jumped down to the road surface, and Ernst followed. The fence stretched to left and right across the road, and off into the fields beyond. A flag, a Stars and Stripes, flew boldly from a pole rising from beyond the fence. A single soldier armed with an automatic weapon stood right before the muzzle of the lead Panzer. He was short, burly, with belt and straps heavy with grenades and ammunition clips. His uniform looked crumpled. Apparently fearless, he was chewing gum.

There was a sign fixed to the fence, neatly lettered. Ernst squinted to make it out:

LUCKY STRIKE BASE
SHALFORD
US EIGHTH ARMY
SOVEREIGN TERRITORY OF THE UNITED STATES OF AMERICA
DO NOT ENTER

'Shit,' said Unteroffizier Fischer. 'We're going to have to pass this back up the line. Even Guderian can't declare war on America on his own initiative. *Churchill*. That wily bastard must have something to do with this. Shit, shit.'

The American soldier grinned. In English he called, 'Can I help you guys?'

II

PRISONER
JUNE–DECEMBER 1941

I

The family were all at breakfast that Monday morning, Fred, Irma, Alfie, Viv, the four of them in the farmhouse kitchen working their way silently through toast and powdered egg, when Ernst walked in with his gift. He placed it on the table, an anonymous cardboard box stamped with swastikas.

'Good morning, Obergefreiter,' said Irma. She pushed her way out of her chair, leaning on the wooden table for support. 'The usual? A bit of toast?' In her forties, she was heavily pregnant, her eyes shadowed, her face drawn of blood. 'The tea might be stewed.'

Alfie's eyes were on the gift. He chewed on rubbery toast, his legs swinging so that his whole body jerked about. He was fourteen but he looked younger, Ernst thought, skinny, always hungry-looking. 'What's in the box, Ernst?'

'Let the poor man get his breakfast, Alfie.' Irma went to the range.

'I'll get the tea,' said Vivien, getting up brightly. She ran to the sink and rinsed out a tin mug. She was a year older than her brother. She wore a blouse and skirt for school today, with thick dark stockings and clumpy shoes. Her mother was a fair seamstress, but you could see the panels of parachute silk where she had let out the blouse as Viv had grown.

Viv came over to Ernst with the tin mug. The drink was fairly repulsive, made from repeatedly stewed leaves and with lumps floating on the surface from the powdered milk. She leaned close enough to Ernst for a few strands of her strawberry blonde hair to brush against his face.

'Thank you.'

She said, in German, 'It's my pleasure.'

Alfie laughed. 'You're a right tart, our Viv, you really are.'

'Oh, leave her alone,' Irma said tiredly, and she set a plate with a bit of toast and a heap of runny powdered egg before Ernst. 'Is that enough, Obergefreiter?'

'Yes, thank you, Mrs Miller.' He made a show of cutting off some toast and tucking it into his mouth. He turned to Viv. 'But, you know, you need not have prepared for school. There will be no school today.'

Fred glared. 'How so?'

'A holiday has been declared. It is the King's birthday!' Ernst smiled.

Fred folded his arms. 'Not my bloody king. I'm a subject of King George, not of his Nazi-loving ninny of a brother who should have stayed abdicated.' He pronounced 'Nazi' the way Churchill always had, 'Nar-zee'. The father of the family was a squat man, his farmer's arms muscular, but his lower body was weaker, his wounded right leg withered, so that he had a rather unbalanced look. His greying hair was slicked back with Brylcreem, making his face angular, hawk-like. He wore his work coat, an old suit jacket from which the pockets had long been removed, leaving ghostly outlines of stitches.

Irma sighed. 'Oh, come on, Fred, have a bit of spirit. Edward's not so bad. He's got his job to do like everybody else. Binding the wounds, as they say. Although I hadn't heard about the holiday, Obergefreiter.'

'Well, we wouldn't,' Alfie said. 'Dad won't buy a newspaper. "Hoare and his bloody collaborators' rag."'

'Language, Alfie,' said Irma sharply. 'Mind you, we argue about that, Herr Obergefreiter. I mean, I can't see what harm a bit of news does. And I do so miss my stars.'

'Well, you are hearing about it now,' Ernst said, keeping up his smile. 'A day off for the whole of the protectorate, except for essential services.'

'I'll go and tell my cows I'm having a day off bloody milking them, shall I?' Fred said.

Irma looked concerned. 'I'd been hoping to get into Hastings today to see if there's any news about Jack and the prisoner release programme.'

'There will be emergency cover at the town hall,' Ernst assured her. He worked there himself, one of a number of soldiers with the necessary skills who had been seconded to supplement the civil servants brought across from Germany to run the protectorate. 'I'm sure that if there is any news you will receive it.'

'Don't know how you'll get down there, mind,' Fred said. 'Buses on holiday too, are they, Corporal?'

'Well, somebody's got to go,' Irma said. 'Viv, maybe you could come with me.'

Viv's anger flared up again. 'Why me? What kind of a holiday is that?'

'I'll come, Mum,' Alfie said.

'You're a good boy,' Irma said.

Fred grunted. 'Good at getting out of his chores around the farm, little bleeder.'

Ernst tapped his forefinger on his cardboard box. 'You still don't know what it is, this present I have brought for you.'

'Let me open it,' Alfie said.

But Viv was too quick. 'I *don't* think so.' She grabbed the box. She wore her nails long for a farmer's daughter, and she used one forefinger nail to slice through the thick packing tape. Inside was a brick of Bakelite, with a speaker grill and a heavy tuning dial. Viv pulled it out eagerly, scattering bits of wrapping paper on the table.

'Cor,' Alfie said. 'A wireless! Can we plug it in, Dad?'

'Actually it runs off batteries,' Ernst said. 'They must be recharged, periodically.'

'"Periodically."' Viv giggled. 'You do make me laugh, the way you talk.'

Fred was dismissive. 'It isn't as good as my old wireless set that they took away with my fowling piece. That's the trouble with you Nazis. Whatever you take away you always give something worse back.'

'Oh, don't be so sour, Fred.' Irma inspected the wireless and quickly found the 'on' switch. Music wafted from the wireless, a bit tinny.

Viv squealed, 'Music!' She got up and started dancing around the room, arms wrapped around her body, making big sweeping steps.

'I know that,' Irma said. 'What was it called, Fred? It was big just before the Germans came.'

Fred said reluctantly, '"The World is Waiting for the Sunrise."'

Irma said, 'Gosh, we haven't heard music for ever so long, not proper music, apart from Doreen on the piano in the church hall, the soldiers' choir singing carols at Christmas.' She began to sing softly: '*Stille nacht, heilige nacht ...*'

Alfie was trying to turn the tuning knob. 'It won't turn. It's stuck.' He looked at Ernst. 'Is it broken?'

'No, no.' Ernst felt faintly embarrassed. 'It's meant to be that way; the tuning is fixed.'

The music ended, and a male voice with the stilted plumminess of the British upper classes intoned, 'This is the Free Albion Broadcasting Service, coming to you twelve hours per day from the Ministry of Information in Canterbury. And now, at eight thirty a.m. precisely, the news ...'

'Free bloody Albion,' Fred said, and he laughed. 'I bet old Joe could bugger it so it picks up the BBC.'

'Language,' Irma said automatically.

'That would be forbidden,' Ernst said. 'Regretfully.'

'You won't, you know,' Viv said to her father. 'I've heard of this, the Promi wireless. One of the girls at school has it at home.'

'It's Propaganda from Hoare and his band of collaborators in Canterbury.'

'Dad, it plays jazz and swing from America!'

Fred said, 'Never mind jazz. I wonder if *ITMA* is still on?' He put on a comedy German accent, glancing at Ernst. 'Funf! Funf! Heil Hitler!'

'Oh, leave it out, Dad,' Viv said. 'You're always picking on Ernst. You know he won't report you or anything. Big man, aren't you?'

'Well.' Ernst pushed the wireless towards the family. 'Here is my gift, for King Edward's day. And I have another. A joint of lamb. I must pick it up. Perhaps we could cook it for dinner this evening.'

'Drool,' said Alfie. 'Lamb! I can't even remember what it tastes like.'

Fred snorted. 'You take away my bloody sheep, and now you give a bit back and expect me to be grateful. Rabbit will do for me.'

'Oh, that's enough, Fred,' Irma said. 'Look, Obergefreiter, you are very generous. If you can get it to me by four I'll have it in the oven. So is it a holiday for you too?'

'I'm planning a drive up to the First Objective.'

Fred grunted. 'A fan of pillboxes, are you?'

'My brother, who is a standartenfuhrer in the SS, has some business with the Halifax government. Prisoner repatriations and that sort of thing. I said I would accompany him; I would like to see the country again, where I fought.'

Viv clapped her hands. 'Oh, let me come with you.' She looked at her mother. 'I'm off school, aren't I? I could practise my German.'

Her father said, 'I've told you, in the stalag in the last lot we only needed four words of bloody German. *Kartoffel. Arbeit. Geld. Verboten.* Spud, work, money, forbidden.'

Viv ignored him. 'It's a lovely day. A ride in a car! I haven't been in a car since before the war. I could take a picnic. Mum—'

'No,' said Fred.

'Mum!'

Irma looked terribly tired. 'Oh, I can't be bothered fighting. It's up to the obergefreiter.'

Ernst felt he had no choice. 'Of course she can come.'

'Yes!' Viv clapped her hands again. 'I've got to work out what to wear ...' She ran out of the room.

'Look.' Irma took her purse from a pocket of a coat which hung on the door. 'Take some money.'

'No, it won't be necessary—'

'Just in case.' She pressed a bundle of occupation marks into Ernst's hand.

Alfie was listening to the news from the wireless. 'Dad, what's "Operation Barbarossa"?'

Fred didn't know, and Ernst had to admit that nor did he. They all listened to the wireless, and learned the almost unbelievable news that Hitler's Germany, in spite of a non-aggression pact, had, the previous day, invaded the Soviet Union.

II

When the car horns sounded Ernst and Viv hurried out of the farmhouse and down the muddy track to the road. It was a little after ten.

The army convoy was a queue of vehicles, two light armoured trucks topping and tailing a dozen staff cars. You always travelled in convoy. Nine months after Sea Lion, the resistance groups the English called 'the auxiliaries', spawned out of the Home Guard stay-behind units, were still capable of doing damage.

Josef was in the lead car, after the armoured vehicle. It was typical of him to drive himself. 'Brother!'

Ernst approached, with Viv holding his arm. Carrying a little picnic basket, she was wearing her mother's big sunglasses, her best shoes and a green crepe dress. Ernst knew how hard she and her mother worked to keep the flimsy material from creasing and tearing. The sun was behind Viv, and caught her pale red hair. As they walked the line of the convoy she was greeted by wolf-whistles and a few obscenities, not words Ernst had taught her in their occasional language classes. Though she smiled back, he could feel how tightly she clung to his arm.

Josef got out of his car, took her hand and kissed it. 'Fraulein, I am delighted.' Ernst saw her eyes widen. Josef's SS uniform, black and silver in the bright light of the summer's day, looked impossibly glamorous. Josef winked at Ernst.

Josef helped her into the back of his car, while Ernst sat up front. With a roar the convoy pulled away, raising dust from the track.

From the farm, two miles north of Battle, the convoy soon joined the main road north towards Tunbridge Wells, and drove steadily through the green heart of Sussex. They made rapid progress across country which had been such a scouring challenge for the advancing armies back in September. Now there were only the farmers busy on their land, and at this rate it would take the convoy only a couple of hours to get to the line before Guildford. But there were signs of the war. They passed fields scarred by bomb craters and heaps of wreckage that might once have been planes, and ruined vehicles hulked by the roadside, still lying where they had been shoved aside in those remote days of September, rusted after a winter's rain.

Josef glanced at Viv in his rear-view mirror. 'So,' he said. 'Good for you there is no room in the barracks. You struck lucky in your billet, you dog.'

'It's not like that,' Ernst said, colouring. 'She's only fifteen.'

Josef shrugged. 'Listen to me. In some of the coastal towns, in Hastings and Rye, you won't find a virgin over twelve, no matter how much you pay. It was the same in France. Oh, come on. Look, this wretched country will soon be empty of its young men. Those who weren't taken prisoner in the war are to be shipped off for labour. England is a country of old people, children, and women – and us, the only men. It is only natural that she, a blossoming beauty, should look at you.'

'I told you,' Ernst said hotly, 'it's not like that.'

Josef just laughed. 'So if you're not poking the daughter, how about the mother?'

'She's pregnant.'

'Really?'

'Nine months gone, nearly. She must have caught about the time of the invasion.'

Josef glanced sideways at him. 'Funny coincidence, that.'

An old English car approached them head-on, driving stubbornly on the left, in defiance of the occupation rule. Of course the German column did not deviate. At the last moment the English car veered away, and Ernst glimpsed a shocked face behind a stern handlebar moustache, before the car ended up ramming itself into a ditch. The German troops cheered mockingly, and made Churchill V-for-Victory signs at the crashed car.

Viv laughed prettily. 'What a lark!'

Ernst said, 'These English aren't like the French, are they? Defiant.'

'Well, the English haven't experienced occupation, not for a thousand years. It's all new to them.'

'Churchill's still a hero to them, even though he was forced to resign over the invasion.' He was thinking of Fred Miller and his 'Nar-zees'.

'We all cheered when that old warmonger was pushed out, after barely six months in office after a lifetime of waiting for it, ha! But it wasn't the shame of the invasion, you know, but pragmatism. There are necessary dealings between England and the protectorate. Churchill adamantly refused to discuss even such matters as prisoners and wounded with us. So he had to step aside for Halifax, an altogether more reasonable gentleman. Churchill's still stirring up feeling against us, though, especially in America. The sooner some collaborator puts a bullet through his thick skull the better.'

'Sometimes the whole business of occupation seems absurd,' Ernst admitted. 'I mean, what are we doing here, so far from home? Who are we to lord it over these people?'

Josef glared at him. 'You always have to *think*, don't you, Ernst? Look, let me give you a bit of advice. Don't go native. If you want a girl, fine. Just remember who you are.'

Ernst, as always irritated at being lectured at, changed the subject. 'It's the issue of the prisoners you are going to discuss at the Objective today, yes?'

'That among other things.' Josef theatrically stifled a yawn with his gloved hand. 'Face to face, me and some pompous British oaf, mediated by a gum-chewing American and a Swiss or two. I have to admit the Americans provide the best lunches, however. Of course it is all a distraction from my work for the Ahnenerbe. You must come visit my installation at Richborough.'

'Still hoping to seduce Himmler with this nonsense of manipulating history, are you?'

'We'll see if it's nonsense in due course,' Josef said, not offended.

'If your work's so important, what are you doing trailing all the way out here?'

'We're all stretched a bit thin these days, aren't we? Now that half the detachments stationed in Britain have been reassigned to the eastern front.'

'You know, I heard nothing about the war against Russia until this morning.'

Josef grinned. 'Well, neither did Stalin. It is in the east that the truth of this war will unfold, Ernst – not Germans against English or French, but the volk against the Slav. It is magnificent, they say. Three army groups are on the move, in a front a thousand miles long – think of it.' He winked at Ernst. 'But spare me from serving there!' He glanced back at Viv, who smiled at him. 'What do you think, shall I drive a bit faster and see if I can make her skirt ride up?'

'You are coarse, Josef.'

III

It was nearly noon by the time they reached the First Objective. In this region the line tracked the main road that ran up from Portsmouth through Petersfield to Milford, and then south of Guildford to Reigate. The barrier itself was a sculpture of wire and concrete that stretched from horizon to English horizon. Watchtowers and searchlight batteries loomed over the fences on both sides. Josef said, 'The shade of Emperor Hadrian himself would be awed by such a monument.'

This was the protectorate's demarcation line, which it was illegal for any subject of the occupation to call the 'Winston Line'. It cut off a slice of south-east England, running from Gravesend on the Thames estuary and south-west towards Portsmouth. The wall roughly corresponded to the first operational objective of Army Group A during the invasion, hence the name that had stuck to it among the German forces. The advance had been halted there when German stormtroopers found themselves facing Americans in their hastily erected bases. It had been Churchill's final masterstroke, in the panicky days after the invasion, to give away such bases to the US all along the objective line; in September 1940 the Reich was unwilling to go to war with America, and the Panzers' advance had stalled.

There was no armistice, and perhaps no possibility of one. England and Germany bombed each others' cities, a desultory campaign of misery – though wise heads said the 'blitz' would have been worse if not for the presence of German troops on English soil, and British subjects under German occupation. At sea, U-boat packs hunted down the supply convoys that crossed the Atlantic, and the Royal Navy harassed the much shorter supply lines to Albion from the continent. Overseas the war was being waged by proxy in a variety of theatres. In southern Europe Britain had opposed Hitler's assault on Yugoslavia and Greece, and Britain had defeated the Italians in Egypt, forcing Hitler to commit the Afrika Corps under Rommel. But once the initial German advance had been halted there had been little active fighting on the British mainland.

And so the situation had held, already for nine months, and the 'Winston Line' had solidified. London, to the north of the line, was in the territory held by the Halifax government, but it was a city held hostage by immediate peril. The government itself had evacuated to York. Ernst had once seen a newsreel of the line as filmed from the air at night. In a country plunged in blackout darkness, the First Objective was like a double wound, parallel lines of light slashed across the passive countryside, extending from coast to coast. It was a genuine division which bisected counties, severed towns from their suburbs, and cut families in two, often quite arbitrarily.

And yet Ernst, by nature an optimist, clung to the line as a symbol of hope. It was the one place where the British and the Germans, two nations at war, were managing to work together peacefully, finding solutions to benefit the most vulnerable. Perhaps the future could be built on such impulses, rather than war, occupation and conquest.

The convoy broke up. The vehicles pulled off the road onto concrete hard-standing areas, and the passengers jumped down. A bridge had been laid across the ditches here and a gate cut into the Objective. Civilians queued on both sides of the gate, waiting to be processed, men, women and children with bags and bicycles, prams and pets. Once the shock of invasion was over, there had been a mass movement of people back from the English territories *into* German Albion: refugees wanting to return to their homes, livelihoods and families.

Surrounded by soldiers, Viv was restless, increasingly nervous. A country girl, she had seen little even of the disruption military life had brought to the towns.

Josef got out of the car and took a slim briefcase from the boot. He pointed through the wire. 'See over there, the Stars and Stripes? That's the Americans. Shalford Base.'

'I fought my way here,' said Ernst. 'This is where the advance stopped, for me. This very spot.'

'I know. Few men got any further. That's why I brought you here. Look, the Swiss flag is flying over that camp too.'

'What have the Swiss got to do with it?'

'Protecting Power for the POWs.' He slapped Ernst on the shoulder. 'My business will probably only take a couple of hours. Look around. Enjoy your picnic with your little girlfriend. Which reminds me.' He dug inside his jacket. 'A letter for you. You might want to keep it from your sweetie over there.'

'Who's it from?'

He grinned. 'Your other lover. Claudine, was she called? It's good news. She's coming to England!'

'You *read* it?'

'Censorship, my boy. A military requirement. Behave yourselves, now.' And with a nod to Viv, he walked towards the gate.

Suddenly planes roared low overhead. Ernst flinched, a reflex that was a relic of the days when he had been under attack from the air. The planes were a schwarm of Messerschmitt 109s, patrolling the line on the German side. And there was a countering roar from the British side, Spitfires augmented by Mohawks of the USAAF.

IV

For all her bravado, Viv had been intimidated by the troops at the Objective, and the bored, mildly hungry looks they gave her. She stayed subdued all the way back to the farm. Ernst, Claudine's letter clutched closely to his heart inside his jacket, was distracted himself, and had little to say.

Viv brightened up once she and Ernst were back home. She practically skipped down the rough track to the farm. They were back not long after six o'clock, and the smell of the roast filled the house. Ernst went off to wash, relieved to be free of Viv for a few minutes. His room was the best in the farmhouse, with a view to the south; it had once been Fred and Irma's own bedroom. As he changed into a fresh shirt, he heard Viv brightly chattering about her day, how she had been chauffeured by an SS officer, and how she saw Americans through the wire like monkeys in a zoo. Elsewhere in the house Alfie was practising his violin. He played 'Lill Marlene'. On Saturdays he busked in Battle or Hastings, playing for pfennigs from homesick soldiers.

When Ernst came downstairs Fred was sawing away at the lamb joint with a carving knife that had been sharpened so often it had been reduced to a sliver of steel. Irma stood at the oven, stirring a pan of gravy. Plates heaped with vegetables, potatoes and cabbage, stood beside her. She looked quite exhausted.

Ernst produced one more present: a bottle of wine, imported by Wehrmacht stores from France. 'So we can toast the health of the King.'

'I'd prefer a beer,' Fred growled. But there had been very little beer about for many months; all of Albion's grain was requisitioned.

'And there's a present for you on the table, Obergefreiter,' Irma said over her shoulder.

Ernst looked. It was a book, a paperback, printed on cheap, pulpy paper. He read the title. *Pied Piper* by Nevil Shute.

'It was in our last parcel from the family in London,' Irma said. 'Story of an old man who has to flee the German invasion of England. He saved some children on the way. You might like the detail. Good story, too. Just a little something for you—' Her hand flew to her mouth. 'Oh – I didn't check if it is on the verboten list.'

'I will enjoy it,' Ernst said quickly. 'Perhaps it will improve my English also.'

Relieved, she turned back to the gravy.

Ernst sat beside Fred as he carved. With Claudine's letter upstairs he felt bright, lively, eager for some conversation. 'So, Fred, how are you this evening? Where is the new wireless?'

Fred's farmer's hands were huge; the knife looked small in his fingers as he sliced through the steaming meat. 'I told you. Gave it to old Joe down the road, so he can bugger it to pick up the BBC.'

Ernst tut-tutted like a mother. 'You'll get it confiscated, you reckless fellow.'

'You'll have to find the bloody thing first, won't you?'

'Any news of Jack?'

Irma turned, ladling her gravy. 'Alfie and I went down to Hastings. They're talking about releasing more cadres. Great War veterans. Postmen. The sons of doctors.'

Fred grunted. 'The sons of bloody doctors. It's always who you know in this country, even under the Nazis. I was a POW in the last lot. I'd give up my liberty again if I could swap places with Jack, I'd do it in a second, I'll tell you that.'

'I'm sure you would,' Ernst said.

Fred stared at him. Then he stood back from the joint and looked at the knife in his hand. 'Sometimes I can't believe what I'm doing. I got my kneecap shot off at the Somme. Now here I am not thirty years later carving a bit of lamb for the benefit of the bloody Wehrmacht, while some black-hearted Nar-zee arse in Kent or France is working out whether my son, *my son*, is to be allowed to come home again.'

'He doesn't mean anything,' Irma said to Ernst, her eyes hollow. 'You know how he is.'

Ernst did not react to Fred's words. He was in authority over these people, even to the matter of life and death, within the military law. And yet he did not feel any such authority.

Viv came bustling in, followed by Alfie. 'Here I am!' She had changed into a more sober black dress, run up from blackout curtain. She wore a yellow star on her breast. She looked at them, crowded around the table. 'Have I missed anything?'

Alfie said, 'Can't we just bloody eat?'

'Language,' Irma murmured automatically.

Fred limped to a seat and sat down. 'God save the bloody King.' He reached for a corkscrew from a drawer, and began to open the wine.

Ernst said, 'I will finish the carving.' He stood and took Fred's place at the head of the table. Hot fat splashed his bare skin, and the smell of the meat rose up, a cosy, family smell. But his own family were very far away, he was reminded.

Alfie sneered at Viv. 'I bet you didn't wear that yellow star in front of the SS officer.'

'Well, that would have been *very* bad taste, wouldn't it? But besides, I know they say you can arrest a Jew for *not* wearing a star, but what are you supposed to do about a Gentile who *is* wearing one?'

'This is a foolish gesture,' Ernst said uneasily.

'There's a girl at school, Jane Mathie, who went up to London on a week's pass to see her grandmother who was dying, and she said they're *all* wearing them up there. Quite the fashion. It's funny how things turn out, isn't it, Ernst? Who would ever have thought I would end up wearing yellow? It just *isn't* my colour.'

'Oh, Viv,' said Irma tiredly.

Fred got the cork out of the wine bottle and took a slug, straight from the neck.

'Do you think I'm being provocative, Obergefreiter?' Viv came closer to Ernst. He flinched away, trying to keep smiling, but now she took a bit of hair at the nape of his neck and pulled it gently.

'Enough!' Fred lashed out from where he was sitting. His big fist caught Viv in the belly, and she went flying back.

Irma screamed, *'Fred!'* She ran to her daughter, and Alfie pushed his chair back and hurried over. Viv was trying to sit up, gasping. She was a crumple of blackout cloth, her legs splayed.

Ernst, stunned, found himself still holding the carving knife in one hand, a serving fork in another. He turned to Fred. 'What have you done?'

'I won't have my daughter turn into a Jerrybag. I won't, do you hear?' He made to stand up.

'Sit still,' Ernst commanded him.

Fred subsided. He took another mouthful of the wine. 'Like being back in the stalag,' he said.

'Ow!' Irma, kneeling beside her daughter, doubled over, her hands around her belly. 'Oh, God!'

Alfie scrambled backwards. 'There's water on the floor. Urgh.'

Ernst put down the knife and hurried over. 'Let me see, Alfie, it's all right. Irma?' He held her shoulders, and tried to look into her face. 'The baby?'

She nodded jerkily. 'I think so.'

'Yuk!' Alfie said.

'The water is normal,' said Ernst, thinking fast. 'There is no telephone here. This is what I will do. I will go to your neighbour, Joe, who has a phone—'

'No. Not you.' Irma grabbed his arm in a claw-like hand; she held him hard enough to hurt. *'Stay here.'*

Bewildered, he said, 'Very well. Then Fred must phone.' He turned to Fred, who sat staring at the wine. 'Fred, call an ambulance. Tell them about your wife. And see if he, Joe, can offer any help before they come.'

He turned back to Irma, not looking to see if Fred complied. But then he heard the chair scrape back, Fred's heavy, uneven step as he made for the door.

Viv was weeping openly now, seeming much younger than her fifteen years, but she didn't appear to be hurt save for a winding. Alfie put an arm around her.

Ernst asked Irma, 'What is it, Frau Miller? What are you afraid of?'

Irma was convulsed by another contraction, and gasped. But she leaned closer to Ernst so the children could not hear. 'My husband, Obergefreiter. I'm afraid of what he might do.'

'About the baby?'

'We've hardly talked about it. I don't know what he'll do – I'm frightened.'

Ernst thought he was beginning to understand. 'The baby is not his.'

'I wasn't unfaithful to him, Obergefreiter.'

'Your relationships are your business.'

'But that's the point. It wasn't a relationship at all. Not like that. It was during the invasion.'

And then he saw it. 'Oh. This was not, um, not your consent.'

She bowed her head, shamed. 'I've told nobody. Not even Fred. But he knows, deep down. I thought if I fought them off, the soldiers, they would take Viv – we had been hiding, you see—'

'What unit were they? Did you learn that, do you remember? Wehrmacht or SS? If you can tell me precisely when this was, I could probably identify them. The Wehrmacht is strict on these matters, Frau Miller.'

'Not the Germans. It was before the Germans even got here, before I'd seen a single wretched German. *They were British.* British soldiers, retreating. They came to the house and just took what they wanted. Food, drink . . . Fred knows, inside, I'm sure of it. But I don't know what he'll do about it, Obergefreiter, truly I don't. I'm frightened, ever so.' Her grip closed around his arm again. 'Stay. Please stay!'

V

In Hastings, because of the various royal birthday events, it was gone nine by the time George got home.

There was a pearl-white glow coming from the living room, and a murmur of German voices, the dull thump of martial music. He kicked off his boots, left his helmet on the occasional table by the door, hung up his jacket, and walked into the living room. Julia Fiveash sat on the sofa, her feet up on a pile of George's books. She wore her black uniform jacket, unbuttoned, but her long legs were bare, looking as if they were carved from marble in the television's cold light. She had a glass of whisky in one hand and a fag in the other, with a heaped ashtray on the arm of the sofa.

'You started early,' he said.

She shrugged. 'Long day.' Her blonde hair was loose, and tumbled around her shoulders when she turned to look at him.

He peered at the television. He saw pictures of German soldiers on the move, and crude maps with bold black arrows thrusting across them. 'Not Walt Disney, I take it.'

She pointed. 'There's Moscow. You can read, can't you? It's a newsreel on our glorious advances in the east.'

George found the television fascinating, whatever the subject matter; he'd only glimpsed sets in shops in London before the war. It was probably one of the Germans' more successful propaganda moves, he thought, to set up a television service in Albion. It made up for the lousy cinema, where all you ever got now was a handful of films from before the war which were deemed 'safe' by the propaganda ministry, shown over and over, or else subtitled German movies, all sturdy farmers and marching youths. Of course the American cartoons on the television helped. George had heard that Hitler liked Donald Duck.

'Anyway,' she said, 'where have you been?'

'Work,' he said bluntly. '*We* didn't get the day off. I've got to go out again in an hour for the curfew.'

'Oh, must you?' She pouted, and uncrossed her legs, parting them slightly. 'It's already been such a long day.'

He turned away. 'Well, mine's not over yet.' He glanced around the room. 'Have you eaten?'

She waved a hand. 'There was a reception at the castle. For the holiday, you know. Quite spectacular, actually. Fireworks. Did you see them? Well, I ate there. Just nibbles. You know me, I eat like a rabbit.'

'Whereas I could eat a bloody rabbit.'

'Oh, don't be such a grump.' She turned back to the television.

He went to the kitchen. He knew there was a tin of Spam in here, unless Julia had swiped it. Since he had lost Hilda he had learned how to rustle up a decent fritter. He rattled around, looking for a frying pan and a bit of vegetable oil, hoping the gas pressure would be up tonight. He was tired, and vaguely annoyed that Julia hadn't prepared anything for him. He clung to his petty irritation. Better to feel like that than to think about what he'd been doing today.

Even on the King's birthday the occupation was churning through its deliberate processes. It was already six months since the orders had gone out to exclude the town's Jews from certain areas of work, such as teaching and policing. Now the process of 'translocation' had begun. At the moment it was simply a question of summoning males of working age to the police stations. Most of them turned up. The Germans always worked through civilian authorities, so it was coppers like George who were interviewing these bewildered-looking young men, some of whom didn't consider themselves Jewish at all. The first transports had already crossed the Channel, taking the men to a holding camp in Drancy, before they were to be sent further east to the Reich's great labour projects out there. It was all bloody, an endless slog of bureaucracy and bewilderment and cruelty.

And George knew what was coming next. According to Harry Burdon it was already happening on the continent, in France and Belgium and Holland. Soon the forcible round-ups would begin. And then it wouldn't be just working-age men who would be shipped out, but old folk, women and even children, and you could hardly tell yourself that they were bound for labour camps, could you, George? He still thought it was best to do his duty. But if the occupation lasted long enough for this sort of thing to be happening on his watch – well, perhaps he would have choices to make.

As he got the Spam slices into the frying pan with a bit of batter, Julia came into the kitchen. She leaned against the door frame, smoking;

she'd taken off her jacket now and wore only her shirt, her legs bare.

'You look filthy,' he said to her.

'I bathed this morning.'

'You know what I mean.'

'I'll take it as a compliment, then. It was quite a do, you know.'

'What was?'

'The King's birthday reception. They were all there. Heydrich was the big star in town.' Reinhard Heydrich was head of the SD, the Sicherheitsdienst, the Party's own security service. He was also the Reichsprotector of the occupied territory. 'And Josef Trojan turned up, brandishing a letter of commendation from Himmler ...' She listed more names.

He half listened, not very interested. The Germans were always politicking. All the great Nazi barons had their representatives here in the protectorate – Himmler, for instance, with this Trojan. 'Do you realise,' he said, interrupting her, 'that every name you've mentioned is a German? They all carry on their plotting and sucking-up and backstabbing among each other as if the rest of us don't exist.'

Julia laughed. 'I imagine it was the same in India under the Raj. Oh, I met one interesting chap. English, I mean. Claimed to be a second cousin of the King.'

'Which king?'

'Well, as Edward and George are brothers, that's rather a silly question, isn't it? In fact this chap is another Edward, viscount something-or-other. Now he's come down from London, and he claimed that there's a theory going around up there that all this is divine retribution.'

'For what?'

She blew smoke out through pursed lips; her lipstick was a little smudged. 'For deposing Edward, of course. That bully Stanley Baldwin – even Churchill thought it was the wrong thing to do. And now England's reaping the whirlwind.'

'What a load of cobblers. This isn't the Middle Ages.'

'Well, it's a point of view. Heydrich rather took to the viscount, I think. He said he admires our aristocracy.'

'A pack of traitors, if you ask me.'

Julia sighed. She crossed to him and wrapped her arms around his waist. He could feel her breath on his neck, the shirt rustling against his back, the smooth firmness of her body only a couple of layers of cloth away from his own. 'Ah, dear George, you are always so browned off, aren't you? You despise most of the English more than you despise the Nazis, I think.'

'Mind my fritters.'

'Oh, to perdition with your beastly fritters.' She pulled at him, turning him around. Her face was close to his, her eyes and mouth wide, and her hair was a golden cloud in the dim light.

'Bloody hell,' he whispered. 'I really am batting above my average with you.'

'You say the most ridiculous things.' Her lips closed on his and her tongue flickered, alive; he tasted cigarette smoke and wine and a hint of spice, the relic of her reception with the Nazis. She grabbed his balls, her moves confident, decisive. 'And do you despise me?' she asked breathily.

'You ask me that every day.'

'You despise what I do. The people I work with. Everything I believe in.' And, it went unsaid, he despised those of her colleagues who had executed his daughter in cold blood. 'And yet here we are. Funny, isn't it?'

'There's nothing funny about this bloody war.'

'Kick me out, then.' She massaged his crotch, while her other hand pressed into the small of his back. 'Go on. Just push me away.'

'You and your bloody games. You're cracked.'

'And you say that every day too. Tell me to leave.'

He took her wrists, and gently disengaged her hands from his body. 'I'll tell you to pack it in for now. Believe it or not I'm hungrier than I'm randy, and those Spam fritters are calling.'

She laughed. She spun away, bunching up her hair behind her head with her hands. 'You do sound your age sometimes. All right, I'll leave you alone. Just make sure you wake me up when you come in from the curfew.'

VI

They were in a muddy field, once the football pitch attached to a boys' prep school, now fenced off with barbed wire and sentry towers and guns. In the grey light the men stood in their rows like tree stumps, shabby in their battered coats and wooden clogs, with their shaven heads. The Wehrmacht guards walked before them, their rifles in their arms. This was the dawn appell.

The stalag commander walked out and stood before the men. Because this anonymous Sunday was Sea Lion Day, he announced, the first anniversary of the invasion, the prisoners would get a boost to their rations, a bit of pork sausage from their cousins in Bavaria, and the work kommandos would be allowed an additional hour off in the middle of the day. There were the usual ironic cheers from the ranks.

Willis Farjeon, standing tall in his blue RAF greatcoat, murmured, 'Good old Boche with all their memorial days. As long as we get a bit of extra kip they can make a memorial out of anything they like.'

'I bet you'd like to make a memorial out of my arse, you bum bandit,' called one of the men.

Willis turned and grinned. 'And you'd like a lick of my pork sausage, wouldn't you, pongo?'

'Bit early in the morning for that, Betty Grable,' murmured Danny Adams, the SBO, actually an NCO in this other-ranks camp, a blunt scouser of a sergeant-major.

The men calmed down and endured the rest of the appell.

Gary couldn't care less about any of it. He just stood there huddled in a greatcoat that still bore the bloodstains from the day he had been captured a year ago, after only a few hours in combat. He did look for Ben Kamen. The men of the work kommandos tended to cluster together, separate from the 'housewives', as stalag slang had it, the men who remained in the camp. Gary couldn't see Ben today.

Breakfast was a bowl of watery potato soup and a tin mug of the brownish liquid the goons called 'tea'. Then the kommandos filed to the camp gates in their work parties, past the solid buildings that had once housed a headmaster's office, and a medical room where nurses had searched little boys' heads for hair nits, and now a German trooper with a machine gun sat in a corrugated-iron shed on the roof.

At the gates they loaded themselves on their lorries. A young man called Joe Stubbs saw Gary coming and made a show of helping him up into the truck. That was the standing joke with the lads, that Gary, at twenty-six, was an old man, in fact an old Yank.

It was a few miles from the stalag to the old Roman camp at Richborough, where the monument was slowly being built. The men endured the rattling journey in silence.

At Richborough Gary and his mates stripped off their greatcoats and jackets. They got to work. Gary had to mix concrete, shovelling sand and mortar into the maw of a grinding mixer. After a year all the men had long lost their flab. Their elbows and knees were prominent, their faces gaunt.

There were perhaps a hundred men working here, prisoners or civilian labour, in parties scattered around the camp. Richborough had been converted into a construction site, with ramps laid roughly down over the Roman ditches. A steady stream of lorries turned up through the day with rubble core and marble blocks and other supplies, to be unloaded by the workers. At the heart of it all was a forest of scaffolding, from which the four great feet of the double-arch monument were already rising.

It was turning into a dismal autumn day, the sky a grey lid, and a hint of the rain to come prickling in the air. The men grumbled, but Gary didn't mind the work. The physical effort made it easier not to think. But you worked slowly; the stalag diet of spuds and swedes and the odd bit of meat didn't provide enough fuel for anything more than that. It wasn't a pleasant thought that the cold today was a foretaste of the winter to come; the last had been bad enough, and Gary had lost his fat since then.

The men worked, the guards patrolled. Mostly the guards were soldiers of the Wehrmacht. But today, maybe because of the Sea Lion anniversary, the Wehrmacht troops were supplemented by men in khaki uniforms. They had armbands bearing the swastika-on-George's-cross symbol of the Albion protectorate, and when they spoke you could hear accents from Kent and Sussex and Hampshire and even London. These were the Landwacht, a German equivalent of the Home Guard, Englishmen who had volunteered to work for the protectorate authorities.

When these characters had first turned up the prisoners had gone out of their way to give them a hard time, trying to knock off their tin hats with bits of hardcore, or spiking the muddy ground with nails embedded in bits of wood. But the Landwacht blokes responded with a ferocity not matched by the Germans, and there had been one occasion when Wehrmacht troops had had to intervene to stop a beating.

After the others were already at work, Willis Farjeon came sauntering over to Gary's group, as blithe as you pleased. 'Morning, pongos,' he said brightly.

'Watch your backs, lads,' said Joe Stubbs.

'Oh, don't be like that, Stubbs, you love me really.' Willis stripped off his coat and took a spade.

Joe Stubbs was only nineteen, a farmer's son from Canterbury, a private who had been captured during the German advance after only a day's active service and barely a couple of weeks' training. To him, it seemed to Gary, war was the stalag, adulthood was being a POW. 'Piss off, Farjeon,' he said now, angry, nervous.

'And the same to you, Stubbs, you lout.' Willis came to work beside Gary. He was tall, rakish, good-looking in a David Niven sort of way. He wore his black hair slicked back, though where he got the Brylcreem from was a matter of rumour, and he had a fine pencil-thin moustache, black as soot. A fighter pilot shot down over Kent during the invasion, he looked mid-twenties but he might have been younger. He said to Gary, 'And how's our resident member of the Dunkirk Running Club this morning?'

'What Stubbs said.'

'Oh, now, now. I am aware you've been ignoring me, you know.'

Willis Farjeon made Gary squirm. Gary had found he simply couldn't stomach a certain class of Englishmen, the public-school types as he thought of them, who sneered at everybody around them from the goons to their fellow prisoners. 'I've nothing to say to you, Farjeon.'

Willis smiled, working as hard as the rest. 'Ah, but I've things to say to you, or so I hope. We have a mutual friend, after all.'

'We do?'

'Hans Gheldman. The little Austrian?'

Gary frowned. 'Hans Gheldman' was the pseudonym Ben Kamen was using in the camp, hiding his Jewishness, posing as a second-generation émigré with an American mother. In the early days in the stalag Gary had quickly made contact with the escape committee crew and persuaded them to run up a fake set of identification documents for Ben. 'I know Hans,' he said cautiously.

'Funny little chap, isn't he? Always scared of something. Well, so would I be, stuck in a place like this with a German accent.'

'Austrian. Hans is an Austrian-American.'

'Yes, but men like Stubbs here are always going to suspect him of being a mole.'

'Fuck off, Farjeon,' said Stubbs. 'They'd never stick a mole in with a Kraut accent. Even the goons aren't that stupid. You're more likely to be a mole than fucking Gheldman.'

'How peculiarly perceptive he is,' Willis said, speaking of Stubbs rather than to him. 'Well, Hans is nervous. He does speak of you, you know,' he said to Gary. 'Quite often – your experiences before the invasion – how you lost your wife.'

'It's none of your business.'

'Hans thinks it's his business, and so it's mine.'

'Christ,' said another man, leaning on his spade. 'Look at that. Another lot of bloody Jugend.' He said the word Jugend, 'Youth', in a cartoon way, as the English pronounced most German words they had borrowed during the occupation: *Joog-end*.

A party of boys, aged perhaps thirteen or fourteen, was being led by an SS officer across the site. They were all in uniforms, and wore swastika armbands. The officer waved his hands in the air, evidently describing the monument as it would one day appear. The Reich was reproducing an arch set up by the Romans to commemorate their own successful invasion of Britain two thousand years ago. It would be embellished with sculptures of the conquering German forces and their vanquished foes; there would be amphibious tanks and barges, Spitfires and Messerschmitts. The SS man had the boys line up before the stub of the arch, while a photographer snapped pictures, and a newsreel cameraman set up his tripod and panned across their smiling faces and up to the monument's mighty legs.

'Look at them,' Willis said. 'Aren't they sweet with their little knees and their polished shoes?'

'I had a uniform like that,' Stubbs said. 'Before the war. I was a Boy Scout.' The scout movement, regarded as propagating anti-Nazi values, had been incorporated into the Hitler Jugend.

'I bet you looked just as pretty as those darlings.' Willis called, 'Hello, little boys. Would you like some sweets?'

That made the boys look around, their smiles faltering, nervous. Some of the prisoners laughed. The SS man glared, and began to shepherd the boys away.

A Landwacht thug came by Gary's group. 'Back to work, you arseholes.'

Willis snapped him a Party salute, and picked up his shovel.

'Maybe you are a fucking mole, Farjeon,' Stubbs said. 'You're too bloody posh to be here, you should be in an oflag.'

'I've been in oflags. I was in one near Canterbury.'

'So why are you here now?'

'I have the right father. My pop is a senior civil servant in Whitehall, or he was; I imagine he's up in York now. You'll never have heard of him, Stubbs, but he's a big wheel in his own circles.'

'So you're a Prominente,' Gary said.

'And so are you. There are plenty of us around. We're here in this commoners' camp because they like to keep us close to the coast. Even you, I dare say, Stubbs, despite your low brow.'

'My dad's just a farmer.'

'Yes, but he's also a big cheese in the trade union movement, isn't he? A mole, me? What a bore that would be. And besides, Stubbs, hasn't it occurred to you that our Dunkirk Harrier here is much more likely to be a mole than I am? After all, Gary, you're a foreign neutral. You could apply to the Protecting Power and get yourself out of here any time you like.'

'The war isn't done. *My* war isn't done.'

'Revenge, is that it?'

'You leave him alone,' said Stubbs. 'The Yank's all right. Every man in here keeps Jerry tied down that bit more, and good for him.'

Willis sneered. 'Well, that's what Danny Adams says to keep your dander up.'

Gary leaned on his spade and studied Willis, trying to understand him. 'Like this all the time, are you, Willis?'

'Like what? Camp? Camp in the camp? Well, why not? I do fit in rather well, don't I? After all this is just like public school and we're all faggots there. Or that's what you think of me, isn't it, Gary? That's the cliché you see stamped on my forehead.'

'I couldn't give a fig who or what you are,' Gary said.

'Actually I'm just playing,' Willis said. 'I mean, what else is there to do?'

'You could try and fucking escape,' said Joe Stubbs.

'Oh, what a bore all *that* is, stooging and planning, stealing and hoarding, digging away at tunnels, mucking about at appells, baiting the goons! No, that's not for me. I'm playing, that's all.'

Gary thought that was possibly the truth of it. There were plenty of 'whackies' in the stalag, as the British called them, men driven slowly mad by their imprisonment. Usually it manifested itself in manias, for excessive exercise maybe, or insane escape attempts, or you would see swings of mood, manic happiness crashing to sullenness and depression.

He tentatively labelled Willis as a 'whackie', then. His baiting and cruelty had no end save for Willis's own entertainment; for a prisoner, there were no ends. But still he could be dangerous, if he really had got close to Ben.

Now there were wolf-whistles, and the men paused again. 'Christ,' Stubbs said. 'It's that SS bird.'

The SS officer who had escorted the Jugend was returning to the monument with a woman at his side, tall, also in a black SS uniform, her hair beneath her peaked cap golden. The prisoners saw very few women. Even some of the guards turned to watch her pass.

Stubbs groaned. 'Look at the way she's swinging that arse.'

'Yeah,' a man said, 'she's doing it for you, Stubbsy, she's noticed you.'

'Hey, look at old Matt!'

Henry 'Matt' Black was in the next party, shaping facing stones. He was another private, a kid no older than Stubbs. He had actually pulled his pants down and had his fist around his stiff cock.

'He's always doing that, bloody Matt,' Stubbs said. 'Never got his hand off the thing.'

'Everybody does it,' somebody said.

'Yes, but not bold as you please in broad daylight.'

The guards were already closing in on Black, and the men yelled, urging him to finish himself off before they got there, as if it was a race.

VII

That evening there was a lot of activity in the camp. Staff cars came and went through the gates, delivering staff in SS uniforms, and boxes of equipment marked with swastikas and Gothic script which they carried into the assembly hall. The men were excited by all this activity, and the escaper types speculated on what they could steal.

But underneath the excitement Gary sensed tension. Whenever there was any break in routine you always worried that what was already a bad situation was about to get worse. Especially when the SS showed up. Even the regular Wehrmacht guards seemed nervous.

Gary made his way to Ben's barracks. It was just two old classrooms knocked together. The school gear was long gone to be replaced by the stuff of a POW camp, bunk beds and stoves and light bulbs dangling from the bare ceiling, and little cupboards made by the prisoners out of bits of scrap wood. But you could still see the mark on the wall where the blackboard had once hung, and sometimes, Gary was sure, you could smell the chalk.

Gary found Ben. He'd hoped to get a chance to talk to him. But Ben, 'Hans', was holding court at the centre of a little group of men, banging on about Einstein, general relativity and the life and death of the universe. Even Willis was sitting on a bunk, smoking a skinny cigarette and listening.

It was always like this inside the camp. The kommando system split the prisoners into two groups, two subcultures. In the kommandos you had the work, and a change of scene, and some fresh air, and the comradeship of those you worked with. The housewives, stuck in the camp, had turned it into a kind of talking shop. They painted and sketched; they kept diaries; they put on stage shows and choral concerts; they organised seminars on everything from German military insignia to surrealism to quantum physics. They even paid each other in lager-

160

marken for their performances. It was just another sort of escape, Gary supposed.

And then, too, there were the love affairs. There was a lot more of that than Gary had expected; the stalag queens who painted their faces and dyed their lips with beetroot juice were just the surface. This was what you got, Gary thought, when men could only turn to each other for comfort. Now he watched Willis watching Ben, and he wondered what the truth was between the two of them.

He waited a bit, but seeing he wasn't likely to get a chance to talk to Ben before lights-out he cleared off, went for a piss and to brush his teeth, and made for his own barracks.

When lights-out came Gary was lying in his bunk. He listened as the stalag creaked its way into the night, a crowded ship. The twenty or so men in the room with him snored and sighed; you slept badly, no matter how tired you were, and only a few of them were asleep at any moment. Sometimes during the night you would hear soft sobbing. But there was no bunk-hopping tonight.

The school's old sash windows had been wallpapered over for the blackout, but the paste was cracking now and the paper peeling, so that Gary could see something of the night outside. There was an occasional splash of brilliance as a searchlight beam crossed the face of the building. The noises of the camp continued, the sharp clip of a patrolling guard's boot, a cry as some whackie or other failed to find peace. But as the hours wore on his senses seemed to expand to fill the night, and he could hear the call of an owl, a rumble of distant traffic, the drone of a Messerschmitt patrolling somewhere over Kent.

And tonight there was something new, unfamiliar German voices talking softly, the voices of the SS working through the night. He wondered how many other inmates listened to the same conversations, and how fearful they were.

It was no surprise when the call for an appell came in the middle of the night.

VIII

Few of the men still owned watches, but one man, holding his wrist up to the glare of a searchlight, said it was after three a.m.

The men pulled their way out of their bunks, looking for their trousers and coats and socks and clogs – no boots in the camp, to impede the escapers. Then they clattered down the stairs, bumping in the dark.

Lights blazed in the camp offices, and in the assembly hall, dining hall, gymnasium and other large rooms. On the chill dewy grass of the football field the men lined up behind the senior officers of their own nationalities; as well as British there were Poles, French, Belgian, Dutch, and empire troops like Canadians and New Zealanders. Gary was the only American, as far as he knew, and he stood with the British, as indeed did Ben, somewhere in the dark, a fake American.

The SS, with the Wehrmacht senior officers, walked up and down before the lines, inspecting the men casually. They spoke softly, too quietly for Gary's bits of German to be any use. SBO Danny Adams and the other senior officers were called for a brief conference.

Then the men were formed up into parties. The British, the largest contingent, were split into three, each of about fifty men. Gary dodged around a bit to be sure he was in the same third as Ben. Willis was here too.

A guard called briskly, 'Come!' Gary's group was the first to be led off towards the assembly hall. As the men shuffled forward Gary could smell mouldy greatcoats and the sweet stink of bodies not properly bathed for a year, and he sensed their gathering fear as they were marched around in the middle of the night by the SS.

The men filed into the assembly hall. It was brightly lit. Gary glimpsed a row of trestle tables set up at the head of the hall, before the stage where schoolboys had once received their school colours. SS officers sat in a row behind the tables, black as rooks on a wall. They shuffled piles of paper. There were a few scientist types too, anonymous in white coats, fiddling with bits of equipment. Wehrmacht guards stood around, their rifles to hand, looking as tired and resentful as the prisoners.

At the back of the hall an area had been fenced off by a curtain. The prisoners were led behind this. A couple of guards stood on chairs so they could see over the group. One guard, a brisk and competent hauptmann, clapped his hands. 'Clothes off,' he said. 'Socks too, gentlemen. Make a pile over there. Then three lines.' He made chopping signs. 'One, two three.'

'Come off it, Hauptmann. What about the blessed Geneva Convention?'

'Get on with it, please.' The hauptmann turned away.

'What larks,' Willis Farjeon said.

Grumbling, moving slowly, the men complied. There was muttering. 'Maybe it's just a delousing.'

'No. Bloody SS. They're probably testing some new type of gas on us.'

'They wouldn't do that.'

'Why bloody not? I don't see any Swiss flags out there. No, we're for it, I tell you. Hang onto your bollocks, lads.'

The heap of clothes quickly grew. The men were all much diminished by being stripped like this, their joints like bags of walnuts, their genitals little knots of flesh beneath their flat bellies. No doubt Gary looked just as bad. And Ben, small and skinny anyhow, looked tiny, even boyish in this company.

They formed up into their three lines. Again Gary made sure he was in the same group as Ben. He ended up right in front of him, with Willis behind Ben. Willis winked, grinning.

The curtain was drawn back. The prisoners were marched in their lines up the assembly hall, until the leaders were at the desks manned by the SS officers. Some kind of testing began on them, and Gary saw the flash of cameras.

As the lead blokes were processed the men shuffled forward slowly, naked, humiliated. The bare shoulders of the man in front of Gary were striped with scars, as if at some point he'd been whipped. It all felt unreal to Gary, a strange incongruity of uniforms and weapons and naked prisoners in a school hall, and all in the deepest pit of the night.

He turned and murmured, 'Hans? You all right?'

'Not exactly,' Ben whispered. 'This doesn't look too good, Gary. Not for me.'

'Oh, he'll be all right,' Willis said, right behind Ben. 'I'll give him a stiffening if he needs it.' He placed his hand on the back of Ben's neck, so Ben was made to lean a bit, and he made thrusting gestures with his hips at Ben's buttocks.

Some of the men looked disgusted. Others laughed. 'Hey, you're getting a hard on there, Farjeon.'

'No, that's a Heil Hitler.' More laughter.

Gary swung an arm at Willis's shoulder. 'Get the fuck off him.' A guard stepped closer, pointing his gun warningly. Gary turned away, and Willis backed off. 'Just leave him alone, Willis,' Gary muttered. He's not some doll for you to play with.'

'It's all right, Gary,' Ben said.

'No, it isn't. I'm not sure this asshole is even a faggot. He's just dominating you.'

'Maybe so,' Ben said, a bit more defiant. 'But it's, well, it's the way it is. You know. I need a bit of contact. We all do.'

'Better an abusive relationship than none at all? Is that it?'

'I think you're jealous, Corporal Wooler,' Willis whispered spitefully. 'But of which of us, I wonder?'

Gary got to the head of the queue. As he stood there before the trestle table with his balls hanging out, he was examined by a team of three men, all bespectacled, all deadly serious. He was asked for his name and army serial number and stalag identification number, which he gave, and then he was asked about his family background, where he was born, his parents and grandparents, and that information he refused to give. He was also asked about illnesses, any congenital conditions, whether he had any relatives who were mentally unstable, any schizophrenia, manic depression or morphine addiction or homosexuality. More questions he refused to answer.

The SS officers and scientists were clerkish, making notes, going through files, barely even looking at the man before them. Gary's refusals seemed to make little difference, for they had a fat file on the table before them, each page stamped with his name and number. Though the text was German, he made out what looked to be family trees. And he managed to see, stamped on some of the files and papers, an acronym: RuSHA.

Next he was photographed, his face in front-and-side mugshot style, his body full length front, back and sides. The scientists used colour charts to establish the precise hue of his skin and his eyes. Then his dimensions were measured, his height, chest and weight, the lengths of his limbs and fingers and toes – even, predictably, the length of his cock. With great care callipers were applied to his head. They measured the depth and width of his forehead, the length, breadth and circumference of his cranium, the length of his nose, the width of his mouth, the distance between his ears. All this was noted down. And the scientists conferred, referring to graphs and a file of photographs, a kind of compendium of people types, erect and stoop-shouldered, large- and small-eared, clear-skinned and dark. It was all routine, efficient, a bit like an army medical, though conducted with an earnestness that was both sinister and a bit comic.

When they were done, one of the men actually smiled at him. 'Congratulations, Corporal Wooler. Now please go to table number one, on the stage, for final logging.'

He had to climb up on the stage, still stark naked. Here five small tables labelled one to five sat in a row, each manned by two more scientist types. At table number one, Gary again had to identify himself. The scientists gave him another cursory inspection, before nodding, smiling, and filling in a form replete with ticks.

'So,' Gary said, 'you're going to congratulate me again?'

'We should congratulate your parents, or your grandparents,' one of them said, an older man with a strangulated accent. 'Your cephalic index is seventy-seven. We have classified you as a Pure Nordic type, Corporal.'

'What the hell does that mean?'

'Look in a mirror one day. Your long head, narrow face, flat forehead, narrow lips, tall, slender body. These are the required characteristics. And all this is backed up by your genealogy, of course, which shows a pure ancestry dating back to the time your forefathers emigrated from England. Why, if not for the present unfortunate circumstances, you would be eligible to apply for the Schutzstaffel itself!' It appeared the scientist was making a joke.

Gary glanced along the row at the other tables. On table five, the furthest from this destination of the Pure Nordics, there was an orderly heap of yellow fabric stars.

Gary was dismissed, and, escorted by a guard, allowed to file back down the length of the hall to retrieve his clothes. But there was a commotion. He looked back to his line. Ben Kamen was at the testing desk. The researchers there seemed agitated; they looked up at Ben and flicked through more files. Then one of them cried out, and stabbed his finger at a photograph. He called, 'Standartenfuhrer Trojan! Standartenfuhrer!' Ben shrank back against Willis, but guards rushed forward and grabbed his skinny arms.

'I'll get you out of this, Hans!' Gary yelled. 'I'll get you out!'

But now the guards came to grab him too. The hall erupted into chaos.

IX

23 September

Gary found out that Ben hadn't been returned to his barracks that night of the processing, or the next. And he learned that 'RuSHA' was the Rasse und Siedlungshauptamt der SS, the SS's Race and Settlement Office.

By the Tuesday of that week, after the Sunday night-Monday morning of the SS processing, something was clearly up. The afternoon shift on the monument was cancelled, and the work kommandos brought home. There was a quick appell on the football field, where the stalag commander told them all they must make themselves as 'presentable as possible in the circumstances'. There was even to be hot water all afternoon in the shower block.

Then as the day ended, around six p.m., the prisoners were called out to another appell, lined up behind their senior officers.

Gary tried to avoid Willis Farjeon, but the RAF man worked his way to him as the ranks formed up. 'Evening, Dunkirk Harrier.'

'What's going on, Willis?'

'Not a clue, old chap.'

'And where's Hans Gheldman?'

'Ah. Don't you mean "Ben"? Oh, don't look so shocked. He told me his secrets long ago. We have been close, you know. Well, he's clearly been found out. Jewish, isn't he? That cute little circumcised willy is a bit of a giveaway.'

'I don't know why the SS were looking for him particularly.'

'It is a bit rum, isn't it?' Willis sighed. 'Well, I'll miss him.'

'I ought to rip your fucking head off,' Gary hissed.

Willis blinked. 'Well, that would be your privilege. But I didn't harm him, you know. Oh, I pushed him around. That's my way. But he took it, for that's *his* way. Surely you know him well enough to see that. Submissive type, our Ben! We both got what we wanted, I think. But

166

none of it matters, you know. None of it got in the way of his relationship with you.'

Gary frowned. 'What do you mean?'

Willis eyed him. 'Oh, come, Corporal. It's you he truly loves, poor Ben. Surely you know!'

Gary, shocked, could think of nothing to say.

The senior officers called them to attention. They were swung around and marched out of the camp, maybe two hundred men, most of the stalag's occupants.

They followed the route Gary was driven every day with his kommando to Richborough and the monument site. But tonight they walked the few miles. Trucks topped and tailed the column, armed troopers sitting in the bodies watching the men, and they were escorted by more guards walking alongside them, both Wehrmacht and SS, some with dogs.

The evening was darkling, and the guards had torches. The air felt fresh, the sky cloudy but dry, and Gary thought he could smell the sea.

Joe Stubbs called out, 'How about a song, lads?'

'Pack it in, Stubbsy.'

'"The Huns were hanged, one by one, parley-vous . . ."'

The Germans near Gary looked anxious.

'That's enough, Stubbs,' said the SBO.

'Oh, come on, sir. "The Huns were hanged, one by one, / Every bloody mother's son, inky stinky Hitler too—"'

An SS officer came storming down the line. The marching men stopped in confusion; there were shouts. With a gloved hand the SS man grabbed Stubbs by the hair, dragged him out of the line and made him kneel. He pressed the muzzle of his Luger to Stubbs's temple.

Danny Adams was there immediately. He tried to stand between Stubbs and the German. 'Don't shoot! *Schiessen Sie nicht!*'

The SS man glared at the SBO. Then he raised his Luger and slammed the butt down on the crown of Stubbs's head. There was a crunch, like the shell of a boiled egg cracking. Stubbs crumpled face forward to the ground. Two Wehrmacht guards, regulars from the camp, hurried forward, picked him up and carried him to one of the trucks.

Adams faced the SS man, his face black. 'After the war, Standartenfuhrer Trojan. *Nach dem fucking krieg.*'

The SS man just grinned. He wiped the butt of the Luger on the grass, and holstered it. 'As may be. Tonight – no more of this.'

The SBO turned to his men. 'Let's just get through this ruddy business without any more dramas. Form up. Attention! . . .'

The men, shocked, angry, subdued, marched on into the night.

Gary heard the murmur of the crowd even before they got to Richborough itself. The area inside the old Roman defences was a pool of light, illuminated by searchlights; in the shadows generators chugged. Somewhere off in the glare a band played, some sentimental German waltz.

The prisoners with their escort were marched to one corner of the compound. Other groups had already formed up in the space around the monument; Gary saw units of the Wehrmacht, Luftwaffe and SS, including a group with the distinctive armbands of the Legion of St George, the British element of the SS. There were even formations of the Landwacht and the Hitler Jugend, all standing proudly under Nazi banners. The flag of Albion flew, the cross of Saint George with a swastika roundel at the centre.

The centrepiece of it all was the monument. Only a fraction of it had been completed, but tonight immense Nazi flags had been draped from the scaffolding. Powerful searchlights had been set up in a ring around the base of the four legs, so that their beams made an arch of light in the sky, a dream of the finished monument that might one day exist.

Now more spotlights picked out a limousine, a Rolls Royce, gliding into the compound. SS troopers jogged alongside, automatic arms ready. The band hurriedly switched to an SS marching song. A ripple of excitement passed through the massed ranks.

'Who the fuck?' the British murmured.

An SS officer stood before the stalag prisoners, and began calling names. As they were called, men stepped forward. Gary was shocked to hear his own name called.

'Wooler. Corporal Wooler, G. Step forward, please.' A man nudged Gary in the back, and he stepped out of the line.

He found himself posted to a row of maybe a dozen others – one of them Willis Farjeon. The SS man and the SBO stood before them, the SBO sombre and angry, the SS man grinning. He was the same man who had clubbed Stubbs earlier, Gary saw.

Willis said out of the corner of his mouth, 'Quite a show, eh?'

The SS man overheard, and stepped over. Willis was taller than he was, and the SS man had to look up. 'Oh, better than that,' he said in fair English. 'Wait and see! What a treat is in store for you fellows!'

Danny Adams said, 'I'd appreciate it if you'd speak to my men through me, Standartenfuhrer Trojan.'

'Yes, yes,' Trojan said dismissively.

The limousine had pulled up at the base of the monument. A trooper opened the passenger door. Various senior officers approached the new arrival, saluting him.

And then the newcomer came walking towards the British prisoners. Standartenfuhrer Trojan stood erect before the line of Gary and the others, and pulled his jacket straight. He looked immensely proud. Yet the man approaching was not prepossessing, despite the gaudy medals he wore. His body looked weak, his feet were pigeon-toed, his face round, his hair dark, his chin receding. He wore heavy round glasses that emphasised the softness of his face.

Willis murmured, 'That's the Reichsfuhrer-SS. That's bloody Himmler. What's he doing here? No wonder these SS thugs look so pleased with themselves, Himmler himself coming all the way to this shithole.'

Himmler, trailed by his entourage, shook hands with Trojan, who bowed, beaming. He waved his gloved hand to indicate the row of prisoners, and spoke rapidly in German. Willis murmured a hasty translation. '"A great honour Reichsfuhrer, welcome to our poor effort at a monument Reichsfuhrer, and blah blah, let me kiss your arse Reichsfuhrer ..."'

'How do you know German, Farjeon?'

'Learned it when I joined the RAF. Useful if I ever got shot down, I thought. Wait ... "Here are the men we have selected from among the Prominente prisoners for the Fountain of Life programme."'

'"Fountain of Life"?'

'The word is *Lebensborn*. Fine Nordic types all, says Trojan! That's us, I guess. Bloody hell. Good Aryan stock!'

'I don't want to be "good Aryan stock",' Gary murmured.

'Don't think you have a choice right now, old boy,' said Willis. 'And as we're standing ten feet from the Reichsfuhrer I'd advise you to hold your peace ... We're to be a symbol of the unity of Nordic races globally, and a demonstration of the theory that Nordic qualities rise to the top, even among prisoners and other riffraff ... Now he's saying something else. Can't quite get it. Something about a loom? A tapestry? That Standartenfuhrer – Trojan? – says he's finally tracked down the one missing component, and the weapon that will cement Aryan supremacy for all future and all past is at hand ... Even for the Nazis this sounds a lot of guff. But look at old Himmler's piggy eyes gleaming behind those glasses. Whatever this rubbish is, he loves it.'

'What component?'

'Him, I think,' said Willis.

Two beefy SS guards dragged forward Ben Kamen. He stood trembling before a laughing Himmler.

X

Mary woke up to music from the Promi. The Nazi propaganda station was proving a furtive hit, even in free England. The announcer said that today was Hastings Day, yet another of the Nazis' endless memorials – and another day off for the lucky denizens of the protectorate. Lying in bed, Mary wondered if Gary was allowed to listen to the Promi.

Reluctantly she got up, to start another day without her son. But she had a faint hope that today might bring her that little bit closer to him.

Her journey to Birdoswald on this October Tuesday, organised by Tom Mackie, was hopefully going to be relatively civilised. A WAAF driver picked her up from her lodgings in Colchester to drive her all the way to Cambridge, where she would take the main east coast train line up to Newcastle. And from there she would be driven further, along the line of Hadrian's Wall to Birdoswald, where Mackie had his office.

The car journey itself was a novelty. You hardly drove anywhere these days, such was the shortage of fuel. They passed lorries and a few packed buses in Colchester itself, but in the open country they saw few vehicles. There were plenty of road blocks though, barriers and barbed wire and pillboxes, manned by nervous-looking Home Guard types. After ten miles or so the WAAF had to stop to show her identification. She took it cheerfully. 'More Home Guard on the road than traffic these days!' she said brightly to Mary. She was rather jolly-hockey-sticks, very English.

And as they set off again a squadron of planes, perhaps Hurricanes, came screaming overhead, flying low, heading south.

Mary was oddly reluctant to leave Colchester, even for a couple of days. It was hardly a comfortable place; nowhere in England was, she imagined. But she was able to carry on her researches here, and she had her duties in the WVS, though they were less demanding now the bombing was reduced. And, only fifty miles or so from Gravesend, she was close to the Winston Line, the dreadful barrier that had cut the country in two, and so about as close as she could get to Gary.

But for the best part of a year she had been badgering Captain Mackie of MI-14 for an interview on the subject of Ben Kamen and his historical conundrums. She had come across Mackie when he sent her a letter after the invasion, offering his sympathy about Gary, whom he had met in those final hours before the cease-fire. It had occurred to her to write back, for Mackie's MI-14 seemed precisely the sort of organisation that might take seriously the mysteries she was uncovering, and figure out what to do about them. She could hardly be reluctant about taking up Mackie's invitation now, even if it did mean she would have to travel to the other end of the country.

She was nervous, though, about the hints of urgency in Mackie's note. Something had changed, and she doubted it was for the better.

The station at Cambridge was crowded. This was now the terminus of the east coast rail lines, King's Cross in London having been abandoned – indeed blown up, it was said, like the capital's other main-line stations. There were a few service personnel on the move from one posting to another, but mostly the crowds were a seepage of refugees from London, a flow still continuing after a year, women and children, old people and invalids, supervised by police and ARP wardens, all waiting for a train to the north.

The WAAF saw Mary to her compartment, making sure her reserved seat had not been taken. Mary would have to share with a mother and her three children, and a couple of older men. The children seemed happy enough, plump little creatures dressed in layers of clothing, each with a colourful gas-mask satchel in the rack above. To them this was an adventure, a day off school. They squealed as the locomotive chuffed into life, and clouds of steam billowed back the length of the train. They made Mary smile.

But the journey seemed long and slow, the overcrowded train hot. Mary peered out, trying to distract herself with a view of a country in the middle of its long war.

Close to London the autumn fields were littered with burned-out vehicles and wire loops, protection against paratrooper or glider landings. The Home Guard manned pillboxes and trenches at every junction and bridge and level crossing, waiting to destroy the rail line in case the Germans should start advancing again. There was a logic to the defence, with stop lines running parallel to the coasts in case the Germans attempted any secondary landings, and other lines cutting across the country to impede any advance out of the protectorate. But Mary felt nervous at the thought of the heaps of mines and explosives the train must be passing through.

In the stations where they stopped there were lots of uniforms, of the conventional services of Britain, the Commonwealth and the US, and of Britain's vast volunteer armies, like Mary's own WVS. Mary didn't like the transformation of Britain into a country of uniforms. It was as if the German way of thinking had infected everybody, as if the Germans had already won.

And the towns were scarred by the war. Though repair work was underway, you could see gaps in the terraced streets, holes colonised by weeds rather than people. There were defensive emplacements everywhere, anti-aircraft guns and barrage balloons. And factories were hastily being erected, relocated from London and the south. There was plenty of labour to do all this work; all of England's major towns had taken refugees from London, homeless and unemployed.

Outside the counties of the protectorate itself, it was the capital that had suffered most severely from the invasion. London was in English hands, but, bombed and oppressively threatened, it was slowly bleeding to death. Its people and factories were being shipped out, its docks barricaded or blown up, and its many state functions transplanted elsewhere: York was now the seat of government, Manchester was Britain's financial centre, the royal family had migrated to Holyrood in Edinburgh, and the seat of the Church of England had been moved to Liverpool. London's museums and galleries had been stripped, their precious contents scattered and hidden. The city itself was turning into an abandoned museum, with only its immovable architectural treasures remaining.

There were some commentators who said that London might never recover from this cruel shutting-down – George Orwell, for instance. 'Oh yes it will,' Mary had heard the old crusties say in the Colchester pubs. 'We'll ship the Cockney buggers back ourselves.'

So the journey passed. Everybody was quiet, save for the children. Mary thought she understood why people were subdued. All the adults in the carriage faced an uncertain future. And everybody in England had lost somebody in the war, even Mary, who didn't belong here at all.

It was a relief when the train pulled into Newcastle, and she was able to leave the stuffy compartment, to find another perky WAAF waiting for her on the platform.

XI

15 October

Wednesday morning at Birdoswald was clean and sharp, the start of a bright fall day. Tom Mackie had requisitioned the farmhouse here to serve as his base of operations, he told Mary as he welcomed her from her hotel. But as he escorted her around the site, Mary saw how the farmhouse nestled at the heart of much older ruins, the remains of a Roman fort set on a bluff of high ground.

'I can see why the Romans came here,' she said.

'Oh, yes, a military man would make the same decision again. Birdoswald – actually they called it Banna – was an integral part of the system of defence based around Hadrian's Wall. Housed a thousand troops at its peak. Seems they had to drain the land, clear a forest, and import the limestone to build it. Kept the peace for three hundred years – which, if you think about it, is longer than modern Britain has existed, since the Act of Union. We'll be doing well if we last so long, eh?'

They walked back to the farmhouse. 'Rather ugly, isn't it?' Its most recent renovation was Victorian. The architects had added crenellations, amid a general look that Mary thought of as 'Gothicised'. 'But they reused Roman stone. I can show you an altar of Jupiter that's been built into the wall of a stable. And there's evidence of occupation of the site *before* the Romans ... But I apologise,' he said.

'For what?'

'For treading on your toes. You're the historian, after all.'

'Not at all, Captain. I'm impressed you know so much.'

'Well, history's always been something of a hobby of mine. I took nat sci at Cambridge – that is, natural sciences, specialising in physics. But I did do rather well at history at my school matriculation. And I've been somewhat keen to find out more about the history of this place since your researches directed me here.'

Something of a hobby. Somewhat keen. After so long in Britain Mary was used to decoding the circumlocutory language of upper-crust types like this Captain Mackie: the more self-deprecating the words, the deeper the passion. 'I'm flattered you took me so seriously. To open up a new Military Intelligence branch here, all on my say-so.'

'Well, this does seem to be a pivotal site for your anachronistic conspiracy theories, doesn't it? And it wasn't all that hard to get the funding, actually, at least for intelligence work. For one thing there's been a general withdrawal from the south-east, as you can imagine. Sites like Bletchley Park are suddenly a lot more vulnerable.'

'Bletchley Park? Where's that? What are they up to there?'

'Oh, you know, war work, the usual. I worked there for a bit myself. And as for the project we're engaged in here, well, the threat you've hinted at seems rather bizarre, but the country is awash with rumours about Hitler's super-weapons. A Nazi time machine isn't even top of the league table of outlandishness, believe it or not. If only for the sake of morale, the government must be seen to be making an effort to investigate all these threats, and, if necessary, put a stop to them. And you do have a certain notoriety in government, Mrs Wooler, thanks to your pieces on Peter's Well. I actually have some quite high-level support. I've a line to Frederick Lindemann, Churchill's personal science advisor. Winston calls him "Prof".

'But even so I do have to compete for funding. Even now, as things seem to be moving towards a certain denouement, I'm desperately short of anything resembling solid evidence to show my superiors. One reason I wanted to talk to you today.'

'What kind of "denouement"?'

'All will be revealed.' He extended his arm and escorted her indoors. 'But first, Mrs Wooler, let me offer you a coffee – generously supplied by your own government as it happens . . .'

'If you're making me coffee, you can call me Mary.'

He smiled. 'And I'm Tom.'

Mackie had set up his office in the farmhouse kitchen; it was by far the best room in the building, he said, and the warmest in winter. The most striking feature was a spear of blackened wood and heavily rusted iron, suspended on the wall over the fireplace. Mary was no expert on the period, but it looked Roman to her.

They sat at a big scuffed wooden table, over which generations must have broken bread together, and spoke of the mysteries of space and time.

He folded his arms. 'Let's start from the beginning. You developed your interest in all this because of your contact with this Austrian fellow, Benjamin Kamen.'

'It was at the time of the invasion.'

'Yes. He was picked up as a prisoner during those eventful days. We believe he was taken at first to a POW camp in Kent. Place near Richborough, on the coast.'

'That's where my Gary is,' she said in a rush.

'Yes, we know,' he said, not unkindly. 'May not be a coincidence; a lot of their more "valuable" prisoners seem to be held there – and that includes Gary, an American citizen. We actually have some intelligence that Gary protected Ben – helped him conceal his racial identity.'

Mary wondered: *helped?* Why the past tense? Had something changed, for Ben or Gary?

Mackie went on, 'Now, your encounter with Kamen set you off on an historical investigation. But once you tipped me off I followed the chap's career from a different direction. Before the war he was, in fact, a promising young physicist ... Bags I go first about all that, and then you can tell me about the history.' He grinned at her. 'You know, I think I'll enjoy this. All rather a jolly game, isn't it?'

She studied him. 'My son is in a POW camp, and I haven't seen him for a year. I lost my daughter-in-law to an SS killer squad. I've followed up this crazy stuff to keep myself busy, this and my WVS work and my bits of journalism. Better than sitting around on my ass while the bombs fall. But a game, it isn't.'

'Sorry. No. Quite right. It's just, you know ...' He sighed. 'Shut up, Tom. Now – Ben Kamen. Nine or ten years ago he worked in Vienna, as a student of a man called Kurt Gödel. I don't suppose you've heard of him.'

'Only in connection with Ben,' Mary said.

'Eventually Kamen made his way to Princeton, the Institute of Advanced Studies, where he met up again with his old mentor Gödel. Who by this time was working with Einstein himself.' Mackie pulled a pipe out of his breast pocket, dug a tobacco pouch from a drawer in the table, and began to fill the bowl meticulously, strand by strand. 'Remarkable chap, actually. Gödel, I mean. One of the top mathematicians of his generation. And Kamen must have been pretty sharp to keep up with him. He was very young.

'Now, Einstein's theories are physical. They concern the nature of space and time, the structure of the universe, that sort of show. But they are couched in mathematics, and when it comes to maths Gödel has a peculiar forte. He is a master of doubt, you might say. He studies formal systems, that is mathematical theories, and niggles away at them until he finds inconsistencies. His most famous result is a proof that even simple arithmetic – you know, just adding and subtracting – can contain a statement you can neither say is true nor false. And so arithmetic, and by implication all of mathematics, can never be made complete and decidable.'

'You're already losing me,' Mary admitted.

'All right. Think of it in terms of a set of laws. No matter how wise your law-making, there will always be cases that can't be decided within that framework. What you have to do, of course, is add another ruling. But that shows that the law can never be made complete. That's not surprising to anybody who's come up against a county magistrate, such as myself.

'But what Gödel did was to find a worm of doubt in mathematics itself, at the heart of what seems the most abstract and logical of all our intellectual pursuits. Even simple arithmetic can never be made complete. I mean, this doesn't stop maths *working*, from day to day; but we know there will always be limits to what we can say about it. There is a gap between our intuition and the truth about mathematics, you see. And having dropped that bomb, Gödel turned his attention to Einstein ...'

As he studied relativity, Gödel became concerned about another gap between intuition and theory, concerning the nature of time.

'We know Gödel read thinkers like Plato and Heidegger. Following them, he thought carefully about our inner experience of time.' He studied her. 'Our intuition is that only the present is real. Yes? Here we are in this farmhouse, as moment after moment ticks by. The future is only potential, undecided; it will emerge from the moment, but does not yet exist. The past too is gone for ever, leaving only traces, just as the long-gone Romans left their footprints here at Birdoswald. So time is like a fabric, built up strand by strand, each new strand coming into existence to be laid over the last.'

'Time's tapestry,' she said, thinking of Geoffrey Cotesford's phrasing.

'Well, quite. That's how time *feels*. Unfortunately that isn't how relativity describes time at all ...'

In relativity there was *no* global time, no single instant that spanned the universe to unite all observers. Instead there were only 'events', points swimming disconnected around a graph of space-time. 'It's all to do with the speed of light. It would be, wouldn't it? And without a global time there *can't* be a common present, coming into existence across the universe for all of us. Relativity is a very well established theory. And yet the time it describes seems to have nothing to do with inner time, time as we experience it.'

'I think I see,' she said.

'You're being very brave, Mary, but you're not fooling me! Now Gödel isn't the only one troubled by this stuff. Some physicists, such as James Jeans, have argued that perhaps there *is* a universal time after all, a cosmic time based on the expansion of the universe, or perhaps the mean motion of matter within it. You see? Some feature of the universe on which all observers could agree, whatever their state of motion.

'But that seemed a bit arbitrary to Gödel; *he* wasn't reassured. So he – and we think in collaboration with Kamen – dug into Einstein's mathematics. I admit I'm winging it a bit here; Gödel hasn't actually written up his results formally, and until he does we're all a bit in the dark. But what he seems to be trying to do is to find a description of a possible universe, consistent with Einstein, in which there could be *no* cosmic time.'

'And he's found one.'

'I'm afraid so. He says that if the universe rotated, in a grand and global way, it would be possible for me to fly around it in some super Spitfire – heading off into the future, but at last arriving in the past.'

'So time travel would be possible in such a universe.'

'Well, that's the implication you and I would naturally draw. I think Gödel, however, doesn't care about time travel. He's a logician; he's simply trying to establish a contradiction. For you see if there is no global time in his model universe, you can't assume a global time exists in *ours*, for there is no difference in principle between the universes. And so our sense of inner time, our most basic apprehension of the universe, is actually an illusion.' His eyes were unfocused. 'Must say that when I lie awake at night, this sort of stuff scares me more than all the Panzers in Germany. Poor old Gödel.'

'But what we have to be concerned about,' Mary said, 'is the practical application.'

'Quite.' He tinkered with his pipe, tucking the last strands of his precious tobacco into place, and lit it. She'd observed this sort of finicky fiddling in smokers ever since tobacco had gone on the ration. He blew smoke up towards the ceiling. 'Now we must come back to Ben Kamen again – and having led you off into the depths of time and space, I'm going to ask you to take another leap in the dark. For at Princeton Ben developed yet another new set of ideas, with a student called Rory O'Malley ...

'Look, Gödel's theory suggests that a path might exist between present and past – between this room, say, and the Roman fort of AD 200 from whose ruins it was built. The question is, how do you find your way along that path? Have you ever heard of a writer called John William Dunne?'

'I think so,' Mary said. 'Something to do with J.B. Priestley?'

Dunne was British, an aeronautical designer. He had served as a soldier, and was invalided out of the Boer war. He had become interested in the perception of time, having had, he believed, a glimpse of the future through a dream.

Mackie waved a hand, a bit dismissively. 'Sort of half-baked stuff that becomes fashionable from time to time in certain arty circles, playwrights and novelists and that sort of crew. That's why you connect him with Priestley, I imagine. But what gives Dunne's work credibility is a patina of science. He was an engineer. So he is methodical even about his dreams; he derives statistics about them; he couches his ideas in language that sounds almost Einsteinian. Dunne says essentially that when we sleep we come untethered in time. He imagines time as an extra dimension, a landscape you can go exploring. Some remember what they see during their dream journeys, some don't. And some may be able to *direct* where their dreaming selves travel.'

It felt very strange to Mary to hear these ideas expressed by a serious middle-aged man in a sober Navy uniform.

Mackie ploughed on, 'It was Rory O'Malley who introduced these ideas of Dunne's to Ben Kamen. Now, Ben may have such a facility, this "dream precognition". Or he may not – interestingly he seems to deny it himself.' He looked at her. 'Perhaps you can see where I'm going with this.'

She nodded. 'If you put it together – Gödel shows that paths from the present to the past may exist. And Dunne argues that it might be possible to explore such paths.'

'To dream yourself from present to past – and perhaps to do a bit of mucking about when you get there. We don't think it would be possible with this method to *travel* to the past, but you could perhaps send back information – perhaps in the form of a dream or a vision implanted in another wandering soul.'

Which, she reflected with growing excitement and dread, was exactly how many of the historical 'deflections' in the testimony of Geoffrey Cotesford were supposed to have originated.

'But it would take a Ben Kamen to do it, perhaps,' Mackie said. 'A man who has, or may have, both this peculiar precognitive facility, *and* the brains to understand Gödel's mathematical solutions.' Mackie smiled. 'It's a wonderful idea, isn't it, to be able to run around in future and past, as freely as one runs as a child loose in a meadow of grass?'

'Wonderful, yes,' Mary said. 'But is it true?'

'We have reason to believe the Nazis take it seriously. Indeed they killed for it.'

Mary was shocked. 'Who was responsible?'

'Actually not a German. A British woman called Julia Fiveash. Holds a rank in the SS. Took part in the invasion – on the German side.'

'I know,' Mary said. 'I met her.'

'Did you, by God?' Mackie listened as she told him the story of how she had run into Fiveash at Battle, with her accomplice Josef Trojan. 'Well, that could be useful. Very nasty piece of work, that young lady. And now,' he said, 'we believe they are at a Nazi research centre at Richborough. And that's where they've taken Ben. He managed to hide away in the POW camp for the best part of a year, it seems. But at last they flushed him out.'

'And that's why you say the situation is becoming urgent – why you contacted me now.'

'Yes. For, you see, if they have Ben, they may have everything they need to make their wretched scheme work – if there's anything in it at all.' He stood up, holding his pipe. 'I feel a bit stale, do you? I could do with a walk, I think. And there's something else I should show you of what we're doing here ...'

He led her to what appeared to be a converted barn; it was stone-built, and she wondered if this was the building with the Roman god built into its wall, but Mackie didn't mention it. Inside, the barn seemed to have been converted into a workshop, the walls panelled with white-washed wood, and a bright light glowed from bulbs suspended from the ceiling; Mary surmised the fort must have its own generator, for no mains electricity bulb burned so bright these days. 'We do try to keep this place clean,' murmured Mackie. 'All the small parts, you know ...'

The centrepiece of the room was a table bearing an elaborate mechanical device, a rectangular array screwed together from fine strips of green-painted metal, with tiny pulleys and gears and motors and threads of string – and, in one corner, two discs of what looked like ground glass. Elaborate graphs had been prepared on drafting tables, set up under the lights for visibility. It was all very complicated, but toy-like, like a model of something else rather than anything significant in itself. But it was being taken very seriously, Mary realised. Around the walls were shelves bearing spare parts, and racks of tiny screwdrivers and spanners.

Mackie asked, 'Any idea what you're looking at?'

Mary shrugged. 'Some kind of game?'

'Not exactly, but you're close. Mary, we live in a mathematical age – indeed, this is a mathematical war. And we need new mathematical techniques to cope with it all. There is a class of analyses based on differential equations, which—'

'Please, Captain. Gödel and his undecidability are enough for me for one day.'

'Quite so. Look – let's suppose you want to compute the trajectory of a shell from a new breed of gun. Very necessary for firing tables, as you can imagine. Now you can list the impulse of the propellant, the angle of the barrel, gravity, air resistance and so forth. But to work out how the shell will fly you must put all that together, step by step, mapping the trajectory as a whole.'

'And that's what this thing does, right?'

'We call it a differential analyser. It's a sort of mechanical brain, if you will. You can input your requirements by using this stylus – you see, you manually push it along the curves, here. The motion is transmitted through these levers and gears and so forth to the glass discs; roughly speaking the spinning of those discs is a model of the variables of interest – I mean, the numbers that describe the shell trajectory, or whatever.'

'All right. So what's it doing here?'

'Well, Einstein's equations of general relativity are just another example of a set of differential equations. It's fiendishly difficult to extract any kind of analytical solution from them. And if you do need to extract solutions of Gödel's kind, describing trajectories from present to past—'

'Oh. You'd need a machine like this.'

'We know that Kamen and O'Malley had access to an analyser in Princeton. And we believe, though we aren't sure, that Fiveash and her Nazi companions are building such a device at Richborough. We, or the mathematical boffins I recruited to work on this, thought we should study Gödel's solutions ourselves, if we were to try to make sense of it all. Hence the beast you see before you.'

'Kind of Rube Goldberg, isn't it?' Mary longed to touch the gadget, to pull the little levers and turn the pulleys. 'Did you have to get these teeny tiny parts specially made?'

'Actually no. They come from a kit called Meccano.'

'A kit?'

'A construction kit for boys.'

'A *toy*? You made your calculating machine from a toy?'

He coughed. 'Rather embarrassing to have to admit that to an American – but, yes, afraid so. Rather British, don't you think? Of course it will make it all the more satisfying if we were to beat the bad guys with it.' He rubbed his hands together. 'Let's go back to the office, and you can tell me all about the history you've dug up.'

XII

Back in Mackie's kitchen-study she opened her briefcase and spread the contents over the table.

'It begins again with Ben Kamen. When he arrived in England he did a bit of research himself – he is a bright boy – and came up with a medieval study of historical anomalies.'

'You're kidding.'

'Nope. He got to know Gary, and found out that his mother was a specialist in the period, and as soon as he met me he got me started on it.'

Kamen had found a memoir by a fifteenth-century monk called Geoffrey Cotesford. She raised a scrap of paper and read out: '"Time's Tapestry: As mapped by myself," that is Cotesford. "In which the long warp threads are the history of the whole world; and the wefts which run from selvedge to selvedge are distortions of that history, deflected by a Weaver unknown; be he human, divine or satanic . . ."'

'Deflections of history,' murmured Mackie.

'Yes. Suggestive, isn't it? Cotesford believed he had lived through one such attempted deflection himself, and had been made aware of others. He did some research – he was a Franciscan monk, a scholar, and he knew what he was doing. Plus he had access to sources, such as from the Muslim libraries in Spain, which have now been lost to us. This is a sound piece of work, considering.

'In all he found evidence of *six* deflections. He went right back to a prophecy supposedly intoned right here at Birdoswald by a Briton some decades before the Roman invasion of the country. It's called the Prophecy of Nectovelin. That's the one I've concentrated on first. Nectovelin itself is lost, at least the original. But Geoffrey was able to find extracts from it, in an old Moorish library in Toledo. Just a few lines – here.' She passed him a paper.

Mackie read:

Ah child! Bound in time's tapestry, and yet you are born free
Come, let me sing to you of what there is and what will be,
Of all men and all gods, and of the mighty emperors three . . .

'We don't know how much was lost, and how much has been garbled in the repeated transcriptions. We don't even know the purpose of the deflection, if it was a deflection. Geoffrey speculated it had something to do with the Emperor Constantine.'

'Constantine? He was centuries later. What's he got to do with the price of fish?' He glanced down the lines again.

Remember this: We hold these truths self-evident to be –
I say to you that all men are created equal, free
Rights inalienable assuréd by the Maker's attribute
Endowed with Life and Liberty and Happiness' pursuit.
O child! thou tapestried in time, strike home! Strike at the root!

Hmm. I'm blowed if that doesn't sound familiar.'

She smiled. 'An American would recognise the reference straight away.'

'Ah. Let me see if I can remember. "We hold these truths to be self-evident, that all men are created equal, that they are endowed by their Creator with certain unalienable Rights, that among these are Life, Liberty and the pursuit of Happiness." The Declaration of Independence.'

'Right—'

'Good Lord.' The implications seemed to hit him then, and he sat silently for a heartbeat. 'I think I'm going to have something eke to keep me awake at night, apart from Gödel's banishment of time . . . So a modern figure sent this back to pre-Roman Britain? Why? To establish democratic values back in the Iron Age?'

'Maybe. But, Tom, the important question is not why but who.'

'Ben's friend Rory O'Malley, perhaps.'

'Yes. O'Malley was an idealistic Irishman who was a great admirer of the US. *And* he was a lapsed Catholic. He had grown up amid a lot of religious sectarian tension. In the US, before he went to Spain, where he met Ben, he wrote a whole series of articles attacking the Church's oppressive nature, and the evils done in the name of organised religion.'

'Hmm. Wasn't Constantine responsible for the establishment of Christianity as the Roman state religion?'

'He was indeed. You can see there's a tenuous case to be made that

182

the Nectovelin document was authored by O'Malley, in order to deflect Constantine's establishment of the Church. He even sent it back to 4BC, the year Christ was born, to establish the link with Christianity.'

'But O'Malley is dead. And if there was ever a record of any material he tried to transmit to the past, that's lost too. We've had agents go over everything O'Malley left behind at Princeton. Like all Nazis, Julia Fiveash is nothing if not thorough ...' Mackie snapped his fingers. 'But then there's Kamen. If Rory used him he ought to know what was sent.'

'Yes,' Mary said. 'Precisely. Ben knew what had been crammed into his head. And it was following up *that* that led him to Geoffrey Cotesford's research.'

'Well, well. So we've another reason to get hold of this young man, if we can.'

'I do wish we had a more complete copy of the Prophecy,' Mary said. 'There could be more internal evidence. For instance, an acrostic.'

'A what?'

'A feature that appealed to classical and medieval scholars. You take the first letter of each line, or the last maybe, and put them together to make a new word or phrase. But this document isn't nearly complete enough to tell ...'

He fingered the papers. So what else did your chum Geoffrey dig up?'

'A lot of material. I'm still exploring it. Not all of it may be relevant. But I think this is.' She produced another document, another prophecy. It was in Old English, with a modern translation. It was called the Menologium of Isolde. 'It's reasonably complete.'

Mackie read a bit.

> *These the Great Years / of the Comet of God*
> *Whose awe and beauty / in the roof of the world*
> *Lights step by step the / road to empire ...*

'Who was Isolde?'

'Apparently a relation of Nectovelin, generations later. The family link may be significant – an inherited susceptibility.'

'And what is a Menologium?'

'A kind of medieval calendar. According to Geoffrey this is another product of Birdoswald, this one produced some time towards the end of the Roman period, the early fifth century. You can see it is organised around the return of a comet to the skies, every seventy or eighty years. It traces through events fated to occur in these years – I've made guesses about some of them. And, it's a little tricky, but you can reconstruct the dates by adding up these "months of the Great Years". And they match to the events they describe – the Vikings sacking Lindisfarne, a terrible fire in Rome.' She paused for effect. 'The ninth verse seems to relate to the year 1066.'

He was startled, and he laughed. '1066? Harold and the Normans, and all of that? Well, you've come on an appropriate day to talk about it, haven't you? And – wait a minute – didn't a comet turn up in that year and frighten everybody to death?'

'So it did. It was Halley's comet. It returns on average every seventy-six years. But the intervals differ a bit each time.'

'Should think they would,' he muttered. 'Deflections by the planets' gravity and so forth ...' He ran his finger down the text of the Men-ologium. 'Don't tell me. The dates of these verses map onto what the astronomers say about Halley's returns.'

'As far as I can tell. But if the text did originate in the fifth century – look, Halley's motion is well understood now, but it wasn't in 1066, or any time earlier. A fifth-century author couldn't have known these dates.'

'Well, well, well. And you think this has something to do with our German chums?'

'Look at the Epilogue.'

He glanced down and read:

> Across ocean to east / and ocean to west
> Men of new Rome sail / from the womb of the boar.
> Empire of Aryans / blood pure from the north.
> New world of the strong / a ten-thousand year rule.

'Well, bugger me sideways.'

'That crucial word "Aryan" – it comes from a bit of Latin in with the Old English, "Imperium Aryanes" ... I'm still working on the inter-pretation of the rest of it, but—'

'So the suggestion this time is that some Nazi has sent this back – perhaps to deflect the events of 1066? – in order, somehow, to establish an Aryan empire, a thousand years earlier.'

'Something like that.' She didn't feel confident enough to tell him of Josef Trojan's boasting at Battle of putting right the defeat of Harold Godwineson. 'The suggestion is that the English King Harold should have made peace with the Danish invaders, and cooperated with them to drive out the Normans. If he had, all subsequent history might have been different. But he didn't take the advice, evidently.'

'Well, it's completely bonkers. But Himmler would love it, wouldn't he?' Mackie laughed, and laced his fingers behind his head and lay back in his chair. 'Funny – the second time we've come across evidence that somebody is tampering with history seems a lot less startling than the first, doesn't it? The mind can get used to anything, I suppose. Well, we're getting somewhere, aren't we, Mary? The question is what we do about it. I believe the objective is clear: we get into Richborough, we find out what these beggars are up to, disrupt it if we can – and we bring Ben Kamen out.'

Mary said, 'You keep saying "we".'

He smiled. 'You spotted that. I think I'm having a bit of a brain wave. Look here, Mary, suddenly you're a jolly useful asset. The fact is, a citizen of a neutral country has a much better chance of passing through the Winston Line, and of travelling reasonably freely once he or she is in the protectorate itself. And we do believe Kamen was held in the same camp as your son, at Richborough. So you have a reason to go to that part of the world, don't you?'

Mary tried to imagine such a journey, coming so close to Gary a full year after seeing him, and all for a lie.

'But even if you do make it to Richborough, you'll need some reason to get close to Fiveash and Trojan and their Ahnenerbe loonies. You say you've met them, but you're a bit notorious among the Nazis because of your piece on the Peter's Well incident. We need something for you to bluff your way in with. Hmm. I expect we'll come up with something.' He glanced at the Roman spear on the wall behind him. 'We have some thinking to do. Come! Shall we walk again?'

She stood. 'A restless type, aren't you?'

'Spent too long on ships to waste the opportunity to stretch my legs ... Do bring your papers with you.'

XIII

They walked across the heart of the Roman camp, heading south. The sun had climbed, but there was scattered cloud around and a bit of dampness in the air. It felt autumnal, in that lovely English word. As they walked he glanced over her papers and scribbled with a stub of pencil on a notepad.

At the camp's southern perimeter the land fell away spectacularly to reveal a river wending through its valley, and a folded landscape beyond. 'On a good day you can make out the hills of the Lake District,' Mackie said. 'Bit too murky today. Autumn mist and whatnot.'

'I wonder if the Germans will ever come this far, if you will have to build pillboxes and barbed wire fences into the line of Hadrian's Wall.'

'Let's hope not, but I suppose it's a possibility. Or on the other hand we might just push them back into the sea where they came from.'

'History really is fragile, isn't it? So many possibilities for the future open out from this very moment, from the position of the war.'

'Well, that's true,' he said. 'But I can tell you that makes it tricky for *us*. Everything is poised. You Americans are supporting us, but you're not yet in the war, despite Churchill's best efforts to persuade you. And there is a real risk of defeat, you know. History doesn't seem to be on our side. I mean, if you look at the global picture, you have these dreadful totalitarian empires, the German and Japanese and Italian, just gobbling up the world. It's quite possible that if Hitler ever did plant a swastika on the Wall, it would be a long time before we could get rid of him. It took centuries for the Christians to kick the Moors out of Spain, didn't it? Rudolf Hess is in York, you know, Hitler's deputy, negotiating away about an armistice. There are many in the British establishment who want to listen to him – and many more, believe me, who sympathise with Hitler's global war aims, who fear and loathe Bolshevism more even than the Nazis.'

'And all this shapes your thinking about our options.'

186

'Quite. We must avoid provoking the military government in the protectorate overmuch; we may after all choose to sign that armistice. And on the other hand we have to try to keep the Americans onside. It's dashed tricky all round. We must be discreet. No parties must be overly alarmed. It will have to be a covert operation, put down to a random act by the auxiliaries, perhaps. We may even be disowned by the government if we get caught.' Even as he spoke he was still doodling on his pad. 'But look, as I say, this is all speculative unless I can get backing from my highers-up, and for that we need some clear *proof* that this material came from the present – proof that we aren't the subject of some hoax, or misunderstanding. I have to tell you that not all the experts I've consulted are finding in our favour.' He dug a scrap of paper out of his pocket. 'Thought you might like to see this.'

It was a letter written in a neat but wavering hand. She read, 'Like Mr Dunne, I fear you have taken my playful description of duration as a dimension of space far too seriously . . .'

'I did hope the old boy would be a bit more supportive; he still has an audience in the government.' His eyes were unfocused, his thoughts chasing.

Mary was mystified. 'Who?'

Mackie came back to himself. 'Oh! Sorry. H.G. Wells. Wrote to him; thought he was worth a try. What we need is proof, just a grain of it.'

'What is it you're scribbling?'

'I'm just intrigued by what you said about acrostics. This Menologium is a lot more complete than the Nectovelin prophecy, and I wondered if I could make something of it.'

'I tried that. Actually it works with the epilogue.' She took a pencil and wrote down:

AMEN

'Why, so it does.' He smiled.

'But I can't make sense of the rest of it.'

'Let's have another crack. I rather enjoy ciphers and such. Got me into Bletchley for my sins.' Still walking, he wrote down the leading letters of the verses, omitting the prologue and epilogue:

TEIN TNSN TTEN TINN TGON TDEN TLKN TAMN TENT

'Nothing,' she said. 'Told you.'

'Yes, but look – there's some redundancy here.'

'Redundancy?'

'A coder's term. Repeated letters. Each verse, save the last, begins and ends with the same letters, T and N. If you were encrypting this lot for transmission you'd put in some kind of summary cipher and cross the lot out. Suppose I try that.' He took an eraser and went through the line, removing the first and last letters each time:

EI NS TE IN GO DE LK AM EN

Mary considered this. 'Is that another AMEN at the end?'

'No,' he said softly. 'Look – if you group the letters differently – ' He wrote out the line again.

EINSTEIN GODEL KAMEN

'Ben Kamen,' she said 'Oh my.'

'He's sent us a message,' Mackie said. 'A message through history. Clever boy, clever boy indeed. This will do the trick, I think. I must call Lindemann.' He turned on his heel and trotted back towards the farmhouse.

She followed more slowly.

She admired Mackie's pragmatism, his determination to deal with this extraordinary problem, his ability to absorb this astounding new development and act on it decisively. But she felt only profound shock at this latest discovery. Could it really be true that this message from Ben Kamen had been waiting, embedded in a document from the fifth century, written down in whatever original had existed and then transcribed into copy after copy – waiting for *her* to detect it, on this fall day in England?

She shivered, and hurried after Mackie, not wanting to be alone.

XIV

The convoy bowled along the Hastings road.

Heinz Kieser was driving the staff car. He was relaxed, the top buttons of his uniform open, but Ernst thought he was pushing up too close to the truck ahead of them. And he insisted on having the top down, although the day was blustery and overcast. Viv had her scarf tied tightly over her head, to try to keep her hair from blowing all over the place.

Beside his sister in the back seat, Alfie leaned forward. 'Can't this old bucket go any faster, Ernst?'

Heinz snapped at him, 'You shut your mouth. And speak respectfully to the officer.'

Alfie flinched back, shocked. He looked small and very young in his Jugend uniform. But he said bravely enough, 'He's not an officer. He's an obergefreiter, and so are you.'

Heinz, barely understanding, scowled at Ernst. 'What? . . . Just shut up, boy, or—'

Ernst said, 'Enough. Sit quiet, Alfie.'

'Yes, Ernst.'

Heinz shook his head, and said in German, 'Wretched little kid.'

'There's no need to speak to them like that, Heinz. Not these two.'

'Are you joking? We're an occupying army, not kindergarten teachers!'

'Look, Alfie has joined the Jugend and Vivien is learning the language, and they've both been given a Tuesday off school for Trafalgar Day. I mean, what more can you ask of them? We're building an empire here. We must win the hearts of the next generation. And the way to do that isn't by bullying kids.'

'"Win the hearts."' Heinz laughed. 'You do talk some shit, Ernst.' He grinned and glanced at Viv in his mirror. 'You know the talk is still that you're giving that little sweetie lessons in more than German. Oh, come on, Ernst, you must see how it looks. All the lads are saying it.'

189

'All the lads are wrong, then, aren't they?'

'Look, we all make this sort of arrangement. I, for example, have an agreement with a lady in Rye. Her husband is a "conchy", as the English say, a conscientious objector. He ended up in prison, up in London, and that's where he still is as far as my friend knows. Let's call her "Mrs X".'

'Let's!'

'Now she has a bad time of it. The English being the English, they despise her for her husband's cowardice far more than they despise us. So they won't help her in all the small give-and-take ways that make life bearable. Not just the black market – nobody will dig her potatoes for her in return for her baking a cake, that sort of thing. And she has a kid, a boy of about ten. Hungry all the time! So it's hard for her.'

Ernst had heard something of this; not all the barracks gossip was about him. 'So you exploit her.'

'No, not at all. I help her out with the ration. Sometimes a bit of chocolate for the kid, that sort of thing. I tell the lads to go easy when they come requisitioning from her little ploughed-up garden.'

'And in return?'

He grinned. 'Let me tell you about Mrs X. She's older than us, Ernst. Late thirties. But she's a strong-looking woman, tall, with a rangy frame. Dark hair, dark eyes. A certain quality, a sad autumnal beauty. And deep, heavy breasts.' He took his hands off the wheel to mime this.

Ernst glanced back uneasily at the children. Cowed, they looked away.

Heinz said, 'We all do it. And I mean, if not for that, why do you stay with these people in their miserable farmhouse? Look, I'm not mocking you, Ernst. I really want to know.'

'I feel responsible, Heinz. It's something like that.'

Heinz laughed. 'Responsible for what? You didn't order Sea Lion.'

'No. But that wretched family has been torn apart. They wouldn't be if we weren't here, would they?'

'These two seem to be embracing the occupation readily enough.'

'I think they're looking for stability,' Ernst said. 'Their mother and father are barely speaking, and the baby— let's just say, I think these two look to me as a pole of order.'

'Ha! There you go again. You take yourself too seriously, you know, Ernst. Obergefreiter Trojan, the successor to Nietzsche! Come on. Stop thinking so hard, and just give the girl a seeing-to. I can see she's longing for it. And probably you are too.'

But there, at least, Heinz was wrong, Ernst thought. He had the latest letter from Claudine in his jacket pocket. He could feel its sharp corners pressing through his shirt to his skin, this little artefact that had been sent from her hands to his. And after the celebrations were done for

Trafalgar Day, the latest in the military government's endless stream of 'morale-boosting' memorial days, he had every hope that he would be able to fulfil the arrangement he had made with her, to slip away before the curfew and—

There was an explosion up ahead, a sharp crack. The truck ahead of them stopped suddenly, and Heinz had to brake. Ernst was thrown forward.

'Shit,' Heinz said.

'I told you we were driving too close.'

There was a rattle of brisk orders, all in German. Ernst saw troopers, Wehrmacht and Waffen-SS, jumping down from the lorries. The vehicles began to rumble forward, but only so they could be pulled off the road.

Heinz leaned out of the car, trying to see ahead. 'What do you think that was, a Woolworth bomb?' An auxiliary special, a bit of gelignite in a biscuit tin.

'Could be.'

'Bloody auxiliaries. We might be here for hours while they search the ditches.' Waiting for room to move forward, Heinz dug a crumpled packet of cigarettes out of his vest pocket. They were Camels, an American brand, and Ernst wondered how he had got hold of them. 'Smoke?' Ernst took a cigarette, and tucked it behind his ear. Heinz turned to the children, and forced a smile. 'You?' he said in English.

Alfie, still nervous, grinned and said, 'Ta.' He leaned forward and took a cigarette.

Viv was shocked. 'Alfie, Mum will kill you. Tell him, Ernst.'

'How's she going to know? You have a light, Herr Obergefreiter?'

Heinz laughed and struck a match.

There was another crump, and more shouts. A blunt, ugly shell went sailing over the column from right to left, landing harmlessly in a wheat field.

'That's a spigot mortar,' Heinz snapped.

'Get down,' Ernst said to Viv and Alfie. He made them crouch in the belly of the car.

There was another boom, the whistle of another shell, and an explosion this time. There were angry shouts in German, and the pop of rifle fire.

XV

That Tuesday night, with the clock past eleven, George set off on his curfew beat around the town centre. He started out from the town hall and worked his way down towards the sea front, taking in some of the side streets on the way.

The October night was crisp, the air fresh; he wondered if there might be a nip of early frost. And it was quiet enough for him to hear the rush of the waves on the shingles, a sound which, he had learned in the last couple of years, was just like the noise a house made when it collapsed, shaken back to its component bricks by a bomb. No sound but that, and a few German voices, all male, a bit of laughter. There was nobody else around, nobody English anyhow, save for plodding coppers like George. The civilian curfew was eleven, and midnight for the German troops.

The town, his town, wasn't quite what it had been even a year ago. Most of the streetlights were out, but not all; the blackout wasn't quite as strictly enforced as it had been before the invasion. You would see chinks in blackout curtains, glimpse parlours and kitchens dimly lit by the low-voltage supply, people straining one last cup of tea out of much-reused leaves before bed. In a few houses he saw the glow of televisions.

In the shopping streets, the walls were plastered with propaganda posters, most of them showing smiling British and German workers standing shoulder to shoulder in the face of a horde of rat-like Bolsheviks. That was the thrust of the propaganda nowadays, stressing the unity of occupier and occupied against a common enemy – and George knew there was an element in the town who agreed with it. And here was another novelty, an official sign plastered onto the door of the Marks and Spencer store in Queens Road: JUDISCHE GESHAFT – Jewish Store.

He checked his watch.

And he saw a figure. A woman in a black, slim-fitting coat, with a dark hat, a scarf perhaps. She seemed to be heading towards the railway station. Her heels rapped on the cobbles with every step, a bright sound, remarkably loud in the dark.

George hurried after her. He called softly, 'Miss! Hold on. Police – don't be alarmed ...' This was why George was out now, along with other senior officers. If there were any curfew-breakers it was better for a bobby to take them quietly into a cop-shop for the night, rather than to leave them to the mercy of the German security services.

But the woman was hurrying now, heading deeper into the dark. She cut up an alley, out of his sight.

'Damn,' he muttered. He began to run, and he put his whistle to his lips, just in case.

When he turned into the alley, he almost collided with her. She had stopped dead, out of sight of the main drag. There was just enough light from a dimmed street lamp for him to make her out. She was quite young, he saw, mid-twenties. She was dressed smartly but sensibly. Her rather square face showed strength.

She looked at him, amused. 'Are you all right, Sergeant Tanner?'

'I don't get out of breath running ten yards, don't you worry. Now look here, Miss—'

'Doris Keeler.'

'I'm quite sure you know all about the curfew. Whatever you're up to I suggest you come with me ...'

There was a half-smile on her lips. 'Three, two, one.'

'Oh. How did you know my name?'

'Mary did say you could be a little low on the uptake sometimes.'

'Mary?'

'Mary Wooler. A mutual friend, Sergeant Tanner.' She held out her hand.

Confused, he took it and shook. 'Now look here,' he said, trying to regain control of the situation, 'I'm not sure what your game is, but the curfew is no bloody joke. So whatever you want from me—'

'Just a couple of minutes. That's all. If any Boche come by you can make a show of taking me in. Please hear me out, Sergeant. You'd do that for Mary, wouldn't you?'

He frowned. 'I wouldn't use words like "Boche" round here. But you're not from around here, are you?'

'I grew up in Colchester. Still live there, or at least I still have a flat there; I've been inside the protectorate for months. That's where I met Mary, in Colchester, during a raid. I used to be with the ARP.'

'Used to be?'

'Things happened. I got fed up with the war, and decided to do something a bit more active. Look, Sergeant, Mary wants your help. And the people she's working for.'

'Who, the WVS?'

She smiled. 'Not them. MI-14. Military intelligence.'

'I don't believe you! Mary?'

'Do you remember a man called Ben Kamen? An Austrian.'

'Of course I remember him. Little chap. Friend of her son Gary's.'

'Yes, and of Hilda's.'

Hearing his daughter's name felt like a blow to the stomach. 'Go on.'

'MI-14 believe Kamen is being held in an SS facility at Richborough.'

'Where's that?'

'Kent. And they want him out of there.'

'Why?'

'Well, I don't know, and I don't need to know. But it was important enough for MI-14 to contact us, through me – I already knew Mary, she mentioned my name – and she suggested I should get hold of you, and ask for your help.'

'Whoa, whoa.' He held up his hands. 'And this "us" of yours, I suppose—'

'I can see you've guessed.'

'The auxiliaries.'

'We call ourselves the resistance.'

'Well, I bloody don't. I have to deal with the consequences of your cowboys-and-Indians indulgences.'

'You're talking about the reprisals.'

'Yes, I'm talking about the reprisals,' he said grimly. 'When the leaves fell last winter and they cleared out most of you lot with your "scally wagging", I cheered, I can tell you. And you're all a pack of lefties anyhow as far as I can see.'

She wasn't perturbed by this. 'It's true a lot of the leaders fought for the Republicans in Spain. In fact, Ben Kamen did, you know. But it's the methods they brought back from over there that count now, Sergeant, not the politics.'

He glanced around, making sure they were still alone. 'I know the bloody Germans have got to be fought,' he hissed. 'I lost a daughter to this war. It's a question of how to fight them. I'm a Sussex copper, Miss Keeler. I keep the peace, that's my job. What makes you think I'd be any use running around in Kent? Is it just that I know Mary Wooler?'

'Well, partly that. And the fact that you're sleeping with an SS-unterscharfuhrer.'

He felt his blood rise. 'You know about that, do you?'

'You're not exactly discreet. And nor is she. She boasts about it!'

'So what does Julia have to do with it?'

'It's just that she is a close colleague of SS-Standartenfuhrer Josef Trojan. And *he* is involved in experiments at Richborough. Experiments for which he needs Kamen, for some reason.'

'What kind of experiments?'

'I don't know,' she said simply.

'And you want me to deceive Julia, somehow, so you can get close to Trojan, and Kamen. Is that it?'

'Pretty much. Why, does that give you a moral problem?' She laughed. 'I mean, you're sleeping with an SS officer!'

'What is this – blackmail?'

'No, no. I'm just trying to understand.'

'I don't pretend to understand it myself,' he admitted. 'Call it lust if you want. Must say I thought I was past all that.'

'Maybe it's the uniform,' she said archly. 'And what does *she* want? I mean, she could have her pick of iron-muscled young SS officers, couldn't she? No offence, but—'

'I think she's lost something too,' he said. 'She's lost her soul, mucking about with all those bloody Germans. Her English soul. So here she is with me. I mean, you can't get much more English than a copper, can you?'

'You're a decent man, Sergeant,' said Doris. 'If I can see that, she must.'

'Best not to talk such rubbish.'

'All right. But the question is, will you help us?'

'I don't know. You clowns in the auxiliaries—'

'Look, if you won't do this for Mary – and you certainly won't do it for me – won't you think about it for the sake of Hilda's memory?'

George felt his fists bunch. 'Don't you bloody talk about Hilda!'

XVI

In the end, it was well after eleven by the time Ernst turned up at the Royal Victoria Hotel, a little way out of the centre of town at St Leonards. And she was later still.

He had booked a table in the restaurant, and he sat, self-conscious as he waited. An unctuous waiter came to take his order, speaking in smooth German; Ernst asked for a bottle of French wine, for he thought it would please Claudine. The waiter brought him a list, the names in German and the prices in Reichsmarks and sterling, and Ernst picked a bottle, more or less at random.

There were plenty of uniforms here, mostly higher rank than his, and a few civilians, business types perhaps, come to investigate the investment opportunities the Reich insisted were to be found here in the protectorate, all blandly ignoring the curfew rules that confined lesser folk. One civilian sat alone at the table next to him, drinking brandy, reading a German-language edition of the *Albion Times*. Everybody spoke German, including the staff, although Ernst detected the stiff strain of an English accent a few times, expensive British types mingling easily with their conquerors.

And then she came in, swaying through the polished wood of the hotel bar as if she owned the place, defying the curfew herself. She wore a slim-fitting dress and what looked like silk stockings, bright red stilettos, a powder-blue jacket, and a small hat like a trilby set at a teasing angle. Her lips, red like her shoes, were the brightest thing in the room. She drew glances, covert and otherwise, from every man in the room. But she made straight for Ernst.

He stood as she approached. 'I can't believe you're here – I mean—'

'I know.' She leaned over the table, letting him kiss her cheeks.

He smelled perfume and face powder, a scent that wasn't like the schoolteacher he had known in Boulogne at all, but under it there was something, a deeper animal scent that he had never forgotten. She sat easily, crossing her legs. She snapped her fingers, and a waiter brought her a glass and filled it.

He said, 'It's so strange seeing you here – it's so different.'

'Well, nothing's the same, is it? Even if you stand still, it all changes around you. That's the war, I suppose. Look, have you got a light?' She produced a slim case of cigarettes.

He fumbled for a match. Oddly he was reminded of the incident in the car, when Heinz had offered Alfie a cigarette. He had lodged the children with an aunt in Hastings for the night; he would take them home tomorrow. It was hard to think of that strange other family of his now; it was another category of reality, he thought, separated from the universe that contained the woman before him. 'I've never seen you dressed so well—'

'Though you'd rather see me undressed.'

The forwardness of that took him aback. 'A schoolteacher's pay must be good under the Reich.'

'Well, I wouldn't know,' she said.

'You gave up your teaching? What are you doing now?'

'Oh, you know, this and that. A bit of translating; there's plenty of opportunity. It's just all so different now, Ernst. I mean, to be a teacher in the middle of all this – how is one meant to explain the war to a child?'

'You used to say teaching was the highest calling.'

'Well, we all say things that don't stay said, don't we?' There was a slight edge to her voice. 'Are you staying here, in the hotel?'

'Oh, no. This is much too grand for me. I've lodgings for the night, a "bed-and-breakfast".' He used the English phrase. 'And you?'

'I'm in a sort of hostel. Look, if we want to go somewhere the hostel will probably be best. The people are discreet – you know.'

Again that seemed oddly forward. He glanced around the bar, hoping that nobody was overhearing. The man with the newspaper sipped his drink, his face concealed.

She reached out to take his hand. 'Oh, let's not be shy. Look, I've been longing to see you. I got all your letters. I kept them.'

'You did?'

'What an extraordinary time you've had. You should turn it into a book one day.'

'Well, it's not over yet. Besides – I meant those letters just for you.'

'I know. I imagined you thinking of me, even under such cir-cumstances. I was touched.' She was looking into his eyes; she was as lovely as ever.

Yet there was something insincere about her. He saw it, in that moment. He pulled back.

'Why, Ernst, what's the matter?'

'I'll tell you what's the matter.' The dapper civilian at the next table folded up his newspaper. 'He's smelled my aftershave on you, that's what.' It was Heinz Kieser.

'Heinz, you bastard, what are you doing here?'

'Spying on you. What do you think? I wanted to see if the lovely Claudine really existed. There are no secrets in the barracks, you know! And now here she is, and well, well.'

'Look, just leave us alone, will you?'

'And guess what,' Heinz went on, 'it turns out I already knew her after all. Except she didn't tell me her name was Claudine, did you, darling?'

'Go to hell,' she said.

Ernst said, 'I don't understand. What are you talking about, Heinz?'

'She's *en carte*.' He used the French phrase. 'Why don't you show him, *Marie*? Show him your card. Come on!'

Claudine dragged hard on her cigarette, glaring at him.

Heinz grinned and stood up. 'My work here is done, I think. Look, don't take it bad, son. We've all been there.' He patted Ernst's shoulder, but Ernst brushed him away.

When he had gone, Claudine stared at the tip of her cigarette. 'Well. This is awkward.'

'You don't have to explain. You don't owe me anything.'

She looked up at him, and anger flared in her pretty, blank eyes. 'Maybe you owe me something, though. Shut up and pour me more wine.'

He obeyed.

'It happened after you left for the barges.'

'What did?'

'I was denounced for my relationship with you. Hard-faced bitch at the school, it was. Probably jealous. Or frigid.' She laughed. 'I got my apartment walls daubed with paint, slogans.'

He nodded. 'Such people use the word "Jerrybags", in England.'

'Do they? Well, I hated them, hated those who would speak out against others that way. What did they know of my heart? So I rebelled further. I took another lover.' She looked at his face. 'I'm sorry. Not a lover. I didn't love *him* . . . I just did it to get back at those who insulted me, really. A childish rebellion, yes? Still, he was there, and our time together was – acceptable. He gave me gifts, as you did. And after the denunciation I could no longer work at the school.'

'Oh. So he paid you.'

'It didn't mean anything. But then he was posted east, and off he went, bleating about his wife and two boys. I never heard from him again.'

'But you needed the money.'

'Another man came. A friend of the first. He said he had heard Hansie talk of me, and, well ... That was how it started. All word of mouth, and all gentlemen, if I may say so. I think they cared for me, each in his way.'

'And then?'

'And then the resistance came. Bastards,' she said with sudden vehemence. 'What brave men they are, to target a woman alone. Much easier than fighting the Germans.'

'You were attacked?'

'They would have cut my face, if I hadn't got away. Well, the police came to me, and when they found out, you know, they passed me to the military authorities. After that it was all very smooth.' She looked at him. 'You're in the Wehrmacht. You know how it works. The army runs the houses. The girls are given their cards. I was checked for infection, and interviewed.' She laughed at that. 'Interviewed! They prefer respectable girls to whore for their soldiers. Well, I passed the test.'

'And you came to England?'

'The authorities are importing French whores for the men here. Think of that! The English are so cold they can't even prostitute themselves properly. Churchill should make a speech about it. And at least the resistance here are leaving the foreign girls alone.'

'So you came for the Wehrmacht,' he said. 'For work. Not for me.'

'No! Oh, Ernst, no. You are so straight in your thinking. It's either one thing or the other with you, isn't it? Nothing in between. Look, I wanted to see you. I still do.' She leaned forward. 'Why don't we get out of this place? We could go to the hostel.

He stood in a kind of panic, shoving back his chair. He tried to calm himself. He took his wallet, drew out some Reichsmarks, and put them on the table, under the wine bottle. 'Will you be able to get back by yourself?'

She looked confused. 'Yes – there are taxis – oh, Ernst, don't go.'

He looked down at her, so beautiful, her bright red lips still shining bright. 'I'm sorry.' He turned on his heel and walked away.

XVII

9 November

The prisoners were woken by bugle blasts.

They gathered for the morning appell. The Nazi flag and the flag of Albion snapped high on their poles, lifted by a chill breeze under a bright blue sky. Bundled in their shabby greatcoats, the men stamped their feet and blew on their hands.

The camp commander announced briskly that the regular Sunday work details would be suspended. Muffled cheers. Once again it was some kind of memorial day. But then Danny Adams announced the British troops would hold a parade and a minute's silence at eleven a.m.

'Oh, it's not just any old memorial, old chap,' said Willis Farjeon, standing beside Gary in the rank. 'This is Armistice Day, when we all down tools to remember our fathers who fell in the War to End Wars. Nice clean military memorial, the kind the Nazis embrace to their bony little hearts—'

'Put a sock in it, Farjeon,' murmured the SBO in his broad scouse. 'And besides, I suspect you and the other superior-breed types might not be spending the day with us after all.' He nodded over to where the commander and his senior aides had been joined by a couple of SS officers, who were, in the usual German fashion, consulting lists.

The men whistled at the SS officers, and called out obscenities in a variety of languages, and those nearby nudged Gary and Willis. The stalag standing joke was that all SS men were in fact raging faggots, and that the racial selection processes had actually been about looking for pretty boys. 'Don't worry, Wooler, I hear Himmler's pecker is even smaller than Hitler's. You won't feel a thing.'

Willis camped it up in response. Gary just stood there.

But it turned out it wasn't all the stalag Aryans who were asked for today. The SS party came over to the British group and spoke briefly to the SBO. He turned and beckoned to Gary. 'Just you, Wooler.'

Gary came out of the line. One of the SS officers stepped forward to meet him.

'Oh, Christ,' somebody groaned. 'It's the SS bird. It's not *fair*.'

From beneath a black peaked cap, a startlingly beautiful face smiled at Gary. 'So you're Corporal Wooler. I've been hearing about you – and your notorious mother, whom I actually met once. We have high hopes for you, Wooler. You're a significant figure. The American fighting for the British. The neutral who refuses a safe passage out of the stalag. You've made yourself prominent, among the Prominente!'

The accent was pure upper-class English. 'My God. What are you?'

Her smile broadened. 'I am SS-Unterscharfuhrer Fiveash. But you can call me Julia. We've quite a day ahead of us, Corporal. Come now.' And she turned and walked away.

Gary glanced at the SBO, who nodded.

Behind him the men, recovering their nerve, got into the catcalling. 'You lucky dog,' shouted Willis Farjeon. 'You lucky dog, Wooler!'

He was led to the gate, where he was briskly searched, first by an SS man and then by stalag guards. The guards, knowing the prisoners' tricks, were a lot more thorough, but he was spared the indignity of a strip search and a cavity inspection.

A small group of staff cars was waiting outside the stalag gate. Julia Fiveash sat in one of these, behind a Wehrmacht driver. The car door was open, and she patted the seat beside her. Gary joined her, bewildered.

The cars pulled away, and formed up into a small convoy. They were heading east, he saw from the angle of the sun, towards the coast. Gary reflexively considered the possibilities of escape. This was no steel-barred truck; this was an open car, and he could just hop over the side. But he had no doubt that weapons were trained on him.

Fiveash said, 'We don't have far to go – a couple of miles.'

'Where to?'

'You'll see.' Fiveash was watching him. 'So how do you feel? What are you thinking? Come, Corporal, I hope you won't cling to that name, rank and serial number routine; I do want us to get to know each other.'

How did he feel? He ran a fingertip along a seam of the leather seat cover. The car was gleaming inside and out, and the woman beside him was crisp and sharp in her jet-black uniform. It was a bright, fresh English fall day, and the car, bowling along, threw up a rooster-tail of leaves that smelled of wood smoke. 'I haven't been in any sort of vehicle outside of a steel-walled prison truck for a year. I feel grimy. Hell, I *am* grimy.'

'Well, you don't need to be grimy. Not any more.'

Soon they approached a cluster of buildings, gathered around a crossroads. Gary's first impression was of whitewashed concrete. It was nothing like the compact little villages of Kent; it looked new, alien, as if it had been dropped from the sky. And it didn't look like another prison, at least, though there was a fence of chicken-wire and barbed wire around it.

They stopped at a barrier, where an SS-schutze, a private, checked papers handed over by the drivers.

Gary studied the sign before the barrier. 'Nova Rutupiae." What the hell kind of name is that?'

'Latin,' said Fiveash. 'Or at least some Party scholar's idea of Latin. Rutupiae, you see, is the old Roman name for Richborough. So it seems appropriate. You know Richborough; you've been working there. I'm told that you will be able to see the invasion monument from the podium of Rutupiae's thingplatz.'

The barrier was raised. They were driven through into the fenced-off inner area, where they climbed out of the car.

'Of course the fence is such a bore,' Fiveash said. 'It will be such a relief when the armistice is signed, and we can tear down all these barriers, even the First Objective itself – don't you think? Now, come, follow me, we've a lot to see.'

She set off briskly. He followed. They were tailed, reasonably discreetly, by a couple of SS men.

XVIII

They walked along a kind of street. The buildings were white-painted with rendered walls, flat roofs, shuttered windows, little scraps of lawn neatly cut. But the houses were odd, built like long halls, stretching back from the street. There was no sense of individuality about them, as if they had been stamped out of a mould in some factory. And none of the houses looked occupied; they all had their shutters closed.

There was nobody about save more SS, and a party of workers, shabby, exhausted, shuffling along under the watchful eye of guards. Gary wondered if they were prisoners on labour detail. None of them looked at him.

'These are residences, obviously,' Fiveash said. 'It's a pity they weren't built in a more sympathetic style, but for now labour and materials are understandably short . . . The larger building is the manor house, where the controlling SS officer will reside.'

'What the hell is this place?'

'A village,' Fiveash said. 'Some of the Ahnenerbe thinkers call it a "colony", but that word has regrettable overtones. This one is meant as a model of its type – a show home, a demonstration of the possible. This is a *lebensborn* village, Gary. Now come and see the public facilities.'

At the heart of the 'village' were unopened shops with their functions displayed on hastily painted signs, and a space with sheds and stock-yards, like an agricultural market. There was even a British pub, mocked up in concrete and white paint; it had no name, but the sign outside carried a stern portrait of Hitler. What Fiveash called the sportplatz was a complex of arenas and facilities, including a soccer pitch and a shooting gallery. There was a large open field which Fiveash said would be a cemetery – very important in this community, she said, a place to honour the dead. 'It's all very Iron Age,' she said drily.

The most imposing facility was the thingplatz, an arena like an open-air theatre with a raised podium. Flagpoles soared, and Gary saw searchlight mounts. You could hold a hell of a rally here. All this was brand new, unused; Gary could smell paint. The only colour amid all the white was the vivid green of the lawns.

'You're one of the first candidates to see this.' Fiveash smiled, her teeth dazzling white in the sun. 'You may not feel this way now, but you're honoured. Really, you are!'

She led him back through the village to the residential buildings, and opened up one of the houses. Inside the décor was functional – more white paint, with false pillars to mask the concrete, and solid-looking furniture of wood and leather. The house was in two halves, he found, looking around, with a family living area at one end, and an open space at the far end that Fiveash said was meant as a barn.

The living room felt cold, all that concrete sucking out the warmth. A television sat mute in one corner, and there was a fireplace, unlit. Standing in this clean space Gary felt even more shabby, like a scarecrow brought in from the field.

There was a knock. A young soldier walked in with a tray laden with biscuits, fruit and a jug of coffee. He put this on a low table and left.

Fiveash smiled at Gary. 'Eat. Drink. Go ahead; there are no strings.'

He hesitated for one second. Then he sat, pulled the tray to him, and stuffed a biscuit in his mouth. It was shortbread coated with sugar; the crystals seemed to burst on his tongue. While he chewed on that he poured out a coffee, slopping it a little, and sucked up a great hot mouthful.

'I'll take mine white,' Fiveash said, good humoured. She took off her cap, revealing blonde hair tightly plaited.

He poured her a coffee and found a jug of cream. He continued to cram his mouth. 'Sorry,' he said. 'Shit, this coffee. Makes the tea we get in the stalag taste like dishwater. Probably *is* dishwater.'

'What do you think of the design? I mean the village as a whole. Himmler himself had a hand in it, you know. The house is based on a Roman era design called a "wohnstallhaus" – the remains of such houses are found all over Germany. You could say this village is an Ahnenerbe experiment. There is a scheme called the Generalplan Ost which will see a great belt of such communities as this serving as a buffer between the Slavic homelands and the Reich. This is when the Jewish-Bolshevik conspiracy is destroyed, and the Slavs pushed back.' She said this as neutrally as if she were describing some feature of the house.

'And who would live here? The racially pure like me, right? What the hell would we do all day? Listen to reruns of Hitler's speeches?'

She laughed. 'What a card you are. No – you would farm. Party ideology is founded on ideals of purity, you see, Corporal. And one such ideal is the nobility of the farmer. In the east there'll be no shortage of land, or indeed labour, and the farms could be quite extensive.'

He picked up the tray and sat back with it on his lap, still eating. He had no scruples about being ill-mannered before this nutcase Nazi. 'Party ideology?'

She smiled. 'Some of it can be a little baroque. But it's hard to argue with Hitler's fundamental thesis. There are three sorts of people in the world, Corporal. Those who create culture, those who preserve it, those who destroy it. There is overwhelming evidence in the historical record that those who create human culture are of the Nordic type.'

'How about the Greeks? I didn't know they were Scandinavians.'

'No, but they were of Nordic extraction. There have been many diasporas.'

'And these destroyers of yours?'

'The Jews. All this Hitler has set out clearly in his own writings. Of course even Hitler drew on the work of earlier thinkers. We have libraries here, you should read up. It was an Englishman called William Jones who in the eighteenth century first identified the Aryan race, you know – indeed he coined the term – based on a comparison of languages, Sanskrit, Greek, Latin. Hitler and Himmler both refer to a recent work by another Englishman called Houston Stewart Chamberlain. A son-in-law of Wagner. Called *Race and Nation*, it—'

'I'll take the scholarship as read. Look, you're English, I still can't believe you swallow a word of this.'

Her smile was thinner now. 'But I have seen these ideas work themselves out in my own life.'

'How?'

'My father, and his father before him, served the empire in India.'

'The white man's burden?'

'Under the British the Indians advanced more in decades than they had in millennia. But my father's properties near Bombay were burned out by insurgents; he was forced to return to England. And then his savings, the fruit of the labour of generations, were destroyed through the criminal incompetence of a financier—'

'A Jew?'

'Almost certainly, though I could not prove it.'

'So that's it. To avenge Daddy, you joined the SS.'

She flared, 'My father died in poverty. Do you imagine that the lands my family had to abandon in India are better off than they were under us? Do you imagine that my family's money is being put to good use by those who stole it from us? You see, I grew up amid *living proof* of Hitler's thesis.'

'Yeah, yeah,' he said. 'So what do you want from me?'

'We're offering selected prisoners of war the chance to come here, lightly supervised at first—'

'You want me to be your poster boy in the States.'

'Well, if you took on the challenge it would create a lot of headlines. I've been over there; I know how it works. It could generate some goodwill.'

'And it might neutralise the news my mother sent back about Peter's Well. Right?'

She leaned forward, crisp in her black uniform. 'I won't try to minimise the harm that has been done to you and your family, Gary. I'm well aware of it. Since I've been stationed in Hastings I've got to know your father-in-law. Rather well, actually.'

'George?' He couldn't believe it. 'You're the SS!'

'Well, I'm also a human being. And he doesn't have anybody else. The civilian police are rather shunned, you know, by those who don't understand. Some call them collaborators, and worse. George needs company – somebody who understands.'

'"Company." My God. So this was why you were detailed to recruit me.'

'We often talk of Hilda—'

'Don't you dare speak of her.'

'Try to keep calm, Gary.'

'I've had enough of this farce. I want to go back to the stalag.'

She stood, setting down her coffee cup. 'Well, that isn't going to happen,' she said with a touch of steel in her voice. 'Not for now, at any rate.' She made for the door. 'Give it twenty-four hours. You'll have the house to yourself. Enjoy. Eat, shower. Watch the television. Wash your clothes, for heaven's sake. Walk around the village a bit; somebody will escort you. Twenty-four hours. Then, if you wish, I'll take you back to the homosexuals and madmen of your precious stalag.' She walked out, closing the door behind her.

He stood there, alone, confused. He grabbed the last of the biscuits off the plate and stuck them in his coat pocket, a prisoner's reflex. And he stared at the television, which gazed back at him, a glass eye focused on his uncertainty.

XIX

This November morning, as every Sunday morning, Ben was brought to Josef Trojan's office. Ben was made to sit on a hard upright chair while Trojan read intently through his latest test results. An SS man stood at the door, a heavy automatic weapon in his arms.

Ben had grown used to this routine. He was just as much a prisoner as in the stalag, but now he was sleeping for the Reich. Once that would have made him laugh. He had learned not to laugh, not at Trojan. He just sat still, trying to settle his breath.

And, out of his windowless cell for these precious minutes, he drank in every scrap of stimulus. They were in Trojan's research block at Richborough. He could hear no birdsong, not today; this was November. But there was a window high in the wall that revealed sky, a rectangle of bright blue, an intense colour never matched by any reproduction, and there was a feathering of high cloud, ice probably, which—

'Rubbish.' Trojan threw the file across his desk and sat back. 'A week's worth of results, and no correlation.'

Ben snapped to alertness, ready to pay full attention to every word, to every nuance.

Every morning, on the moment of waking, Ben had to recite whatever dreams he had had to a waiting psychologist. The transcript was analysed and matched with the results of deep interrogations of Ben's past life, as well as a register of likely future events, all in the hope of finding some evidence of psychic dream-wandering. But no significant evidence had turned up.

'I'm sorry, sir,' Ben said.

'You've been eating the programmed food, consuming the drink? The drugs – the aluminium cap?'

'Yes, sir.' The Nazi scientists had been varying the 'input' as they called it, his food and drink and other stimuli, even the stiffness of his mattress, to see if there was any change in the 'output', his dreaming.

As if he were a machine producing sausages. And they had tried shrouding his skull in an aluminium cap, in order to see if there were tangible radiations that could be screened out, or perhaps focused.

Trojan got up and walked around the room, hands behind his back. 'I trust we're not wasting time. At least the negative results prove you're not lying about your dreams, which would be easy enough to do.'

'I wouldn't dare.'

Trojan looked at him, surprised, then laughed. 'I'm sure you wouldn't. And what's next on the list of trials?' He ran a finger down an open page in the files on his desk. 'Human contact. *Gach.* I see these gun-shy dolts I employ propose putting a companion or two in your bed with you. Girls, a couple of plump boys. You'd like that, wouldn't you, you repellent little faggot? Pah, what rubbish it all is. But I need this experiment to work. I need my Loom! And you need it too, or you're for the ovens, my friend.'

Ben flinched.

'If only you weren't a Jew,' Trojan mused now. He strutted around the room, a peacock. 'If only you were a good German, even an English. You would then perhaps have the mental discipline to control this talent of yours, if it exists, to tame it. Of course if you were French you would only dream of pornography. Ha! All right.' Trojan sat again. 'I have been reconsidering our approach here. After all this is an experiment in psychology, is it not? Your psychology in particular. And up to now you have been motivated entirely by fear. Would that be true to say?'

Ben hesitated. 'It's undeniable, sir.'

'Yes, it is. Undeniable. Good word, that. But there are other sorts of motivation, aren't there? Look, Kamen, you and I are going to get to know each other a little better. I want you to understand what it is I want, and why I want it. Perhaps I can make you *share* my desires, to some degree, or at least sympathise with them. And if so you will have a *positive* motivation to make the experiment work, as well as negative. So what do you think? Will that work?'

'I've no grasp of psychology, sir.'

'Well, that doesn't surprise me. Do you know anything about me, Kamen? No, of course you don't. Suffice it to say that I have been politically active since I was a boy, when I worked for a nationalist group in the Rhineland. I was motivated, you see, by the humiliations heaped on my father, who fought honourably in the last war, only to be betrayed by the very politicians whose lives he had protected.

'My petty grouping was absorbed into the Party, and then – I was still only twenty – my true career began. I worked for a time as a

208

reader in the Official Party Department to Protect Writing. But I was drawn to scholarship – I had studied history, you see. I was part of a research party that visited the Canary Islands. It is believed that these are fragments of Atlantis, and a homeland for an Aryan race. After that it was a natural step for me to join the SS, and come to work for the Ahnenerbe ...'

'You need to find something to impress Himmler,' Ben said. 'Sir.'

'Got a sharp tongue in that rodent head of yours, haven't you, rat-boy? But, yes, it's true. We are all jostling for position in the Reichs-fuhrer's court.'

'And that is why you need the Loom.'

'Yes.' Trojan eyed Ben. 'I wasn't planning to reveal this to anybody, not until your precognitive abilities are proven – until we have proof the Loom can work. But in the interests of motivation – ' He opened a drawer and extracted a brown card folder. 'You do understand,' he said casually, 'that if you ever breathe a word of this I will personally cut out your tongue and feed it back to you?'

'Yes, sir.'

'Good boy. Now, take a look at this.' He spun the folder across the desk. 'I know you're no historian ...'

Inside the folder was a kind of poem, nine stanzas with a prologue and epilogue, rendered in German and what looked like Old English. '"The Menologium of the Blessed Isolde",' Ben read.

> These the Great Years / of the Comet of God
> Whose awe and beauty / in the roof of the world
> Lights step by step / the road to empire
> An Aryan realm / THE GLORY OF CHRIST ...

He looked up. 'What is this?'

'A kind of calendar. Authentic-looking document for the time. And a prophecy, if you will – or it would be, if you were stuck in the sixth century. Entirely faked, of course. I've been working on it with various scholars – linguists, astronomers.' He sounded paternally proud, and he wanted Ben to understand. 'It must span centuries. My para-psychologists assure me that its most likely recipient will be a relative of the hapless pagan afflicted by O'Malley, generations before my own target. The document is encoded to ensure its own survival – for instance, in the hands of monkish scribes – and has an embedded chronology. Look – can you see? It is structured around the repeated visits of a comet to the skies.'

'What comet? I don't understand.'

'Halley's comet,' said Trojan, and he grinned. 'Now, Halley's comet might not mean much to you or me, Kamen, but it means a lot to the English—'

'The Norman Conquest.' Ben looked at the Menologium, piecing it together. 'Halley's comet returned in 1066. This is what you want to send back to the past, isn't it? This document.' It seemed unbelievable. 'Are you planning to, um, *adjust* the outcome of the Norman Conquest of England?'

'Think of it,' Trojan said ardently. 'Hastings! What a catastrophe that October day was, so long ago! England, you know, was thoroughly Nordic. Why, only a generation before 1066 it had been part of Cnut's Scandinavian empire. King Harold himself was half-Danish! But William, that creature of the Pope, defeated Harold; the Jewish-Christian conspiracy defeated the Nordic race that day. And now the Aryan stock of the English is polluted by cross-breeding with the degenerate French. Quisling, the wise leader of Norway, argues this cogently, by the way.'

'And what if that could be reversed?' Ben said evenly.

'You have it,' Trojan said. 'Exactly! The Normans would have been smashed for a generation, and Harold secure on his throne. England, Scandinavia, Germany – the Nordic countries would have remained strong, and dominant over the Jewish-Christian south.' His eyes were misty, almost as if his own rhetoric was making him cry. 'Think of it. I would shine in Himmler's eyes. And I could become a hero of the English – Harold's grave was the first place I visited after the invasion. They would tear down the Objective wall and strew my path with petals ...'

Ben saw that this man had no real idea what he was meddling with – no idea that if this prophecy did what he intended there was every possibility that he would be erased from existence, along with Ben, Himmler and the applauding English.

Trojan turned to him. 'Now do you see the scope of my ambition? Even a Jew can think. And I hope that you will share some of my intellectual excitement.' Then his expression shifted, becoming more calculating. 'Of course the gesture is the thing. Even if the Loom *doesn't* work the very effort will grab Himmler's imagination. So what do you think?'

'I think I have no choice but to work with you.'

'But I need you to *want* to work with me, Benjamin Kamen. Can you do that?'

'Oh, yes, sir, I can do that,' Ben said. He glanced down at the Menologium, thinking fast. 'Perhaps I could study this draft. Polish it a bit. Make it more mine.'

'Yes!' Trojan clapped his hands. 'Good idea. Keep it, work on it. Perhaps that will help you make the whole project part of you. I think that's enough for today. I have other duties. But you have only one duty, Benjamin – sleep! And sleep well.' He was already turning to other papers.

Clutching the Menologium to his chest, Ben turned and made for the door. And he began to plan how he could use this opportunity to make a cry for help.

XX

There was bottled beer in the fridge.

Bathed, wrapped in a dressing gown, having eaten his fill and then some, and mildly drunk after sipping his first alcohol in more than a year, Gary sat before the television. Earnest German voices spoke over images of spectacular advances in the east and in Africa. Gary had no way of working out how much of it was true. Other voices spoke of gloomy news from the rest of Britain, of a hungry, cold and demoralised population, the famine to come in the winter, the flight of the people from cities like Birmingham and Manchester. There were even pictures of queues at the Winston Line, defeated English folk clamouring to come into the Reich protectorate, smiling Wehrmacht troops handing out cans of meat and chocolate for the children.

Now a documentary programme came on. Sponsored by the SS, it illustrated the cosmological ideas of one Hans Horbiger, an Austrian engineer. Gary understood little of the German commentary, but he soaked up the general ideas from the pictures.

Horbiger said the universe was driven by heat, like a giant steam engine. A cartoon sky filled up with tiny stars so cool they were clad in ice, and hot giant stars. When the icy stars fell into their hot neighbours there were spectacular explosions that sprinkled planets and moons, like sparks from a firework. That was how the earth had been born. Initially earth had had a whole family of moons, which were made of ice – as was the existing moon, the last survivor. One by one the moons fell to the earth, causing immense cataclysms. Gary watched as the earth was repeatedly plated over by ice, save for a central belt where giant tides were raised by the falling moon. The most recent of these disasters had been eleven thousand years ago, said Horbiger; life had survived only in a few refuges.

This amazing cosmology explained a lot, from the true meaning of the Scandinavian creation myths to the destruction of Atlantis. And it was the reason why, even after years of ardent searching, nobody had found a trace of proof that the primordial Aryan race, source of all high civilisation on Earth, had ever actually existed.

If he'd been watching this with friends, with his buddies from the stalag, Gary might have laughed. As it was he was chilled. Most Germans he had met were as sane as he was, more or less. But there must be somebody high up in the Nazi hierarchy who believed in this garbage sufficiently to have it researched and dramatised. They're crazy, Gary thought. And they are in control. I'm trapped in a world of the mad, as if the whole planet is a vast stalag run by lunatics—

There was a tap on the door.

Reflexively he hid the beer under his chair, as if he was in the stalag and a goon had called for a late-night inspection. He checked himself, deliberately picked up the beer, and set it on the coffee table. He stood, turned off the television, and wrapped his dressing gown tight around him as he walked to the door.

A young woman stood there. She was dressed plainly, in a knee-length black skirt and a modest blouse with a kind of neckerchief. She wore her dark hair pinned back in a bun. The whole effect was of a uniform, like a Girl Guide troop leader. She had a face that was more handsome than beautiful, he thought. She looked strong.

She grinned at him. 'What's wrong with you? Never seen a woman before?' Her accent was some English variant unfamiliar to him.

'Not hardly, for a year. Look, I'm sorry.' He stepped back, impossibly awkward. 'I guess I left my manners back in the stalag. Come in.'

She swept past him. 'You weren't expecting visitors.'

'Hell, no. I mean – sorry. I guess you know who I am, right?'

'Yes, Corporal Wooler.'

'Call me Gary.'

'Thanks,' she said, amused. 'I'm Sophie Silver. But you can call me Doris Keeler.'

That threw him completely. 'What did you say?'

She glanced around the room, at the beer, the empty food plates, the television.

'You've been making yourself at home. Good for you. Mind if I sit down?'

'I—'

'Have you got any more of those beers?' She sat confidently on one of the easy chairs. 'Needs a bit of colour, this place, doesn't it?'

'Um—'

'That beer.'

'Oh. Sure.' He went to the kitchen.

She called after him, 'I don't want to drink up your treat. But then again, I'm supposed to be your treat too, aren't I?'

Again he was thrown. He brought her a glass of beer, and sat on the sofa. 'Look, Miss Silver – or Keeler—'

'Doris will do.' She sipped her beer. 'Yum. Better than the shitty wine we get back home.'

'Where's home?'

'Colchester.'

'Colchester. Look, Doris, I've had kind of a bumpy day. You're talking in riddles here. Who are you? Did Julia Fiveash send you?'

'She sent Sophie Silver. She didn't know Doris Keeler was here for the ride too.'

'So start with Sophie Silver. Who is she?'

'She's supposed to be your, well, your *mate* is probably the right word. Did Fiveash tell you this show village is *lebensborn*?'

'I don't know what that means.'

'This is a love camp. *Lebensborn* means the fount of life. Another of Himmler's ideas. He wants to purify Aryan blood. The Fuhrer approves; he's named Himmler the Reich Commissioner for the Strengthening of the German Race. So Himmler's setting up a programme of breeding, where Aryan men, especially SS officers, can couple with suitably chosen females of the right sort. And if you and I successfully reproduce, there will even be a new sort of religion into which we can baptise our little Nordic runt.'

'Well, that's another bloody stupid idea of the Nazis.'

'True. But you've got to admit it's more fun than invading Poland.' She winked at him. 'They must like you.'

'I'll say. But I take it healthy Aryan copulation is out of the question—'

'Come near me and you'll be posting your balls home to America,' she said. 'No offence.'

'None taken. So that's Sophie Silver. Who's Doris Keeler?'

'Resistance.'

'Ah.' He took another drink of his beer. 'You must have taken a hell of a risk to get in here.'

'You don't need to know the details,' she said evenly.

'Then tell me why.'

'For you. Or rather, for your friend Ben Kamen.'

'Ben.' He sat up straight. 'They took him out of the stalag.'

'Well, he's alive. But the SS have him. They mean to use him.'

'For what? – No, I guess I don't need to know that.'

'I got a briefing through the Special Ops Executive – you know it supports the resistance. We, or rather the British military intelligence,

214

are putting together a plan to get him out. We want you to help.'

'How?'

'Well, we don't know yet. But you're connected. You know Ben. And your mother is involved in the analysis of the situation.'

'My *mother*?'

'She sends her best, by the way. I've already spoken to George Tanner.' She looked at him; perhaps he was showing his shock. 'Your father-in-law.'

'I know who he is, damn it.' To have these names fired at him, the names of his family and friends in this extraordinary place, was very disconcerting.

'All these people,' Doris said, 'have a relationship with Ben Kamen, and can plausibly be positioned close to him as assets during the retrieval attempt.'

'You make us sound like pieces on a chess board.'

'Well, that's military intelligence for you. All you have to do for now is stay out of the stalag.'

He said immediately, 'I've been refusing release programmes and exchanges since the day I was brought to the stalag. I was a soldier; I am a POW; that's how I want to be treated.'

'All right. But the fact is you'd be a lot more use to the war effort if you stay here. Actually I'm not interested in your agonising,' she said briskly. 'I'll stay an hour, if I may, for form, and then you can do what you want.'

'Well.' He sat back. 'Kind of business-like, aren't you?'

'Isn't it better to be?'

'So what shall we talk about? How did a girl like you finish up in the resistance?'

'It's best if we don't talk,' Doris said. 'What's on your television? I've watched a bit of it from the other side of the Winston Line. It's quite popular, funnily enough. Any more beer going begging?'

XXI

12 December

The Wehrmacht transport dropped Ernst off, and he walked up the drive to the Miller farmhouse. It had been snowing this December Friday, though it wasn't desperately cold; the snow was moist and sticky.

He walked slowly. He was tired tonight, his imagination worn out by all the briefings following Hitler's sudden declaration of war upon America.

The declaration itself wasn't a shock; the Fuhrer had been infuriated for years by the Americans' bending of the meaning of neutrality in its support of Britain: 'Roosevelt is picking a fight,' Josef always said. And the Japanese attack on Pearl Harbor was a good time to go to war, for suddenly America found herself fighting on two fronts.

And he was reluctant to go into the house, so sour had the mood been that morning, after the post had come with the bad news about Alfie. This isn't my problem, he told himself. That was what Heinz and his officers told him every time he tried to talk about this. It's just a billet. Walk away. And yet he was bound up with these people. So he walked to the house and in he went; what else could he do?

He hung his greatcoat and hat on a hook in the hall, items of a German soldier's military issue beside Fred's battered farmer's overcoat and the children's school blazers and gabardines. He left his slushy boots in the hallway, so that he had to walk into the kitchen in his socks. The kitchen was warm, and full of cooking smells. It was yet another memorial day, Coronation Day, the anniversary of the crowning of King Edward previously denied him by his abdication. Ernst had been able to provide another bit of meat, a pork joint; he could smell it in the oven, while pans of vegetables sat on the range, steaming.

Only Irma was here, with baby Myrtle, six months old, in her cot. Irma was hanging decorations on her Christmas tree, a fir about five feet high. There was a Nativity scene too, a stable and little wooden

216

figures carved in wood, set up on the mantelpiece over the stove. Myrtle's baby bag, her haversack-like protection from poison gas, sat on the floor near the cot.

'Hello, Obergefreiter,' Irma said. She looked tired, as always, and she pushed a lank bit of hair out of her eyes. 'Do you need a cup of tea?'

'Thank you. I will wait for supper. I can smell the pork.'

'I've salted it for crackling, the way you like it. Thanks for the joint, Ernst.'

'Don't thank me, thank the King . . .'

The truth was that Ernst wasn't sure how much longer he was going to be able to provide treats like this. At war with America, life for all of them in the protectorate, German and English, was going to get harder. But there was no need to bring that into the family home, not tonight, with a Christmas tree and a roast in the oven.

Dutifully he inspected the tree. There were garlands of some kind of tin foil, and bits of paper made into chains, and balls of wool scraps, multi-coloured. One odd touch was a set of little wooden battleships, suspended on bits of thread from the branches. There was even an angel, carved of wood and clumsily hand-painted, strapped to the top of the tree with a bit of string. 'It is pretty.'

'Well, I'm doing my best. We have a box of stuff we bring down from the loft every year. Fred made the angel, and his father made the Nativity scene. His father was a real woodworker.'

'What is this tinsel?'

'Chaff, from the RAF bombers. You find it all over the fields.'

'Why the little battleships? These were issued for *Scharnhorst* Day, last Monday. You should use the King's coronation medallions.' One of these, stamped in wafer-thin tin, had been issued to every child under sixteen.

Irma tutted. 'Tell that to Fred. "I'm not having that bloody usurper's image on my bloody tree." Besides, little Myrtle eats them.'

Viv came bubbling in. She was still in her school uniform, but Ernst could see she had put a bit of lipstick on, no doubt for his benefit. 'Good evening, Ernst! I heard you come in.'

'I must have noisy socks.'

'What do you think of the Nativity? I set it up.'

'It is very nice.'

'See what I did?' She picked out the infant Jesus from His crib. The tiny doll, small enough to fit in the palm of her hand, was quite delicately carved, though worn from handling. And it had a yellow star on its breast, cut out from paper and fixed with a spot of glue. Viv winked at Ernst, as so often trying to draw him into a private connection.

Ernst said nothing. She put the model back in the crib, and got to what she was clearly longing to ask. 'I just wondered, you know, if there was any more news about the exchange programme.'

In fact he had enquired at the town hall in Hastings that day. 'As far as I am aware, nothing has changed. Although, look, the war situation is changing daily, even hourly. Everything is' – he hunted for the colloquialism – 'up in the air.'

'I don't see why the Japanese bombing a lot of American boats in Hawaii should make any difference. I'm so glad I'm going, ever so. I mean, it will be *ever* such fun, to see Berlin!'

Irma said wearily, 'Oh, you're such a silly girl, Viv. And so selfish. Don't let your father hear you talking like that.'

Viv sniffed. 'I'll say what I like.'

Ernst touched Irma's arm. 'It is all right. She is young, after all—'

It was the wrong thing to say. 'I'm not *young*!' Viv turned and stormed out of the kitchen, and almost collided with her father. Fred walked in and glared at Ernst.

'Good evening, Fred.'

Fred scowled, the dirt rubbed deep into his lined face. 'Battle. I suppose you've heard.'

'What?'

'The auxiliaries blew up an ammo store there. It's on the German radio. There'll be reprisals, won't there?'

Ernst knew nothing about what had happened at Battle, but he was sure that this was another consequence of Hitler's declaration of war against the Americans. But the news was grave and depressing. In Albion resistance attacks had blossomed, bombs and assassinations and attacks on collaborators. And the reprisals had been harsh.

'They're taking one from every house, they say,' Fred said.

'It is best not to speak of this until necessary,' Ernst said stiffly.

Fred turned to his wife. 'And what's wrong with that empty-headed little bitch upstairs?'

'Don't speak of her that way.' Irma used a fork to test how the swedes were cooking. 'She's just fretting about her exchange trip, that's all.'

'She can't think she's still going to Berlin. Not after Alfie. And not after the way everything's blowing up.'

'You know what she's like, Fred.'

'Yes, I know what she's like, she's bloody selfish and she couldn't care less about her brother, and I know she's not going to Berlin.'

'Yes, well, you let her work that out for herself if that's how it's going to be. Don't go wading in and calling her names.'

He walked to the sink, his limp pronounced. He stepped over baby Myrtle as if she was no more than a heap of firewood. He never acknowledged the baby's existence, not even by a glance. He rolled up his sleeves. He dumped out washing from the sink, underwear and smalls, shoving aside the box of Rinso, and began to wash hands and arms grimy from the fields. 'I tell her the truth, that's all. You're too bloody soft.'

'I wish you'd wash in the yard,' Irma said. 'Look at the mess you're making. And never mind calling me soft. I'm just trying to protect Viv, is all.'

'Protect her? What about protecting Alfie, eh?' He glared over his shoulder at Ernst. 'How can it be right to call up a fourteen-year-old boy for forced labour?'

Irma opened the oven to draw out the roast. The air was filled with greasy steam, and the heat of the kitchen was oppressive. Ernst suddenly felt very weary. Fred had been just as angry this morning, when Alfie's call-up letter had come; Ernst imagined him raging all day, inwardly, taking it out on his family, and himself.

Ernst pulled out a chair and sat at the table. 'Look, Fred. You have to see the context. Since the declaration yesterday, we are at war with a power that already has military assets in position just the other side of the First Objective. Suddenly there is an enormous amount of defensive work that must be done, along the Objective, at the coasts. Airfields must be rebuilt, ports extended. And in Albion there is a shortage of young men of working age. There were the casualties of the invasion, the prisoners taken, the labour drafts for the continent—'

'If Hitler needs fourteen-year-old English boys to defend himself against the Americans he shouldn't have declared war on them. Alf's not even going to get paid, is he?' Wiping his hands, Fred jabbed his finger for emphasis. 'I let him join the Jugend because I thought it might spare him this sort of thing, but no.'

Irma snorted. 'I'm surprised you don't tell him it'll toughen him up. That's what you used to say to Jack. "I had to do my time in the last lot and now it's your turn." You called him a *girl*, for wanting to go to technical college.' She laughed, bitter.

'You leave Jack out of this.'

'Fred, I understand,' Ernst said hastily. 'Truly I do. But I am an obergefreiter, a corporal. I have little influence on policy.'

'You're a bloody useless little prick, is what you are.'

Irma turned on him, suddenly furious. 'Oh, you're such a big man, aren't you? You sit here night after night beating up Ernst. Why don't you take on the Gestapo? No, you won't, because you're a coward and a bully, and you take it out on kids and women and—'

'Now see here, I won't be spoken to like that.' Fred's face was crimson, a vein in his neck bulging.

'I heard shouting.'

The three of them turned.

Alfie stood in the doorway. He was growing fast, but he was so thin his ill-fitting clothes hung off him, his cuffs and ankles showing. His face was blotchy, as if he had been crying. He actually had his letter from the Obligatory Work Service programme in his hand. Ernst imagined him carrying it around all day, as his father had his anger.

Fred made an obvious effort to calm down. 'It's all right, son. We weren't shouting.'

'Yes, you were. It's my fault, isn't it?'

Fred crossed to him and took his son in his massive arms, his sleeves still rolled up. 'Oh, no, son, it's not like that. We're upset about you having to go off to work, but it's not your fault, don't ever think that.'

Ernst couldn't meet Alfie's yearning eyes. They both knew that Alfie's best chance of being spared was to get a medical certificate, but such exemptions tended to favour the well-connected and wealthy. He said, 'Alfie, it is only work. It will not be so bad. You will be with others of your age, and older.'

'You see,' Fred said. He mock-punched Alfie on the chest, and pinched his arms. 'A bit of outdoor work. Better than school, eh?'

'Will we get more food?' Alfie asked Ernst.

'I do not know. I will try to find out.'

'Well, there's food now,' Irma said. She had the roast on a big serving plate; the crackling was golden brown. 'And that's enough fuss for now. Fred, come over here and carve. And Alfie, will you tell your sister to—'

There was a knock at the door.

They all froze. Fred caught Ernst's eye, and Ernst knew what he was thinking.

Viv came running down the stairs. She seemed excited, not alarmed. 'Was that a knock? Who is it?'

'Shut up.' Fred walked heavily to the door, and opened it.

The voice was a woman's, her English heavily accented. 'I am looking for Ernst Trojan. I – he used to lodge here—'

Ernst ran to the door, pushing past Fred. '*Claudine*?'

XXII

She was dressed in a slim-fitting coat, stockings and black hat: a smart outfit but mud-splashed and torn. She looked exhausted. And an immense bruise marred one side of her face. 'My God, Claudine, what happened to you? Come in, come in out of the cold—' He took her arm and led her into the kitchen. In the light the bruise on her face looked even worse, and he could see how her stockings were snagged.

The Millers stood around staring.

'I'm sorry,' Ernst said in English. 'Fred, Irma, this is a friend. Her name is Claudine Rimmer, she is from France.'

'I didn't have anywhere else to go,' Claudine said in German. 'I couldn't think—'

Fred snapped, 'This is my house, and you'll speak English.'

'Yes,' said Ernst hastily. 'I am sorry. Of course.'

Irma got over her shock. 'Oh, never mind him. Come in. Let's get that coat off you. My, it's pretty.'

Claudine forced a smile. 'It is torn,' she said in English.

'Nothing that a bit of make do and mend won't see to.' Irma handed the coat and Claudine's hat to Viv. 'Here, love, hang these up.'

Viv took the clothes with a scowl and flounced out.

'Now you come and sit down. Fred, you put that roast back in the oven.'

Alfie stared at the meat. 'Aren't we going to eat?'

'There'll be time for that later. Fred, put a bit of paper on the meat so it doesn't dry out.' Irma bustled off to put the kettle on the range.

Ernst sat with Claudine. He had not seen her since that October day at Hastings, when he had fled from her. Seeing her now, in this condition, he felt ashamed. And it was very, very strange to have her sitting here now, the girl he had fallen in love with in sunny Boulogne, a year and a world away. But that was the war for you, the endless, overpowering, abhuman war, mixing everything up.

221

He said, 'So you ran away. Yes?'

'Me? Run? In these shoes?' That was the old Claudine.

He smiled at her. 'Do you want a cigarette?'

'Please.'

Irma came over now and inspected Claudine's face, pushing back her hair. Claudine flinched. 'That's a nice shiner you've got, love.'

'I walked into a lamp-post. The blackout. You know.'

Fred just glared, disbelieving. But Irma said, 'Well, we've all done that. I could send Fred or Alfie for the doctor—'

'No,' said Claudine quickly. 'It is just a bruise.'

'Well, I'll get you some iodine, and a sponge to clean you up a bit. You just sit there, darling. Fred, you make some tea. Get some fresh leaves from the caddy; that last lot are as old as last Christmas.'

Fred was still putting the roast in the oven. He said, 'Bloody hell.' But he complied, fetching down a fresh mug from the shelf

Viv came back in. She sat beside Ernst, as close as she could get, and she glared at Claudine. 'So what's your name again?'

'Rimmer. Claudine Rimmer.'

'*Claudine.* How do you know Ernst? What do you do for a living, *Claudine*?'

'I work as a translator for the occupation authority.'

'Oh, yes? I'll bet I know what you *really* do.'

'Viv!' Irma came back with a bottle of iodine solution and a rag; she poured hot water from the kettle into a bowl. 'You don't speak to people like that.'

'Come on, Mum, look at her! She's French!' She wrinkled her nose. '*And* she's drenched in perfume.'

'Enough. Your room, Vivien. Now.'

Viv stood up. 'I'll be glad, I can't stand the *stink* in here.' She marched out, lips pulled into a pout. She had come and gone in a minute; it was as if a storm had passed through the room.

Fred set a mug of tea before Claudine. She closed her hands around the mug, as if grateful for the warmth, but did not drink.

Irma started working at the bruise with the iodine and water. 'You mustn't mind Viv. It's just that she's, well, she's fifteen.'

'I was fifteen once,' Claudine said. She drew on her cigarette and eyed Ernst. 'But she likes you, I think. She is jealous, perhaps. Of course she was right about me.' That stunned them all to silence, Ernst embarrassed, Fred and Irma shocked, Alfie wide-eyed. 'It is best to be truthful, is it not? Not to hide behind lies.'

'Bloody hell,' said Fred. 'Bloody, bloody hell. What's it coming to, eh? That's what I want to know.'

Irma, resolute, kept on with her first aid. 'Don't mind him. We don't all get pleasant choices, do we, in this war?'

'That is true.' Claudine flinched as Irma dabbed on the iodine.

'And whatever you've, you know, you didn't deserve this done to you, did you?'

'Who was it?' Ernst asked.

'English,' she said. 'A Landwacht. In the closed houses we are expected to entertain them too. When I would not do what he asked – well. He grew frustrated.'

'So why did you leave?' Ernst said. The military brothels were supervised, and the girls given medical attention. 'You could have reported this.'

'But he would have reported what I did to *him*. I did fight back, Ernst.'

'Good for you.'

'My punishment would have been harsh. I have not always obeyed rules before. So I fled.'

'Can we eat now?' Alfie asked pitiably.

'In a minute,' his mother said. 'Maybe Miss Rimmer would like to join us? There's enough meat for another plate.'

'Now wait a minute,' said Fred, and he loomed over the table. 'Wait just a bloody minute. I hope you're not thinking of letting this frog *stay*.'

'Fred,' Irma snapped.

Ernst said quickly, 'She has nowhere else to go, Fred.'

'We ought to hand her over to the bloody Gestapo, that's what we should do, or we'll all be for it!'

'Let it just be for the night, then. I will sort something out.'

'Oh, you'll sort her out, but you won't get my little boy off the OWS levy, will you?'

'That's different.'

'I bet it bloody is. Shall I cut him a hole so you can fuck him, will that make you help him?'

Ernst stood, furious. 'That is *enough*.'

Irma pushed herself between them. 'For God's sake, Fred! Please, Obergefreiter—'

Viv came running down the stairs. 'Ernst – Dad – there's somebody coming. I saw them from upstairs. Cars and torches and dogs. There's shouting. They're coming here, Dad!'

XXIII

Fred paced around, limping heavily on his damaged leg, punching one fist into another. 'Oh Christ Jesus. One from every house, that's what they take. Oh Christ bloody Jesus, not here, let them not come here.'

Viv peered out of a chink in the blackout curtain. 'They're walking down the drive. One fat man just slipped in the slush.' She actually laughed.

'You stupid little baggage!' Fred would have lunged at her.

Ernst caught his arm. 'Fred! We must get the children away, out of sight. And the women.'

'I'm not going anywhere,' Irma said. But she was shaking, her face empty.

And anyhow there was no time even for that. There was a hammering on the door, a shout, in German, 'Open up! Out, out!'

Viv screamed and ran upstairs. Irma grabbed her baby from her cot, and went to Alfie, who was still clutching his OWS papers, as if they were a shield. Fred just stood there motionless, hands bunched into fists.

Ernst made to go to the door.

Claudine got up and grabbed his arm. 'No,' she said in German. 'Let me go.'

'You? But—'

'Maybe I can confuse them. I will start shouting in German, and demand to see the oberleutnant in charge of the closed house, or something.' She managed a small smile. 'You know how you Germans are. Bureaucratic to a fault. If they're confused they might forget why they came here.'

'But—'

There was another slam on the door, like the heel of a boot, and dogs barked.

She flashed him a smile. 'I do this for you,' she said. She made for the door.

Ernst glimpsed an officer and an enlisted man, both in SS black, with a dog on a rope leash. When it smelled the roast pork the dog went crazy. Claudine spoke softly to the SS men in what sounded like English, not German, and showed them a bit of paper that to Ernst looked oddly like a British identity card. The officer inspected the paper. 'Good. Come.' He grabbed her arm and pulled her away, so roughly she stumbled.

Fred stood, unmoving. 'Is it over?'

Irma was patting at her apron. 'My identity card is gone. She must have— I thought what she showed them looked a bit familiar. How did she do that?'

In an instant Ernst saw what Claudine had done, that she had taken Irma's place. 'Claudine!' He lunged forward.

But Fred stood in his way and grabbed his arms. 'Let her go,' he said. 'She did it to spare us. For God's sake—'

Through the open door Ernst saw they were dragging her to a truck, in which a dozen people already stood passively, their heads bowed. He struggled. 'Get your hands *off* me!'

'Please. I'm begging you.' The man was crying, Ernst saw. Fred wrapped his big farmer's arms around him, as if he was hugging him rather than restraining him. 'Let her go! Oh, God, let her go.'

XXIV

It was an hour before Fred would let Ernst out of the house.

They all sat in the kitchen, as if stunned. Irma cut Alfie some of the pork. None of the others could eat.

When the hour was up Ernst pulled on his greatcoat and boots and ran out of the door. It had stopped snowing. The sky was full of cloud, but the air was cold, clear.

Ernst went to find Alfie's bike, the one the boy rode every day to school, the only transport available. The bike was a bit small for him, but Alfie's legs were long, and Ernst was able to make it work. There was a little dynamo that powered flickering lamps front and back.

The bike was hard work, the slush and the mud dragging at the wheels. It was pitch dark aside from the light of his lamps, but he was able to follow the tracks of the truck easily enough. As he passed more farmhouses he saw where the footprints of the men and dogs diverged from the main track.

As he rode on he began to hear the shooting, rough volleys clattering through the still air.

The killing site was at a place called Netherfield, little more than a road junction a couple of miles north of Battle. The only light came from the trucks' headlights; the vehicles' engines were running, rumbling. He saw people being lined up, ten or a dozen at a time. There seemed to be more SS men than captives. The men stood around, helmets of smoke around their heads in the cold air. One man bent to pat his dog. He heard laughter.

A man, an SS-schutze waving a torch, stopped him a hundred yards from the site. 'Halt, Herr Obergefreiter. You have your card?'

Ernst got off the bike, and fumbled in his jacket pocket for his papers.

The schutze inspected them by torchlight. 'What are you doing here, Herr Obergefreiter?'

'There is somebody here I know,' Ernst said. 'Not British – French. A mistake.'

Another volley of gunfire.

'I wouldn't go down there if I were you,' the schutze said. 'It is nearly done, the work. If your friend was ever there, well . . . The einsatzgruppen are not fond of being interrupted.'

Ernst took a step forward. 'But—'

The schutze put a gloved hand on his chest. 'Please.'

Another group was lined up. They stood at the edge of a pit. Ernst wondered how it had been dug out, for the ground was frozen. Perhaps it had been prepared in advance; the SS were nothing if not efficient. Ernst saw the silhouettes of the men with their pistols, standing behind their targets. When the order came to fire there was a spray of blood and brains, you could clearly see it, vivid crimson by the glow of the trucks' lamps. Some of the victims fell cleanly, others quivered and trembled before they dropped, and some screamed, not yet dead. Men stepped forward and pistols cracked, as the work of clean-up was finished.

The schutze watched this impassively. 'Would you like a cigarette, Herr Obergefreiter?'

'No.'

'Um. Then, do you have one to spare?'

Ernst dug a packet out of his greatcoat pocket.

The man took a cigarette gratefully. He lit it within cupped fingers, and the glow illuminated his face. He was very young, Ernst saw. 'It is not as easy as you might think,' the schutze said slowly, 'to kill a man.'

'It is a mistake,' Ernst said. 'She should not be there.'

The schutze nodded. 'Such things happen. I once read of a pope who, when receiving complaints about the unfairness of the Inquisition, said that he would leave it to Saint Peter to sort out saints from sinners. Do you believe in God?'

'Do you?'

'Not any more, Herr Obergefreiter.'

The men dispersed from the edge of the pit, and the trucks' engines roared.

XXV

24 December

The Sea Lion monument was already astonishing, Mary thought as she was driven up with George. Even incomplete, it was a henge of concrete and scaffolding that utterly dominated the Richborough site. All around its base the ground was churned into ruts, and rainwater stood everywhere, glimmering, scummy.

'All this must be playing merry hell with the archaeology,' she said.

George sat beside her in the car, the buttons on his uniform polished to a gleam. He twisted his head to see the arch. 'Look at that bloody thing. These Germans really are crackers.'

'The SS scholars know their history, though. Claudius would have been impressed. But I'm surprised the RAF haven't bombed this monstrosity to bits.'

George grinned. 'Oh, their way is to wait until the thing is nearly finished, *then* bomb it to bits.'

New buildings huddled at the feet of the arch, neat but boxy. Staff stood in rows, mostly uniformed. As Mary's car drew up, flashbulbs popped. Evidently they were expected.

And Gary was here, somewhere in this strange complex.

Mary would have been nervous anyhow, even if not for Gary. She'd never been involved in an operation like this before, and the fact that Germany and the US had gone to war with each other since Mackie had cooked up his plan had made things 'a tad more complicated', in Mackie's dry words. Still here she was, the show was on the road. But when she thought of Gary being close by, the day seemed distant, unreal, even the mass of the unfinished monument transient and illusory.

The car drew up at the base of the arch. The SS driver opened the door and Mary got out. The driver took a package from the car trunk. It was Mackie's Roman spear, preserved within a beautifully crafted wooden box. The box was heavy, but George carried it easily.

Under lumpy cloud it was dark, Christmas Eve turning out to be one of those English midwinter days that never seem to gather the strength to break into full, honest daylight; at noon this was about as bright as it was going to get. But the monument somehow looked right under such a sky, four mighty silhouetted stumps. She could smell the sea, and that reminded her that Tom Mackie was not far away, standing offshore in a motor boat, waiting to take her to safety.

A small party of SS officers approached, trailed by photographers.

'We'll get through this,' George said to Mary. 'Just a couple of hours and it will be done.'

'I'm glad you're here,' she whispered.

One SS man closed on her, hand outstretched; he was not tall, but slim and unreasonably good-looking. 'Mrs Wooler? I am Standartenfuhrer Josef Trojan. Merry Christmas! I am really so delighted to see you again. We have worked together a long time now, haven't we?' Trojan took Mary's hand and shook it; the grip of his gloved hand was firm, warm. He turned with practised ease to face the little party of photographers. There was a blizzard of popping bulbs. 'And Constable Tanner, we meet again.'

'Sergeant Tanner now, thanks very much.'

The photographers were close enough for Mary to make out their accreditation. Some of them worked for Reich information agencies, but there were reporters from neutral-country newspapers – Swiss, Spanish, Irish. She knew that part of Trojan's objective today must be to bind her up in a Reich-friendly story that might mitigate the impact of her report of the Peter's Well atrocity. Let him think that. One way or another the day wasn't going to unfold as Trojan expected. She smiled for the cameras.

Now Trojan made more introductions. 'Mrs Wooler, you have met my colleague Unterscharfuhrer Julia Fiveash. And this is my brother, Obergefreiter Ernst Trojan.'

The obergefreiter wore a Wehrmacht uniform. He bowed to Mary crisply. He was a younger, paler version of his brother, she thought, less vivid – less certain – a more interesting character, perhaps. But there was no time to speak to him.

And Julia Fiveash, when she walked up to Mary, was extraordinary, a mass of contradictions, a beautiful Englishwoman in a mannish SS uniform. 'Mrs Wooler? I'm delighted to meet you again.' She bowed to George, who nodded back, more stiffly.

Josef Trojan clapped his brother's back. 'I dragged Ernst here, away from his other vital duties for the protectorate, because this is Christmas! A time of friendship and family. A time to demonstrate loyalties that transcend the temporary barriers of wartime. And today here we are, American, German and English, all gathered to celebrate intellectual endeavour.'

Mary thought she ought to say something. 'You do understand I'm not representing my nation.'

'Of course.'

'I'm here for the scholarship. Whichever sides we find ourselves on temporarily, your work here deserves praise and encouragement,' she deadpanned. 'For it is only scholarship, education, learning, that will ultimately remove the shadow of war from mankind.'

'I could not have put it better myself,' Trojan said. 'I won't keep you waiting any longer. Come now.' He turned and led the group back towards the largest of the new buildings.

George and Julia walked together, stiff, not looking at each other. Mary knew there was something going on between them, unlikely as it seemed. And George in fact was troubled by his 'betrayal' of Julia today. Mary didn't understand it. She had always thought of war as a simplifying process, a lining-up of good against evil. But on the ground things were messy, in just about every way you could imagine. Mary couldn't figure out George and this Julia, and maybe she never would; it was best to look away.

The brick building was unprepossessing, a couple of storeys with a flat roof, like an office building. But once they passed through the big double doors Mary found herself in a grand space, with a floor of polished pink granite and oak-panelled walls. A rather over-ornate staircase led up to the upper storey, and down to a basement. The hall was dominated by an enormous Christmas tree, a towering affair covered with silver balls and tinsel and little swastika medallions. The Nazis did everything big, it seemed, even Christmas.

Once they were out of sight of the cameras, just for a minute, Trojan asked them to submit to a search. Their bags were opened, their bodies briskly patted down.

Then the party was lined up for more photos, before a wall which bore a proud name plaque – 'Richborough College – SS Ahnenerbe – 1941' – and an embossed swastika and various other insignia. Above all this clutter Mary made out two hooks, neatly fixed.

Trojan grinned. 'You can see we are ready for your gift.'

'I think that's your cue, George,' Mary murmured.

George stepped forward, and made a ceremony of handing Trojan his wooden box. Trojan opened it to reveal the battered Roman spear that had once graced a farmhouse wall at Birdoswald. For the sake of the cameras Trojan cradled the spear, earnestly inspecting it. All this as the flashbulbs popped, and the photographers called him to look this way and that.

'And the provenance – this is authentic, a spear that witnessed the Crucifixion, so to speak.' Trojan stroked the spear tip, caressing it, almost sexually. 'Astonishing to think, isn't it? The Reichsfuhrer will be delighted! Here, Ernst. See if you can get this mounted. It will make another good picture.' He passed the spear to his brother.

The young obergefreiter sent another soldier running; he returned with two short step-ladders.

'I don't know what the Nazis want with an old spear,' George murmured.

Mary whispered back, 'It's quite neat. Tom Mackie did his own research about Birdoswald, since it seems to be so pivotal to this whole saga. There is a fragmentary story that the fort served as headquarters to one of the officials involved in the construction of Hadrian's Wall. An auxiliary commander called Tullio, a Bavarian. And this Tullio had some kind of contact who was present at the Crucifixion.'

That jolted George. 'Really? What's this based on?'

She grinned. 'A good historian's question. Very little. Grave markers, that sort of thing, and a lot of speculation. But Christ had died less than a century earlier. Given that, it's at least plausible that Tullio would have had in his possession some sort of relic of the Crucifixion. A soldier's trophy. A spear, perhaps – like the Spear of Longinus, said to have been used to wound the dying Christ.'

'Ah. Hitler's got that, hasn't he? And Himmler and his crew are always on the look-out for holy relics.'

'Yep. But if Tullio did have such a spear, and he was stationed at the Wall, and his descendants stayed on after him—'

'It might have finished up buried at Birdoswald. Only to be dug up by a Navy bloke two thousand years later.'

'That's the general idea.'

'This is an utter pack of lies, isn't it, Mary?'

'Absolutely. But Himmler's toadies have been fooled by much less convincing frauds.'

The photographers took more snaps, of the party as a whole under the spear, then of Josef Trojan and Mary together, and Trojan alone. He had the photographers crouch, so they looked up at his handsome face, his crossed arms, the spear on the wall behind him.

Mary watched this, fretting, light-headed. Knowing what was to follow, she felt furiously impatient with this buffoon and his show-boating, even though she knew it was that quality about him that had got her in here in the first place.

At last Trojan was done. He straightened his uniform and approached Mary again. 'This day is perfect, for me – perfect. And now let me make it perfect for you, my dear Mary Wooler.' He turned and nodded to his brother, who, looking a bit embarrassed by all the song and dance, opened a door to a staff room.

And Gary walked out. There was a young woman as his side. He wore a smart suit and tie, his shoes were polished, his hair cut and combed.

Mary ran to her son and grabbed him. She hadn't seen him since the invasion, since his capture. Gary hugged her back, hard; she felt his strength, an echo of his father's. Flashbulbs popped. Trojan and the other Germans applauded. Mary ignored them all.

Gary drew back and held her arms. 'Mom. Hey, no tears. You'll mess up the suit.'

'I wasn't expecting— when I thought of you, I imagined you in your uniform. Seeing you in a suit, it's as if the war never happened.'

'Yeah, but my uniform don't look so good after a year in the stalag, believe me.'

She looked at him intently. 'And you're well?'

He shrugged. 'Life in Rutupiae is pretty good. Their doctors gave me a good check-over. Compared to the stalag, I'm well off.'

'And of course he has me.' The young woman approached tentatively. She was dressed in white, attractively if soberly; her face was square, sensible, and quite well made up. This was Doris Keeler, and one eye flickered, a subtle wink at Mary, her old friend from Colchester. 'Sophie Silver,' she said boldly. She held up her left hand and waggled her ring finger. It bore a band of silver. 'Though, with your blessing, it will soon be Mrs Sophie Wooler. And hopefully *before* any little Aryans come along.'

'Oh, my dear.' Mary embraced her. 'It's so good to meet you. Gary told me all about you in his mail.'

'All good, I hope.' She plucked at Gary's lapel. 'Though he didn't listen to me about this suit. A bit spivvy, don't you think?'

More flashbulbs popped as they talked. Gary Wooler, American veteran of the invasion, was now the poster boy of Himmler's crackpot breeding programme. It had all been perfect, Mary thought, immaculately set up by MI-14 and the resistance – a trap of publicity and achievement this vain, ambitious Josef Trojan couldn't resist falling into.

But Julia Fiveash was staring intently at them, her eyes narrow, her face expressionless. Trojan might have taken the bait, Mary reminded herself, but he wasn't the only player here.

Delicately Trojan approached them. 'I am delighted to have been the agent of this long overdue reunion,' he said. 'But now I must ask you to come with me. Mrs Wooler, I have a number of scholars eager to discuss with you their work on the implications for the medieval age of the Norman Conquest – I know that is an interest of yours. Many of our scholars are English, you know – indeed many have come into the protectorate specifically to work at this institute! And we have good links with several English universities, including both Oxford and Cambridge. As you remarked, there are bonds of scholarship which, eternal, transcend the petty political squabbles of the day. And then you must let me treat you to lunch . . .'

He walked on with Mary, with George, Doris and Gary following, the rest of the German staff and the patient photographers, on deeper into the bowels of his brand-new college, their footsteps echoing on the granite floor tiles.

XXVI

The space under the floor was only about three feet deep, and full of water and gas pipes and electricity cables. Gary had to climb through this jungle from joist to joist, ducking past the pipes and cables, fearful that at any moment he would put his foot through the basement ceiling under him and ruin everything.

Doris seemed able to squirm through it all with remarkable ease. By the light of the torch strapped to his head, Gary saw her wriggling away ahead of him, her legs bare save for her stockings, her skirt tucked up without self-consciousness into her belt. She wasn't even getting her white outfit dirty. 'Come on, keep up,' she whispered back at him.

'I haven't had your training.'

'What about all that tunnelling out of the POW camp?'

'That was for the English,' he said. 'The public school types. Anyhow the Germans kept a close eye on me. A Prominente, remember.'

'What a rotten excuse. We're close, I think.'

It hadn't been hard to slip away from his mother's group and out of sight of the various German guards. Once they were alone, in a kind of reading room, Doris had shown him the diagram the resistance spies had assembled of this Ahnenerbe facility. They knew that Ben was being held in a kind of laboratory tucked away in the basement. 'Of course it would be the basement,' Gary had remarked. 'Nazis like basements.' It had taken Doris only minutes to lift the carpet, prise up a couple of floorboards, and slip down into the space between the ground level floor and the basement ceiling.

'Here.' She came to a stop. With care she unscrewed a light fitting, pulled it back, and peered through the hole in the ceiling plaster. 'Bingo. And there's nobody around. Probably all watching the show upstairs ...' She took a knife from under her skirt and briskly cut a circle in the plaster, a couple of feet across. She looked down again. 'Only six or eight feet. Piece of cake.' She grabbed a wooden joist and swung her feet down through the hole. She dangled by her arms from the joist. Then she let go and dropped, bending her legs so she landed without impact, and virtually no noise.

Gary came to the hole. The room below was brightly lit. He glimpsed mechanical equipment, a glass wall. Doris stood directly beneath him. He could see plaster dust on her hair. 'Now you.'

He landed heavily, with a noisy clatter, and nearly stumbled over.

'Idiot,' she hissed.

'Show-off.' He straightened up, brushing the dust from his suit jacket, and looked around. The room was a box, brightly lit, the walls white-washed. The central area was walled off by glass, a room within a room. There were desks, work tables and chairs, mounds of paper heaped up – and, incongruously, a big bookcase that contained mouldering history titles. There was a hum of fans; the air was dry, cool.

But the place was dominated by a bank of mechanical gadgetry that covered one wall, side to side, floor to ceiling. It was as he imagined a telephone exchange might be, all relays and wires in an aluminium frame.

Doris asked softly, 'Is this Ben?'

He whirled around. She was looking into the glass-walled inner chamber. There was nothing much in there but a bed, he saw, with white sheets, and a table and chair and a washbasin, a piss-pot on the floor. And on the bed, over the sheets, lay a man in striped prison pyjamas, small, hunched over with his legs up by his belly, his arms folded, mussed black hair dark against the pillow. He wore a kind of cap of silvery metal, connected by the wires to a metal cabinet beside the bed. He was bathed in brilliant white light.

Gary hammered on the glass wall. 'Ben. Ben!'

The sleeping figure stirred resentfully, mumbling.

'Keep it down, for God's sake. Let's get him out of there.' The glass box had a door, a lock embedded in its transparent structure. Doris produced another tool, like a fine screwdriver, and began to work at the lock.

At last Ben opened an eye. When he saw Gary, he lurched up to a sitting position. His shirt hung open, showing his belly. He got out of bed and ran to the glass wall. The metal cap was ripped off his head by the trailing wires. His crown had been shaved, like a monk's tonsure, and his scalp was prickled by an array of crimson dots. He stood there flattened against the glass, his mouth open. 'You came for me.'

Gary was inches away, but could not touch him. 'I told you I would, didn't I? It's OK, Ben. We'll get you out of this fucking zoo. Christ, I think they've got him drugged up. His eyes—'

'Gary! Gary!'

Doris still worked at the lock. 'Try to keep him quiet.'

Gary made calming motions with his hands. 'Ben, it's OK, just take it easy.'

The door swung back soundlessly, and Doris, tucking away her lock-picking tool, hurried into the glass room. When Doris reached for him Ben flinched back, hammering his head on the glass wall. 'Christ,' Doris said. 'Gary, get in here, for God's sake.'

Gary pushed past Doris. Ben threw himself at him. 'Gary, oh my word, you came, I thought I would never, I thought . . .' He buried his face in Gary's chest.

Gary wrapped his arms around him. Ben felt almost podgy, with fat over his ribs and belly. 'They've been feeding you up. Christ, what have they done to you?'

Ben looked up, his eyes glazed. 'It's what they've done *with* me . . . Drugged up, asleep most of the time. *Dreaming.* Past and future, past and future. We're a bridge across time, a computing machine and my poor wandering psyche. You don't want to know, Gary, I mean it. Although your mother knows, I think, she might understand by now.'

'Never mind that,' Doris hissed. 'Come on. Out.'

Ben didn't want to let go of Gary, but they persuaded him to grab Gary's arm so that the two of them could walk, awkwardly, with Doris's help.

Doris, all business, shepherded them to the heap of plaster dust under the hole in the roof. 'Out the way we came. Gary, get back up there. Use that chair. I'll give Ben a boost back up. I'll follow, after I've done a bit of business in here. And then—'

'No.' Ben had been passive for a few seconds, but now he started panicking. He twisted away from them both and ran to the bank of mechanical gear at the back wall. 'I must see if they've done what they threatened, if they've *done* it . . .'

'We don't have time for this,' Doris snapped.

Gary grabbed her arm. 'Look, Doris, take it easy. He'll be a lot easier to get out through that roof space conscious than unconscious.'

She bit her lip. 'All right. But quickly.'

Ben found a paper-tape punch. He scrolled through its output, and pawed through heaps of notes, handwritten in German, some tech-nician's orderly journal.

Gary stood by him. 'We have to go, pal.'

'Not before I know if they've used this thing.'

'For what?' Gary looked up at the bank of gleaming equipment, the relays and wires, rods and gears. It was beautiful, he thought, a beautifully made machine in the midst of all this madness. 'What is this, Ben?'

Ben snorted. 'Actually it's a Z3. An electromechanical calculating machine. The pride of German engineering. They use it to calculate the Gödel trajectories, you see, the paths back to the past. They come here, you know. Technicians from the Zuse Apparatebau in Berlin. Zuse sends technicians from Berlin to service it! Can you believe that? They get *paid*. And I, I must dream ... *Unh*.' It was a grunt, as if he had been struck in the stomach.

'Ben?'

'They did it.' He held up a length of paper tape. 'See? There's the proof, right there. And the date stamp.'

'They did what?'

'*They sent it back in time*. The Menologium. Just two days ago. Tell your mother. Make sure she understands, that she knows. Tell her I signed it.' He grinned. 'I signed my name in their fucking Menologium. Now my name must be in the history books. Think of that! But if only you'd come earlier – it's too late, they did it again, like Rory, and I died, I died again—' And he slumped into the corner, his back to the shining machine.

'Enough,' Doris said. 'Help me, Gary.'

They each grabbed an arm and began hauling, but Ben was limp now, just a burden. He said, 'To wipe out all of history, at the push of a button, the close of a relay – billions upon billions of lives, snuffed out and *swapped* for a whole new set – the close of a relay – what could be more fascistic than that?'

Gary could hear noise coming from above, shouting, heavy running footsteps – the thump of an explosion somewhere, a rattle of gunfire. 'It's coming apart,' he said.

'You surprise me,' Doris said. 'We might still get out of this. Up you go.'

Gary hopped on a chair, jumped so he got his hands onto the joists, and pushed himself up. 'Pass him up.' Sitting with his legs dangling through the ceiling, he reached down with his arms.

The door slammed open. SS troopers burst in, six, eight, ten of them, all with automatic weapons or pistols. Julia Fiveash was at their head, waving a silver pistol of her own. The SS troopers screamed German phrases that Gary knew well from the stalag: 'Down!' 'On your knees, on the floor!'

Doris looked up at Gary. Ben was slumped in her arms, almost unconscious. She mouthed, 'Go!' And suddenly she had her knife at Ben's throat.

Gary lifted his legs out of the hole and scrambled back.

Doris turned to face Fiveash. 'Back off, you traitorous bitch, or I cut his throat!'

The troopers hung back uncertainly.

Fiveash advanced, step by step, her pistol held out straight before her in her two hands. 'I knew there was something wrong with you people. The way the Woolers greeted each other – that was more than a mother greeting her prisoner son – I knew there was an agenda! I admit I didn't spot *you*, Silver—'

With a grunt Doris shoved Ben at Fiveash. He fell against her, tangling her up. And Doris ran at the big calculating machine, the Z3. Fiveash yelled at the troopers.

Suddenly Gary saw what Doris was going to do. He ducked behind a roof joist for cover.

The explosion was a pulse of light, the concussion a punch in the gut. Over the Z3 the roof plaster blew upwards, and Gary tried to shield his face.

XXVII

He could feel himself rock back and forth, and the breeze on his face was fresh and cold and salty. He opened his eyes. Uniforms, all around him, at odd angles. A grey sky above, heavy with cloud.

He was in a boat. He sat up with a lurch.

'Gary?'

His mother was beside him. He had been lying with his head on her lap. She stroked his forehead, but he flinched, his skin tender. The boat was small, and full of marines. One older man, an officer, sat opposite him, peaked cap, trenchcoat, watching him steadily.

His mother asked, 'How do you feel?'

He grabbed her hand. 'Like one big bruise. And I've a head that's ringing like the Liberty Bell.' He touched his ears; his hearing was muffled.

'I'll get you some water.' She passed him a canteen.

He glanced down at himself, at plaster dust, blood, rips. 'I've ruined my suit.'

'You'll answer to Moss Bros for that,' said the officer, his voice very cultured British.

'Who?'

'Never mind. Bad joke.' He stuck out his hand. 'I'm Tom Mackie. Captain, RN. Seconded to military intelligence for the foreseeable. I know your mother, and I've heard all about you, Gary, but it's the first time we've met. Apart from when I slung you over my shoulder to get you out of Richborough.'

'I'm embarrassed,' Gary said. 'Um, where am I?'

'The English Channel, old chap. Don't worry, you're quite safe.'

His mother said, 'The doctor who looked at you on the shore said you had concussion, you were suffering from shock. It's amazing you found your way back out of that roof space at all.'

'I don't remember,' Gary admitted.

'What, none of it?' Mackie asked drily. 'The marine assault on Rich-borough, perfectly timed incidentally, the gun fight with those SS goons, the dash to the beach?'

'Sorry.'

'Ah, well. Just your average Christmas Eve, really.'

Gary shivered. A marine threw him a green blanket. 'Here you go, chum.' He wrapped it around his body gratefully, and let his mother embrace him; he supposed she deserved that. The day was darkling, he saw, the light seeping out of a leaden sky.

Mackie leaned forward. 'Are you up to a little debrief?'

'I'll try.'

'Ben Kamen?'

'We found him. He was sleeping. Wired up to a machine, an, um, "electromechanical calculating machine", he called it. A Z3, yes.'

'All right. Good. You didn't manage to get Ben out?'

He shook his head. 'Last I saw of him, that SS officer came – Fiveash. I was looking down into the cellar room from the roof space. Doris challenged her. They could all be dead by now.'

'We'll have to assume they're not, until proven.'

'I think Doris must have done for the Z3.'

'Good girl,' Mackie said, nodding. 'She'll get a medal for this, if posthumously. But it may not do a lot of good,' he said to Mary. 'Not if they still have Kamen.'

'What I don't understand,' Gary said, 'is how Doris managed to smuggle in that much explosive. I mean, we were all searched on the way in.'

His mother said, 'It was George.'

'George?'

'That wooden box containing the spear – it wasn't as solid as it looked.'

Gary shook his head. 'I never knew. What happened to George?'

'Sergeant Tanner kept out of the fighting,' Mackie said. 'Sensible chap. Now he's stayed behind to help clear up the mess. He's on our side, fundamentally, of course. Look, you did all you could, all that was asked of you. But the operation will be judged a failure, I think.'

Mary said, 'Why? They have Ben Kamen, but Doris destroyed the Z3.'

'Yes, but they can rebuild. We've been receiving reports of paratroop raids on high-technology establishments. Bletchley Park. Radar research sites. Places like that. We're pretty sure they are planning a Loom Mark II - were, even before the events of today. Bigger and better. We haven't stopped them, just slowed them down a bit. Of course that's something. But the fact that we acted against the Loom might, paradoxically, convince Trojan's SS superiors to take it more seriously. Ben was the key, really. We hoped to save him. That was a mistake. Should have gone in specifically to kill him.' He sighed. 'May be a while before we get a second crack at it.'

'The Menologium,' Gary said suddenly.

They both looked at him sharply. 'What was that?'

'I remember. Ben talked about something called the Menologium. He was terrified.' He stared at his mother. 'Look, what's going on here? What are you mixed up with, Mom?'

'We'll brief you properly in a secure environment,' Mackie said. 'But for now, please – if you are beginning to remember—'

'He said it had been "sent back". This Menologium. He showed me a paper tape to prove it. As if I'd understand ...'

His mother looked at Mackie. 'It *had* to have been sent back. I mean, I found traces of it in the literature. Records of it going back to the fifth century. With Kamen's name embedded in it.'

Mackie asked, 'Gary, *when* was this Menologium sent back? Did Ben say?'

'Two days ago. He was clear about that. He said the bit of paper tape confirmed it. He said I had to be sure to tell you, Mom.'

His mother grabbed the side of the boat, her face white.

'Mom? Are you OK?'

'Yes, yes. It's just – Tom, *two days ago*. But I was finding evidence of Ben's tampering with the Menologium, I held it in my own hands, I copied it out, *months* ago. The evidence existed, in a sense, even before the Menologium had been sent – perhaps even before Kamen did his bit of coding in the acrostic – perhaps even before any drafts of the Menologium had been prepared at all. Now you tell me, how is that possible?'

Mackie stroked his stubbly cheeks, pulling his lips. 'Perhaps I should write another letter to Mr Wells.'

'So Trojan saw through his scheme to meddle with Hastings. *But he failed* - the Menologium didn't work. It can't have. Because Harold lost, didn't he?'

'That's what I remember being taught at school,' Mackie said drily.

'Nothing happened, two days ago, when Trojan closed his switch. No flashing lights in the sky. I remember two days ago, and three, and four; my memories are continuous.'

Gary stared at her. 'What on earth are you talking about?'

'But now we live in a history in which the Menologium was sent back, but failed to deflect Hastings. Maybe there was another history that existed before Trojan threw the switch – gone. It never existed, and never will. And the people who inhabited it – copies of us, but different from us—' She shuddered. 'It could be that way, couldn't it? That could be how the history change works. I don't know if I can deal with this.'

'You're scaring me,' Gary said. 'Ben was scared. I've never seen such terror, and Ben was a Jew in Nazi hands. He had a lot to be scared about. I promised to get Ben out when he was taken from the stalag. I failed. I'll have to go back.'

'Well, you could get the chance, old bean, although it might be a while,' Mackie murmured. 'And while this Menologium may be a busted flush, they'll no doubt start off on some new history-bothering project altogether, and we'll have to start from scratch too. More research on your agenda, Mary. What a bloody show this all is, what a show. We really have got to put a stop to it.' He glanced over his shoulder. 'But that's for tomorrow. Soon be at the ship. Hot cup of tea, that's what we need.' He pulled out a pipe and began to fill it.

His mother grabbed Gary and buried her face in his collar. He put his arms around her. She was trembling. But even now he didn't understand what she was so scared of.

The motor boat forged on through the fading afternoon light.

III

WEAVER

MAY–JULY 1943

I

13 May 1943

The air in the farmhouse kitchen was a mass of cigarette smoke and
steamy cooking smells.

'I'm telling you you're not going out again dressed like a bloody little
tart.'

'What are you going to do, Dad, thump me again?'

Sitting at the kitchen table, Ernst sighed. He was tired tonight, tired
from the rounds of combat training. His ears rang from the gunfire. Not
enough, however, to shut out the raised voices.

Irma worked listlessly at the range. Little Myrtle, now nearly two years
old, was bundled-up skin and bone on the floor at her mother's feet,
playing with worn wooden blocks. Fred and Heinz sat together at the
table, two shapeless lumps hunched in their grimy shirts, smoke curling
up to the ceiling from their cigarettes. Glasses and a half-empty vodka
bottle sat on the table between them. The television set was on, its screen
a lens showing indistinct figures, walking, smiling, shaking hands, while
jolly martial music played.

Viv was before the mirror. She wore one of her smarter dresses, the
powder-blue, much let out with her mother's help. She was working at
her lips with her little finger. Seventeen years old now, she had blossomed into an attractive young woman – if a slim one, but everybody
was skinny nowadays. Ernst knew how much of her glamour was faked,
tricks learned from the girls in town: a pencil line to mimic a stocking
seam, a bit of beetroot juice and Vaseline smeared on the mouth in lieu
of lipstick.

As usual she was the centre of the arguments.

Heinz took a drag on the cigarette he held between the stumps of the
fingers of his right hand. 'Can't say I blame the father,' he said to Ernst.
'She really is a Jerrybag now, that one.' He used the English word amid
his guttural German. He had come back from the east with his voice

shot, whether by gas or Russian cigarettes he wouldn't say.

'And how long have you two been at the stuff?'

Heinz shrugged. 'An hour, maybe more. Ever since the feld-gendarmerie called again.' The military police were trying to get Fred to train with the Volkssturm militia. 'He told them where to shove their helmets, and they cut the rations again, and that was that.'

Viv turned to the door. 'Right, Mum, I'm off.'

Irma asked, 'What time will you be back, love?'

'Now don't you encourage her,' Fred said. 'Don't you bloody make it seem as if this is all *normal*.' Fred's voice was heavy. He was a stubborn old man who could defy the German military police, but he had no control over his daughter.

'Oh, Fred, what am I supposed to do? She's seventeen, she can do what she wants.'

'Well, thank you very much,' Viv said heavily. She fixed her hat on her head; it was a small trilby. 'I'm glad somebody in this house treats me like an adult and not a *criminal*.'

'Just be careful, love.'

'Yes, yes.' Viv walked past Ernst, not even looking at him.

When she slammed the kitchen door behind her Ernst winced. He felt guilty; he felt that the kindness he had tried to show the girl when he had first been billeted here had somehow gone wrong, that she had at last become what her father had feared. But what else could he have done?

Heinz topped up Fred's glass.

Ernst crossed to the sink, and stood with Irma before the open window. As the English midsummer approached the days were long; it was after seven in the evening, but the sun was still above the horizon, the sky a deep but brilliant blue, the world green and full of birdsong. It often struck him how resilient nature was. It took only days for weeds to colonise a bomb site, far faster than any human agency could clear debris and rebuild. And some men did not recover at all. Look at Heinz. He had come back from his winter on the eastern front wounded in body and mind – come back aged.

Irma handed Ernst a glass of cold water. When she took a step her clogs clattered on the stone floor. The clogs were made by Fred from wood and a bit of old leather; shoes were another item the civilian population found ever harder to replace. 'You can't blame Viv. Poor girl! It's not much of a time to be growing up, is it? No wonder she goes after a bit of glamour. You can't blame her.'

He sipped his water. 'Any news of the boys today?'

She shook her head. It had been a month since they had had a letter from Alfie, now sixteen, who had been working on a bombed-out airfield in Kent. But now there were rumours that anybody who had been involved with the Hitler Jugend was to be drafted into the Volkssturm or even the British units of the Wehrmacht, and trained to fight the expected counter-invasion. As for Jack, three years after he had been taken as a POW, there had been no word at all of him for months and months, not even through the Red Cross.

'Fred always gets worse after the post comes. In a way he frets more about Alfie than about Viv, or even Jack. Alfie's so young, you see. He can probably barely remember a time before the Germans came. It might be hard for him to shake it all off, when the Americans come.' She glanced over. 'They're starting in on the vodka earlier every day.'

Ernst forced a smile. 'Well, Heinz says he lost the fingers of his right hand at Stalingrad, but came back with a bottle of vodka in his left.'

'I hope you ate well today, Herr Obergefreiter.' She stirred the watery stew. 'Potatoes and turnip again I'm afraid. Not even any whale meat tonight! They cut our ration again, the feldgendarmerie.'

'Heinz told me.'

'Fred's a war veteran. They can't expect him to take up arms against his own countrymen. You'd think they'd have the respect not even to ask. I know he's heading for trouble. I mean, the way he swears at them! Well, maybe the Americans will be here before it all comes to a head.'

'I am sure we will cope,' Ernst said vaguely, hoping to reassure her.

She smiled and pushed hair out of her eyes. She too had lost weight; the bones of her temples were prominent, her hair thinning. 'You're always so kind, Herr Obergefreiter. It's a strange thing – I never thought I'd feel this way in that time after the invasion – I miss those old days, ever so. When it was just you. I know Heinz is your friend, but with him here, and the other soldiers in the towns, you know . . .'

He understood. The movement of troops in anticipation of the counter-invasion had upset the web of obligations and compromises that had grown up among the local people and the troops stationed among them. He himself had been irritated to have Heinz foisted on his billet, after the business over Claudine. But Claudine was long dead, and Heinz was damaged by his own war; it didn't seem to matter any more. 'Heinz isn't so bad,' he said gently. 'There are worse.' Some of the men had been brutalised by their time in the east.

'Oh, I'm sure,' she said. 'In fact he's company for Fred, in a way.' But her voice was flat, a sign that she was hiding something from him, as she often did. She shooed him away so she could finish her cooking.

Ernst sat with the men and grudgingly accepted a small shot of vodka. The television showed a newsreel, a Nazi grandee in a long leather coat touring an armaments factory. He could have been anywhere in Albion, as it seemed the whole protectorate was given over to such industries.

'Herr Goebbels,' Fred told Ernst. He pronounced the name the comical way Churchill did, 'Gobbles'. 'Poking his nose around Canterbury.'

'We are honoured,' Heinz said mockingly. He raised his glass. 'To the Reichsminister!'

'At least he's here,' Fred said. 'It's a bloody long time since Hitler showed up.'

'It is not Goebbels we need,' Heinz growled. 'Not him and his speeches and his slogans. It is tanks and guns and shells and bullets we need to face the Americans.'

'You've got reinforcements,' Fred said. 'You're a bloody reinforcement, man.'

Heinz laughed. 'Yes, and I still have one hand left that I can shoot with! God save the Fuhrer.'

But Ernst knew that Heinz's tanks and guns were unlikely to come any time soon. Despite the rumoured Allied build-up on the other side of the First Objective the Reich's resources were increasingly being diverted to the astonishing battles being fought out in the east.

Now Goebbels calmly watched a row of blindfolded auxiliaries being executed by firing squad. The music swelled to a brittle climax as the bodies shivered and fell.

'I will tell you one thing,' Heinz said. 'I would not want to be a British partisan in the hands of the SS. From the Fuhrer down, they are saying it's all your fault, you British, the troubles we are having.'

Fred laughed. 'What, even Stalingrad? Uncle Joe and his T-34 tanks might have had a bit to do with that.'

'Yes, but if you buggers had not been so stubborn, if you had made peace as any sensible person would have done, we would not have so many men tied down on this absurd little island.'

Buggers. Ernst suppressed a smile. Heinz had picked up a good deal of English from Fred. Fred said, 'And so those bloody SS thugs take it out on English children, while they hide from the Russians like the cowards they are.'

'You won't hear me defending the SS, that's for sure.'

Ernst stood, downed his vodka and picked up his jacket. 'I probably ought to pack before dinner. The truck's coming for me at midnight.'

'Where are you going now?' Heinz asked.

'I have a posting on the coast in Kent. Richborough. Five days.'

Heinz eyed Ernst. 'Is this your brother pulling strings again?' Even before his return from Stalingrad Heinz had always been a hugely suspicious soldier, endlessly perceiving favours done and postings manipulated. He got up unsteadily and lurched over to Irma at the range. 'Where's that blessed stew, woman?'

'Coming,' Irma said without emotion.

Seeing Ernst was leaving, Myrtle gurgled and raised her little arms to him. With his jacket slung over his shoulder, he squatted down. He picked up her Mickey Mouse gas-mask from where it sat on the floor and waggled it. When she grabbed for it he picked her up, his hands under her armpits. She laughed when he bounced her gently, and plucked at the buttons on his shirt. He could feel her ribs, her elbows and knees were lumps of bone, and he could make out the shape of her little skull as she smiled at him. He knew little about the development of children, but it seemed to him she was behind with her walking and talking. It was strange to think that this child had always been hungry, every minute of every day of her short life.

Heinz's shadow fell over him. And when he looked up, he saw Heinz's left hand, his good hand, rake upwards over Irma's hip and settle on her breast. She elbowed him away, with a nervous glance at Fred. Heinz just laughed and staggered back to the table.

Irma saw that Ernst had seen all this. She glanced again at Fred, and hissed, 'You won't tell him, will you? It's not what you think. I mean – it's just for the rations. Heinz brings me extra, you know, I need it for the child.'

He stood, keeping his face blank. 'I could have helped you. There was no need.'

She shook her head. 'I would never beg favours of you. I have my pride, Herr Obergefreiter.' She began to ladle out the stew.

II

14 May

Ben Kamen heard voices. Trojan, the monstrous woman Fiveash, another he did not recognise. He struggled to wake, to focus on their words.

'Vril,' Trojan was saying. 'Vril is the power which underlies the universe, Ernst. So it is written. And it is vril that has woven history. In the greatest age of Atlantis, the first building that ever stood upon the face of the earth housed a vril time lens. It was a calendar, but it did not record time; it *created* time. I believe my petty Loom is a poor imitation of that mighty lens – and yet it is surely vril essence that I have captured here!'

'You actually believe all this, don't you?' A young man's voice. 'And you, Unterscharfuhrer Fiveash?'

'Of course,' came Fiveash's silky, hateful tone, her German mildly accented with the tight vowels of the English. 'I would not work here at your brother's side without that faith, Obergefreiter. I would not have brought him the Loom technology from America otherwise.'

But she did not believe, Ben thought, lying there, eyes closed. She spouted this dreary hotchpotch rubbish merely to control the fool Trojan, for she, English-born, needed a German puppet to exert full influence within the SS. In Ben's opinion all Nazis were either fools or in the thrall of fools. But could none of them see what a menace this woman was?

Their voices murmured, meaningless, falling away. He listened, his eyes closed. He longed to be anywhere but this place. He longed even to be back in the solitary-confinement cell in which he had been kept for month after month, while Fiveash and Trojan rebuilt their devilish machinery, until they were ready to bring him back to this hell of drugs and artificial sleep. He longed even to escape into sleep, and yet he dreaded it for the damage his dreams might do.

Trojan was talking again, boasting to his brother. 'The new calculating equipment is remarkable, isn't it? Much of it is British, frankly; this is one technological area where they seem to be ahead of us. They are building powerful electronic machines, clearly intended for some such purpose as code-breaking, or command and control. We have raided a country house called Bletchley Park, for example, where they call their machine the "Colossus". And the British Post Office has a research establishment at a place called Dollis Hill north-west of London. Such gadgets as this are manufactured there.'

'The Post Office?'

'They are used to handling this kind of equipment in their telephone exchanges. Look here, Ernst – see the valves, the glass tubes? We have over two thousand in this machine alone, each capable of switching from one state to another in just a millionth of a second. It is this speed of switching, you see, which enables the machine to carry through its computations so rapidly.'

'And how do you express your problems to it?'

'Ah, good question. You "speak" to this beast in a physical language. It is a question of setting switches and plugging in cables, as if reordering its very brain. These are the most advanced thinking machines in the world! And with such devices the computation of Gödel trajectories becomes trivial.'

'"Trivial." You mean that in the academic sense, don't you? "Not an intellectual challenge." But perhaps one should apply the word to your whole enterprise, Josef.'

Fiveash laughed. 'Your muddy foot-soldier of a brother has a brain in there, Josef.'

'Unterscharfuhrer Fiveash, yes, I am a muddy infantryman, and proud of it. That is the reality of the war to me. Mud and guns and blood, hunger and death. All this talk of ancient powers and time travel is so much claptrap. You already failed once – that nonsense over Hastings!'

'But we will not fail again.' And can you not see,' said Josef Trojan earnestly, 'that if we succeed we will transform the fortunes of the war at a stroke? For we will cut down our most powerful opponent—'

'America.'

'Yes. Cut it down at the root! Let the Americans shuffle their tanks and ships around the world; it will avail them nothing. We have a plan, you see, a new plan to do with Christopher Columbus, and the beginning of it all. Believe it or not, our historical research is taking longer than the technical. But we are making progress. And then we

251

will see how it goes for the Reich, in a new and transformed world in which America *does not exist at all.*'

And nor would the Reich exist, Ben thought. You unimaginative fool.

The voices fell silent. Perhaps he had spoken aloud.

He opened his eyes. The lamps' glare dazzled him, and he blinked away tears. He could see the three of them standing just outside the glass wall of his chamber, two black SS uniforms, a uniform of the Wehrmacht. Ben tried to see the brother's face, Ernst's. He imagined himself as Ernst must see him. His skinny frame lying above the smoothed-out sheets. The shackles that bound his wrists and ankles and neck. The tubes that snaked under his striped prison-issue pyjamas and into veins in his arms and legs, into his penis and into his mouth. The metal cap that had been fixed to his scalp, attached with screws that had been tapped into the very bone of his skull.

Josef Trojan's face loomed like a moon. 'Good morning, little fellow. Or is it good afternoon? *You* never know, do you? Don't you have anything to say, Ernst? Remarkable sight, isn't he – a triumph for modern medical science. He never leaves his little glass room, save in the imagination, of course. He can't *do* anything. He can't even play with his own circumcised, cathetered cock, poor fellow. All he can do is sleep – and I control even that, for by turning this switch I can administer drugs to him at will, do you see? Sleep, and dream the dreams I command through the loudspeakers that surround his pillow. And as he sleeps he guides the teasings of the Loom of history, and by doing so he wins the war for Hitler. What do you think, Ernst? Even you must be impressed.'

'What I see here is cruelty. Arbitrary, pointless cruelty. Such ambition and vanity will bring us down in the end, Josef.'

'If you believe that you really are a fool.'

But Ben heard uncertainty in his voice. As the months had turned into years, others had expressed similar doubts over Trojan's elaborate project and the resources it was consuming. It was a long time indeed since Himmler had shown any support, let alone visited Richborough. Trojan had even once been hauled in by the Gestapo for an inter-rogation. The experience had left him shaken and unsure. But Julia Fiveash was always on hand to stiffen his spine.

'Enough,' Trojan said. 'Let's put him back to work.' He turned his switch. Ben felt the opiates course into his blood. The brothers and Fiveash walked on around the facility. 'You should come work with me here at Richborough, you know, Ernst,' Trojan said. 'There are Wehrmacht guards here. I'm sure I could fix a transfer.'

'My duty lies elsewhere.'

'Your trouble is you never got over that wretched French girl, did you? It's muddled your thinking. You always were a fool . . .'

The world spun away, as if he were tumbling down a well, and Ben, trapped inside himself, fell into fragmented dreams.

III

18 June

Mary's train into York was late.

When she got to the little tea shop on Low Petergate they were waiting for her, sitting at a window table, drinking tea and eating cake: Tom Mackie, slightly crumpled and donnish as always despite his Navy uniform, and Gary, his own British Army uniform fitting him closely. Both men got up when Mary squeezed her way to the table, hot, flustered, tired. 'Mom—' Gary embraced her. He smelled of cigarette smoke, earth, a whiff of cordite, a soldier's smell. But the arms around her were strong. It made her ache that she would only have a few minutes with him.

Mackie pulled out a chair. 'Good to see you, Mary. Tea, is it, a scone or two? You might have to wait a bit, I'm afraid; all these GIs are rushing the girl off her feet.' He turned and raised his arm, trying to catch the waitress's eye.

'Thank you. Sorry I'm late.' She sat, setting her handbag and gas-mask pouch on the floor beside her.

The shop was crowded with servicemen, talking loudly, smoking, most of them apparently American. And music played, a sentimental Glenn Miller ballad. It was probably the Promi; you heard it played everywhere for the music, which everybody agreed was a better selection than the BBC's. She was right in the big picture window; it was a surprise such a window had survived the bombing. Looking along a street crowded with military vehicles and black government saloon cars, she could just make out the angular ruins of the minster.

'You look a bit hot and bothered,' Gary said.

'The train's a trial at the moment, isn't it? Packed with servicemen, en route from A to B.'

'You do get a sense of the mobilisation, don't you?' Mackie said. 'Lots of pieces being moved around the board, ready for the chess game to begin.'

It was all hush-hush, but it was impossible not to know what was going on. Troops had been pouring into the country for months. In the north and in Scotland farms and villages had been evacuated, vast tracts of land set aside for training. It was said that the US Eighth Air Force had pretty much taken over East Anglia. At night, across a vast swathe of countryside north of the Winston Line, you could hear the rumble of tanks and mobile weapons, of studebakers and jeeps, trundling to their marshalling points under cover of darkness.

And here was her own son, preparing to throw himself into the cauldron. He seemed so much less boyish than when she'd last seen him. Now he had a man's heavy body, a thickening neck, even slightly thinning hair like his father's. And he was full of nervous energy. He kept glancing at a clock on the wall.

'You've filled out,' she said to him.

'Well, I'd hope so,' he said patiently. 'Mom, it's eighteen months already since I got sprung from that *lebensborn* camp in Kent. They do give us decent rations, you know.'

Mackie tamped his pipe tobacco. 'Better in the US Army, I hear. You could always swap sides.'

Gary shook his head firmly. 'I started this thing in these colours, and I'll finish it in them.'

'From Dunkirk to Berlin, eh?' Mackie murmured. 'Good for you.'

The girl came over and took Mary's order. No older than sixteen or seventeen, she wore rouge, eye liner, lipstick, and what looked like real stockings. Pushing back through the tables she ran a gauntlet of leers, whistles and wandering hands.

'Remarkable,' Mackie said, watching her go. 'Here we are not half a mile from the seat of Halifax's government, and there's a girl like that, a walking demonstration of the way the GIs have distorted the British economy, with their ration-busting cigarettes and sweets and silk stockings, all pumping up the black market – their rather coarse glamour—'

Gary laughed and sipped his tea. 'You sound as if you'd like to be rid of your allies, Captain. How did Churchill put it? You'd carry on the fight "until, in God's good time, the new world, with all its power and might, steps forth to the rescue and the liberation of the old". Well, here we are.'

'Yes, thanks very much. And the sooner we get you lot packed off back to the land of the free the better.'

'I'll drink to that.'

'Let's get down to business.' Mackie said to Mary, 'We need to talk more fully. But I've already given Gary an outline of what we're up to. And an indication of the role I'd like him to play.'

Gary eyed her. 'History books and time machines!'

Mackie glanced around uneasily. 'Walls have ears and all that, old chap.'

'Well, all right.' Gary spoke more quietly. 'Look, Mom, Captain Mackie got me seconded to his operation, though I have an assurance it won't be until W plus three.'

'"W"?'

'W-Day,' Mackie said with a cold grin. 'Operation Walrus. Eats sea lions. One of Churchill's.'

Gary said, 'I'm struggling to believe that I'll be more use following up this fruitcake stuff than I would be with my buddies kicking Nazi butt around Sussex and Kent.'

Mary nodded. 'I understand. I generally have trouble believing it myself. But I do have evidence, Gary.'

'Historical stuff.'

'Yes. That's what I'm here to discuss with the Captain, in fact. I've spent three years on this now, on and off. The likelihood of this project of the Germans coming off might seem low. But if it did, the consequences could be – well, catastrophic.'

Gary frowned. 'If you weren't my mother I'd walk out of here right now. You hear too much of this guff about Hitler's secret super-weapons.'

Mackie said, 'I've made it plain to Gary that he's under no obligation to carry this through. Indeed he's under no obligation to return to front-line combat at all.'

'I don't want a damn staff job,' Gary said fiercely. 'That would kill me off faster than any Nazi bullet.' Mary flinched, and he was instantly regretful. He covered her fingers with his. 'Mom, I'm sorry. But you can see how it is. Especially as we're so close to the off. Or so I heard.' He drained his tea, and swept up the last of the cakes from the plate and stuffed them in his pocket, an old prisoner's reflex. 'Listen, I got to go. I do wish we could have had more time, Mom.' He leaned over to give her another hug; he let her hold him for a long minute. When they broke he said, 'I'll tell you what. If I were going to go back and fix the past to resolve this damn war, I know where I'd go.'

'Where?'

'Versailles. The lousy settlement after the first war. You speak to any German, and I spoke to enough in the stalag, and he'll tell you that's where it all began. A just peace and you'd get no Hitler.'

Mackie murmured, 'I'll take it on advisement.'

'You do that.' Gary stood and took his gas-mask pouch from the back of his chair. 'Good day, Captain. Mom.'

'Godspeed, son.'

He walked away. Once outside the shop he fixed his cap on his head, straightened up and marched off. She watched him until he was out of sight.

Mackie waited patiently. 'He's a good young man. I'm sure he'll fulfil the mission we have for him.'

'I just want him to get through all this without getting shot up again.'

He tapped his saucer with a clean fingernail. 'Look, let's wait for your tea. Then perhaps we should get out of here. I think I'd feel more comfortable if we talked on the hoof, so to speak.'

Mary sat back. 'Come on, Tom. You can't seriously believe there's a German spy in here. We're surrounded by GIs!'

Mackie grunted. 'Believe you me, there are circles in the British government who are more wary of our allies than our enemies. No offence. Where *is* that girl?'

IV

So they walked, heading through the heart of the city towards the minster.

It was a hot June day, a little after three. In the centre of the city the shops were busy, the place bustling even on a Friday afternoon, full of military and pinstripe-suited civil service types. A British Restaurant, a self-service café ostensibly for the use of the bombed-out, was doing brisk business. Mackie and Mary, both bookish, paused by a W.H. Smith's whose window was piled high with Penguin editions of Graham Greene and Agatha Christie novels, and pot-boiler crime and romance.

It was the GIs who caught the eye, though. You saw them everywhere, hanging around on street corners like unruly kids, endlessly chewing gum, and ostentatiously smoking their Camels and Lucky Strikes at a time when smokers in England mostly had to put up with foul Turkish brands. They had a kind of loose casualness about them that was just this side of slovenly, and it made you realise how prim and proper most British servicemen looked by comparison. In England's cities and towns, 1943 would always be remembered as the GI summer, Mary thought.

York was busier than most towns in free England, because it was the emergency seat of government. But it shared with the rest the marks of the long war: the ack-ack gun emplacements, the pillboxes, the sandbags around the public buildings. The major air campaigns had been abandoned after those frenetic months of the invasion in 1940, but because it was the seat of government York had taken more than its share of the sporadic Luftwaffe raids – the Brits called them 'tip and run' raids. So there were gaps in the streets, marked by stubs of walls and broken pipes, the rubble cleared away and piled up in vast mounds in the parks. Some of these bomb sites were four years old and were choked with greenery; the weeds loved the brick dust and the ash. Mary supposed glumly that when W-Day came the bombing would resume in Britain, just as it was about to resume, so she'd heard, in the heart of Germany, and that York and other cities would soon have fresh scars to add to the old.

Some of the changes wrought by the war seemed positively medieval. Every park, playing field and flower bed was given over to growing crops or raising pigs: it must have been five hundred years, Mary mused, since the farmyard had penetrated the city in such a way. And there was a pervasive atmosphere of neglect. The city was stripped of railings and lamp-posts, the metal turned over to the armaments industry. After nearly four years without a lick of fresh paint the homes and shops and offices looked shabby, slowly decaying, their blacked-out windows like closed eyes. Mary thought she saw a similar round-shouldered shabbiness in the people, in their patched-up clothes and shoes, now enduring the fourth year of a war that had become, worse than grinding, *boring*.

The most spectacular bomb site of all was the minster itself. In one week in the summer of 1942 the Luftwaffe had launched a series of particularly spiteful raids against the grand old building, evidently meaning to make a symbolic strike against Halifax's seat of power. When they reached it, Mary and Mackie stepped cautiously through the main entrance on the northern side, with flags of St George, Britain, the United States, Poland and France flying over their heads, and into the shadow of ruin. The central tower had been pretty much demolished, and the rest of the roof was blown in, the stone floors smashed to shrapnel. But the minster was still a working church. A small open-air altar had been set up beneath the Great West Window which had, by luck or a miracle, survived the bombing. But most of the interior, cleared of rubble and swept for unexploded shells, had been dug up to form allotments. Today squads of Land Girls toiled in the shadows of the broken walls.

Mary and Mackie sat on a fallen pillar in the shade of the ruined north transept, their feet in the long grass, and watched the girls working. They were cheerful enough, their young voices echoing from the stone walls.

Mary said, 'Looks as if they are fighting a losing battle against the rosebay willow herb.'

Mackie shrugged. 'I'm told it's more a symbolic effort than anything practical. Morale booster, you know. I mean it's rather too shady in here to grow anything worthwhile. Of course the archaeologists have been crawling all over this place since Hitler conveniently blew it up for them.'

'Well, they would. There are roots here going back to a Roman military headquarters, the centre of power in the whole of the north of England.'

'And now York finds itself the locus of a world empire. Remarkable how things come around. I wonder what archaeologists of the future will find of our time. A layer of ash, I suppose. Rubble and bones.'

'Geoffrey Cotesford visited the city many times, according to his memoir. In fact his first monastery was just outside the walls.'

'Ah, our friend Brother Geoffrey! I thought he might have done. So to business, Mary.' He dug out his pipe and began the usual rather theatrical business of filling it, shred by tobacco shred. It occurred to Mary that she hardly ever saw Mackie without the pipe. Perhaps he needed this prop for reassurance; perhaps he was less calm than his urbane British surface would have led her to believe. 'Tell me first how you are getting on with your counter-history. What was your hinge of fate?'

'Dunkirk,' she said immediately.

This was an exercise the two of them had set themselves. In an effort to delve into the minds of history-meddling Nazis, Mackie had proposed that they try to devise their own 'counter-histories'. If you had a Loom, what tweaks to history would you consider making? It was not so much the results that were of interest, he argued, but the habits of thinking and the types of research, a bit removed from the conventionally historical, that he wished to understand.

Mackie nodded sagely. 'Dunkirk. I should have guessed you would wish to spare your son the consequences of living through that horrendous defeat.'

She said fiercely, 'Let it be done to someone else's son, not mine.'

'Fair enough. How could that calamity have been averted?'

'If Hitler had hesitated . . .'

She had had access to remarkably thorough briefings. Mackie's MI-14 had moles that penetrated all the way, it seemed, to the top of the Nazi Party. And she had learned that in those dark days of May 1940, when the BEF and the remnant French forces were trapped on the beaches, it had been a full day before Guderian had been authorised to unleash his Panzers for the final assault and his resounding victory. The delay was obvious even to the allied soldiers on the beaches; Gary had spoken of it.

'There seems to have been a debate at all levels within the military and the Party,' she told Mackie. 'Guderian himself had some concerns about the nature of the ground they would have to cover. The blitzkrieg had advanced so fast he was short of proper intelligence.'

'Ah,' Mackie said around his pipe. 'Germans never did like a heavy pitch.'

'Meanwhile Guderian's superiors were well aware that France was not yet conquered. The BEF was beaten; so let it go, and keep back Guderian's forces, let them rest and re-equip for the French campaign. And then Hitler was still dreaming of peace with England. He thought that sparing the BEF from slaughter might demonstrate to you Brits that he was a civilised kind of guy after all. But in the end they concluded that the destruction of the BEF was too good an opportunity to miss.'

'So how would you make the change? You remember the rules we set. You're allowed to go back and whisper in one person's ear.' This was, from Geoffrey's evidence, how the Loom seemed to operate.

'I'd reach back to Hitler's court in those hours when they were debating whether to unleash Guderian. And I'd mess about with the head of Karl Ernst Krafft.'

'Who's he?'

'An astrologer.'

'I thought Hitler didn't believe in astrology.'

'Yes, but there are those around him who do, Himmler and Goebbels to name but two. In 1939 this guy Krafft sent a prediction to Himmler's intelligence service that there would be a bomb attempt against Hitler. Well, the prediction came true.'

Mackie snorted. 'Pure coincidence!'

'Of course. But it gave him an in at court. Mess with him, and you can influence at least two Nazi barons.'

'And if the decision about Guderian was so close, that might be enough to swing it. What would you say to him, though?'

Mary shrugged. 'Some suitable gobbledygook, couched in Aryan-mythos phraseology. Hitler is a Taurus, which is supposedly ruled by the element earth. Hitler is a lion on land but lost in the water – so he should spare Britain, an island nation, and concentrate on the ground he can conquer, which after all stretches all the way to Russia. Something like that.'

'Um. So what next? If the BEF had been reprieved—'

'I think everything would have been different,' Mary said. She hesitated, then plunged on, 'I think the German invasion might not have happened at all.'

Mackie raised his eyebrows.

A different Dunkirk would have altered the mood on both sides of the Channel, she argued, and so affected the chains of decision-making that led up to the invasion itself. A saved BEF might have boosted British morale. Churchill might have survived politically – and then, emboldened, he might have forced through such belligerent actions as disabling the French fleet, to prevent it being absorbed by the German navy. As for the Germans, facing a tougher, more resolute Britain, and with the balance of power less in their favour on both land and sea, the invasion might have seemed that bit more daunting.

'They were always disunited at the command level,' she said. 'Each service seeking to shuffle off responsibilities onto the others. If the invasion had seemed more difficult, the infighting might have got that much worse.'

Mackie nodded, but looked doubtful. 'You know, actually I'm not sure how much difference the invasion has made, up to now at any rate, in the bigger picture of the war. Essentially the land war in the west has been stalled since September 1940. It doesn't matter much whether Hitler's troops were held up on this side of the Channel or the other. Without an armistice, he couldn't have withdrawn too many units for the eastern front – I doubt if he could have launched Barbarossa any earlier or more violently. And in the meantime he still had the Luftwaffe. He would have been able to strike at us even without an invasion. Hammer the cities – London especially. And he could attack the Atlantic convoys. In some ways we might have suffered more.'

'That's true,' Mary insisted, 'but with an unoccupied British mainland the allied western front would have been a hell of a lot stronger. You wouldn't have to go through a W-Day counter-invasion to scrape the Germans back into the sea before you could even contemplate going into France, for instance.'

'Perhaps. And with Britain intact, the Japanese might not have been bold enough to launch their invasion of Australia, for instance ...' He pulled his lip, clearly not convinced. 'The trouble is, Mary, all the military logic of the time dictated invasion. In that summer the Germans had the momentum of blitzkrieg, and we were the last pawn to be taken. One way or another they'd have had a go, I think, whether the BEF was spared or not. Nice try, Mary, but invasion was inevitable, whatever happened at Dunkirk! Tell you what, though: if I may, I'll hand this to my tame boffins back at Birdoswald. See what they make of it. All right?'

'Sure. I'll give you my notes. So how did you get on? Where would your turning point be?'

'1938,' he said without hesitation.

It was hard to think back that far, to remember what was going on in the world before the great shock of the war. 'That was the year Britain was trying for peace, right?'

'We call it appeasement now,' Mackie said, his face hard. 'Bloody great mistake. We should have declared war when Hitler marched into Czechoslovakia, thereby tearing up all the guarantees he'd given up to that date.'

'But Britain wasn't ready for war – was it?'

'We were in a damn sight better shape than Hitler. He couldn't have mounted a blitzkrieg. He didn't have the tanks or the trucks. Why, he

262

only had three months' fuel! He'd placed orders for ships, for instance, that could have overwhelmed the Royal Navy a few years later. But he couldn't wait, had to move fast. His Nazi economic expansion was heading for a bust, and at court there was plotting against him, according to our spies. And that's also why he's kept on moving – it was no surprise to *me* when they took on Russia. Nazism is a bankrupt ideology sustained only by endless expansion and conquest. In retrospect we muffed it; we should have struck when the balance of power was at its most favourable for us. By waiting another year we gave him the chance to arm to the hilt.

'As to what would have followed if we *had* gone to war then, there are many uncertain factors. I can't imagine the French poking their noses much beyond the Maginot Line, for instance. But at worst it might have been a war like the close of the last show, a lot of infantry manoeuvres. And at best it could all have been over by Christmas, and that would have been that for Hitler and his crew. It certainly would *not* have been the catastrophic collapse in the west that we actually saw.'

But it would have been politically impossible to have gone to war then, Mary thought. She remembered the mood in Britain, and indeed America. Only twenty years since armistice, another European war was a horrible prospect, and Chamberlain had been a hero, briefly, when he produced what looked like a peace deal. But Mackie was showing a side of himself she had perceived among other Brits, especially in the military. These were a people who believed themselves destined to rule the world. Hitler had humiliated them the first time he put a tank-tread on a south coast beach. Anything to reverse that.

She asked, 'So how would you make the change?'

'Actually we haven't got that far. Not as far as you! I must sack my historians.'

But he was being cagey, and suddenly she wondered if he was lying, if he had some team of military thinkers working on this counter-history for real, just in case. Which made him as bad as the lunatics in Richborough – and as bad as herself, for she had been seduced into seriously contemplating how her Dunkirk project would work. The power implicit in the idea of the Loom was just too tempting.

He smiled. 'Well now, look – enough of the fun stuff. Tell me what you've found out about this old fossil Geoffrey, and his inventory of history-botherers.'

V

She opened her handbag and drew out a stack of papers, neatly folded. She spread these out on the pillar between them.

'Not such an old fossil. Quite an imaginative chap, our Geoffrey. Look – this is the summary table he appended to the front of his memoir.' It had been translated into modern English: *'Time's Tapestry: As mapped by myself ...'* 'We have a couple of versions, actually, but the earliest seems to have been written down in 1492.'

'The year Columbus sailed.'

'Yes – and as it turns out that's no coincidence. I'll come to that. The *last* version was found in Geoffrey's coffin, though that copy has been lost.'

'This was a man determined to speak to the future,' Mackie murmured.

'Oh, yes. He was asking for our help, actually; he wanted rid of the menace he called the "Weaver". Now, look. Geoffrey has listed no less than *six* deflections of history, revealed to him by his researches – and, he says, deriving from his own experience. But I'm going to propose, Tom, that we neglect two of these ...'

She spoke of Geoffrey's account of the 'Testament of al-Hafredi', in which a strange visitor to the court of a petty Frankish duke had deflected an eighth-century Muslim invasion of France.

'And an entirely Muslim Europe,' Mackie murmured.

'Quite so.' And she described the 'Amulet of Bohemond', through which a time meddler appeared to have arranged the murder of the Mongol Khan in the thirteenth century. 'If not for that the Mongols would surely have swept on into western Europe, laying waste our cities – wrecking Europe for all time to come, as they wrecked so much of the east.'

'Good God almighty,' Mackie said. He worked at his pipe. 'So why do you say we should exclude these possibilities?'

'Because the technology seems to have been different. The Loom depends on feeding information directly into a subject's brain. But the Amulet of Bohemond was some kind of gadget that "spoke" to its subjects.'

'Like a recording device. A tape or a phonograph.'

'Perhaps. Sent back to the thirteenth century.'

'All right. And this al-Hafredi?'

'He seems to have been a man who was hurled bodily across time – *the man himself,* not just his words.'

'Well – gosh. Hard to know what to say to that. But look here, if these cases are *not* to do with our Nazis and their Loom, then what *are* they to do with? Who else is building a time machine – the Japs?'

'I think it's stranger than that,' she said carefully. 'I can think of two possibilities. One, that these interventions come from our own future. More advanced technologies. Or, two—'

'Yes?'

'That they come from different histories. Ones that were, um, obliterated by the changes in the past. Geoffrey seems to hint that this al-Hafredi was a witness to a Muslim empire that stretched as far as Hadrian's Wall.'

'Which never came to pass in our world.'

'No. But his own history vanished, when he went back in time and blocked the Muslim expansion in France. And that left him stranded, I suppose. The last relic of a reality wiped into oblivion, into non-existence, the moment he threw himself back in time.' She said all this forcefully, hoping Tom Mackie would find it as scary a thought as she did.

'Oh my good golly gosh.' He got up and walked around in the long grass, his right hand cradling his pipe, his left slapping at his uniformed leg. 'Every so often – these extraordinary matters – speak to me, oh spirit of Mr Wells!' But he sounded more excited than appalled. 'All right. Then Geoffrey's remaining four instances, you believe, *are* to be dealt with.'

'I think so.' She spoke of the Prophecy of Nectovelin, which was apparently the result of meddling by Rory O'Malley, using a prototype of the Loom in Princeton before the war. And then there was the Menologium of Isolde, sent back by the Nazis at Richborough – and with Ben Kamen's name surreptitiously coded into it.

Mackie sat again. 'Well, we know all about those. And Geoffrey's two remaining cases, then -' He squinted at her document. '"The Codex of Aethelmaer". "The Testament of Eadgyth". Ah. And I see that Geoffrey links them both to the destiny of Christopher Columbus.'

'That's the idea. Columbus was a significant figure, but one striking point is that Geoffrey couldn't possibly have known *how* significant Columbus would become – he wrote down his account in the year Columbus sailed.'

'Um. And the purpose of these deflections?'

'I'm speculating,' she said warily.

He smiled. 'Speculate away.'

'I think the Nazis have moved on from all those baroque Aryan dreams – the reversal of Hastings, the establishment of a northern empire deep in the past. They're too bruised by the war for all that. So what is the problem for the Germans right now? America, with all her resources and might. I think Trojan and Fiveash are trying to muck about with the founding of modern America – to abort it completely, or at least change history to such a degree that no entity like the modern United States could emerge. And they're doing it by meddling with Columbus.' She described the Codex of Aethelmaer. 'It's essentially a weapons programme,' she said.

'A very Nazi idea!'

'They seem to be trying to implant seeds of weapons technologies, anachronistically advanced, centuries before Columbus – giving them enough time to come to fruition.'

'Ready to be placed in the hands of Columbus, yes? But after centuries of development, who would know what to do with the stuff?'

'That's where the Testament of Eadgyth comes in. The second of the Columbus prophecies. Unfortunately it only survives in fragments.' She showed him some of this. The "Testament", supposedly whispered into the ear of an eleventh-century Christian woman, was a kind of poem in old English. 'It refers to Columbus, I think, if elliptically.'

'Not that elliptically. "The Christ-bearer" – Christopher. "The Dove" – Columbus.'

'It mightn't have seemed so obvious to contemporaries, and certainly not to anybody in the eleventh century. There are lots of references to "God's engines" and coming wars, and finally the main commandment: "All this I have witnessed / I and my mothers. / Send the Dove east! O, send him east!"'

'And these two messages would, you're arguing, set up chains of events which will converge in the career of Christopher Columbus. And then what?'

'You have to remember that Columbus was a militant Christian as much as an explorer. He thought he was going west to Asia, yes? He was after wealth from new trading routes. But he also dreamed of taking on Islam, which was then on the march across Europe. He carried a letter from the Spanish monarchs to the Mongol Khan, hoping they could team up.'

'And squeeze Islam in a pincer movement. Good plan. Shame for him the Americas were in the way! But I think I see where you're going with this. If he had these super-weapons from friend Aethelmaer—'

'He mightn't have felt the need to enlist the Mongols. With such weapons he could conceivably have given up his dreams of sailing west, and turned east instead, to launch a direct attack on Islam. Europe would have been consumed by a new age of crusading and jihad, fuelled by anachronistic weaponry. The destruction would have been horrific. And though others would surely have sailed to the Americas, nothing like the modern United States might have emerged.'

'So, America aborted – but Europe destroyed in the process. Why would the Nazis want that?'

Mary shrugged. 'They don't approve much of Islam, or the "Jewish-Christian conspiracy". The usual Aryan nonsense. It's a bit drastic, but they might be quite happy to see medieval history expunged.'

'Remarkable. Intricate. Audacious! But it didn't work, did it?'

'Apparently not,' she said. 'But then, in our present, these messages *may not yet have been sent back.*'

'But we see traces of them in Geoffrey's memoir.'

'Well, we saw the Menologium before Trojan sent *that* back. I don't pretend to understand it all, Tom!'

'All right. I'll put the squeeze on my intelligence sources, and try to find out what Trojan is up to – in particular if he's working on anything like these messages you've discovered in the record. And then we must decide what to do about all this.'

Mary folded up her notes. 'I'd say that's clear enough. Destroy the Loom before it can be used again.'

'Yes, of course,' he said sagely. 'And that's why I've asked for your son Gary. Security around Richborough has been as tight as a mouse's arsehole since our raid in '41. But Operation Walrus gives us an excellent chance. If we send in a small team, highly trained and motivated, going in perhaps ahead of the main counter-invasion front – hit them before they even know we're there.' He tapped his teeth with his pipe stem. 'But we must plan for all contingencies. Suppose, for instance, we're too late to stop this Codex being sent back. What then? Do we block the Eadgyth material?'

She frowned. 'I'm not sure. I've no idea what harm the Codex engines might do to history *without* the Eadgyth testament. It might be better to make a minimal change in the record. Sabotage the testament rather than destroy it. Turn it into a mandate to send Colombus west, not east.'

'In war it always pays to have back-up plans. I wonder if you'd work through these possibilities for me.'

She thought that over. 'Perhaps I could work out a warning about what might have followed a destructive fifteenth-century European war. A conflict with China, perhaps. A counter-invasion by the American cultures, the Incas or the Aztecs ... But I'm no expert, Tom.'

'Well, who is, in this peculiar field?' He sucked on his pipe, and brushed bits of ash from his trousers. 'You know, all this mucking about with the past by one side or another – it's as if our modern war with the Nazis is folding down into the past. Remarkable thought. Tell me this, though,' he said. 'Purely hypothetically. If *you* had the power to make a change – say, your Dunkirk intervention – if it was just a matter of pushing a button – would you do it?'

She'd thought about that, long and hard. Having studied Geoffrey's agonised testimony, she'd become convinced that nobody really under-stood the deep structure of the tapestry of time, even though so many hands eagerly plucked at it. And when they did meddle, they left flaws. She didn't want to mention to Mackie evidence she thought she had unturned of *holes*, where it seemed entirely plausible a figure had been torn from the weave of centuries. Robin Hood, for instance – a shell of legend around a character that *ought* to have existed. Bubbles of remnant causality.

'I don't know,' she said honestly. 'I think it's possible that even the slightest change might wreak the most devastating consequences. You might be like al-Hafredi, deleting your own history entirely, cut away at the root you tamper with. You might create a world in which nobody like you would ever be born ...'

'That seems a drastic point of view,' Mackie murmured. 'My gut feel is that history might be a bit more resilient than that. I mean, it seems to me it's possible that if you were to make some sort of change, the consequences would just sort of ripple through. The tapestry of time must be a hefty piece of work. The patterns would persist, wouldn't they, even if you pulled out the odd thread? The physicists have nothing to say, incidentally. Nothing sensible anyhow, which is typical of that crew.'

'So if *you* could push the button?'

He pursed his lips. 'I'd like more data. But it seems to me that it might be possible to calibrate the effects of interventions.'

'Calibrate?'

'It would mean turning history from an art to a science, but still! Think what a boon for good such power could be.'

And there, she thought, was the difference between herself and men like him. Mackie was an instrumentalist, who saw in this technology only a weapon. She saw horror. But then she thought of her own Dunkirk counter-history. Only if one were sufficiently desperate, she thought. Only then ...

'Of course,' Mackie said, 'all this mandates us to keep this technology, if indeed it exists at all, out of the wrong hands.'

'You mean the Nazis, the Russians—'

'And the bally Americans, my dear, no offence! Now come, let's get out of here. Can I offer you a lift anywhere?' She stood. He took her arm, and guided her out of the ruins of the minster.

A liberty bus drew up outside the minster, a 'passion wagon' that took young women to dances at the GIs' bases. The Land Girls flocked that way, colourful, grimy, laughing.

VI

3 July

The marshalling area for the British Second Army was south of Guildford.

It was late afternoon when Gary reached Guildford, having been driven down from Aldershot with Willis Farjeon and Dougie Skelland and the rest of their platoon in the backs of studebakers. When they got there a river of men and machines was pouring through the town's old centre. MPs and NCOs stood at every junction, directing the flow according to some complicated scheme. Even the roads had had to be rebuilt to take the traffic, bridges strengthened, junctions widened, the tarmac reinforced to withstand tank tracks. Gary could smell the fumes of the engines, like a vast traffic jam.

It was like this all the way along the Winston Line, from coast to coast.

South of the town, as they neared the marshalling area, the spectacle was even more amazing. The column broke up, and the vehicles swarmed off the road looking for a bit of hard standing to park up. From the elevation of his troop carrier Gary saw vehicles crowding as far as he could see, their backs glistening green or American olive in the dusty afternoon sunlight, with men moving everywhere and dumps of weapons and ammo covered in camouflage netting. There were more complicated machines too, such as the bridge-building gear of the Royal Engineers, who had been training to provide roadways over the concrete trenches of the Winston Line. Tanks moved through this crowd like elephants at a waterhole. Gary recognised the profiles of Shermans and Centaurs, and even a few squat Soviet T-34s; the Russians had insisted on making a contribution to this crucial push in the west. All this was going on under a cloud-littered sky through which fighter planes soared, Spits and Hurricanes and Mustangs and a few Soviet MIGs, there to deter the Luftwaffe from any ideas it might have entertained of disrupting the

270

build-up. It was a spectacle that battered all the senses.

There was no secrecy now, no creeping around in the dark. Gary, lost in the middle of it, had a sense of huge energies gathering, a vast coiled spring about to be released. The war had turned. The Germans had been defeated in Africa and at Stalingrad, the Allies were winning the Atlantic war against the U-boats, and the Japs were held at Midway. Now Roosevelt and Halifax had done a deal, to sort out Europe first before resolving the Pacific war. This July the Allies were effectively opening four fronts against the Nazis. In the Mediterranean an invasion force was closing on Sicily, the beginning of an operation planned to knock Mussolini's Italy out of the war. British and American bombers were beginning an intensive campaign of assault on the German homeland; the first great target was Hamburg. In the east the Russians were taking on the Germans in a gigantic tank battle on the Kursk salient.

And here in Britain Operation Walrus was ready to be launched. Gary knew there had been plenty of muttering in the British press about the time it had taken to get the Nazis out of England. But you wanted to assemble an overwhelming force before you could consider such an operation. Here, today, was the result. And it was remarkable to think that all this was just a prelude to the main event, when England would be used as the platform to launch the invasion of Europe itself, next year or the year after.

Marshalling Area A-C, only a few miles north of the great gash of the Winston Line itself, consisted of two camps set out to either side of Quarry Street, the main road that led south out of Guildford and on to Horsham. The camps were surrounded by triple fences of barbed wire, and the troops, lugging their gear, were marched through gates manned by American guards. The sappers had colonised Pewley Green to the east of the road and a golf course to the west, and in the distance Gary saw water glisten; the camps tapped into the River Wey. NCOs directed the troopers through a city of tents clustered around central wooden buildings. Everything was green and brown, canvas and khaki and paint, the colour of the English ground.

They found the bell tent Gary was to share with Willis and Dougie Skelland. Inside, duck boards covered the grass, and there was a tortoise stove. The three of them dumped their gear. 'This isn't bad,' Willis Farjeon said. He inspected the stove. 'Anybody got any water left? We could have a quick brew up.' The others handed over their canteens.

Dougie Skelland already had his boots off, and a fag in his mouth. Dougie was a veteran of campaigns in Africa and the Middle East. He'd been reassigned after a spell at home recovering from malaria.

His skin was weather-beaten dark, with ingrained dirt that didn't seem to shift no matter how hard he washed, and his eyes were narrowed from too much wind and sun, so that he had an oriental look about him. They were all misfits, in a new battalion welded together from survivors of other, long-disrupted units: Gary the Dunkirk veteran, Willis a POW escapee, and Dougie who had fought with Montgomery. Dougie didn't seem to care where he was sent, save that he was aggrieved to have missed el Alamein, which the commentators all called the first great victory of the war. But he could get his boots off and a fag in his mouth faster than any other man Gary had ever met.

'Americans manning the fence,' Dougie said now. 'See that?' He had a faint Scottish lilt. 'Security over W-Day, see. The Yanks don't trust anybody.'

'Who cares?' Willis asked. 'In American camps you get the best, that's what I heard. A great big NAAFI.'

'PX,' Gary murmured. 'They call it the PX.'

'Briefing halls like theatres. Hot showers. Cinemas!'

Dougie growled, 'You really are a wanker, aren't you, Farjeon?'

'I sure am,' said Farjeon cheerfully. 'But it's a big camp. I'm hoping for a bit more action tonight than Johnny Five-Fingers, frankly. I hear some of the Poles are up for it for the price of a packet of fags.' He winked at Gary. 'Just like the stalag.'

Dougie looked disgusted.

Gary shook his head. 'Don't let him get to you, Dougie. He just says this shit to wind you up.'

'The trouble is,' Dougie said coldly, 'I don't know if you're a bloody sodomite or not, Farjeon. I saw you trying to pull those Yank bashers in Aldershot. What do you want a bird for if you're a shirt lifter?'

'He goes both ways,' Gary said.

'Well, I've never heard of bloody that,' said Dougie.

Willis grinned. 'Don't they have people like me in Edinburgh, Dougie? I'm a breaker of hearts. And of sphincter muscles.'

Gary said, 'It's all just a game to you, isn't it, Willis?'

'I've seen men like him,' Dougie said. 'Who can kill a man hand to hand and make a sport of it. Arseholes like him don't live long in combat. That's what I've seen.'

Willis laughed at him. 'I'll remember that when I'm singing "Auld Lang Syne" and shovelling dirt on your cold dead face, Dougie. Give me your mugs.'

Danny Adams stuck his head into the tent. 'Evening, ladies. I see you're settling in.' Gary had known Adams since the stalag, from which the former SBO had escaped in 1942 with Willis; his accent was as broad Scouse as ever.

'Could be worse, Sarge, could be worse,' said Willis.

'Shut up, Betty Grable. Right, two things you need to know. This is a sealed camp. That means if General Brooke himself tried to leave he'd get his arse shot off by the US Army. Security. Got that?'

'Noted,' said Gary.

'Second. You'll get your final operational instructions in briefing marquee F.' He waved vaguely in the direction of the golf course. 'You'll find it, just follow the other ladies. Eighteen hundred, and if you're late *I'll* shoot your arse off. Oh, and at twenty hundred the padre is coming round. Any questions?'

'Yes,' Willis said. 'Come on, Sarge. What's the plan? Now we're all tucked away inside the barbed wire—'

Adams gave him a look. 'Well, it's simple. In the west you've got us, the British Second Army and the Canadian Third, under General Brooke. In the east, the US First and Third under Hodge. We'll skirt the high ground, cutting south of the Weald, and meet up somewhere near Hastings, us coming from the west, the Yanks from the east. A pincer movement, see? With the Nazis cut off from the ports, and the air forces and the Navy already battering them, it will just be a question of mopping up. First one to Hastings gets the beers in.'

'Let's hope it's the Americans then,' Willis said.

'Don't forget to take your malaria pills, Skelland. And don't be late for the briefing.' He ducked out of the tent.

'Yes, Mother,' Dougie said.

'What an exciting time we have ahead of us,' Willis said drily.

'Kursk,' said Dougie Skelland reflectively. 'Now that's the place to be if you want a bit of drama. A million men on each side, a single battlefield bigger than Wales. It's in the east this war will be decided, not in this tin-pot operation.'

Willis said, 'Let's just be glad we can leave that to Uncle Joe, then.' He pulled his boots off with a grunting effort.

VII

4 July

Few of the men in the slit trenches had been able to sleep that night.
You could tell from the soft voices in the dark.

As dawn neared, Ernst huddled with Heinz Kieser and Carl Fischer.
Heinz smoked obsessively, clutching the cigarettes between the stumps
of his ruined fingers, hiding their light with his good hand. They were
not far south-east of the First Objective at a place called Shamley Green,
on a straight line between Guildford and Horsham. They were in a scrap
of forest, and a mild breeze rustled the branches of the trees above them.
Everything was dark, with not a scrap of torchlight to give away their
positions.

Though it was a summer night, and though they had had the time to
line their trenches with bits of wood and corrugated iron, Ernst felt
cold, and he was grateful for the warmth of the other men close to him.
It had been like this night after night, as they waited for the Allied push.

At about five they were served stew and soup, brought up by runners.
The field kitchens were so far behind the lines the stew was always
lumpy and cold by the time it got to you. The men ate the stew
with their Kommisbrot, hard Army bread, their murmured conversation
counterpointed by the clink of tin spoons in bowls.

'Listen to them,' murmured Fischer. 'The men. They fret, you can tell.
They know they need to sleep. When the Americans come, who can say
when any of us will sleep again?'

'*If,*' growled Heinz. 'If any of us will sleep again.'

'And they become anxious when sleep does not come. In a way all
the inactivity, all the waiting, makes it harder.'

This was Fischer being typically soft about the state of his men's
mood. But Ernst knew it was true. There was only so much trench-
digging you could do, so many telephone cables you could lay, only so
many times you could polish your leather boots and belt.

He looked north-west, to where the Allied armies must be slumbering this night, only a few miles away. The mood could not have been more different from the 1940 invasion, the last time he had been posted to the front line. In the last months, after the Stalingrad disaster and the mounting losses in the east, the Albion garrison had been steadily stripped of men and materiel. Now, who was left to face the Tommies and the Amis? Rear-echelon types like himself, who had spent much of the war on office work in Hastings, second-raters like Fischer, whose softness and sentimentality had blocked any chance of promotion, and eastern-front veterans like Heinz, damaged in body and mind. Them and a few prisoner battalions shipped over from Poland and Czechoslovakia, and whatever conscripts the SS had managed to drum up from the local population – Jugend, most of them, it was said. Second-liners, second-raters, prisoners and kids.

He thought he heard an owl call. He wondered if he might get some sleep tonight.

'Oh,' Fischer said. He was looking up, and orange light bathed his face.

Ernst turned. To the north-west he saw a signal flare, yellow-orange, climb into the sky from beyond the Allied line. The night remained silent. Even the men in the trenches fell quiet, like children watching a firework display.

Ernst asked, 'Another morning concert, do you think?' Just another example of harassing fire, if that was so.

'I don't think so,' Heinz said softly.

Then it started, a noise like thunder that smashed the silence. They all dropped on their bellies. Ernst pressed his face to the dirt and covered his head with his arms.

Birds rose into the sky, great flocks of them, alarmed.

The first shells landed somewhere to Ernst's rear. The ground shook with the impacts, as if huge doors were being slammed. These were high-explosive shells hurled from guns that might be miles away, a bombardment meant to destroy the German defences before a single Allied boot had crossed the First Objective.

It was only seconds since the silence had been broken. The screaming of the wounded began.

In a fragmentary lull, Ernst dared to look up. There was plenty of light now. Through the trees to the north-west the whole sky was in flames, from horizon to horizon. Smoke billowed up, illuminated by the sparking of the great guns themselves, and more signal flares scraped across the sky. It was a sudden dawn, rising hideously on the wrong side of the world.

He twisted. Behind him the neat zigzags and diamonds of the trenches had been broken by fresh pits, neat and round like craters on the moon, and fires were burning. Across this smashed-up landscape he saw engineers trying to reconnect severed wires, and medics struggling to get to the wounded, men buried in the trenches they had dug themselves. And more shells fell, the explosions seeming to burst up out of the ground. Ernst saw men thrown up in the air, men and bits of men, limbs and torsos neatly pulled apart.

A hand grabbed Ernst's shoulder and dragged him back under the cover of the trench's corrugated iron roof – it was Heinz, of course. A shell burst somewhere over Ernst's head, shattering the trees, and wood splinters hammered on the iron. Aiming for the trees was a gunner's tactic; you could kill and maim with shards of wood as well as with hot metal.

'July the fourth,' Heinz yelled through the noise.

'What?'

'July the fourth! Of course the Americans would start their war today. We should have known.'

Another shell screamed close, and they ducked again. And then came a new sound, a whooshing, screaming roar, and machine-gun fire pocked the dirt around the huddling men. It was an aircraft, a ground-attack plane, roaring along the line of the defences. Ernst saw by the light of the fires that the plane had red stars on its wings.

'That's a Shturmovik,' Heinz said. 'By Goebbel's balls, I never thought I'd see one of them again—'

There was a roar of engines, a rusty clatter of tracks.

'They're coming,' Fischer yelled over the din. 'Positions, lads!'

They had trained for this. Ernst grabbed a panzerfaust and rested it against the northern wall of the trench, the weapon raised at his cheek. Heinz was on one side of him, Fischer the other, prepared.

The forest ahead was full of smoke now, a bank of smoke and mist and dirt illuminated by lights. The men in the trenches were already shooting back, with panzerfaust grenades rocketing into the mist and the clatter of small arms fire. Though he could see no vehicles yet, Ernst saw trees felled, just pushed over and crushed under the advance.

Then the first of the tanks burst out of the trees and through the smoke barrier. It was like something mythical, Ernst thought, a monster emerging from the woods, from the cradle of all human fears. He could see something scrawled on its turret, white paint over the camouflage green: REMEMBER PETER'S WELL.

'Fire!' Heinz slapped Ernst's neck. 'Fire the bloody thing!'

Ernst hefted his panzerfaust, aimed, and fired. The roar of the rocket-propelled grenade was loud, the tube hot, and he could not see what damage he had wrought.

VIII

In Hastings George was woken by the sound of the guns. It was like thunder coming from the north, from far inland.

But the first thought in his head was that they were out of bread. He checked his alarm clock by the light of a pen torch. Not yet six thirty. Early, but he knew the baker's ought to be open at this hour. With any luck he could beat the queues. He turned on his bedside light; the power was down again, but there was enough light to see by. He slid out of bed. He'd got used to doing this without waking Julia. He pulled on his shirt and trousers.

She turned over, away from him, grumbling a little in her sleep. In the soft yellow light the skin of her long back was smooth, unblemished, the sheets draped over her like the posing of an artist's model. She really was quite beautiful, when she slept.

He slipped out of the room, went downstairs, used the bathroom, and pushed his bare feet into his shoes. He paused in the hall and glanced in a mirror, scratching at the grey stubble on his jowls. Then he turned the latch key, opened the front door, and stepped out, testing the morning.

He was in the shadows of the narrow, steep street, but the sky above was a deep blue, crusted with bits of cloud. The sound of the guns was louder out here, the noise echoing from the blank walls of the boarded-up houses. It was chill, dewy, but he'd survive outdoors for a few minutes without a coat. He pulled the door closed.

He walked down the road, breathing deep of the fresh air. Grass was pushing through the paving stones; clearing it was the sort of chore nobody tended to these days. The street was quiet, though he could hear a rumble of traffic off in the distance: heavy stuff, a throaty roar, military vehicles probably.

A door opened as he passed, and a woman emerged – Mrs Thompson, a Great War widow, fiftyish, he knew her slightly. She was clumsily

278

pushing a baby's pram, piled up with goods and covered by a blanket. She locked her door and set off up the road, away from the coast, muttering to herself. For days the occupation authorities had been moaning about refugees getting in the way of military vehicles on the routes out of town in every direction. But the Germans in these latter days seemed to have no will to do anything about it, and George certainly wasn't going to try to resist the tide with his few officers. He worried a bit for Mrs Thompson, though. It would have been better for her if she'd stayed put in her home until it was all over, following the British coppers' quiet instructions.

At the baker's an SS officer came striding out clutching a loaf. The baker himself chased after him. He was a small man of sixty, bald, with the sagging face of one who had once been overweight. 'Here!' he called at the German, indignant. 'You ain't paid for that!'

The SS man shrugged. 'By tomorrow Tommy will be here. He will pay.' And he strolled off, not looking back.

'Blithering cheek,' the baker said to George. 'The usual, is it, Sergeant?'

'If you can manage it, Albert.'

As the baker went back into his shop a squad of soldiers marched through the crossroads up ahead – at least they looked like soldiers, fellows in ill-fitting Wehrmacht uniforms led by an SS officer. But they were short, skinny, their helmets too big on their heads. They were Hitler Jugend, young English boys seduced from scouting into training to serve the Reich. The ultimate expression of Nazi madness, George thought, kids going to war. He paid for his National Loaf.

When he got home Julia was making coffee in the kitchen, with her SS ration. Her hair was still down, she wore her uniform blouse, and as he came into the kitchen he could see the soft curve of her buttocks above her slim legs, her bare feet on the flags of his kitchen floor. He got a knife from the cutlery drawer and began to cut into the loaf.

There was a particularly loud explosion that made them both flinch.

'A storm is coming,' Julia said, not looking round.

'Sounds like it to me. I'll be glad to get it bloody over.' He spread a scraping of marge onto a bread slice, and opened a little pot of jam made by a neighbour from the year's early strawberries. 'Calm is what I like. I don't much care if it's calm under the Jerries or calm under the Yanks.'

'What a tidy sort of chap you are. Well, I too will be glad when the balloon goes up. I'm rather tired of shepherding cowardly members of Hoare's government down to the port and packing them off to France.'

'Ah. That's why you're here.' She didn't always tell him what brought her to Hastings, and he didn't generally want to know.

'The sooner I can get back to Richborough the better. Is there any of that jam left?' She pinched the bit of bread from his hand and licked the surface, digging her tongue into the jam.

He could smell her, unwashed, the scent of bed still on her. Even the way she ate jam and bread was quite unreasonably erotic. 'If the Americans are coming, that's it for us, I suppose.'

'I suppose it is. Been a funny sort of business, hasn't it, Sergeant George? *Us*. And yet it's lasted three years.'

'I don't understand it,' he said stiffly. 'Don't suppose I ever will.'

She kissed him now, lightly. Her tongue flickered into his mouth, and he could taste the strawberries. Her tongue withdrew and his followed, and she bit down on its tip, quite hard, and he flinched back. She laughed at him. 'You despise me,' she said. 'You must do. I'm a traitor, by your lights. But to me you're the traitor, you see. You and the rest of the complicit, complacent English, for allowing our destiny to slip away through sentimentality and false loyalties. You should be joining Germany in the great war on Bolshevism!'

'I think you're a bloody nutter. And I think I am too.'

'A paradox, isn't it?'

They stood there, their mouths close, their breaths mingling. There was another crash, powerful enough to make the crockery on George's dresser rattle.

'Fuck,' he said.

'*That* one came from the south.' She went to the window. 'They're bombing the harbour.' She brushed her hair back from her face and peered up at the sky. 'There are planes up there, bombers. This is what we expected the Allies would do. Smash the harbours to bottle us up, while striking overland from the north.'

'Julia. Look – don't go back to Richborough. Stay here.'

'With you?' She sounded quite incredulous, as if the idea was absurd.

'Give yourself up. You must see the war is lost.'

'I don't see any such thing.' She looked him up and down. 'You know, suddenly I feel I'm waking from a nightmare. Why have I been wasting my time on a fat old fool like you? Oh, the war's not lost yet. And once I get back to Richborough *I'll* win it for sure. Mind if I use the bathroom first?' She hurried out. The steam from her half-drunk coffee curled up into the air.

There was another explosion, another shuddering shock, and George clamped his hands to his ears.

IX

The retreating Germans were leaving a mess behind them. Bridges were routinely blown, the roads churned up, the villages torched.

Gary's troop marched past a burned-out truck. The driver still sat behind his wheel, on the left hand side of this German vehicle. He had been reduced to a stick figure by the flames, just a blackened husk. His teeth gleamed white behind peeled-back lips, and his hands still clasped a melted steering wheel.

'Look at that.' Willis used his rifle to point at the driver's wrist, where there was a white band, a bit of flesh. 'How about that, Dougie? Some bugger's nicked this poor bastard's watch. How's that for heartlessness?'

'Shift your arses, ladies,' said Danny Adams.

The troop had to get off the road to let a column of tanks go by. The tanks were Shermans. They had bedsprings and other bits of iron strapped around their bodies with bits of rope. The junk was there because it caused premature explosions of the panzerfausts, rocket-propelled grenades. The troopers predictably mocked the tank crews as the vehicles rolled past.

Gary was glad of a chance to sit for a bit on the soft ground and have a smoke, although Dougie Skelland had a ciggie in his mouth most of the time anyhow. Their blackened faces were streaked with sweat.

'Just let them go by, lads,' Danny Adams said. 'A tank's all right. But what counts in war is feet on the ground. One bloody footstep after another. And that's us. Winning England back step by step. Come on, let's get on with it.'

They clambered back onto the road and carried on. The road surface had been churned up by the tank tracks, so you had to watch where you stepped.

It was mid-morning. After the dawn bombardment they had quickly broken through the smashed crust of defences behind the Winston Line itself, and now they were pursuing the retreating Germans hard, to give them as little time as possible to regroup. But Christ, he was tired, Gary thought; he'd been on the go for eight or nine hours already.

It could have been a lot worse. There were rumours that the Germans had concentrated their mechanised divisions in the east of the protectorate, to take on the Americans; in the fields of eastern Kent a massive tank battle was being waged, and the Germans' deep defence was concentrating on holding the major ports, such as Folkestone. But even here in the west the Germans were putting up a determined resistance, for which they had had three years to prepare.

Although lead units had already surged through the countryside there were plenty of pockets of Germans left, and the advancing troops knew they were surrounded by the enemy, by peril. In this closed-in landscape of fields and hedges and trees and lanes, there was little visibility. Every tree, every window of every one of these bucolic cottages could hide a sniper; every furrow in every field could shelter a machine gun nest or a mortar. Further out the Germans had some big guns emplaced which could spit their vicious shells miles, aiming for the dust plumes of the advancing columns. As a result the vehicles were crawling along at not much better than walking pace. The lead units had stuck signs to telephone posts and trees: GO SLOW. DUST MEANS DEATH.

Everything was mixed up. Sometimes you came so close to the enemy you would hear German voices, or the clatter of their horses' hooves.

But in the middle of all this, it was still England, and those civilians who hadn't fled were carrying on with their lives. Once Gary saw a tank detachment stopped to allow a farmer to drive his cows across the road for milking. Cows!

They came to an abandoned German position behind a crossroads, a complex of interconnected slit trenches protected by a minefield. The sappers had marked out a safe path with white tape. Gary saw a gruesome monument lying in the road: a human leg blown clean off at the knee, the booted foot shredded. Somebody had paid dearly for the path he followed now.

Danny Adams was poking in the dirt. 'Over here, lads. The trench has been pretty much stripped, but I think there are weapons. See, buried in the dirt where the wall collapsed?'

Gary went to see. 'Panzerfausts.' They had been trained up on these; it turned out that a panzerfaust's rocket-propelled grenade, designed to take out a tank, did a good job of smashing in the walls of a house.

'Come on, let's dig them out. I'll call for a truck.'

The trench itself was a bit of a mess, when Gary got into it. Grenades had clearly been used, you could see the cratering in the trench walls. Most of the bodies were intact, more or less, killed by the blast, but some had been ripped apart, and you had to watch where you stepped. In one place Gary saw that one fellow had fallen over another when he died, with bits of medical kit scattered around, bandages, syringes, even a stethoscope.

'A doctor,' Willis said. 'Killed as he treated another man, you think?'

'Looks like it.'

'Odd, isn't it? He stayed to do his duty, and got killed for it. Sort of thing that rather proves there's no God. Now then—' Using his rifle barrel as a scoop, he got hold of the stethoscope. 'That's a souvenir you don't see every day.'

'Yeah,' Dougie Skelland growled. 'You can use it to find out if you've got a fucking heart, you faggot.'

Danny Adams said, 'Shut up and get these panzerfausts stacked.'

X

5 July

By midnight, as the fourth of July gave way to the fifth, the retreat was in full flight.

They were kept marching through the night, in the pitch dark, moving on south step by step, following the little English country lanes. The dark was the only cover they had, from the planes that buzzed constantly overhead and from the heavy English guns. They weren't allowed so much as a torch beam to see their way forward, and Heinz was slapped down when he tried to light his cigarettes. So it was a question of stumbling forward in the dark, endlessly tripping over tarmac churned up by tank treads, and everybody bumping into each other with soft curses.

By the time the dawn seeped into the sky, Ernst was exhausted. Practically since the softening-up bombardment it had been twenty-four hours of this clumsy, uncoordinated flight, when you were barely able to rest either physically or mentally, not for a moment. He couldn't remember the last time he had eaten, and for hours had had nothing to drink but water from his canteen, refilled from brackish puddles in the ditches. In the grey dawn light, as the hulking, grimy shapes of the men coalesced around him, he felt unreal, distant, as if he were watching some black-and-white cinema film.

At about nine o'clock in the morning they heard a roar of engines, a rattle of treads coming from the rear. They rushed for cover, thinking that the Allied army had overtaken them. But the column's lead tank was a Tiger. The men emerged from cover, their legs splashed with mud and dew.

The vehicles drew to a halt, pulling off the road into bits of cover. The column was a ragtag bunch, a couple of tanks, some self-propelled guns, and a chain of open-backed trucks crowded with troops. The men clambered down. The troops swapped cigarettes; one man passed around a bottle of sloe gin he had stolen from a farmhouse. Officers, NCOs and feldgendarmerie from the column and the infantry units stood in a huddle, negotiating. Most were Wehrmacht, but some of them were SS, and others, very agitated, wore the brown uniforms of the Party. Mechanics worked at one of the trucks, whose exhaust smoked blackly. It was clearly breaking down, so they siphoned off its fuel and stripped it of its tyres and spark plugs and other parts, cannibalising it. What they could not reuse they began to wreck, systematically.

Men stood by the vehicles, or leaned against trees, their rifle butts on the ground. They all had blackened faces. You could see that some of them were asleep standing up. For a moment it was calm, no engines running, not even a distant buzz of aircraft engines to disturb the peace. It was a fine morning, if misty. Ernst breathed in the scent of honeysuckle.

'It was just like this after Stalingrad,' Heinz muttered.

'What was?'

'The retreat. Our front just collapsed. So it is here. No coordination, no proper communication. The calmer officers trying to impose a bit of organization. Just a headlong flight, really.'

Fischer approached them. 'You keep talking like that, Kieser, and we'll leave you with that broken-down truck.'

Ernst asked, 'So what's going on, Unteroffizier?'

'The hauptmann over there says the Americans have broken through at Faversham. Their tanks are heading for Canterbury, and then on to Folkestone. It will all be over by nightfall.'

'They have learned the art of blitzkrieg,' Heinz said without emotion.

'They will find nothing but rubble left of Canterbury. And there's talk of a fighting withdrawal, making a stand at the Hastings bunker. I think—'

There was an explosion, out of nowhere.

Ernst dived for cover behind a truck. Fischer almost landed on top of him, his heavy bulk thudding into the dirt. Bits of twisted metal clattered from the truck's body, and a wall of dust and heat swept over them. There was a stink of petrol and oil and rubber.

When the shock wave had passed, Ernst twisted sideways and looked out, under the truck's body. One of the tanks was burning, still sitting where it had been parked. Flames shot out of its open hatch. Ernst could smell oil smoke and cordite, and the sour, awful stench of burning flesh. But then another explosion broke open the tank turret further, and Ernst had to duck again. Now there was a rattle of machine-gun fire.

One of the officers from the motorised column came running by, a Schmeisser machine pistol in his hand. 'Partisans! Fucking partisans! X

Company with me, we'll clean these bastards out. The rest of you stay under cover.' So Ernst huddled with Fischer under the truck, while the troopers stormed the resistance hold-out. There was a crackle of small-arms fire, the chatter of machine guns, the thump of grenades – and screaming, plenty of that.

But even as men fought and died Fischer dug a pack of field rations out of his pocket. It was wrapped in a bit of newspaper, one of the last editions of the *Albion Times*, with a picture of Goebbels' visit. Fischer unwrapped the paper and handed Ernst a bit of army bread. Ernst had some water in his canteen, so he got that out to share. 'Quite a picnic,' Fischer said, chewing on his bread. 'We must do it again—'

Another explosion, and a clatter of shrapnel against the truck sides.

After that Ernst thought he might have slept for a while, despite the extraordinary situation.

At last they were called out of hiding. Men emerged from the vehicles and the ditches, and slowly began to form up into marching order once again.

Heinz nudged Ernst. 'Come on. Let's take the chance and go and see how those partisans have been living.'

They crept forward, past the burned-out tank.

The auxiliaries' bunker had been broken open by grenades. SS men were rifling through the junk. Built of railway sleepers and corrugated iron, it was quite extensive, with rooms and tunnels, and bits of equip-ment scattered everywhere – weapons, tinned food, paraffin lamps, radio gear. Bodies were curled up in the ruins. One SS man picked up a thick booklet marked 'Countryman's Diary 1939'; it seemed to contain instructions on sabotage and guerrilla warfare.

A German medical orderly was tending wounded, mostly German but one British with a shot-up kneecap. Some prisoners had been taken, men in battledress sitting with their hands on their heads, watched over by more SS troopers. The captured men were a mixed lot, mostly older men but some younger, aged eighteen, nineteen, twenty perhaps, men who had grown up during the years of the occupation.

And one man, aged perhaps twenty-two, looked familiar to Ernst.

Ernst spoke to the SS guard, offering him a cigarette. 'May I talk to that man?'

The guard took the smoke. 'Makes no difference to me or him. Par-tisans get nothing but a bullet, you know that.'

Ernst stepped forward and squatted down before the man.

The Englishman watched him with a kind of insolent curiosity. 'What's your problem, Fritz?'

'My name is Ernst Trojan. I am an obergefreiter of the Wehrmacht. You are surprised at my English.'

'Not that you speak it. You sound like you've picked up a Sussex accent.'

Ernst smiled. 'That would not be unexpected. I have spent much of the three years since the invasion billeted with a family, in a farmhouse near Battle. And you I recognise from their photographs. You are Jack Miller.'

Jack raised his eyebrows.

'Your family believe you are a prisoner on the continent. Or, perhaps, dead. They have not heard from you for a long time.'

Jack looked angry, as if he had been reprimanded. He was a young man, but Ernst saw in him something of his father's stubbornness. 'Well, you can see how I'm fixed, Obergefreiter. I broke out of a stalag in Hampshire pretty sharpish back in '41, and got picked up by this lot, and I've been with these blokes ever since. I had to stay off the radar, see. I've become a UXB specialist, if you want to know. These old men need somebody with a bit of military expertise to give them backbone.'

This banter was directed at his comrades. They grinned. 'Yeah, yeah. You tell it like it is, Windy.'

'And did you receive any of the letters sent from your family?'

'Not since I left the stalag. This isn't the kind of location you can send a postcard to, is it? But we've all got our duties to do, haven't we, Obergefreiter?'

'That is true.'

Jack hesitated. 'So how are they, the family?'

Ernst sighed, and wondered how to compress three years of family news, and such difficult news, into a few sentences. And yet he must try. 'Your father is well. He rages against the occupation.'

'So he should.'

'Your mother – you have a new little sister. Myrtle, born in 1941.'

That perplexed Jack. 'That's a shock.'

'Your brother Alfie joined the Jugend. He had little choice.'

'And Viv? Wow, she must be seventeen now.'

'She is fine.'

'I did read about you. Those early letters to the stalag. They said you were a decent man, for a German.'

'Praise indeed.'

Fischer nudged Ernst. 'Time to move on, Trojan.'

Ernst stood.

Jack said, 'Herr Obergefreiter – my family—'

'Yes?'

'If you find a way, will you tell them, you know ...'

Ernst tried to keep his voice level. 'Yes, of course. I will write. I will tell them how I met you. And when all this nonsense is over you and I will drink English beer together, two old men talking about the war.'

'You're bloody paying,' said Jack.

Ernst walked back to his unit, which was ready to move out. The conferring officers seemed to have come to a decision.

'So now what?' Heinz asked Fischer.

'We have new orders,' said Fischer. 'We split up. We Wehrmacht elements will make for the Hastings bunker, with the tanks. Meanwhile the SS and the Party men will make a dash for the town, hoping to get to the transports before the harbour is closed.' Everybody knew what he meant: the Wehrmacht men were expected to lay down their lives to cover the escape of the SS. Fischer said, 'The SS are going to take these prisoners with them.'

Heinz asked, 'Why not just shoot the bastards here?'

'The SS officers are concerned about due process.'

'Rubbish,' Heinz said. 'They're concerned about their own arses. They don't want to leave another mass grave, not with Tommy and the Amis half a day away.'

'Well, whatever, these are our orders. Form up.' Fischer walked around, blowing his whistle, calling for his men. 'Form up! Form up!'

Ernst looked for Jack again. But the prisoners had already been loaded onto a troop carrier, which roared away, dashing south.

XI

It was about three in the afternoon by the time Gary reached the strongpoint. It straddled the Battle road two or three miles north of Hastings, near a hamlet called Telham.

It was a formidable bunker, a concrete block set down uncompromisingly in the middle of English countryside. A triple wire fence surrounded it, and the bare earth between the fence and the building was no doubt riddled with mines and other nasties. The Germans did build well, you had to say that for them. An impressive anti-aircraft gun installation had been mounted on the roof, but that was a twisted tangle of metal, already taken out from the air.

There was a fire fight going on, closer in. Stray shots came pinging, and occasionally there would be the thump of a mortar. The Germans in the bunker were evidently still putting up a decent fight. But Gary could see that a Wolverine, a big mobile gun, had been drawn up to face the bunker. It was firing shell after shell, and was making craters in the concrete wall. A Sherman stood behind the Wolverine, quiet, its shoulders massive. It was like a huge beast waiting to pounce, Gary thought.

The countryside around was littered with the wreckage of battle. Gary and his mates approached along a road lined with burned-out tanks and mobile guns and armoured cars and trucks, shoved aside to clear the way. There were bodies too, stacked up in a field. Some had their faces covered by their jackets, but others had been stripped of boots and shoulder boards and other mementoes.

They were halted beside a burned-out Sherman tank, some way short of the bunker. While Danny Adams crawled forward to find out what was what, Gary, Willis and the rest of their platoon huddled in the cover of the tank.

They swapped cigarettes; the smoke dispelled the stench of burned oil and rubber from Gary's nostrils. Willis napped a bit. They were all exhausted, even though the exhilaration of the advance pepped them up.

Adams came crawling back. 'All right, lads, here's the picture. We've surrounded the bunker, the wireless masts have been shot up, the telephone lines cut. The Jerries are isolated in there and have got to be running out of ammo and fuel. But they're still fighting.' He sketched on a bit of paper. 'What we've got is actually three houses in a terrace, farm workers' cottages. The Nazis plated over the whole terrace with concrete. Inside you're going to find lots of little rooms, doorways, cellars. Outside, you've got this triple wire fence around the perimeter, and this whole area between bunker and fence is mined.'

'Lovely,' said Willis.

'Shut up, Betty Grable. Now here's what's what. As soon as that wall gives way we'll be one of the lead units going into the compound.' Adams drew stabbing marks on the paper with his pencil. 'We'll go in through the west fence, here. We'll have a sapper unit with us to cut the wire, and we'll make our way across the mines with a few Bangalores. At the bunker, in we go if we can, and the sappers will have a go at the wall with their picks. And meanwhile in the rear, more sappers will be clearing a channel for that Sherman. At the same time a Marine commando will be going in from the east side. Any questions?'

'Can I go back to the stalag?' said Willis.

'No.'

There was a throaty rumble, a ragged cheer from the men. Adams looked around. The concrete wall of the bunker, riddled by Wolverine shells, was crumbling, revealing a dark interior shrouded by dust.

'No time like the present,' Adams said with a grin. 'At this rate we'll be in Hastings before the pubs are open. All ready? Go!'

Gary, Willis and Dougie scurried across the open ground towards the bunker, always keeping low, bullets singing around them. They lobbed smoke grenades ahead for cover. They were in an assault group of eight men, armed with grenades, sub-machine guns and daggers. They were followed by reinforcement groups with heavier weapons and flame throwers, and then by sappers with explosives and pickaxes, and finally by reserve units.

The going was slow. They all carried bits of a 'Bangalore torpedo', steel pipe crammed with explosive. It was awkward to carry, and Gary had always felt nervous of this crude bit of kit anyhow.

Willis, though, seemed fearless, as always. He soon outstripped Gary, and was one of the first to reach the fence. Gary watched as the sappers prised back the layers of wire. Amid a hail of covering fire, the men fitted the torpedo together, then pushed it through the wire.

The torpedo went up, detonating the mines. Earth was thrown up in a string of muddy fountains.

Willis was already scrambling ahead. Gary followed in Willis's tracks over the ground into the minefield, head down and feet tucked in under his body, praying that all the mines had been cleared. It was hard going. The ground was broken by trenches, and now it was churned up by the craters of the mine detonations.

At the wall, he and Willis threw themselves flat on the ground. The upper edge of the broken wall was only about three feet above them.

Gary glanced back the way he had come. More men were following under covering fire. They swarmed over the muddy, broken ground, looking oddly rat-like. Around them the sappers were working to clear more mines and to bridge the trenches for the tanks to follow.

Willis grinned, his teeth white in his blackened face. He hefted a grenade. 'Ready for a bit of the old Stalingrad two-step?'

Gary pulled out a grenade of his own. 'After you.'

Willis counted down on his fingers. Three, two, one. They pulled the pins out of their grenades and hurled them over the wall, and huddled during the double explosion. Then they stood up so they were looking over the wall, their Thompson guns raking fire into the room. A machine gun emplacement had been wrecked by the grenades. Two men lay dead, but another ducked out of an open doorway, firing a pistol at the invaders.

Gary and Willis swept their legs over the wall and clambered in.

They pushed forward, moving from room to room. It was a routine, throw a grenade, follow it up with automatic fire, then on to the next. Gary made sure he raked the walls and even the ceilings. Some of the rooms were crowded, and they used concussion grenades, smoke or phosphorus to cause confusion and panic, before wading in with their weapons, leaving behind corpses, wounded and prisoners. They had been trained up for this sort of operation by Soviet advisors, who had learned hard lessons about a new kind of infantry warfare in the streets of Stalingrad, and they had exercised in bombed-out districts of London.

The complex was quite elaborate, with communications gear and a range of weapons, including mortars and some larger pieces. The individual houses under their shell of concrete were connected by knock-through doorways and tunnels. Many of the rooms were lit only by slit windows in the concrete shell. Under one window, Gary found a sketch of the countryside painted on the wall, with ranging information for the guns.

He crashed at last through one more doorway, grenade in hand, ready to draw the pin.

A soldier of the Wehrmacht faced him, a torch in his hand, his arms aloft. 'Please.' The man swung his torch around. The room was full of people in civilian clothes, many of them women; their faces swam in the dark before Gary, their eyes wide, their mouths open. There was a stink in here, of urine and shit and vomit. The Wehrmacht man said, his English good, 'I am Obergefreiter Ernst Trojan. I am the only military personnel here. These are civilians. German civilians. There is no need to injure them.'

Gary hesitated. 'Don't I know you?'

Trojan stared at him. 'From Richborough? A Roman spear, a raid? Another life . . .'

'What the hell are these people doing here?'

'They are civil servants. Brought from Germany to Hastings to help run the protectorate. You see? They are clerks, telephonists, typists. When the counter-invasion came they were brought to this bunker for safety. Where else were they to go?'

'How about back to fucking France?'

Trojan actually smiled. 'Ah, the boats are reserved for SS and Party members.'

'That doesn't surprise me.'

There was a crash; the whole bunker shook, and the civil servants screamed as plaster rained down from the roof. Gary heard an engine roar, a grind of pulverised concrete, a scream of twisted metal. And then a big gun barked, unmistakably the Sherman's seventy-five millimetre.

Trojan said, 'Your tank is inside the stronghold – well, the game is up, yes?'

Gary heard English voices calling. 'Put it down!' 'Hands on heads!' 'Back up, against the wall. Back up!' The gunfire ceased all over the building, as if a rainstorm was ending.

XII

George, uniformed, plodded through the heart of Hastings, looking for Julia.

It was late afternoon. It had been a day from hell. And it wasn't over yet.

Not a single Allied soldier had yet set foot in the town. But the battle raged all around. You could hear the boom of the big guns firing out at sea as the Kriegsmarine struggled with the Royal Navy to keep open the evacuation corridor across the Channel. In the air, Luftwaffe fighters flying from France were trying to fend off the Allied bombers striking at the harbour. You could hear air battles going on inland too, as the RAF attacked the columns of German personnel and vehicles heading for the coast. Royal Navy ships out at sea were also using their heavy guns to strike at the harbour, but their accuracy was predictably poor. You would see great waterspouts thrown up where the shells fell short – and, worse, some of them fell into the town.

Caught in the crossfire, Hastings was having its worst day since the invasion itself. There were few civilians around, nobody out of doors who didn't need to be, and the air raid shelters built earlier in the war were all full once more. The ARP and the fire service, the WVS and Home Guard and ambulances were all out in force at each bombed-out house.

And meanwhile the Germans were all over the place. The town swarmed with Party members and SS, crowding to book places on the last boats to the continent, men who had so brutally imposed their own sort of rule now running in fear of the 'Tommies' and 'Amis'. And in these last hours the SS were going crazy. Bodies dangled from the lamp-posts of Hastings, most of them English civilians punished for some misdemeanour, but some in the uniforms of the Wehrmacht and Luf-twaffe, even the SS themselves. The only fresh soldiers George had seen thrown into the defence of the town today were the wretched children of the Jugend, and the Legion of St George, English volunteers fighting for the occupying army under the banner of the SS, men with no future.

For a policeman this final collapse of order was a nightmare made real. George felt as if he were the only sane man left in a town of lunatics. He longed to cut down the corpses from the lamp-posts, but he knew he dare not while the SS still had any vestige of authority.

In the end he spotted Julia close to the town hall. Here a line of muddy-looking men, probably resistance brought in from the country, were being roughly lined up against a wall by the SS. The wall was already pocked and splashed with blood. A nervous-looking SS officer walked along the line offering cigarettes and blindfolds. A gang of civilians, watched over by armed Waffen-SS, stood by uneasily, no doubt detailed to remove the bodies when the work was done.

Julia, in her uniform, stood watching this spectacle, her arms folded. George hurried to her. 'Julia, for God's sake—'

'George.' She turned to him, oddly calm. 'I've been expecting you. Believe it or not, I'm glad to see you.'

'What do you mean? – Look, everything's unravelling. The British will be here in an hour. What's the point of this? Can't you stop it?'

'I could not if I wished to. These deaths mean nothing.'

He saw the bleak coldness in her then. In some sense none of this was real to her; the men being shot might have been mannequins. He wondered, not for the first time, how he had managed to share her bed for three years. 'The game's up,' he said. 'You won't get out of here. It's already too late.'

'I don't think so.' He felt something press at his belly. It was the muzzle of her silver pistol.

'You can't be serious—'

'I have a car waiting,' she said. 'You see how it'll work. Our two uniforms will get us past any barrier we are likely to encounter. And if we cross into Allied territory I will change out of my uniform – I am English after all; we can concoct some story or other.'

'My job is here. I'm a copper, for Christ's sake.'

'Well, you will be a dead copper unless you do as I say, and what good will that be to anybody? I will kill you if you refuse, you know.' And he knew she was telling the truth. 'Come with me now . . .'

There was a commotion among the doomed men. One of the civilians waiting to process the bodies, a burly older man, came rushing forward, limping a bit, breaking past the line of SS men. George could hear him call, 'Jack! Jack Miller! It's me!'

'Dad? No ... go back ...' There was horror in the younger man's voice, even as he embraced his father.

A young SS man came up, pistol drawn, and tried to pull the older man away. But he stood his ground, hanging onto his son. 'Shoot him and you shoot me, you black-hearted bastards.'

The SS man tried a bit longer, and the son tried to push his father away. But the old man was stubborn. At length an officer snapped an order, and the trooper pushed the old man against the wall beside his son. Father and son clung to each other, both weeping now, until the rifle shots echoed.

XIII

The German prisoners were marched along the coast road from St Leonards into Hastings. It was evening now, the sun casting long shadows through air laden with dusty smoke from the bombings. And as the day ended, so did the battle, it seemed. The gunfire on the land had stopped, though you could still hear the deep guttural booming of ships' guns rolling in from the sea like distant thunder.

This was a road Ernst had walked many times, but never as he walked it now, one of a hundred or so prisoners, all stripped of their helmets and weapons, and some of boots and belts taken by the Tommies as souvenirs, walking with their hands on their heads. Nobody spoke, and it was hard to tell what the men thought as they plodded along. Ernst himself longed for sleep. But aside from that he felt only relief that he was alive, and that he would presumably see out the rest of this wretched war in a prisoner-of-war camp rather than be shipped off to an even more brutal front. Relief, mixed with a good dose of shame, that so many had died where he still lived.

On the outskirts of the town they came on a German column that had evidently been caught in the open by RAF planes. The tanks, guns, trucks, horse-drawn carts were blown up and burned out, and bodies were littered everywhere, sprawled over dashboards or dangling from the back of the trucks. Horses had died too, their great bodies smashed and splashed. You could see where some vehicle, a bulldozer perhaps, had cut right through this mess to clear it, leaving track-marks stained with engine oil and the brown of drying blood. The men walked through with eyes averted. You could shut out the sights but not the smells, the endless stink of blood and cordite and oil and soot that seemed to soak through all of this corner of England. The Allied guards allowed the Germans to lower their hands and hold handkerchiefs to their faces.

It was only a hundred yards past the destroyed column that they started to come into the town.

British flags hung out of the windows of the houses, and Ernst wondered where they had been hidden all these years. People leaned out of upstairs rooms and shouted at the British troops as they walked by below, women came out with trays of tea, and the soldiers were given kisses and handshakes. One girl in bright lipstick called as they passed, 'Any Americans? Have a go, Joe! Any Americans here?'

Heinz plodded beside Ernst, hands clamped to his head. 'All this only a hundred paces from the dead. What's the word I'm looking for?'

'Surreal.'

'That's the one.'

They were walked along the sea front road. The beach, to the prisoners' right, was littered with the wreckage of boats and bodies, spread over the shingle. An old man was picking his way among the corpses, taking watches or wallets or even just cigarettes. Ernst wondered where the British police had vanished to; the 'coppers' he had got to know wouldn't have tolerated such disrespect. As they walked on Ernst heard the sound of a violin, played jerkily but sweetly. The tune was a simple one, but familiar: 'Lili Marlene'. 'Just as Alfie Miller used to play,' he murmured to Heinz, but Heinz didn't care. Some of the marching Germans began to hum the melody, or even sing the words, softly. After a few paces some of the British guarding them joined in.

They were marched to the Marine Parade, beneath West Hill with its brooding castle. It was crowded; people were congregating, looking for somewhere to celebrate, and there was a sound of laughter, as if some vast party were about to start.

The prisoners were halted and lined up regulation style, backs against a wall, too far apart to be able to conspire, faced with armed guards. It was a relief just to be able to lower your arms.

An English officer called out, 'Now you chaps just hold your horses here while we work out where you're to be kept for the night. I know there's no fight left in you, any more than in me, so let's just get through this business without any more drama. All right?' He called to a German officer, a hauptmann, who translated this for him.

Ernst leaned against the wall, exhausted, relieved he hadn't been called to translate.

Still the violin played. It was coming from the sea front. Ernst looked that way. He saw a boy playing, at the centre of a circle of English soldiers, the smoke from their cigarettes rising up around them. They were drinking, watched tolerantly by a couple of MPs. The boy seemed to be in the uniform of a Jugend. And now there was a fuss, as a girl with a shaven head tried to break into the circle, shouting. It was very remote, and Ernst couldn't make out what she was saying.

Heinz, a couple of yards away, called to him, 'Hey, Ernst. It's the second time today we've run into the bloody Miller family.'

'What do you mean?'

'The girl, the Jerrybag with the shaved head. Isn't that Viv?'

Ernst saw that it was true. And the boy at the centre of the circle of men must be Alfie. Looking closer now, he saw how Alfie wept as he played, and blood trickled from his fingers.

Ernst didn't think about it. He just ran, out of the line, across the road.

He heard running footsteps behind him. 'Oi! You get back here!' There was a shot, but it was in the air. People scurried out of his way, a woman screaming. He saw military police and soldiers converging on him; if not for the crowds he would surely have been gunned down. He got to the circle of soldiers before he was grabbed by a huge military policeman. 'That's as far as you're going, Fritz.'

Struggling, he called, 'Viv! Vivien!'

The girl turned, confused. He saw how her scalp was scraped where it had been brutally shaved. A drunk soldier was holding her arm, trying to get her attention. Ernst had heard of this; soldiers from both sides saw a shaved head as a sign a girl was available. She called, 'Ernst! Oh, Ernst! Make them stop, make them stop! They say they'll kill him!'

'Vivien!'

'Now what the Sam Hill are you doing here, Obergefreiter?'

Another familiar face swam before him. It was Gary Wooler from Richborough, who had taken him prisoner in the bunker. Ernst said, 'Corporal – please—'

The MP made to drag Ernst away, but the corporal held up his hand. 'Hold on, Angus.' He glanced at the girl, the boy who held the violin in his bloody fingers. 'What's going on here?'

Alfie blurted, his accent strong Sussex, 'I've got to play, and when I stop they'll shoot me. That's what they said. I've played for hours already, and I can't, my fingers, I can't—'

'Oh, come on, Gary, it's just a bit of fun.' Another man came out of the circle of soldiers. 'Look at the little prick. He's a Jugend! I mean we weren't really going to do it. But these lads say this pretty-boy took a pot-shot at them, out on the Folkstone road.'

The corporal's face darkened. 'You asshole, Willis.'

'Anyhow we're celebrating. Think of it. England's been invaded before, but not once have the invaders been chucked out. Boadicea couldn't get rid of the Romans, the Saxons couldn't kick out the Normans. We're the first!'

'Never mind bloody Boadicea.' Wooler waded into the circle, dragged out the boy, and pushed him into the arms of his sister. 'Just clear off home, and take that fucking Nazi jacket off. And you, Willis – come with me.'

'Where are we going?'

'Richborough. We've got another job to do.'

Viv and Alfie walked away. Viv put her arm around her brother's thin shoulders. She looked back once, at Ernst. Then she said, 'Come on, Alf, let's find Mum and Myrtle. But, listen, I have to tell you about Dad. Dad and Jack . . .'

The MP dragged an unresisting Ernst back across the street, and threw him hard against the wall, back in the line.

'You arsehole,' said Heinz. 'Get your bloody head shot off doing that.'

'If I hadn't been here you'd have done the same.'

'Well, that's true. But it's the principle. Hey, Tommy! How about a cigarette for an old man?'

The MP ignored him.

The soldiers who had been tormenting Alfie gathered in their circle again, passing around cigarettes and alcohol. A few girls came out to join them. One couple danced, though there was no music. The light was fading now, but the town was brightening, the lights of candles and oil lamps and even electric bulbs glowing out of windows, as for the first time in years blackout curtains were torn aside.

And Gary Wooler was coming back to Ernst. 'On second thoughts, Obergefreiter, I think you should come with us.'

XIV

6 July

Ben woke to a symphony of gunfire: the boom of heavy artillery, the angry cough of mortars, the popping of small-arms fire. Was it 1940 again, had he finally come unstuck in time and drifted into the past?

But he felt the bed under him, the prison-camp pyjamas that covered his nakedness. He was still here, still in the laboratory. Still embedded in the Loom, a Jewish fly caught in a Nazi spider-web.

His mouth felt sour, and there was an edge to his consciousness, a brittleness – a kind of false colouring to his sight, a high-pitched ringing in his ears, a scent of antiseptic in his nostrils. He knew these signs. Julia had made him sleep again. She had put him under and brought him back with opiates and stimulants, controlling him with a smooth expertise that had grown over the months, and yet left Ben with a sense of fizzing disorder each time.

And just as every time he woke, he felt a gathering dread of what Julia Fiveash might have used him to achieve while he slept.

One big crump, a shell landing nearby, was enough to make the bed shudder. That gunfire was real enough, then. The war had come to this place of horror, at last.

He opened his eyes.

The hard light of the electric lamps above him glared into his head. The glass wall of his cage was only a foot from his face. It wasn't as pristine clean as it used to be; a patina of dust covered it, plaster shaken from the roof. He could see his own reflection, a face half-buried in a pillow.

And he saw another face beyond his. Beautiful, hard, on the other side of the glass, it was Julia. He remembered how in Princeton he had woken to see that lovely face looking back at him, blonde hair tousled, how his helpless heart had hammered. In the end it had been just another supine seduction by a monstrous figure who had sought only

300

to use him, in a long line of such seductions, such monsters. But even so he would never have imagined then that the two of them would be reduced to this, that she would use him so.

'He's awake,' he heard her say. 'I think it worked. So that's Aethelmaer's Codex sent back, Josef.' She glanced away; Ben saw the curve of her neck, the supple muscles above the collar of her uniform. 'Step one complete. Come on, man, show a bit of enthusiasm. We have changed history – again!'

Ben's vision was misty, blurred by drugs and dusty glass. Beyond Julia he could see the calculating machine, a wall of glistening metal and wire, and the hunched figure of Josef Trojan before a flickering grey screen. There was another man too, in a dark blue uniform, sitting silent in a chair Ben was shocked to recognise George Tanner.

'You might explain that to the Allied units who are even now besieging Richborough,' Trojan said. 'Whatever we've done hasn't made a blind bit of difference, any more than the Menologium did.'

'You know very well this is a two-part process. We have sent back the weapons; we must still send back the motivator, the Testament of Eadgyth. Then it will be done – America defeated before it is spawned. Kamen just needs a bit of time to get the drugs flushed out of his system and a brush-up from the mnemonic tapes before we send him under again.'

'We may not *have* the time.' He sounded panicky. 'We have rushed this programme, rushed to complete the research, the calculations. And now it comes down to this, the last hours, and still it is not done—'

'I can't believe you're drinking. At a moment like this!'

'It is our last bottle of the Fuhrerwein. A gift from the Fuhrer to Himmler on his birthday, and from Himmler to me. Drink, drink! Do you want to leave it for the English? Maybe your pet policeman lover-hostage would like some too. Or Ben Kamen!'

'Try to conceal your cowardice,' Julia said. 'You know, Josef, the only thing I ever admired about you, the *only* thing, was your brashness. The way you used to bully your brother pointlessly – I liked that. I saw something of me in you, I suppose. Now you merely disgust me. Ah, let us work; we still have that in common.' She turned back to Ben, looking into his eyes. 'The work! How marvellous it is, how intellectually bracing. Don't you agree, Ben Kamen?'

Ben, restrained and drugged, barely able to move a muscle, did his best to meet her stare. He knew what reaction she was looking for.

She knew that Ben remained convinced that changing the past was an all-or-nothing affair. Every time he was put into his drugged sleep – if the Loom worked, and he still wasn't prepared to concede that it did, that this wasn't all some foolish illusion – *then he died*, as all of history folded away like a crumpled bit of paper. And the Ben who had just woken had, in a sense, existed for only a few minutes, since the implementation of the change, and all his memories were of a history that was entirely new, a fabrication. This was his conviction, and it filled him with a deep existential horror.

And this hellish woman knew this. As she peered now into Ben's head she was looking for the terror that penetrated his soul. She relished it, a connoisseur of pain.

But the lab shuddered again. She still had Ben in a cage, but now it was Julia and all her projects who was under threat. He met her stare and grinned. Her face twisted into a snarl, and she turned away.

'Look at this,' Trojan said. 'The television broadcast is back! The Allies have taken over the Promi station.'

'How enterprising of them,' Julia said. 'Ah. American and British soldiers shaking hands. How convenient that there was a camera there to record the historic moment when their twin thrusts met north of Hastings ... Oh, and here's Churchill, walking the cliffs of Dover – of course he would be there. The great opportunist stands amid the ruins of his country, celebrates a victory that is not his, and looks out to sea towards his next conquests. And they call Hitler a warmonger!'

'Do you think all this is a foretaste of what is to come, Julia? The resources assembled against us – is this the pattern we must endure for the rest of the war, until Americans shake hands with Russians in the ruins of Berlin?'

'You are a fool, Josef Trojan. A fool and a coward. Just remember, now that we have got this far I can finish the job myself. I don't need *you*. Not any more.'

'I do not forget that,' said Trojan. 'Not for a minute. Oh, look – a flyby by Spitfires. Such a pretty aircraft, don't you think? ...'

Julia checked the dials on the monitors by Ben's cage. 'The specimen is ready. A few more minutes with the tapes and we can send him off on his final journey into the past.' She grinned. 'Listen well, little fellow.' Out of Ben's sight she snapped a switch.

A recorded voice began to speak in his ear. He tried not to listen, to think of other things, to empty his head. But he felt a mild sedative slide into his veins, washing away his determination, as the Testament of Eadgyth poured into his head:

> *In the last days*
> *To the tail of the peacock*
> *He will come:*

The spider's spawn, the Christ-bearer
The Dove . . .
Send the Dove east! O, send him east!

Another shuddering crash as a shell fell close, and the small-arms fire grew louder.

XV

The Sherman tank's great gun fired one round after another into the carcass of the squat concrete tower, the central fortification of the Richborough complex. The defenders seemed to have nothing left to respond with, nothing but machine guns and rifles whose bullets rattled off the tank's oblivious carcass. The booming of the tank's gun was huge, and though Mary kept her hands clamped over her ears she could feel it in her chest, the cavities of her skull.

Mary was huddled with Gary, Willis Farjeon and the young German prisoner, Obergefreiter Ernst Trojan, in a captured trench. More troops, a total of eight in the group, rested nearby. They were waiting for Tom Mackie. The trench smelled of blood and cordite, the stink of battle.

Gary touched her shoulder. 'Mom, are you sure you're all right?' He had to yell over the sound of the gun.

'What do you think?' she shrieked back. She felt self-conscious in her 'siren suit', her blue WVS coveralls, and her pack on her back contained the results of her researches into Geoffrey Cotesford's memoir – a pack of academic documents in a war zone.

Gary said, 'I never even got to see the arch I spent a year of my life toiling over. And now they've pulled it down to build a flak tower!'

'Same thing happened to Claudius's monument. When the tide turned against Rome, they tore that down too, to build the Saxon-shore fort.'

'I guess England's not a place you want to invade,' Gary said.

Perhaps that was true, she thought. And how strange it was that today, the last moments of one immense invasion might be played out on the scene of another nineteen hundred years earlier.

Ernst Trojan stirred. He wore his grubby Wehrmacht uniform, but he had been given a British army helmet for his safety, and he had his hands tied behind his back.

Willis yelled at him, 'You OK, Fritz? Anything I can get you? How about a beer?'

'Leave him alone, Willis,' Gary said.

There was another crash, and they all ducked.

Tom Mackie came crawling along the trench. He crouched down with them, holding onto his Navy officer's hat. 'Afternoon all.'

'About bloody time,' Willis said. 'Sir.'

'We're all doing our best, Farjeon,' Mackie said, unperturbed. 'Well, we're fit to go at last,' he said to Mary. 'The boffins have arrived.'

She risked a glance out of the trench. She saw that an armoured vehicle at the rear of the field was disgorging military types and civilians, some quite elderly. 'Who are they?'

'Some of my MI-14 colleagues. There are a few chaps from Bletchley Park who want to see if the Nazis have made any improvements to their Colossus calculating machines. And some American boffins.' He pointed. 'That is John von Neumann. An egghead among eggheads. He worked at Princeton in the time of Ben Kamen and Gödel. Knows more maths and physics than they did, probably. Actually we have him on loan from the Americans' atomic bomb project. And *that* is a man called Thomas Watson. Head of International Business Machines. You know – IBM, the big calculating-machine corporation in the States. Not terribly ethical, so the rumours go. Got a medal from Hitler.'

Willis Farjeon said, 'Bloody Yanks, Captain? Over here stealing our women and now our calculating machines. What can you do, eh, sir?'

'All right, Farjeon.'

Mary spotted some other men in more unfamiliar uniforms, with cogwheels and spanners on their shoulder boards. They stood apart from the rest. 'And those?'

'Ah. Red Army technical experts.' Mackie smiled ruefully. 'All a bit delicate, isn't it? Can't shut Uncle Joe out of what we're offering to share with the Americans. Anyway let them have the Colossus and so forth; *that* doesn't really matter. In fact our pals here believe this is all part of a Nazi chemical weapons research programme. Sarin and Tabun. The *verzweiflungswaffen.*'

'The weapons of despair,' Ernst Trojan murmured.

'A lot more plausible, don't you think? Now, look, *we* don't have to wait until the tower falls. What we plan to do is take this group in ahead of the main party and break into the Loom bunker itself. We've always had pretty good intelligence about this place, and we're confident that right now in the bunker there's only Standartenfuhrer Trojan and Unterscharfuhrer Fiveash. They've always kept the Loom technology to themselves – waiting to pass it on as a gift to Himmler.' He glanced at

305

Gary and Willis. 'Two Nazis, that's all, one of them a British woman. Think we can deal with them, boys?'

Willis grinned in that disturbing way of his, face blacked. 'Show us the way in, sir.'

Gary checked his weapons, but he was more circumspect. 'I think it would be a mistake to underestimate those two. Julia Fiveash in particular.'

'I agree,' Mary said warmly. 'But I'd like to get this over before I lose my nerve altogether.'

Gary said, 'I'll keep you safe, Mom.'

'I'll stay out of the line of fire, don't worry.'

Tom Mackie said, 'Right, let's get on with it. We can reach the bunker entrance by following this trench, and then hopping over that bit of wire over there. Corporal Wooler, if you bring up the prisoner – Farjeon, you lead the way, if you would.'

Willis grinned again. 'Aye aye, Captain.' He turned and scurried down the trench.

The rest followed, splashing through mud that stained their boots with blood and oil.

XVI

The door blew in. In his chair, handcuffed, George cowered.

'Drop your weapons! Hands up, *hande hoch*! Drop your weapons!'

Running figures, silhouetted by daylight, came through the smoke and dust, fanning out quickly, rifles raised to shoulder height, shouting. Their faces were blackened. They were soldiers with guns, soldiers in British battledress, six, seven, eight of them, and other figures behind. Josef Trojan backed up to the Colossus machine uncertainly, his Luger in his hand.

Julia ran to George. She grabbed him under one armpit and hauled him to his feet, with a strength like a rugby player's. She pressed the barrel of her silver pistol to his temple.

And with her free hand she turned a switch on the glass tank. Ben had been struggling to stay awake; he had been fighting his restraints, if feebly. Now he was sinking into a deeper sleep. George had seen this done before, the medication automatically fed to the boy. It would take him some minutes to succumb.

One of the soldiers, blond hair under his helmet, peered into the glass tank. 'That's him, Gary, that's Ben Kamen! My God, he must be the unluckiest man alive.' He actually laughed at Ben's plight.

The other called, 'Ben, I told you I'd come back for you.' His accent was American. George recognised the voice; he couldn't believe his ears. *Gary?*

'Dunno if he can hear you,' the blond one said. He came closer to the tank, rifle raised.

Julia snapped, 'Another step and I'll kill the policeman and the Jew. Is that clear?'

George, dizzy from lack of food and water and sleep, crusty in a uniform he hadn't changed for two days, tried not to laugh. 'So we're reduced to this, Julia? What on earth did I ever see in you?'

His reward was an elbow in the kidney.

Another of the intruders stepped forward. He wore a peaked Navy officer's cap. 'All right, lads. Lower your weapons. Let's get this mess sorted out without anybody else dying. I said, lower your weapons.'

The others looked at him uncertainly before they complied. Julia, though, kept the pistol muzzle at George's temple.

The captain was distracted by the calculating machine. 'Look at that bloody thing. Puts my bloody bits of Meccano in the shade, Mary!'

Mary?

George called to the American soldier, 'Gary Wooler? It is you, isn't it?'

The American grinned at George, his teeth white in the black on his face. 'Should have known you'd be up to your neck in it, George.'

'I haven't heard from you since you got out of the stalag.'

'Sorry about that. Blame the Reich post. Hey, Mom. Guess who's here?'

And George was stunned when Mary Wooler stepped forward. She was wearing a blue coverall, the kind the WVS girls wore, and she had a pack on her back. Her greying hair was tied back, and her face was blacked.

'Mary? My God!'

'I suppose I should have expected you, George. You're still in thrall to Miss Fiveash here, are you?'

'Unterscharfuhrer to you,' Julia snapped.

Seeing Mary and Gary together brought memories flooding back to George, memories of Hilda he thought he had buried for good. 'I've been lost, Mary,' he said, hearing the gruffness in his own voice. 'I guess a lot of us have, this side of the Winston Line.'

'You always did your job, Sergeant,' murmured the Navy man. 'So our intelligence informs us. I'm Mackie, by the way. Captain, RN. Mary, I suggest we get on with what we came here for. We may not have time to interrogate these two. But the documentation here – look, there are heaps of it – that may be enough to tell us how far they've got.'

Mary walked to a set of shelves, where documents were piled in neat stacks. She began dragging papers down and spreading them out on a desk, and she dug out reading glasses from her blue overalls. She was a frumpy middle-aged woman preparing to study, George thought, while armed soldiers stood around with weapons raised.

Julia was getting more agitated. 'Do not touch our work – do something, Josef, you coward!'

But Trojan was distracted too. 'Ernst?' He sounded bewildered, and spoke in German. 'It's you, isn't it?'

Another figure stepped forward from the rubble of the doorway. He wore a Wehrmacht uniform, and had his hands tied behind his back. 'Josef. I think I imagined we would never meet again . . .'

'Do stick to English, you fellows,' Mackie said laconically.

'Well, well,' Julia said sourly. 'It's a day of reunions.'

Trojan seemed outraged. 'What is the meaning of this? Why have you brought my brother here? If he is a prisoner of war he should be treated as such.'

'Like Ben Kamen?' George spat, and got another jolt from Julia.

'Isn't it obvious, Josef?' Julia said. 'He's here to make you dance to their tune.'

'Oh, I wouldn't put it quite like that,' Mackie murmured.

'Liar,' Julia said calmly. 'Ernst is a hostage, just like Sergeant Tanner here. You are a hypocrite, Captain. It's the one thing I've always despised most about the English. The sheer bloody hypocrisy, when we are the worst butchers of all.'

Mackie studied her. 'Do you really loathe yourself so much, madam? Is that what this is all about?'

Ernst said to his brother, 'Josef, even on this day of all days, you skulk in the ground with women and absurd machines. What would Father have said?'

Trojan looked hurt. 'I am trying to win the war. And cement the Reich's power so that it will truly last a thousand years – ten thousand! If you understood, you would see.'

But to George, he didn't sound as if he believed it himself, not any more.

'My God, Tom,' Mary said now. 'They know all about us.' She held up sheaves of paper. 'Even the simulations we did. Here is your 1938-war counter-history. And – oh my Lord – my Dunkirk study.'

Josef said, 'We are the SS. Do you imagine your work was immune to our intelligence? I must say that MI-14 in particular was very prone to leaks.'

'Actually,' Julia said, 'we found your studies useful. You kindly worked out the corresponding Gödel trajectories for us. We used these ideas as rehearsals.'

'Rehearsals?'

'You do understand how the Loom works?'

'I believe we have a good idea,' Mackie said.

'Ben Kamen is our messenger, our sleeping child. We have used your solutions as exercises, using hypnotic, mnemonic and other techniques to force the information into his addled head, the Gödel trajectories and the counter-historical mandates.'

Mary looked at Julia over her reading glasses. 'My God. You actually, um, *loaded in* my Dunkirk scenario?'

'And the 1938 study. Of course we never let him sleep until these were out of his short-term memory.'

Mary leafed through the papers on the desk beside her. 'And this is what you have sent back. Yes?' She produced a set of papers covered with diagrams, like engineering sketches. George squinted to see. Aircraft with wings like birds', submarines like metal fish. 'Weapons designs, sent into the past. And gunpowder. You're sent back a recipe for gunpowder.'

'We call it the Codex,' Julia said. 'Rather proud of our research, actually. Not easy coming up with weapons that would make sense to a grubby-arsed monk of the Dark Ages.'

Ernst was staring at his brother. 'What is this madness, Josef? Into whose hands did you hope to place these weapons?'

'Ah,' Mary said, and she produced another paper from the pile. 'That depends on the second of these missives, doesn't it, Standartenfuhrer? The Testament – which I now see,' she said, reading, 'was to go back into the head of a woman of the eleventh century. A wife of one of William the Conqueror's warriors, called Orm Egilsson. So that's who Eadgyth is. Wasn't Egilsson involved with an English priest called Sihtric, one of Harold's inner circle? So that's the way in.'

Julia frowned. 'You know a great deal about our work. Who were your spies?'

Mary shook her head. 'I didn't get this information from spies. I'm a historian, not a detective; I got all this from historical research. Whatever you have done has left traces in the past.'

'And are we too late, Mary?' Mackie asked grimly. He glanced around. 'Is history changing around us, because of these criminals?'

Julia went straight on the attack. 'Criminals? You patronising slug, Mackie, Captain, Royal Navy. Men like you have always disgusted me. You abuse the Party. You bleat about our treatment of the Jews. But who devised the blood libel? The English. Who expelled Jews in the thirteenth century? The English. Who set up concentration camps in Africa? The English. And you Americans are no better, Wooler. You bleat about our racial laws, but there are marital segregation laws in your southern states which the Party used *as a model* for its Aryan-Jewish laws. Everything Hitler has done is in the context of history – *your* history.'

Mackie listened to this, stone-faced. 'I really do think we should get you to a bump-feeler, my dear.'

'Do not speak to me!' she yelled, a hysterical edge to her voice.

Gary glared at Julia. 'Why is this Nazi woman keeping us talking? There's something wrong here—'

And suddenly George saw Gary was right. This was all a performance, he knew Julia well enough to see that. He glanced around. Ben, in the tank, was still stirring, his eyelids lifting like heavy curtains. He was fighting the drugs.

George said quickly, 'Listen. Gary's right. She's stalling. She sent the first lot back, the Codex. I heard her. But the second lot, this Testament, she loaded it into him but—'

The butt of Julia's pistol slammed down on the back of his skull. It felt as if his head exploded. He was on his knees, on the floor, but he was conscious. 'Ben – in the tank – keep him awake—'

It all kicked off.

XVII

Josef Trojan made a rush at the tank. But his brother blocked him, arms behind his back, getting in his way bodily. Then the British soldier, Willis, the blond one, jumped on them both.

Julia screamed her frustration, swinging her silver pistol wildly.

Gary charged her. She aimed her pistol. She fired.

George saw it clearly. Gary lumbered on, his legs still working as if by reflex, his limbs uncoordinated, his head lolling. But his forehead was a shattered mass of blood and bone. He tumbled into Julia, knocking her down. George was pushed sideways; on his back, stunned, handcuffed, he could barely move.

Mary fell on the body of her son, and the woman who had killed him. Her face was contorted, a mask of grief and rage. She clawed at Julia's throat, her hair coming loose from its tie, a cloud of grey around her twisted face.

Mackie dragged her away. He grabbed Julia's hand and crushed it, making her scream, until he had forced the silver pistol out of her fingers. He looked across at George. 'Sergeant. Help me. Hold this woman.'

George willed himself up onto his elbows. His head rang, and his vision was blurring. But he rolled over and lay on top of Julia. Mackie dug keys out of Julia's pocket and released George from his cuffs. His hands free, George got her by her wrists, his heavy arse pinning her legs. She stared up at him, stunned, the bloody marks of Mary's hands on her throat.

Mackie pulled Mary to her feet. 'Mary. Mary! Listen to me. *Listen.* I know it's hard, my God. But you have to help me. The job's not done yet. The mission.'

Slowly she replied, 'The mission.'

'The Loom. You heard what George said. God, how can I have been so stupid? She was stalling – why didn't I see it? They didn't finish the job. Fiveash sent back the Codex. But she's still in the middle of sending back Eadgyth's Testament. We still have a chance.'

'But Gary, look at him, he's not even got his face covered—'

'Mary, we have to make his loss worthwhile.'

She pulled away from him. 'Don't you speak to me like that, you manipulative prick.'

He held up his hands. 'All right. I deserved that. But, Mary, for now – please.' He began to tinker with the bank of controls beside the tank. 'What if we stop the supply of opiates? Fiveash, which is the switch?'

'Too late for that,' Julia said, pinned on her back, her mouth twisted into a sneer. 'Too late! The Jew will be under in a minute, and everything will change.'

Mackie looked around. 'Trojan? Is she right?'

'I am afraid so,' said Josef Trojan.

'Plan B,' Mary whispered. 'Turn Columbus west. Not east.'

'Yes.' Mackie said. 'That's it. Good. Good, Mary. Come on, work with me now. We prepared for this eventuality, didn't we? If you can feed him your alternate version of the Testament, maybe that will be enough. Trojan, is this a microphone? Can Ben hear us? You can do it, Mary. Come on. Speak into his ear as he falls asleep. Do you remember what you worked out? The Aztec feathered serpent, the Chinese dragon—'

'They could just kill him. Kill the little fucker. But that hasn't occurred to them, has it?' Julia whispered this to George, as once she had whispered erotic promises.

He pinned her down harder. 'Shut up. For the last time, shut up.' He held his face over hers, close, as if he might kiss her. But a drop of blood from the wound she had inflicted rolled over his scalp and splashed on her cheek.

Mary lowered her head to the microphone. The body of her son was sprawled at her feet, and George could see how she was drawn to him, as if by elastic cables. But she spoke into the mike, improvising. 'Egilsson. Orm Egilsson. Can you hear me? *Are you there*? Are you there, Orm Egilsson? Orm Egilsson! Listen to what I have to tell you. Listen, and remember, and let your sons and their sons remember too . . .'

Mackie whispered, 'Mary. Old English. Speak to Egilsson. Make him hear you through Eadgyth.'

'Yes . . . Egilsson. Orm Egilsson. Hīerst þū mē? Bist þū ðǣr? *Bist þū ðǣr*, Orm Egilsson? Orm Egilsson! Hlyston ond mune, for þon ic þū recce. Hlyston ond mune, ond giefst to þīn sunum ond to hira sunum . . .'

EPILOGUE
JULY 1943

'My son didn't deserve this, George.'

'I know, Mary, I know.'

'To be killed by practically the last shot of the conflict.'

'Oh, the war's not over yet, Mary. And, look – well – he's with my Hilda now. *His* Hilda. That's something, isn't it?'

'Do you really believe that?'

'I was brought up to believe it. And, you know, I think if I try really hard I can believe it again.'

'Well, you're going to have to teach me.'

'Mary – George – please.'

'Tom? What now?'

'I know you don't want me around. But I have to show you this ...'

If he could hear their voices, Ben knew he must be waking. If he was waking, he had been asleep.

And if he had been asleep, he must have implemented another of Julia's grisly historical changes. He had died and had been reborn. *Again.* That deep fear stabbed at him. It was a fear at the transience of life, at the impermanence of it, the fragility. A fear like being suspended over a thousand-foot cliff.

He put it aside, and kept his eyes closed. Sleep hovered about him, a loose blanket. Perhaps if he willed it he could bring it back, fall away from the world again.

But if he slept again, could he control his dreams?

'Mary. Look. These are your own notes – look, your transcription of Eadgyth's testament, taken from Geoffrey's memoir, written out *in your own hand.* Can you see?'

'It's changed. It no longer reads as it did. "Send the Dove west! O, send him west!" *West, not east.*'

'History has shivered around us, Mary. The past has changed.'

'And yet we remember.'

'And yet, yes. It may take a century of tinkering with this Loom of Trojan's, and even more theorising, before we understand any of this . . .'

Ben had a good memory. He always had. It had only been enhanced by Julia's hypnotism and the mnemonic tapes. He thought he could remember every word of the time-manipulating chunks of doggerel she had beaten into his head, every one of the attempts she had made to change history. Even the 'dry runs', as she had called them.

And Mary's Dunkirk counter-history had intrigued him. He'd had plenty of time to think this over, lying in his tank.

What might have happened if, for some reason, the Germans had not pressed home their advantage in the spring of 1940, and had allowed the BEF to survive? There would have been a ripple of changes, he had concluded in the end, a chain of different decisions on both sides. People would have died. Of course they would. Ben knew the Nazis. If they could not conquer a slice of England, they would have struck at it another way – with terror, probably, with bombs on London and the other cities, a blitzkrieg against civilians. People would have died. But not the same people. Not Hilda Tanner, for instance.

And, perhaps, not Gary Wooler. Gary who had kept his promise to save Ben, Gary who would not have had to grieve over a young wife butchered by a Nazi thug. And he, Ben, would not have had to lie in this absurd glass box and listen to Gary being shot dead, his life unlived. Gary whom Ben had always loved above anybody else. All he had to do was fall asleep, and dream of an eccentric astrologer at Hitler's court. If he did that Gary might be spared all that pain.

He could do this, Ben Kamen, the helpless boy in the box, who had been used and abused by all of them. Even now he could save them all, and himself. Perhaps he could create a tapestry of time with a little less blood on it, a little less Weltschmertz, a world with a little less sorrow. Even though he would have to die, once again, to do it.

'You know, Mary, if we could find a way to control this technology – I mean, to compute and moderate the effects on history correctly – perhaps we can exploit it to make limited, controlled changes. I'm still drawn by my scenario of the 1938 war. If we were to implement that, all of this suffering could be avoided—'

'No. Listen to yourself, Tom! We must stop this now. Demolish this monstrous thing, this Loom. Why, it's what Geoffrey Cotesford begged us to do in his memoir. I mean, even if you could be sure your change was pure, your motives just – what happens when somebody else gets hold of this technology? Stalin, another Hitler? What then?'

'Um. I suppose you're right. We'll let the sappers take it apart, and the man from IBM can have the Colossus.'

'Are you serious? Do you promise me?

'Of course. Just as soon as the medicos get Ben Kamen out of this glass box.'

'Speaking of whom—'

'Yes, George?'

'Is Ben smiling?'

The boy slept beside the calculating engine.

And then—

Afterword

Possible alternate outcomes of Dunkirk have been analysed by, for example, Andrew Roberts in his essay in *Virtual History*, ed. Niall Ferguson (Picador, 1997). Panzer General Heinz Guderian (in his book *Panzer Leader*, 1952) said he believed the order to hold back at Dunkirk was a mistake, and that 'only a capture of the BEF ... could have created the conditions necessary for a successful German invasion of Britain'.

Hitler's planning for 'Operation Sea Lion', the invasion of Britain, was recorded in German archives and has been well documented, not least by Churchill himself in *Their Finest Hour*, the second volume of his monumental six-volume history of the war (Cassell, 1949), and by Peter Fleming in *Invasion 1940* (Rupert Hart-Davis, 1957). More recently Derek Robinson's *Invasion, 1940* (Constable, 2005) focuses on the importance of naval power in the defence of Britain.

The first speculative accounts of a successful Nazi invasion of Britain appeared during the Second World War, for example the novel *When the Bells Rang* by Anthony Armstrong and Bruce Graeme (Harrap 1943). Norman Longmate's *If Britain Had Fallen* (Hutchinson 1972) is a careful account of a successful invasion. Richard Cox's *Operation Sea Lion* (Thornton Cox, 1974), based on a war game played out by veterans from both sides, post-predicted a German failure. More recent studies include Martin Marix Evans' *Invasion! Operation Sea Lion 1940* (Pearson, 2004).

Sir Samuel Hoare, ambassador to Spain in 1940, had been a favoured candidate of Hitler's to take over as Prime Minister had Britain fallen (see *Hitler's Table Talk*, ed. Hugh Trevor-Roper (1953)). Himmler's SS did establish *lebensborn* Aryan breeding camps in the occupied territories, notably in Norway. A recent reference on Nazi science and pseudo-science is *The Master Plan: Himmler's Scholars and the Holocaust* by Heather Pringle (Fourth Estate, 2006).

A useful reference on conditions in wartime Britain is *Wartime Britain 1939-1945* by Juliet Gardiner (Headline, 2004). A recent reference on the German occupation of France (my model for some of the portrayal of 'Albion' here) is Richard Vinen's *The Unfree French* (Allen Lane, 2006).

My sources on prisoner-of-war camps included P.R. Reid's Colditz books, particularly *The Latter Days at Colditz* (Hodder & Stoughton, 1953). The Germans had a habit of referring to their British enemies as 'the English', and I have reflected that here.

Kurt Gödel's speculations on the nature of time in rotating universes were published as 'An Example of a New Type of Cosmological Solutions of Einstein's Field Equations of Gravitation' in *Reviews of Modern Physics* vol. 21, pp447-50 (1949), and the philosophical implications explored in 'A Remark about the Relationship between Relativity Theory and Idealistic Philosophy', in *Albert Einstein: Philosopher-Scientist*, ed. P.A. Schilpp (La Salle, Illinois, 1949). In a recent review of Gödel's work and his relationship with Einstein, Palle Yourgrau argues passionately that the implications of Gödel's insights have yet to be fully assimilated by the scientific and philosophical establishment (see *A World Without Time*, Basic Books, 2005).

J.W. Dunne's notions of 'dream travelling' in time were taken seriously in the interwar years (see his *An Experiment With Time* (1927), recently republished by Hampton Roads Publishing, Charlottesville, VA). J.B. Priestley dedicated plays including *Time and the Conways* (1937) to Dunne. H.G. Wells was interested in Dunne's ideas and corresponded with him, but was critical of some of Dunne's notions.

British researchers really did build Differential Analysers with the toy kit Meccano, beginning in Manchester in 1934 and continuing until the 1950s. Their most significant use during the war was probably in developing Barnes Wallis's 'bouncing bombs' for the Dambusters raid (see www.dalefield.com/nzfmm/magazine/differential_analyser.html). The machines have been studied by 'Meccano men' ever since.

I'm very grateful to Adam Roberts for his expert assistance with the Old English of the 'Testament of Eadgyth', and his invaluable support throughout this series.

Any errors or inaccuracies are my sole responsibility.

Stephen Baxter
Northumberland
May 2007